GIRL ABROAD

Elle Kennedy

Bloom *books*

This one's for all the Londoners.
Each time I visit your magical city,
I feel like I'm coming home.

Copyright © 2024 by Elle Kennedy
Cover and internal design © 2024 by Sourcebooks
Cover illustration by Amber Day
Cover design by Hannah Wood

Sourcebooks and the colophon are registered trademarks of
Sourcebooks. Bloom Books is a trademark of Sourcebooks.

All rights reserved. No part of this book may be reproduced in any form or by
any electronic or mechanical means including information storage and retrieval
systems—except in the case of brief quotations embodied in critical articles or
reviews—without permission in writing from its publisher, Sourcebooks.

The characters and events portrayed in this book are fictitious or
are used fictitiously. Any similarity to real persons, living or dead,
is purely coincidental and not intended by the author.

All brand names and product names used in this book are trademarks,
registered trademarks, or trade names of their respective holders. Sourcebooks
is not associated with any product or vendor in this book.

Published by Bloom Books, an imprint of Sourcebooks
P.O. Box 4410, Naperville, Illinois 60567-4410
(630) 961-3900
sourcebooks.com

Originally published in 2024 by Little, Brown and Company,
an imprint of Hachette Book Group.

Cataloging-in-publication data is on file with the Library of Congress.

Printed and bound in Canada.
MBP 10 9 8 7 6 5 4 3 2 1

AUGUST

1

HE FOLLOWS ME EVERYWHERE. I THOUGHT I'D DITCHED HIM WHEN I climbed through my bedroom window and doubled back around the pool deck to the laundry room—only to be confronted by my father's disembodied voice telling me about the latest stabbing near a London Tube station. Via the Echo speaker on the counter, he proceeds to cite crime statistics at me from somewhere in this house.

But nope. Not listening. I tune him out as I gather clothes from the dryer, then haul them back to my room, where a sizable fort of suitcases and boxes has overtaken much of the floor. I've had weeks to pack. Yet somehow, I've managed to delay the most time-consuming tasks until barely an hour before my ride to the airport arrives.

"Knife crimes have risen to more than six thousand—"

I mute the Echo in my room when my father starts up again. Once I'm safely out of the zip code, I'm talking to someone about having his internet cut off. He's going to give himself a heart attack.

My phone buzzes. I expect to see Dad's name on the screen, but it's my best friend, Eliza, so I put it on speaker and toss it on my bed.

"I'm sorry I couldn't make it," she says in lieu of hello. "We were supposed to be back by now, but my mom had to get into a huge fight with the valet about a dent I'm pretty sure she put in her own bumper backing into the landscaper's truck again, so we're still not—"

"It's fine. Really. Not a big deal at all."

I start folding shirts and leggings, stuffing them hastily into packing cubes in a frantic race against the clock that begins to negate the point of folding them at all. Everything becomes a crumpled act of desperation to make forty pounds of clothing fit inside my bursting suitcase. The vision I had a few days ago of a well-organized departure is now slipping through my fingers.

"But you're leaving me," she mock whines in the dry, reluctantly invested way she has. Every day she's ever woken up and the world hasn't ended yet is a complete drag, but I'm one of the few people in it she doesn't entirely despise. It's endearing. "I won't see you again for a year. I'll miss you."

I snort out a laugh. "That sounded painful."

"It was," she sighs. Fact is, Eliza's never needed or missed anyone in her life.

"I appreciate the effort." It's how I know she cares.

Truthfully, I envy her self-reliance. Her general comfort with herself and indifference to things like anxiety, doubt, or fear. She could be dropped anywhere in the world at a moment's notice, and as long as she could find a decent cup of coffee, she'd be content.

My phone beeps with an incoming call. I promise to call Eliza before I get on my plane and answer the other line without looking at the screen, expecting my future roommates' call. With the time difference and travel time between Nashville and London, this will likely be the last chance I have to speak with them before I arrive at the doorstep of my new flat.

"Hello?"

"In London, women between the ages of sixteen and twenty-nine are eight times more likely to be the victims of—"

"Dad, seriously? Did you talk with Dr. Wu about your raging paranoia and separation anxiety?"

"Baby girl, listen. London can be a dangerous place for a young woman. I lived there for six months, you know."

Yes. Everyone knows. He was there while he wrote and then

recorded his third album at Abbey Road, for which the Beatles titled their eleventh studio album and, thirty-two years later, I was named.

"You do realize that in much of the rest of the world," I tell him, struggling to zip another suitcase, "the U.S. is seen as a violent and barbaric society overrun by crime, right?"

"This isn't like going to the movies in downtown Nashville," he returns, ignoring my argument. "London is a major international city. You can get into a cab and never be seen or heard from again."

"I don't think Dr. Wu would consider bingeing the *Taken* series before your daughter's semester abroad a healthy coping mechanism."

"Abbey."

"Dad."

"You're nineteen years old. That's old enough to drink in the UK. I can't help if I'm not thrilled at the idea of my little girl on a different continent with people I don't know, at some nightclub, getting drinks shoved in her face by a bunch of English assholes."

"As opposed to American assholes."

"Abbey."

Now I know he's careened right over the ledge. My dad never curses in front of me. He'll barely sip a glass of wine at dinner if I'm there. Since the day he retired from touring when I was eleven years old, he's gone to extreme lengths to neuter the rock star persona of Gunner Bly and fashion himself into the perfect father figure. I still think those tabloid photos of him carrying me as a toddler off a tour bus at four in the morning, a cigarette hanging out of his mouth, a bottle of Jack in one hand and me in the other, sent a shock wave through his very being. Scared him straight. Made him afraid I'd grow up to be one of those burnt-out, degenerate celebrity offspring who does alternating stints on reality TV and rehab before a crying jag on *The View*, only communicating with him in the pages of the gossip section.

Which is to say I love my dad, but he's becoming an emotional basket case, and the overbearing father routine is wearing on me.

"Dad, as much as I'm sure you'd prefer me to spend the rest of my college education locked in my bedroom, I can take care of myself. Time to cut the cord, buddy. I'm a big girl now."

"You don't get it. I know how easily a few drinks turns into a few lines of coke…"

Oh, for the love of…

"Yeah, can we circle back on this? I'm kinda in the weeds over here."

I end the call without waiting for a response. If I indulge him, he'll only work himself into a frenzy.

When I applied for this program to spend my sophomore year at Pembridge University London, it was at the suggestion of my European history professor and in a stupor induced by *Peaky Blinders*, *The Crown*, and *Love Island*. And although my grades from freshman year were excellent and my professors were happy to write letters of recommendation, I didn't believe for a minute I'd actually be accepted. Getting the email sent my entire life into a tailspin. Suddenly, I had to break the news to my hyper-protective father that I was not only moving out but leaving the country.

With D-Day now at our doorstep, he isn't taking it well.

"Maybe there's an online program."

I nearly jump three feet in the air when I emerge from the closet with heaps of clothes in my arms to see him standing in the middle of my room.

"Jesus, Dad! You're disconcertingly stealthy for a man your age."

"How about it?" he pushes. "Online learning would suit you."

"No, it would suit *you*. And forget it. This is happening. The car will be here any minute. I've already sent the first month's rent to my roommates."

Which reminds me I still haven't heard from them, so I grab my phone to find I have a couple of missed texts from a very long phone number. That'll take some getting used to.

> Lee: Cheers, babe. Can't wait to meet you. We've got your room ready and some housewarming gifts Jackie and Jamie think you'll love. Emailed directions to the flat. Don't follow the Google directions. They're shit. See you tomorrow. Today? I've lost count xx

"And why haven't I talked to these roommates?" Dad asks, the worry lines on his face growing deeper. "We don't know anything about them. You could get there and find out your apartment is a warehouse by the docks and some men are waiting to throw a bag over your head."

"Ugh, you're exhausting."

I type out a quick response to Lee, then pocket my phone.

"I found them on the same site Gwen used to find a house share for her semester abroad," I remind my father. "Everyone on there is vetted with a background check. The university even recommended it. It's legit."

Because I can't get a grip on time zones, we haven't yet gotten on the phone or video chat for the formal introductions. Just emails and text messages usually sent while the other is asleep. But the digital conversations Lee and I have exchanged over the last couple weeks were encouraging. So far she seems nice. A senior, so a couple years older than me. And there are two other girls already living there.

"I'd feel better if I could speak to them," Dad says. "Maybe talk to their parents."

"Their parents? Really? I'm not spending the night for a sleepover. These are adults."

He narrows his eyes at me, his lips flat. "That doesn't make me feel any better."

"And I suggest you work on that with Dr. Wu."

I give him a little smirk over my shoulder, which he definitely doesn't appreciate.

Dad takes a seat on the end of my bed. He runs his hand through his shaggy hair and scratches at his stubble. It's moments like this—for no particular reason—that I remember how weird it is to be Gunner Bly's daughter. It's a big part of the reason I didn't want my roommates to know who my father is before I was able to move in. It only makes things…complicated.

My whole life, I've been surrounded by people pretending to be my friend so they could get closer to him. Never knowing who to trust. Constantly disappointed by empty relationships. He moved us out of LA, out here to the ranch outside Nashville, to get away from the fame seekers and sycophants in favor of a quieter kind of life. And it is. Mostly. There's still the odd groupie or two that slips through. A fan or someone hoping to launch their own career. Sometimes an entrepreneur in the market to sell photos and gossip to TMZ.

I learned at a young age that there are pitfalls and vipers everywhere. It's why I don't even use social media. So I don't begrudge my dad his neuroses. I just wish he'd give me a little room to breathe while I work out my own.

"Listen, baby girl," he says after a sigh. "I know I've been kind of a drag, but you gotta remember I've never done this before. You're my kid. Letting you run off and start your own life is pretty scary for a father. When I was your age, I'd just signed a record contract and was in a different city every night getting up to all sorts of trouble."

"So I've heard," I say dryly.

He smiles and drops his head in response. "So you know that means I've seen all sorts of ways a young woman can find herself in over her head alone in a big city."

"Yeah. I'm under the assumption that's how I came to be."

He coughs, furrowing his brow. "Something like that."

It's no secret that Nancy was a groupie who followed Dad around until she finally made it up to his hotel room. They weren't together long. The rest is rock 'n' roll history. Terribly fickle, those groupies.

Truth is, I'm due an adolescent indiscretion or two. Another drawback to being Gunner Bly's daughter is growing up hearing the stories of his many exploits but having no stories or exploits of my own, coddled and sheltered in the hermetic seal of his guilt and regrets. I appreciate he only wants the best for me, but I'm a college student now. I'd like to experience at least a little of the rowdy debauchery that is customary for a girl my age.

"What I'm trying to say is I worry about you. That's all." He gets up and reaches for my hand. "You're just about the only thing I've gotten right."

"I think *Billboard* and the wall of Grammys would beg to differ."

"That stuff doesn't matter even a fraction as much as being your dad, you hear me?"

A tear comes to his eye, which gets me all choked up. Nothing gets me crying like seeing my dad emotional. We're both softies that way.

"I love you," I tell him. "And I'm going to be fine. It means a lot to me that you're on board with this, okay? It's important."

"Just promise me you'll make good decisions. And remember that nothing good happens after midnight."

"I promise." I give him a hug and kiss on the cheek.

"You know you can always come home, right?" He won't let go of the hug, so I don't pull away because I know he needs this. "Any time. Day or night. Say the word and I'll have a ticket waiting at the airport."

"I know."

"And if you get in any trouble at all. No matter what it is. You find yourself somewhere you don't want to be or you end up in jail—"

"Dad…"

"Whatever it is, you call me, and I'll help you out. No questions asked. We don't ever have to talk about it. That's a promise."

I wipe a tear from my eye and smear it on his shirt. "Okay."

My phone chimes. It's a text from the driver saying he's outside. I release a nervous breath. "Time to go."

Right. This is really happening.

Until now, all I've thought about is the freedom and adventure of moving across an ocean. Suddenly, the dread and uncertainty rush in. What if I hate my new roommates? What if they hate me? What if British food is gross? What if everyone at my new school is much smarter than I am?

An urgent instinct to dive under my bed grips my chest.

As if hearing my anxieties bubbling over, Dad manages to snap himself into parent mode. Somehow, he's the one reassuring me now.

"Don't sweat it," he says, throwing my backpack over his shoulder and grabbing my carry-on roller. "You're gonna leave them breathless."

Together we load up the waiting airport limo. What's left will get shipped to the flat. I'm not sure I'm even breathing as Dad gives me one last hug and shoves a wad of cash in my pocket.

"For emergencies," he says. "I love you."

For most of my life, this ranch house felt like a comfortable prison meant to trick me into forgetting I was shackled to its confines. Finally, I've broken through, except I never stopped to ask myself what I'd do once I was free. It's a whole terrifying world out there full of ways to get my teeth knocked in.

And I couldn't be more excited.

———

It's after midnight local time when we touch down in London, the lights of the runway blurry in the window speckled with rain while a voice overhead tells us to set our watches forward.

After a nearly ten-hour flight, I can't get off this plane fast enough. My bladder's screaming at me and my feet are swollen. A delirious kind of urgency grips me while I stand in the aisle, anxious and fidgety, with my bags in hand to deplane. The hatch opens, and I scurry down the gangway to the terminal and nearest restroom.

It's past 1 a.m. when my driver loads the last of my bags in the trunk of the black town car. I offer him Lee's directions, to which he assures me he can find Notting Hill just fine.

My body still thinks it's not even 8 p.m. as I plaster my face to the rear passenger window to watch the lights of London fly past.

I'm not well traveled by any means, thanks to an overprotective father who sees murder around every street corner, so I'm still struck when places look exactly as they do in the movies. The architecture, landmarks. Those red phone booths. It's almost surreal. I devour the city with my eyes, every few seconds glancing forward to suck in a startled breath at oncoming traffic, only to remember we're on the other side of the road. The driver chuckles at me in the rearview mirror.

Fair, sir. Fair.

I decide to get it all out of my system on the ride to my new home, embracing the wide-eyed American yokel stereotype as I gawk unabashedly at double-decker buses and ask my driver dumb questions just to hear his accent. Without rush-hour traffic, however, the journey ends all too quickly on a quaint residential street of row houses in brick and pastel palettes.

We slowly creep up on a stucco-fronted two-story eggshell Edwardian town house. Both apartments have pillared porches and waist-high iron gates encasing tiny potted gardens before rising up their steps to covered entrances. A tickle of nervousness starts in my feet when I read the number 42 on the front door of the one to the left.

The porch light is on, waiting for me.

"I better make sure someone's up," I say to the driver but more to myself as I force my hand to grab the door handle.

The front windows glow behind the white curtains. Evidence

enough that I'm expected, though I now question if I should have caught a red-eye to arrive at a reasonable hour. Keeping the whole house up maybe isn't a great first impression.

Here goes nothing.

With a knock, I hold my breath. I've considered a dozen times how horribly this could go. We could hate each other on the spot. From what I gather, the roommates are all a year or two older than me. What if their patience for the clueless American wears out in a week or so?

I get myself worked up again just as I catch a blur of movement inside. The curtains sway before the door creaks open.

To my great confusion, a slender Black guy in a loose tank top and long wide-leg bohemian silk pants stands at the threshold.

"I knew you'd be a redhead." He smiles at me, bright and friendly.

"Is, um, Lee home?"

"Occasionally. I'm about two-thirds into a bottle of merlot, however, so no promises."

Was that an answer? I'm still baffled.

"I'm Abbey." I bite my lip. "I'm supposed to be moving in."

"Of course you are, luv." He looks over my head and nods at the driver.

"Sorry to keep everybody up. I should have considered the time difference when I booked my flight."

"Not everybody. You'll meet the other lads tomorrow. They're out tonight."

I blink stupidly. "Lads?"

"Jack and Jamie." Shoving open the door for me, he tugs me inside. "Best not to wait up. You'll hear them stumbling in around four. Try to reserve judgment until they've had their morning toasties."

He leaves the door ajar for the driver, who's got the trunk open and is piling my bags up at the curb.

My confusion is slowly giving way to unsettling clarity. "You're Lee?"

"Since I was a baby." He peels my backpack off my shoulder and slings it over his, striking a catalog model pose. "I know, I'm more radiant in person."

The interior of the flat is bright and airy. A relief, given the dreary weather. There's a small foyer at the base of a staircase, then a tight hallway with a living room off one side and a kitchen at the end. It's a hodgepodge of expensive-looking mismatched modern furniture, as if the pages of an interior design magazine got all jumbled and thrown together in one house.

"But Lee's a girl," I say emphatically.

He arches an eyebrow at me. "Don't let these flawless cheek-bones fool you."

"No, I mean, I'm supposed to be rooming with girls. Is this the wrong house?"

"Not if you're Abbey Bly." He regards me with skeptical concern. Like I'm the hysterical woman fighting with a shopping cart in the cereal aisle. "I'm Lee Clarke. Welcome to London."

2

My father is going to kill me.

Forget London crime. In about ten hours or so, I'll have a murderer from Tennessee on my doorstep, straight up ready to strangle me for this boneheaded mistake. Well, innocent error, really. But semantics aren't going to save me from imminent death here.

I continue to gape at Lee. "And the other housemates are guys too?" I mutter more to myself as I notice the sneakers in the corner and the jackets hanging on the hooks behind the door.

"Afraid so, luv." He gives me a pitying pout. "But don't let their smell put you off. They're really quite lovely otherwise."

I start rereading emails and text messages in my head, searching for clues. I'd checked the box for female roommates when I signed up on the house-sharing site. I just assumed…

"Wait, but why would you ask for a female roommate?"

Not that Lee's giving off creeper vibes, but this is exactly the kind of thing my dad's vivid paranoia warned me about.

"Online you mean? Didn't make a difference to us. I left the gender preference open."

Great. I've never felt so personally attacked by androgynous names.

That's it. This whole plan is blowing up in my face. Not only will Dad be furious I'm sharing a house with three dudes, he'll take it as evidence I can't be trusted to fend for myself. One simple task and I manage to screw it up.

"You okay?" Lee is frowning at me.

I rub one temple, feeling a headache coming on. "This is embarrassing."

"I've got the cure for that."

Then he's off to the kitchen, coming back a moment later with a glass of wine that he places in my hand.

"There you go. For the nerves."

I take a hasty gulp. I don't know if it helps, but when the driver places the first load of bags in the doorway, I accept this isn't a jet-lagged hallucination. I'm not still on the plane, suffering a fevered dream brought on by champagne and airline food.

Well, shit.

"I'm fine," I lie, because a complete meltdown ten seconds after walking in the door seems rude. "Just tired. Long flight. Anyway, these things happen, right?"

"Happy accidents." He shrugs. "I like to think I'm an everything-happens-for-a-reason person. I mean, I'm not, but I like to think I am." Lee smiles to himself and mimes flipping his hair. "Who knows, Abbey Bly. This could be the start of a gorgeous friendship."

Sure, if I'm not hauled back on a plane by this time tomorrow. Lee seems great and all, but I don't see how I'll be allowed to stick around long enough to become more than an anecdote.

Apparently sensing my growing discomfort, his smile falters.

"Hey, it's all good," he assures me. "This isn't what you expected. I promise we're not a bunch of weirdos. And you're welcome to stay. But if you'd feel better in a hotel tonight, I totally get that. Take a night to yourself, see how things look in the morning?"

I do consider his offer. I could turn around and get back in the car. Spend the night contemplating my situation and approach it again when all the roommates are here. But then I'd have to put a hotel on the credit card, and the statements go to my dad. Plus I'm pretty sure at this point he's got alerts set up if I spend more than fifty bucks. Before my head even hits the pillow, I'll get a frantic call wondering what the hell I'm up to.

No. Despite this hiccup, I remind myself that I've spent the past several weeks conversing with Lee via email. And he was fully vetted by the house-sharing site. Besides, I don't get an axe-murderer vibe off him or anything. I'd like to think I have a good radar for homicidal maniacs.

"If it's all right with you," I tell him, "I'd like to stay."

"Right then." Beaming at me, Lee jerks his head toward the stairs. "We'll save the pleasantries and tour for tomorrow. Let's get you off to bed."

At the top of the steps, he informs me that Jack's and Jamie's rooms are down to the right. We go left toward three doors.

"Bathroom at the end of the hall. You and I will share."

I don't think I make a face, but Lee's quick to interject.

"Trust me, you don't want to see what Jamie does to theirs."

We stop at two doors across from each other.

"That's me," he says as he points to the left one. Then, opening the other, "This is you."

My breath hitches in surprise. I expected blank walls and maybe a quilt tossed on the bed, but this room is so much more than that.

"Hope you like it." Lee shrugs modestly. "I couldn't help myself."

Decorated in tones of white, gray, and cream, the room offers a peaceful, cozy atmosphere. The bed is made with a duvet, throws, and plush pillows. Overlapping rugs cover the hardwood floor. On the windowsill, small potted plants dangle tendrils toward the floor. There's an armoire, a desk, and a dresser with a small TV.

"You did all this for me?"

I turn to him in shock and awe. It's really too much. I mean, it's perfect. But so much effort.

He rolls his eyes. "The last girl had shit taste." Lee sets my backpack down beside the dresser. "Anyway, it's only the essentials. Couldn't well let you sleep on a bare mattress."

"Thank you. This is awesome."

He snorts a laugh, then waves it off.

"And for being here to meet me," I say. Because all things considered, it could have gone worse, given the circumstances. "Thank you."

"You're quite welcome, Abbey Bly. Bathroom's all yours if you want to shower or freshen up. I'll get your bags up here."

Travel has me feeling grimy and exhausted, so I take him up on the offer and we decide to save the rest of the nice-to-meet-you conversation for tomorrow. Afterward, I lie in bed, my hair still wet as I take in the new sounds of the house at night. Staring up at the ceiling, I have no idea what I'm going to do about my dad.

I love this neighborhood. I spent weeks obsessing over photos online of the walkable tree-lined streets, the cafés and bookstores. Finding a place near enough to campus wasn't easy with real estate in London at a premium. If I give up this house, chances are slim I'll find something else that ticks all my boxes. Not this close to the start of the semester.

But Dad is going to flip. No way he lets me stay once he finds out.

And if I don't have a place to live, he'll be thrilled to drag me back home.

Goodbye, London.

———————

It's the strangest thing. I wake to the sounds of passing cars outside my window, of bicycles and people walking their dogs. The aural intonations of a community rousing itself to meet the day, something I haven't experienced with regularity in years. Out at the ranch, there's just the birds and my dad's heavy footsteps, with no other houses in earshot. Not since we lived in LA when I was a kid have I heard the garbage trucks or car stereos outside my bedroom window. All these cues that remind me how far I am from home and how very near to one of the great cities of the world. It starts to feel real, this journey I've set out for myself.

It's enough to shake the jet lag from my brain. Then I catch whiffs of bacon, sausage, eggs, and toast, and my stomach snarls at me. Guess those pretzel sticks I saved from the plane weren't much of a dinner.

Downstairs, I'm slightly hesitant heading into the kitchen, where I hear the noise of utensils on metal pans and someone banging around from one cabinet to another. It's like the way a bed-and-breakfast always feels intrusive and oddly inhospitable. I live here, but not entirely yet.

"Good," Lee says, lifting his gaze from the stove to notice me over his shoulder. "You're up. Wasn't sure if you'd sleep most of the day."

"Jet lag usually hits me the second or third day. I'll be up all night most likely."

I'm a bit distracted by his appearance. He's transformed. As if last night was a hallucination, today he's dressed for an afternoon in the city: crisp navy khakis and pressed button-down shirt under a vest, finished with a silk bow tie and brown leather belt. Behind his thick-rimmed glasses, he's almost an entirely different person.

"Have a seat." He sets out a plate with a fork and knife at the breakfast bar. "Probably not ready for the full English. We'll start small."

He then proceeds to load up my plate with enough cholesterol to put down a hippo. Not that I'm complaining.

"Smells awesome." I've got a mouthful of eggs before he's even stopped shoveling food from the pan. I don't taste so much as absorb every bite.

Lee laughs to himself, shaking his head.

"What?" I say from behind my hand over my mouth.

"Americans. Everything is *awesome*."

"Oh." There's a carafe of milk with some empty glasses, so I help myself and wash down my eggs. "These eggs are brilliant."

"Better."

"All right, mate?" A tall, leanly muscular guy with short brown bed hair saunters into the kitchen from behind me. He's barefoot in wrinkled jeans and a rumpled T-shirt that appear slept in. "Who's this then?"

"Abbey, Jamie," Lee introduces, preparing another plate for the newcomer. "Jamie, Abbey."

The quintessentially pale Englishman I've come to expect from rom-coms goes to the kettle on the stove and makes himself a cup of tea, which he brings over to the chair beside me, then picks a piece of bacon off my plate with a flirtatious wink.

"Hi, Abbey." He bats his eyelashes, and I'm sure that routine, coupled with his aristocratic features and prep-school posh smile, works every time. "Sleep well?"

I nod fervently. "Brilliant."

That gets a chuckle out of Lee.

Jamie nods back. "Lovely."

With spatula in hand, Lee hovers over the plate of sausage. "Shall I fix her a plate?"

Though Lee addresses the question to him, Jamie doesn't look up from spreading jam on his toast. "Who's that?" he says, dismissive.

"Are you asking me because you don't remember her name?" Lee's tone is wry.

"Who are we talking about?" I ask curiously.

"That's the question, isn't it?" Lee cocks his head when the floor creaks above our heads. We hear quick footsteps followed by a hastily shut door. "Can't tell me those are Jackie's pitter-patters."

Jamie, apparently speaking to his toast, shrugs. "Must be mice."

A series of much slower, heavier footsteps trudge down the stairs. I soon discover they belong to a whole mountain of a tanned shirtless blond guy with stubble around his jaw and more abs than I have eyelashes. Jack, I presume. Though he could easily pass for Thor. Only thing missing is the big hammer.

Maybe he keeps that in his pants…

I swear I hear Eliza's voice in my head.

"You know there's a half-naked woman running around upstairs?" he drawls in a thick Australian accent, dropping down in the chair on the other side of mine at the breakfast bar.

As he reaches across me for the serving plate of eggs, he flashes a charming smile that knocks me right off my axis.

Holy smokes. I've never seen a more attractive man in person. Perfect square jaw and endearing dimples. Biceps the size of my thighs.

"There seems to be some confusion as to whether she's several mice in a person costume," Lee says, flaring a sarcastic glare at Jamie, who remains steadfastly committed to his breakfast.

Jack peers at me. "You're not several mice in a costume, are you?"

I shake my head. "I'm Abbey. You can call me, um, Abbey."

Oh my God.

Really? What the hell else would he call me? Susan?

His lips twitch with humor. "I'm Jack." A beat. "Call me Jack."

Lee snickers from the stove. I can only imagine how red my cheeks are at the moment.

Fortunately, Jack puts me out of my misery by breezing past my bout of insanity without further comment. "Right. So Abbey and I aren't mice. Glad that's sorted."

His eyes are impossibly, mesmerizingly blue. So cosmic and glittery that I only realize I'm staring when he grins knowingly and winks, telling me I've been caught out.

Nice, Abbey. Subtle.

"I'm only worried for the poor girl." Lee stands on the other side of the bar and starts picking at his breakfast but mostly daring Jamie to look at him. "Do you suppose she's lost?"

"There isn't any girl." A stubborn Jamie salts his eggs, growing more indignant.

Jack has the wingspan of a 747. As he eats, his elbows bump

mine, though he doesn't seem to notice. "You suppose she crawled out of his wardrobe?"

Jamie leans in to speak softly at my ear. "Be a doll and change the subject, yeah?"

"Abbey…" Lee warns, his voice grave. "Remember who made you bacon."

I am a sucker for the desperate and downtrodden, so I toss Jamie a lifeline. "So catch me up. How long have you all lived together?"

Lee rolls his eyes. "Typical."

Jamie leans in and smacks a kiss on my cheek. "You're a rose, Abbs."

"We moved in here last fall," Jack supplies as he chews.

"How'd you all meet? You've been friends a long time?" I ask.

He glances at the other two. "It was that holiday do, wasn't it? At the Spanish place with the fucked-up heads on the wall."

I lift a brow. "Heads?"

"There weren't any heads," Jamie tells him. "And it was before spring term. That girl Cara's flat in Chelsea. You remember the one."

Jack piles eggs and sausage on a piece of toast, folds it, and shoves the whole thing in his mouth. He gulps it down, then says, "I remember you nicked a shipment of crisps off a lorry."

"I left him forty pounds."

"How much do you think a bag of crisps costs?"

"You're both wrong," an exasperated Lee interjects. "The place with the masks on the wall was where Nate had his gig the night Jack showed up with that rugby bloke. The one who was put off when his girlfriend walked out of the loo with her lipstick smeared all over Jamie's face."

"That's right." Jack smacks his hand on the counter and points at Jamie. "You got your arse kicked." He laughs, and the deep sound makes my heart beat a little faster.

"Oh, fuck off, Campbell," Jamie says.

"Oh no." I try to contain my nervous laughter at the idea of Jamie getting into a bar brawl with a friend of Jack's. Because I assume all Thor-sized men travel in packs. "You didn't really fight him."

"Ha!" Lee chuckles, nibbling on a piece of toast.

"No." Jamie balks. "I aptly sized up the situation and determined self-preservation was the more prudent course."

I smother a grin. "Meaning what?"

"Meaning he paid Jack's mate fifty quid not to damage his pretty face," Lee answers. "Which essentially means he paid the bloke fifty quid to snog his girlfriend."

The three of them go at it for a bit, arguing over the particulars of Jamie's financial diplomacy, which is how Lee comes to explain that Jamie is "quite well-to-do." As in connected to the British aristocracy. Back home, that would mean some kind of celebrity or maybe an heir to a corporate fortune. Here it comes with fancy titles and castles and whatnot.

As we spend the rest of breakfast breaking the ice and engaging in all that get-to-know-you stuff, they inevitably desire to know something about the American in their midst. And thus we arrive at the tricky part.

"Well, I'm majoring in European history. So that's why I'm here—obviously. I'm originally from Los Angeles, but now I live outside Nashville. That's in Tennessee."

"Los Angeles? Like Beverly Hills?" Lee perks up, stars in his eyes. I know the look well. "You know anyone famous?"

This is always how it starts. Verbatim. And it inescapably ends with people fawning over my dad for hours until I cease to be a real person anymore. Just a vessel for their fandom. A conduit to my father. So I lie. Constantly. It's exhausting.

"Uh, no, not really. I thought I saw Ben Affleck in a Dunkin' Donuts once. But it was just a guy in a Red Sox hat."

Lee goes on to tell the story about the time he hooked up with a guy from *Love Island* at a drag show in Brighton, mercifully letting me off the hook. I'm sure the subject will come back around eventually, but I'm not in any rush for it to arrive. Which again reminds me that I'm not only keeping my dad a secret from them but the other way around as well. Because I still haven't decided if I can stay.

We're well into Lee's catalog of every remotely famous person he's ever encountered and he's yet to realize the rest of us have tuned out.

"He's happy to entertain himself," Jack murmurs to me. "But I'm still interested in hearing about you."

I completely fail to conceal the redness that blooms over my cheeks when he says that. The way his lips turn up in the slightest smile. He doesn't even have to try, and I lose all control of my higher functions. Attractive men are the worst.

"Do you all go to Pembridge?" It's the first thing that comes to mind in my pathetic attempt to maintain conversation.

"No, that's just Lee. I'm in my third year at St. Joseph's. Jamie is in his last year at Imperial College London with the other poshes and future prime ministers."

"The real question is…" Lee rejoins the conversation, leaning over the counter to rest both elbows. "Will Abbey be sticking around, or is she running back to the States?"

"What, you're not staying?" Jamie wrinkles his forehead. "Why?"

Lee heaves a dramatic sigh and answers for me. "Daddy dearest was under the impression she'd be rooming with other women. But lo and behold…"

Jamie shrugs. "Daddy's across the pond, is he not?"

I nod. "Well, yeah."

Another shrug. "So lie."

"That's a pretty big lie." I've never lied to my father. Not about anything real.

"You only need to dodge the subject for, what, a month or two?" Jack points out. "By then, you can tell him, and it'll be too late to withdraw from school, right?"

"You don't know my dad. He's pathologically protective."

On the other hand, I'm starting to feel comfortable here. The guys have made me feel welcome, like I'm already part of the house. There's none of the awkward stiltedness I'd feared could result from this enormous miscommunication.

Besides, I've been looking forward to this opportunity for months. The chance to explore London and all its history and architecture. Access to a world-class library at Pembridge. And most of all, a chance to exist outside the constant watchful gaze of my father. I know his intentions are good, but it can be suffocating in his shadow.

Here, even under the dreary skies of a late English summer, there's daylight.

So when the guys gently prod for an answer, I hold my breath and furlough the consequences.

"Okay. I'll stay."

Lee's entire face brightens. "Yesss! I'm so excited to—"

He stops abruptly when hurried footsteps clatter down the stairs and scurry across the foyer, accompanied by a blur of color. After the front door slams shut behind the exiting smudge, we look to Jamie, who simply offers yet another shrug.

"Huge mice."

3

THE SUN'S BARELY PEEKING ABOVE THE TREES IN NASHVILLE WHEN I text my dad after breakfast, but he still responds right away.

> Dad: Hang tight. I'll video call you.

I'm not sure how well I can carry off the lie face-to-face, so I dodge.

> Me: Knee-deep in unpacking. Just wanted to check in and let you know I'm good.

> Dad: The flight okay? How's the house? Nice as the pictures? You've got your own room, right?

With hours to obsess since we last talked, he's worked himself into a frenzy. As usual.

> Me: Yep, it's all good.

> Dad: How are the new roommates? Nice girls?

I hate this. It puts a pit in my stomach knowing what I'm about to do.

> Me: Yeah, great. We all had breakfast this morning. I think I'm going to like it here.

Not one of my proudest moments. Lying does cast a pall over what is otherwise an extraordinary opportunity, the chance for me to expand my horizons while furthering my education.

But knowing the truth now would only compound his already heightened state of separation anxiety. A few weeks, though. A month or two. He'll have adjusted by then, come to terms with the empty nest. I'll tell him then. At which point, I'm sure he'll understand why I had to fudge a few facts.

> Dad: Well, don't like it too much. Counting the days till you come home.

He's such a softy.

> Me: Christmas will be here before you know it. Don't decorate the tree without me.

> Dad: Deal. Call me later. Any time. Never too late or early.

Maybe I should look into an emotional support rabbit or something for him.

> Me: Will do. Love you. Bye.

There's a quick knock at my door, and then Lee cracks it open to inform me there's a house meeting in ten minutes. That gives me enough time to reply to Eliza, who'd sent a few texts last night.

> Me: Guess who ended up in a house with three dudes?

To my total astonishment, she's awake.

> Eliza: Are they hot?

> Me: I think one is gay, but yeah.

> Eliza: Slut.

> Me: This one, Jack, he's Australian and plays rugby.

> Eliza: And you want to have like 10,000 of his rugby babies.

> Me: I'm pretty sure he could bench-press my horse.

> Eliza: Super slut.

> Me: I haven't told my dad. He still thinks they're girls. So keep this on the DL, k?

> Eliza: Lol. Yeah, don't tell him. At least not before you insert-suggestive-rugby-reference-here with Hot Jack.

I really need to learn something about rugby.

Downstairs in the living room, I find Lee in an armchair beside the fireplace. Jack and Jamie sit on either end of the sofa, Jamie's finger compulsively swiping across his phone's screen.

When I enter, Lee not so subtly nods for me to take my place between the two. I sit down and tell myself I'm not disappointed that Jack has put on a shirt.

"Right," Lee says, glancing at his watch. "I've called this meeting to reiterate a few house rules."

"Could we hurry this up?" Jack grumbles. "I was about to go work out."

Jamie groans. "You're always working out."

"Exactly. You should try it. Put some muscle on those puny pencil arms."

"Why?" Jamie scoffs. "I look like this without even trying."

"Yes, I know. That's the point."

Pinching his nose, Lee lets out a long sigh. "Are you both done, or do you require that Abbey and I validate your respective masculinities and tell you how devastatingly hot you both are?"

"Nah," Jack says, flashing that cocky grin. "I know I am."

Damn right he is. I'm liable to self-combust sitting this close to him.

"As do I," Jamie says with the haughty tip of his chin.

Jamie does have a certain metropolitan chicness about him. Attractive, definitely. But he's not my type. I'm not into guys who spend more time on their hair than I do.

"As I was saying," Lee tries again. "The house rule."

Oh, okay. Apparently we've whittled down our list of "a few house rules" to just one.

He then looks directly at me as though wrapping his fingers around my very soul. "There is absolutely no fraternizing among housemates."

Oh.

"Otherwise known as the Jamie rule," Jack says helpfully.

Jamie doesn't choose to respond, still swiping at his phone and looking deliberately uninterested.

Lee rolls his eyes. "Thank you, Jack."

"Why the Jamie rule?" I ask when they don't elaborate.

Crossing his legs, Lee cocks his head at the chastised Jamie. "Care to explain, Lord Kent?"

Jamie prefaces his explanation with a weary sigh. "Well, you see, Abbey, some would have you believe our previous living situation became untenable following a brief and not at all remarkable liaison between two cohabiting, consenting adults."

I bite back a laugh. "What did you do to her?"

"See?" Beside me, Jack bites back nothing. His deep laughter makes my heart skip. "She gets it."

"Why does everyone assume I'm the guilty party?" demands Jamie.

Lee grins at him. "Babe, during your last row, that girl broke my flat iron and two of the good plates."

"Your flat iron?" I echo.

"For my wigs," he says like it should be obvious. "Anyway, I don't entirely blame her."

"You mugged her off good, mate," Jack agrees.

"It could have been handled better on all sides," Jamie concedes. "Let's leave it at that."

Lee, however, is more willing to expound on the topic. He's quick to tell me how the two of them hooking up got complicated when Jamie's tendency toward polyamory came as an unwelcome surprise to her.

"He's a tricky rat bastard," Jack says to sum up. "Sneaking girls in and smashing two doors down from her bedroom."

"So in your mind, once I've slept with a girl, I'm to be exclusively bound to her for the rest of my existence then. Is that it?" Exasperated, Jamie now employs a full-throated defense. "I wasn't aware I'd married her."

"I'm sensing it got ugly." I direct this to Lee, whose answering expression suggests that's a gross understatement.

"Toxic," he declares. "This one was a little shit about it. Not even an apology to keep the peace. So once they stopped talking, she started throwing things. Couldn't get her out fast enough."

"To be clear," Jack interjects, "I'd have chosen Fiona to stay."

Jamie throws up his middle finger. "Cheers, mate."

"She wasn't an unpleasant girl," Lee says in her defense. "Jamie just has that effect on people."

"Right." Jamie gets to his feet, clearly over this roast of his character. "If my presence is no longer required for this, I'll be going."

"Darling," Lee calls after him, "don't be angry with us."

Then it's just Jack and me on the sofa, still squished together, looking more conspicuous with the space vacated by Jamie. Lee's full attention is now trained on me, as though he's heard my pulse racing.

Or maybe that's my guilty, lustful conscience talking. Which is nuts, because it's not like I've done anything, nor would I. In fact, I'm totally jumping the gun here to assume Jack would take any interest in a somewhat awkward younger woman.

"Good," Lee says once I've been tucked inside my own mind spiral so long I don't know if either of them has noticed. "Glad we got that sorted."

At that, Jack pats my head as he stands, like I'm a Labrador. "Dodged that bullet, eh?"

Stupidly, I smile and nod. But what does that mean?

Was Jamie the bullet? Was I?

Is Jack talking about himself?

I'm more anxious now than when this talk began. But Lee's right. The secretive circumstances of this living situation are fraught enough without the added messiness of *feelings*. Better to banish any notions right out of my mind. Box 'em up and shove them in the attic with my childhood crushes.

This never would have been a problem if Jack had just been a girl like he was supposed to be.

4

THE TIME DIFFERENCE IS STILL WINNING THE WAR WITH MY internal clock. Couple that with anxiousness about my first day at Pembridge, and I'm up and dressed before the rest of the house has even hit their snooze buttons. I take advantage of the head start to walk the neighborhood, just down the street and around the corner to a café where I grab a muffin and coffee. There, I realize I'm still a little iffy on the difference between pence and quid, though thankfully almost everywhere accepts mobile pay.

I take my breakfast to go. It's a two-mile walk to campus in Paddington. There are ample Tube stations to make the trip, but I want to get a sense of the place. Get my bearings and whatnot. I join the pedestrian brigade traversing the tree-lined sidewalks past row houses and hotels, centuries-old apartments and modern glass office buildings. I shuffle along the north end of iron-fenced Kensington Gardens among tourists and joggers and moms with strollers.

The skies are clear and the temperature mild when I reach campus. It isn't the traditional self-contained compound of typical American colleges but rather a series of buildings tucked in among the urban environment, a hodgepodge of baroque architecture and shiny steel. Most of my classes take place in the newer Colburn College, which is home to general education requirement courses. My program-specific work, however, and my first class this morning are in the older Albert Hall, a French-inspired four-story building with ornate carvings over the heavy bronze-embellished doors. It's breathtaking, really, ducking under the portico. Not the kind of thing we get much of in Nashville.

I'm early for my research and composition class. Basically, it's an essential introduction to academic writing necessary for all history majors. I have to tamp down my eagerness as I stake out my spot at the end of the fourth row. Close enough to be engaged in discussion but not so close as to brand myself the try-hard on the first day. With the class filling up, eventually another girl scans the room, then makes eye contact with me as she tracks down the aisle.

"Mind if I sit?" she asks in a crisp British accent.

I tuck in my legs and scoot my bag out of her way. "Go for it."

"Wasn't sure I'd make it," she says, dropping into a seat one over. "I wasn't minding where I was walking, popped into a shop and looked around quite confused."

I know the feeling. "I thought this building was a hotel at first."

She introduces herself as Amelia, a recovering Russian lit major now transitioning to revolutionary France. She confesses that becoming obsessed with an Instagram photo of a dead author is no way to pick a major. I tell her I'm not sure it isn't.

When class gets underway, our professor is a chic middle-aged woman in a scarf who looks like the type you might see at the ballet holding court in the lobby during intermission. Some retired prima ballerina who's left kings and tycoons in her wake.

She explains the course will require us to propose a research topic and spend the better part of the semester preparing a paper on our subject. We have until the end of September to identify our topic and present a strategy. Simple enough, though the enormous breadth of possibilities has me somewhat paralyzed with indecision already.

"Have you been to the Talbot Library yet?" Amelia asks as the teaching assistant walks the aisle handing out the syllabus.

"No, not yet. I heard it's extraordinary."

The Talbot Library remains one of my primary motivations for attending Pembridge. Since I was little, I've adored libraries. My babysitters as a kid, who stayed with me when Dad was touring, would take me to reading camps and book fairs at the local public library. Later, I'd take sightseeing trips just for an especially unusual or historic one, begging my dad for detours on trips together to investigate another library I'd read about online. The one here at Pembridge, while architecturally and aesthetically typical of its era, is notable for its collections in art, history, and primary sources.

"There's a nook on the third floor, near the entrance to the special collections wing. It gets great light," Amelia tells me, and I make a mental note of it.

She and I exchange phone numbers at the end of class, after which I find a bench in the concrete courtyard to sit and call my dad. I know if he doesn't get regular updates, there isn't much that will stop him from getting on a plane and showing up at my front door.

"Hey, baby girl."

"Hi, Dad."

"How's the first day going?"

"Good. I just sent you a picture of the building. It's incredible up close. Built in 1854 and dedicated by Prince Albert."

"I ever tell you about the time I played a gig at Royal Albert Hall? Our guys showed up to load in the same day another crew was loading out, so there's a major traffic jam at the loading dock. I'm on the bus because we've got a short turnaround and need to get a sound check in before lunch, and I see our roadie Rusty outside looking like he's about to kick the hell out of some driver."

My life is measured not in years but in my father's anecdotes. He's got a story for every occasion. Once he gets going, there's no interrupting the memory train.

"Anyway, I go inside to have a look around, and they're telling me I can't go to the stage because John Mayer's out there. He's got his guitar and he's playing, getting some footage or something. But when Rusty gets up there to snatch the guitar out of Mayer's hand and tell him to move along, turns out it isn't him. Just some dude off the street with a thin, patchy beard who somehow snuck into the venue," Dad finishes with a laugh.

"I'll be sure to keep an eye out for John Mayer impersonators," I reply as my phone beeps in my ear.

It's a text from Lee. He's on campus and wants to meet up for lunch by the flower box building. Then he drops me a pin to his location. I study the screen—he's a couple blocks from me.

I hop off the bench and walk and talk until I find Lee looking dapper in another vest and bow tie ensemble, a brown leather messenger bag slung across his chest.

"You finding your way around okay?" Dad is asking in my ear.

"Yep," I answer, then mouth to Lee it's my dad on the line.

Lee grins and waves at the phone in greeting.

"Lee says hi, by the way. We're grabbing a bite before my next class."

"You two going to have any classes together?"

"Not likely. She's in her last year and majoring in biochemistry." Lee brushes his hand over his head to mime sweeping his hair back. "I rock a savage lab coat."

I shush him for fear my father will hear him. Rolling his eyes, Lee animates locking his lips shut.

"Gotta run, Dad. Give you a call tomorrow."

"Be careful," he tells me as a matter of ritual. "Love you, kid."

Lee links his arm through mine and guides me to an Egyptian café a few doors down. The owners are a young married couple who greet him with waves from the kitchen behind the counter. The three of them converse in Arabic, and I catch the word *American* as Lee nods toward me. Before I can reach for a menu from the stack on the counter, Lee waves my hand away and orders for me.

"Trust me," he says as we take a seat at a table outside. "You'll like it."

"I'll try just about anything." And I'm starving. A pastry and some coffee hardly seem sufficient to tide me over for the morning after that walk to campus.

The girl at the register comes out with two glasses of water and our utensils. She also puts down a plate of flatbread with various ramekins of dips.

"Are they friends of yours?" I ask once she's gone.

"Friends of the family, from back in the old neighborhood. This place got me through my first year at uni," Lee says. "They gave me a job washing dishes and bussing tables, then line cook. Hager would be in late most nights roasting lamb for the next day. I'd pop over after the library closed at night, and she'd meet me around back with a plate to take home. Took care of me, being my first time living away from home."

"Your family's Egyptian?"

"My mum. Dad's from Manchester. Mum taught my sister and me to speak the language because she said she wanted us to feel connected to the culture. Really I think she didn't want to feel alone. Dad never much wanted to try. Doesn't have the patience."

"Are you tight with your parents?"

"We're a close family, yes. Our parents threatened to move to London when we applied to university, but we managed to talk them out of it by promising to come home on the weekends. Well, every other weekend maybe." Lee pushes a green dip at me. It sort of resembles chimichurri in texture and appearance but tastes altogether different. "How about you? Both parents are American?"

"My dad was born in LA. My mom…" I pause, tearing off a piece of flatbread. "Come to think of it, I don't think I know where my mom's from."

"You're not close?" He clucks sympathetically.

"Something like that. The birthday cards she sends me never even have a return address. If they arrive at all. Which is usually a couple weeks late. At this point, I don't remember her much."

"What of your dad?"

"Yeah, he's having a tough time letting go. He wasn't much into the parenting thing at first—I sort of got dumped on him full-time when I was two. It took him a few years before he came around to the idea. Since then, it's like he's always trying to make up for it. I love him, but that's a lot of pressure, you know?"

Lee nods. "I reckon."

When our food arrives, I have trouble not gaping at everything. It seems a lot for lunch. One dish after another Tetrised onto the table.

"They always do this." Lee sighs, shaking his head in amusement. "Hager's way of saying I'm too skinny."

I grin. "I've always wanted to order one of everything off a menu."

As we start eating, I discover that Lee is a dictatorial lunch companion. He insists I try this thing first. Then that. Put this one with this other thing. Now try this sauce on this thing. I appreciate his coaching through the culinary adventure, but at a certain point, I feel like I'm in a time trial. Before long, I'm stuffed and groaning when he asks if I'm ready for dessert. I'm convinced Lee has an incinerator where his stomach should be.

"Sorry I missed you this morning," he says as we're finishing our meal. "I meant to ride in with you. Make sure you didn't end up halfway to Leicester."

"It's all good. Gave me a chance to explore a little."

"Getting on then?"

"So far. Class was good, and I think I made a friend. She didn't get up and walk away when she heard my accent, so that's something."

"Well done." The check comes, which Lee snatches before I can look at it. "This one's on me, luv. Call it a welcome gift."

"Oh, okay. Um…thank you." I hate letting friends pay for things. It's sort of a tic of mine, like when someone is embarrassed at receiving compliments. I don't know how to accept it.

"Well, don't strain yourself." He laughs, noticing my discomfort. "You can take me somewhere expensive next time." He signs the check with a flourish, then flashes me a wink. "And speaking of welcome. My friend's band is playing in a pub tomorrow night. You're coming."

"They any good?"

I mean it as a joke, but Lee considers the question before offering a rueful shrug. "No, not really. But my sister will be there." His expression lights up at that. "You two have to meet. I just *know* you're going to love each other."

5

THE FOLLOWING EVENING, OUR ONCE-PROMISING FRIENDSHIP IS near shambles. Lee alternates between sighs of disgust and groans of impatience while he surveys my wardrobe, half of which is still crumpled in suitcases. My room is bursting with boxes that arrived from Nashville this afternoon. I barely started cracking them open before it was time to get ready for his friend's gig.

"Babe, you know this is silk?" He pulls a blue peasant top from one of my crushed packing cubes. "You don't treat good fabrics this way." Then he finds one of my favorite vegan leather jackets, which I'd considered wearing tonight. "This, on the other hand..."

He holds it up by the lapel pinched at a distance between two fingers, his nose scrunched as if he'd found the garment stuck belly-up in a storm drain.

"Are these patches ironic?"

"I love that jacket," I protest. Fine, so maybe it's a little derivative and passé, but I still love it.

Lee walks it across the room and drops it in an empty cardboard box. "We'll call that the *maybe* pile."

I get the feeling that box will be sitting at the curb this time tomorrow.

His passive-aggressive approach to personal styling continues as I try on different iterations of curated outfits. Each one elicits only slight variations of disappointed grimaces until I'm standing in my bra and underwear amid a knee-high pile of war crimes Lee apparently regards as personal insults to his taste.

There's one bag he hasn't opened yet, so he tears into it with a disappointed huff. I'm taking a second glance at the clothes still hanging in my closet when he gasps.

"What is this?" Lee holds up clumps of fabric in two fists.

Apprehensive, I respond, "Clothes?"

He beams at me. "Finally!"

From the bag, he lays out a black graphic T-shirt, a long cardigan, and a dark gray pair of cutoffs. Basically something I'd wear to ride my horse or do chores. He then grabs a handful of necklaces from my dresser and throws them at the outfit with a pair of booties compiled on my bed. The relief that washes over him is visibly intense.

"Clothes," he declares happily.

His phone buzzes on my nightstand. As he goes over to read the message, I notice a secret smile tug at his lips.

"Who's that?" I ask, because I'm nosy.

"George. A new friend."

"A special friend?"

His smile grows wider. "Could be."

"He coming to the show?"

Lee laughs at me and shakes his head. "Not that kind of friend."

"Ah. I see."

"We're meeting up after the show, though."

"Got a picture?"

Lee beckons me over and opens Grindr to show me his new friend's profile. I lean in for a better look. George is handsome, except for one glaring deformity.

"What's with the cop 'stache?" I demand, aghast.

"Oh, babe, I know," he grouses. Lee places his finger over the lower half of George's face. "But see? Perfect."

I laugh. "Maybe you can talk him out of it."

"If things go really well, I'm shaving that thing off once he falls asleep."

"Lee, mate!"

Jack suddenly bursts into my room while I'm still standing in nothing but my bra and underwear. My hands fly up to fight over what to cover more.

"You got any ibuprofen? I've a headache throbbing behind my left eye. What's up with that? It's driving me mad."

I turn sideways in the hopes I might become invisible to him. Like camouflaged prey in the forest. Except I'm more like a pale, freckled deer in the headlights. Our eyes meet in the mirror on top of my dresser. His quickly flick away at realizing I'm not exactly dressed for company. They return, though. Only for a second. Something flashes across his expression that I can't read. Then it's gone.

"Put some clothes on, ay?" Jack says with an unbothered grin. "This is a family establishment."

Oblivious to my mortification, Lee answers Jack with, "Top drawer of my vanity."

"Lee in there?" Jamie appears in my doorway, entirely naked. A towel is slung over his shoulder. "Have you used my trimmers? I've just gone to find them, but they're not in my cabinet."

My hand flies up to avert my gaze, but it's too late. The image of Jamie Jr. is burnt on my retinas.

Barely a week in and already my father's worst nightmares are coming true.

"Go on, darling. Have a gander," Jamie says with humor in his voice. "Surely you've seen a knob before."

"Oh," I say, coughing a laugh. "Isn't that quaint."

Jack keels over with laughter. "Oh no, mate. She called it quaint."

"I think she meant the euphemism."

"No, she's said your willy's sweet and delicate like Grandma's knitting."

Truthfully, my experience with a penis by any name is limited to a one-night stand in high school and a guy freshman year I could generously call my boyfriend. The sex was good, but neither of us were devastated when we moved on.

"Yeah, so can I have my room back now?" I ask, arms strategically placed, talking to the floor.

"Right, you lot." Lee corrals the boys away from the door with arms out wide. "Time for a house meeting about knocking first."

Relief trickles over me once they're gone, and I allow my hands to drop to my sides. Cohabitation will take some getting used to.

And door locks.

We catch a ride to the pub, which is itself a fraught ordeal. Lee seizes the front seat and leaves me sandwiched in the back between Jack, Jamie, and Jamie's penis. But it's Jack, with his sculpted arms and muscular legs pressed against mine, that has me running warm. Both from embarrassment and nervousness.

Like a scratchy throat warning of a coming cold, I feel the fizz of a budding crush bubbling in my gut. He looks utterly edible in a pair of faded jeans and a T-shirt with a surf logo stretched across his broad chest. And he smells really good. So good I have to force myself not to breathe because I'm worried I'll sigh dreamily each time I inhale.

Except not breathing isn't conducive to staying alive, so before long, I'm forced to suck in an abrupt gulp of air. Which makes me cough for a few seconds and draws an amused look from Jack.

Check her out, folks. The weirdo American who hasn't figured out oxygen.

I'm practically jumping out of my skin by the time the driver pulls up at the curb. The moment I'm out of the car, I breathe in the fresh evening air and pretend I'm not at all affected by the hot Australian standing next to me.

Inside, the pub is crowded but not bursting. Most of the commotion surrounds the bar and dartboards toward the front of the room. We bypass them to the tables arranged in front of the tiny vacant platform just large enough to squeeze in a drum set, mics, amps, and a couple monitors.

Lee leads us to a table with two young women already seated. A pale willowy blond with a severe pixie cut sets down her martini when he walks up. She's wearing a satiny dress with a deep vee neckline and a ton of funky silver jewelry. She lifts her large seafoam eyes to mine, and I'm already feeling small and underdressed.

Beside her, a taller girl stands to kiss Lee on both cheeks. This one wears a tight ribbed tee and leather pants that encase her endless legs. She's gorgeous. Like easily the most attractive person I've ever seen in real life.

The similarities between her and Lee are impossible to miss. They have the same mouth. Same dark eyes and high cheekbones. They're not identical, but you'd know these two were related from across the room.

"My twin, Celeste," Lee says by way of an introduction. "Cece, this is Abbey."

"Ah. The American."

I get that a lot lately. "One and the same," I answer shyly. "It's nice to finally meet you."

"Likewise. This is Yvonne." Celeste nods toward the elegant blond, then gives me the up and down.

While she examines me, I wonder if Lee's assistance earlier helped or hindered. Both Yvonne and Celeste are dressed far more glamorously and sexier than anything I would have come up with. I suddenly feel like a little kid.

As Jack and Jamie run off to the bar, Yvonne rises to greet me with double air-kisses. I zig when I should zag and we end up in this awful dance trying to get out of each other's way. She ends up kissing my ear, then my nose, and we are both worse for the entire exchange. At this point, I'd prefer to leave the country and never come back.

Her eyes flicker with amusement. "Right. That certainly was awkward."

At least she has a sense of humor about it. "Very discouraging," I agree. "Doesn't bode well for the rest of the night."

That gets me an airy laugh. "Oh hush, darling. It's going to be a smashing night."

"What are you drinking?" Lee asks me.

"White wine?" I hadn't given much thought to what *my drink* would be now that I'm legal on this side of the Atlantic. This seems the safest choice.

"Pace yourself," Yvonne mocks. "Wouldn't want to risk having a good time."

So it's going to be like that.

Yvonne asks for another espresso martini and Celeste orders a pint. Armed with our drink orders, Lee leaves me under the unshielded scrutiny of the two women.

"You're probably not much of a drinker, right?" Celeste guesses. "You're not legal in America."

"True. But I also think it's sort of a PTSD," I find myself confessing. "I can't tolerate the smell of beer and liquor. Makes me sick. I was around too much of it when I was a kid."

"Why's that?" Celeste asks. "Parents alcoholics?"

Subtle. She certainly shares a brashness with her brother.

I shake my head. "No, not like that. But my dad was kind of a partier back in the day. Came with the territory."

I'm not sure why I keep talking. I don't actually want to have this conversation. But something about Celeste's penetrating stare creates a persuasive cocktail that pulls the words from my lips, and I lose control of my better instincts. A terminal case of wanting to be liked by everyone.

Celeste narrows her eyes. "What territory's that?"

"No, I mean…" Shit. I don't know what I mean. I walked myself into this corner, and now I'm struggling to find my way out. "Like his job…" *Seriously, Abbey?*

"His job," Celeste repeats. "What does that mean?"

I could dip and dodge all night, but she isn't going to let this go. The intent in her eyes tells me she's got a whiff. And now, if purely for sport, she's getting this bone.

I let out a quick breath and capitulate. "He was a musician."

One perfect eyebrow arches. "What, like, would I know him?"

I hate this part.

"Gunner Bly."

Her mouth falls open. Yvonne cocks her head. I know exactly how it goes from here. This is usually the moment they start gushing. Telling me my dad's hot. Which, no, gross.

Then they'll go on about their prom song or graduation song or breakup song or that time they lost their virginity in the Dairy Queen parking lot. Why people think I want to know these things is beyond me.

And then, inevitably, one of them is a budding music producer. Their cousin is a singer. Their boyfriend has a band. Everyone wants something that I have zero power to give, and I become a prop, a means to an end. Whatever relationship we had or could've had devolves into a quid pro quo. Doesn't make it easy to have friends.

It's lonely as hell, actually.

The boys return to the table with our drinks. Celeste ignores the plea in my eyes and instantly turns on her brother.

"Why didn't you tell me Abbey's dad is Gunner Bly?" she accuses.

"What?" Lee chuckles as he looks at her sideways. "Who said that?"

"Abbey."

"What, really?" Jamie blinks at me.

I nod reluctantly.

"Should I know that name?" Jack scans the table. I knew there was a reason I liked him.

Yvonne hands him her phone. And if I'm not deluding myself, she's watching me with a newfound respect, perhaps? It's better than contempt, so I'll take it.

Jack holds the phone up to his ear, listening intently as a Spotify track plays. Then his attention jerks to me. "Oh, the 'heart is a windmill' bloke."

I hate that song. It's one of Dad's first singles and at this point a cliché staple of every commercial, saccharine TV soundtrack, and instrumental elevator background score. How the hell is a heart like a windmill anyway?

I asked my dad that once. He said he was probably high when he wrote it, then gave me the just-say-no-to-drugs talk.

"Really?" I glance around the group. "None of you are going to make a big deal out of it? Because you have no idea how refreshing this is."

"We're English, Abbs," Jamie replies in his crisp, posh accent. "Englishmen only make a big deal about pints and footy."

"You seriously don't care?" I glance at Lee, who seems most likely to suffer from celebrity obsession syndrome. He grilled me hard when he found out I grew up in LA.

"I listen exclusively to pop stars and power ballads," he says gravely.

I hide a smile and turn to Celeste, who shrugs. "I've never been a Bly fan. But that one track he has? 'Acrimonious'? Not terrible."

I'm tempted to type that out as a quote and text it to my father. *"Gunner Bly: not terrible"—Celeste Clarke.*

To my immediate relief, no one presses me for salacious details or some vague promise of a favor. There's no gushing at all, in fact, and the group quickly moves on to a nostalgic cataloguing of their middle school playlists.

I am well off the hook when the lights in the room dim as the band takes the stage. They get decent applause from the audience.

Proving they're capable of caring about more than soccer and beer, Lee and the boys whistle and holler, which elicits a nod from the bassist while he plugs in. A couple of stage lights above our heads flash on, at which point my attention becomes transfixed.

For perhaps the first time in recorded rock history, the bassist is hot.

6

MY ENTIRE LIFE, I'VE BEEN BAFFLED BY THIS CULTURAL INFECTION of rock star worship. Groupies sleeping in cars on cross-country pilgrimages. Teen girls staked outside hotels. Waiting hours in the rain, distraught and hysterical, for an autograph. Obsession as disease.

Then this dark-haired bit of poison slings a bass guitar over his shoulder, and I'm entranced. Utterly dumbstruck. Riveted by the way the instrument hangs low at his hips. His shoulders hunched over as he plays. The silver rings on his fingers. Leather bands and bracelets of string around his wrist that all have a story, a meaning, but you don't ask because he won't tell. You don't want him to; it would ruin the infinite mystery.

While not Jack-sized, he's tall and lean with perfectly sculpted arms, biceps flexing when he begins to strum. My throat goes dry as he closes his eyes, nodding his head to a melody I'm scarcely hearing. I'm too distracted by the way he's biting his lip. He's feeling the chords as his fingers rip across the bass line. Rhythm and poetry.

I'm mesmerized by the dumbest things. How one lock of hair drips in front of his eyes. The shirtsleeve riding up his bicep. The worn, raw marks on his guitar that each encompass a memory. I hardly hear a single song in their set. For twenty full minutes, I'm in a trance, until they leave the stage and I snap out of it. I hastily look around, worried that everyone has noticed my intense preoccupation, but they're all chatting among themselves, oblivious to my pounding heart and damp palms.

The bassist eventually reemerges and makes his way through the maze of tables in the pub.

Toward ours.

He's coming this way.

A jolt of nervous panic surges through my limbs. Stupid scenarios of him picking me out of the crowd run through my head as he flashes a wry smile, jerks his chin the slightest bit in recognition, and—

Kisses Yvonne, who eagerly rises to meet him.

I feel flattened.

Run down and backed over.

Frantically embarrassed, I avert my gaze and stare into my barely sampled wine. My pulse remains wild and frenetic, so insistent I feel it in my feet, my teeth. I hope nobody can see my mortification.

"Nate," Lee says as the bassist pulls up a chair beside Yvonne to throw his arm over her shoulder. "This is our new flatmate from America. Abbey, this here's Nate."

I don't know what to do with my hands. Thankfully, Nate doesn't bother with a proper shake. He offers a nod as Jack hands him a pint.

"All right, Abbey," he says in a deep, husky voice.

I never know if that's a question with Brits. "Uh, yeah. Great set."

I inwardly cringe, kicking myself. Already, I sound like a stupid fawning bass bunny. I've played dolls in Steven Tyler's house and ridden horses at Skywalker Ranch, but here I am starstruck by some guy playing gigs in a West London pub. I hate me.

Approaching something like nervous nausea, I down my glass of wine. In the chair beside me, Jamie raises an amused eyebrow in question.

"Another?" he asks.

Why not. "Please."

As he stands, the shouted drink orders pile up. Jamie makes his trip to the bar while the others talk and I struggle to appear engaged as their competing accents become more difficult to distinguish the more glasses they empty.

"Ask Abbey," Celeste suddenly says. Ask me what, I don't know. I glance over. "Huh?"

"She's a bit of an expert." Celeste looks at Nate, which means I look at Nate. And my pulse rushes again.

"You a musician, Abbey?" His eyes are dark brown and inquisitive.

"No, not even a little." I dabbled on guitars and drums when I was younger. Even briefly took up piano and violin lessons when my dad thought it was a change of genre that might spark some creative interest and latent talent. That was not the case.

"Her dad's Gunner Bly," Yvonne informs him.

"That right?" Nate sits forward. He drags a hand over the stubble shadowing his chiseled jaw, his inscrutable expression giving nothing away. "He recorded all the instruments on *Apparatus* himself, didn't he?"

"Um, yeah."

Nate becomes more animated. "I heard he laid down the rough cut on the back of his tour bus during the second leg of a European tour."

I nod. "Some of the original masters were confiscated by Polish police when they searched the bus while he was on stage in Warsaw."

Jack, who's been typing on his phone, lifts his head with interest. "What, they stole them?"

"He got them back, didn't he?" Nate asks, those curious eyes locked on mine.

I find it hard to look away. "My dad's tour manager, Tommy, damn near got arrested fighting these cops for them. He's my godfather, actually. Still has a scar from where they clubbed him."

"Clubbed him? What the hell happened?" Jack grins as he raises his pint glass to his lips, drawing my attention away from Nate's eyes to Jack's mouth.

My erratic pulse is now confused as to which guy it's pounding for. Both, it decides and careens harder. Awesome. I'm caught in a love triangle fabricated entirely by my overactive imagination. Because in real life, Nate is clearly with Yvonne, and Jack treats me like a little sister.

"Abbs?" Jack prompts.

I try to remember what we were talking about. "Oh. Right. So Tommy watches the officers walk off the bus and put the tapes in a police car. He tells my dad, and Dad goes to one of the riggers and says, 'I need a pipe or whatever. Something heavy.'"

I realize midsentence that I'm doing that thing I always cringe at from other celebrity kids: making my entire personality about who my father is. I almost never tell these stories at home. Maybe because for most of my childhood, his name was everywhere.

Now, it's like I'm stuck in his cycle of word vomit. I can't shut up, even as I listen to myself speak like an out-of-body experience.

"The rigger hands him a shackle, like what they use to hang truss and chain motors. He takes this steel shackle and smashes the passenger window of the car, and Tommy grabs the masters. Except then he gets clubbed and hits the ground. He tosses Dad the tapes, shouting, 'Run, man! Forget about me.'"

Everyone at the table breaks out laughing. "This is wild," Lee raves.

"So Dad hightails it out of there. He flags down a random car outside the arena with the cops running after him. Tommy manages to get back on the bus, and the driver takes off. Dad gets dropped off at the airport and calls Tommy, like, 'Get your ass here. We're getting the hell out of the country.'"

I look at Nate, who's shaking his head in amusement. It's not lost on me that my most interesting stories are not of my life at all.

"Anyway, my dad can't go back to Poland. He likes to tell people they put an Interpol warrant out for him, but that's just a rumor."

Jamie comes back in time for another wave of laughter. He sets several drinks on the table. "What'd I miss?"

"Abbey's dad is an international fugitive," Lee explains.

Jamie waves that off, as if to say, *I can top that*. "Did I tell you about the time my mate brings this girl back from Ibiza on his plane to find a bunch of massive blokes in suits and black SUVs waiting at the airport? He'd practically kidnapped a crown prince's daughter."

The group soon tears through the fresh round of drinks and dives right into another. I don't try to keep up, though the more I run a distant second, the more the wine calms my brain. Until there's just the warm embrace of gentle inebriation.

At some point, we migrate to the dartboards. Turns out Jack and Jamie are bitter rivals where pub games are concerned.

"What strategy is that then?" Jack says, collecting the darts Jamie just flung at the board. "Going to hit everything but the money spaces?"

"Keep it up, ya twat." I'm discovering that Jamie loses control of his tongue after a few drinks. I sort of love it.

They go at it to a draw. Neither are satisfied, and the skirmish soon becomes a battle of attrition in the war of trash-talking.

"As enthralling as this is," Lee says, sliding up to me, "I'm dipping out. Don't let these fools kill each other."

I give him a coy smile. "Tell Mustache George I said hi."

He winks in response, then kisses his sister goodbye on his way out.

"Face it, yeah? There is no world in which you beat me." Jamie's on one now. I don't know what he's been drinking, but he's consumed a lot of it, the belief in his invincibility now total.

"You're welcome to put down those darts and put your elbow on the table." Jack cracks his knuckles and then flexes his biceps, as he apparently challenges Jamie to an arm-wrestling competition.

"Bring the darts and I'll take that action," I mutter to myself.

I don't realize until I hear a muffled chuckle that Nate has come up behind me. I glance at him over my shoulder. Bad idea. In his amused gaze, I become stuck. There's a flicker of, I don't know, awareness of sorts. Then it vanishes with Jack's bellow of victory at throwing a bull's-eye to end the game.

I'm drafted by Jack onto a doubles team against Jamie and Celeste, leaving Nate and Yvonne to cozy up undisturbed. At some point, they duck out together, and that's how I met and lost the crush of a lifetime in a single night.

I think I love London.

I think I hate it.

SEPTEMBER

7

MY HEAD'S TAKEN A GOOD POUNDING, AND I MIGHT HURL IF I SIT up too fast. Last night's makeup is smudged on my pillow. Sharpie doodles cover my hand after Lee got hold of a marker somehow and we took turns drawing on each other over a plate of bacon when we all stumbled in from the pub last night. I smile as I remember us sitting in the kitchen listening to the walls creak from Jamie's latest conquest upstairs.

Which is to say I'm finding my place here.

My first week of classes are over, and aside from several reminders to adopt British spelling conventions, I'm keeping up. A part of me was worried I wouldn't make it a week. That pessimistic little bitch sitting in the shadowed corner of my psyche said I couldn't cope outside the protective confines of Daddy's house, that I'd wither and crumble out on my own. Hated by my roommates, resented by classmates, and shunned by professors.

Despite any reports to the contrary, I am not, in fact, a complete disaster.

Hell, I'm practically a functional adult.

Slowly, I peel myself out of bed, throw on a pair of sweatpants and slippers. I hesitate at my door, remembering I'm not wearing a bra beneath my loose tank top. I debate putting one on before heading downstairs, then remind myself this is my home now and I need to get comfortable with going braless. Because bras suck.

The house is quiet when I make my way to the kitchen. We left a mess last night. Most of which I blame on Jamie trying to make pancakes at 3 a.m.

I feel the ground rumble beneath my feet as I fix myself a bowl of cereal, signaling Jack coming down the stairs. He's shirtless, as usual. His perpetual Gold Coast tan and undulating abs obliterate the remnants of sleep from the corners of my eyes. I promptly grow distracted by the way Jack's sweatpants cling to his ass as he saunters toward the sink.

It isn't fair he just…does that. I don't know how I'm going to survive this living arrangement if he keeps flaunting his physique like some Aussie Magic Mike. Every time he walks into a room, that giddy, stupid energy surges up in my gut all over again.

It doesn't help that I've made myself come to fantasies of him almost every night.

The reminder brings heat to my cheeks while at the same time puckering my nipples. Great. Where is that bra when you need it?

"Morning," Jack says, turning to face me.

"Morning."

He pours granola into a bowl of plain yogurt, then drizzles honey on top, licking some excess from his finger while meeting my eyes.

"Did you know your nipples are poking out of that shirt?" he says helpfully.

Oh my God.

"Your observation is noted," I grumble. "Perv."

"Just saying."

"Say it quietly and in your head next time," I suggest in a saccharine tone.

Jack chuckles and shoves yogurt in his mouth.

"Apparently Australians need to take some etiquette lessons from the Brits," I add, rolling my eyes at him.

"We're a very vocal bunch," he agrees. "If you think I've no filter, you should meet my older brother Charlie. Chronic foot-in-mouth syndrome, that one. And our eldest brother, Noah, holds the record for getting his teeth knocked out at bars for talking shit."

I furrow my brow. "How many siblings do you have?"

"One sister and three brothers."

"Wow. That's a lot. You're saying there are three other Hot Jacks walking around—" I stop, cursing myself when I realize what I'd said.

A half smile curves his lips. "Hot Jacks?"

My cheeks are on fire.

The grin widens. "You think I'm hot, do you, Abbey?" he drawls.

"Shut up. You know you are."

He props his hip against the counter and drags a hand through his sleep-mussed hair. "Honestly? Nobody's ever said that to me before."

I stare at him. "You're fucking with me."

He bites his lower lip. There's something very vulnerable in the way he's—

"Yeah, I'm fucking with you," he confirms, that brash glint returning to his expression. "Most women agree with that assessment."

"Cocky much?" I try to distract from my red cheeks and thundering pulse by pretending this has all been a bit of banter.

He brings his bowl over to lean across the breakfast counter where I sit. "Hey, you're the one going on and on about my good looks."

That devastating smile should be a war crime. In fact, no man should be so handsome and charming at once. Like, one or the other, buddy. Save something for the rest of the guys.

"G'morning." Jamie strolls in looking all shiny and new.

It's remarkable how well he cleans up after a night out. No puffy eyes or signs of a hangover. Still manages to make a T-shirt and jeans look couture. He's got a runway model build and effortless cool. It's very annoying.

Jamie goes to start a kettle for tea and turns to look at us. "Lee and I are off to Surrey today. I need to drop in at the estate for a few things. You're both welcome to join if you don't have other plans."

Jack shakes his head. "Can't, mate. Got a match this afternoon."

"Abbs?" Jamie asks. "Care for a drive out to the country?"

I'm not exactly claustrophobic in the city already, but I could use some greenery and blue skies. Might be nice to get out from under the gray buildings and car exhaust.

So I say, "Sounds delightful."

"Lovely."

"And on the way, maybe you let me try a little of that driving on the other side of the road?"

It came up last night, though from the puzzled look on Jamie's face, he doesn't recall our conversation. He laughs, shaking his head.

"Not bloody likely. I'd sooner lose a foot than give you the keys of a machine like that. American drivers are notorious."

"You know movies aren't real, right?"

"Isn't crashing cars literally a sporting event there?" he responds.

"Depends who you ask."

Jamie pours himself some tea, defiant. "Americans are the most destructive force the world has ever known, and I won't have one behind the wheel of my car. Especially not a teenage girl."

"The most dangerous kind," Jack says with a mocking ominous voice.

"I'm turning twenty in January," I protest.

"It's September. Ergo, today you're still a teenager who won't be touching my car."

"Forget him." Jack winks at me as he carries his empty bowl to the sink. "I'll take you driving when we get a chance."

A flush of excitement warms my cheeks. "Really?"

"Sure. What's living without the imminent threat of death?" Jack elbow-jabs me on his way out of the kitchen, leaving Jamie to chuckle to himself as he scrolls Insta.

Boys are dicks.

———————

Once Jamie, Lee, and I are on the road headed south out of London, I come to understand why Jamie is so militantly protective of his car. The Jaguar is gorgeous on the inside and rides like it's on a cushion of air. Of course, this makes me more determined to break down Jamie's resistance. I've got time. He hasn't seen me put my mind to a task yet.

"Nate's got another gig at the Polly next weekend," Lee says from the passenger seat, reading off his phone. "Should he put us on the list?"

At the mention of the hottest bassist on planet Earth, my heart does a very predictable somersault.

"That depends. Are they going to play a song I've not heard forty times?" Jamie asks dryly.

"They'd have to write a song that isn't one of their eight thinly veiled Bob Dylan covers, so I doubt it."

"Okay." I laugh with relief. "I didn't want to say anything, but I thought I was the only one."

"They try so hard," Lee says. "Does have the feeling of a child's school recital, though, don't it?"

"Shame, because Nate's bloody damn good," Jamie tsks. "Come to think of it, Kenny's a fine singer. And Rodge kills it on those drums."

"Perplexing," Lee agrees.

"My dad always talks about how he was in this band in high school. They were all fine individually. Together, they were a dreadful mess." I shrug. "I guess it takes more than standing on the same stage to make a band."

"That's quite good," Jamie says. "I like that."

Now that they've brought it up, however, I can't help being a little curious about their friendship with Nate.

Or…okay, fine. Maybe I'm more than a "little" curious. The memory of his dark, mysterious eyes is haunting me.

"How do you all know Nate?" I ask lightly. "School or…?"

"Met him through Yvonne," Lee says. He doesn't elaborate, which impedes my fact-finding mission.

"Okay. So how do you know Yvonne then?"

Jamie glances over at Lee. "Yvonne was your friend first, wasn't it?"

"We hung out my first year at uni, yeah, but eventually she became more Celeste's friend."

"How long has she been with Nate?"

Trying to put together a picture of him in my head, it's hard to reconcile the guy I met with someone who would date her. Those two seem so entirely incompatible. Nate is very chill, albeit broody. There was something equally enigmatic and lustful about him, a hint that beneath his hard-to-read exterior lies something wilder, raw. Yvonne was elegant, posh, and outgoing, with a hint of drama beneath the surface. She also came off a bit snooty.

"I don't know," Lee answers. "Like six months, maybe."

Jamie, proving to be more perceptive than I gave him credit for, meets my gaze in the mirror and smirks slightly. "All academic there, right, Abbs? Just being thorough."

I narrow my eyes at him.

Lee turns in his seat to stare at me. "Oh dear. Does someone have a crush?"

"Absolutely not."

Even if Yvonne wasn't in the picture, how could I go home telling my dad I'd fallen for a bassist? He'd disown me.

"I knew this one would be trouble from the out," Jamie says with a chuckle. "Yvonne had better be wary."

"I don't have a crush," I mutter, scowling at them both. "Just catching up on the histories."

It isn't long before the concrete buildings and city streets give

way to small villages, trees, and sprawling green hills. Estates delin-
eated by wooden fences and hedgerows. It's not so different from the
secluded suburbs outside Nashville. The roads become narrow and
winding as the homes grow larger and farther from the road until
they disappear entirely behind iron gates and tall foliage.

"That's the Allenbury estate," Lee tells me as we pass a narrow
driveway. "Their eldest son had to be plucked from the Ligurian
Sea by the Monaco coast guard after he was tossed off the yacht
of a Genoese billionaire. Rumor has it the husband flew out on his
helicopter to find the lad sunbathing naked on the bunny pad with
the missus."

"What, seriously?" I ask in disbelief.

"That's the story," Jamie confirms. "He floated east for three
hours on a life ring the crew tossed him after the husband ordered
them to cut it loose from the boat."

"Wow. That's terrible but, like, also sort of gangster."

Coming around a bend, we see a sign for an estate sale.

"I can't imagine what a garage sale out here looks like," I remark.
"Whose estate is that?"

"The Tulleys," Lee supplies with a graveness in his voice. "Few
have fallen further."

"What does that mean?"

"Was a time they were quite chummy with the royal family, but
they fell out of favor with the Crown over the years. Those poor
Tulleys have been in a slow-motion free fall for the better part of a
decade."

"Money troubles?" I guess. When rich people let strangers pick
over their life's possessions, it usually means one thing.

"That's part of it," Jamie says. "More a symptom than the illness,
perhaps. That whole clan's rife with black sheep. Drug addicts,
adulterers."

"That doesn't seem so bad." There are worse sins, after all.

"For commoners, no. In private even, not that unusual. British aristocracy flaunting their skeletons in public, however? There's no greater faux pas. The levee broke, as it were, when the duke's brother was arrested with a prostitute overdosing in his Bentley outside the gates at Kensington. After that, the palace had no choice but to disavow the whole lot of them."

"Yikes."

Lee glances at me over his shoulder. "Yikes indeed."

"Excommunication hasn't stopped them from name-dropping like they're doing Christmas at Sandringham," Jamie says derisively. "To hear them tell it, it's all a simple misunderstanding that'll be cleared up any day now. Never mind a series of poor investments and fraud investigations has left them near squalor. I'm surprised they've kept the estate this long."

"Well, now we have to take a look," I say, sitting forward to poke my head between their seats. "Can we go to the estate sale? Just for a few minutes?"

"Yes, can we, darling?" Lee bats his eyelashes.

"Right. Hang on." Jamie makes a sudden U-turn. "If you both promise to behave yourselves."

Lee's quick to quip back. "I wouldn't dream of it."

8

Jamie parks his Jaguar beside a Bentley and a beat-up Volkswagen coupe on the gravel car park in front of the manor house. It's astounding, this place. Four stories of ornate original architecture surrounded by green lawns. A pond on the east side is ringed by willow trees dipping their limbs in the still water.

"Are you serious?" I mutter the exclamation to myself, though Lee hears me and chuckles.

"Shoulders back, chin high. Act like you belong."

"People actually live like this," I say in continued astonishment. I've seen these places in movies, but they're so much more elaborate and impressive in person.

"It's all right," Jamie says dismissively.

A young woman in a blue pantsuit approaches with a blinding white smile to hand us each a registry of items available for sale. She escorts us around the west side of the main house, through a river stone–paved garden, until we reach a brick courtyard where tables are set out to display silver serving sets, jewelry, books, paintings, and the various collected possessions of one of Britain's once-great families.

It's sort of depressing.

Like picking over a corpse.

Jamie is unfazed. Immediately he's on the scent of a cute brunette admiring the vases and candleholders. In seconds, he has her twisting her hair around her finger and leaning on one hip. Incredible.

As he's been doing most of the morning, Lee has his head bowed over his phone.

"George?" I ask while we peruse a table of carved jade candleholders.

Lee nods absently.

"Did he shave that horrid mustache?"

"What? Oh, no, luv, this is a new one."

"A new what?"

"A new George."

"What happened to Mustache George?"

"Too clingy." Lee picks a couture silk kimono-style robe sheathed in plastic off a clothing rack. Then he sees the price tag and throws it down like it tried to bite him. "New George is more chill. A go-with-the-flow kind of bloke."

I shake my head. "I swear, everyone in England is named George."

We drift over to another table. Most of the stuff arrives at a weird intersection of seventeenth-century English country and eighties Miami drug dealer. Then I spot a hardbound encyclopedia of the trees of France and decide, well, no sense letting material go to waste. I have my research project to think about, and this estate could provide ample inspiration.

I browse the stacks of leather-bound first editions and obscure volumes about the most random of topics. From the history of English carpentry to great ships of the empire. Modern fashion to mapmaking. I find a leaf pressed between the pages of an account of an early expedition to Greenland. Minutes later, my arms are full, and another attendant of the sale offers to set my shopping aside for me while I continue browsing.

"I won't be mad if you want to slip a few rubies in your pockets." Lee sidles up to me in front of several paintings propped up against the brick-faced wall of the servants' entrance to the kitchen.

"Is that the good crystal I hear clinking around in your pant legs?" I tease.

"Did you see those porcelain goose things?" He makes a gagging noise. "A thousand pounds. What on earth possessed these people?"

Most of the paintings are what I'd imagine as fancy British interior design: Hunting horseback behind a pack of dogs. Landscapes. Still life and gardens. But then a small portrait in an ornate frame catches my eye. It's of a young dark-haired woman looking off her shoulder. Her eyes are a deep chocolate brown. A simple gray dress covers her slight frame and drapes over the side of the antique chair she's perched on.

Lee whistles softly. "They're tossing the ancestors out with the old linens. This is dreadful."

My gaze remains glued to the painting. The girl is around my age, maybe a year or two older. She appears preoccupied. Not lost in thought but as if listening to a conversation just out of frame. That look you get when people are talking about you like you aren't in the room. She's trapped in this pose, though she doesn't know why. Doesn't know how she found herself here or what else her life might have been, might still be, if she had the nerve to decide otherwise.

It's mesmerizing.

"Hello?" Lee snaps his fingers inches from my face. "Babe, you in there?"

I gesture at the painting. "She's sort of captivating, right?"

Staring at her, he makes a face like he's stepped in something. "It's a sad white girl."

"I don't know. I like her."

He shrugs. "Whatever. I don't kink-shame."

The registry says little about the painting itself. Oil on canvas. Not even a date. By the hair and dress, I'd guess World War II era, but I can't be sure. It's perfect for further research, however.

"Hi there," I say, approaching the woman in the blue pantsuit.

She looks up from her clipboard. "May I be of assistance?"

"I hope so. I have questions about one of the paintings."

"Oh, lovely. Let's see if I can answer them."

She introduces herself as Sophie and offers that pearly-white smile again. She's gorgeous, I realize. Her brown hair is arranged in an elegant chignon, and she has warm hazel eyes and cheekbones I'd kill for.

"Do you work for the Tulleys?" I ask as we fall into step with each other. "Or are you just organizing the sale for them?"

"I work for the duke's eldest son. Benjamin," Sophie clarifies, as if I should know this information. "I'm his executive assistant." She laughs dryly. "My duties range from attending to business matters to running his entire household."

"Sounds exhausting."

"Sometimes," she relents.

I lead her back to the painting of the dark-haired girl. "This one. Can you tell me anything more about it other than what's on the registry?"

Sophie studies the painting, pursing her lips. Then she flips through the pages on her clipboard, stopping to read.

"I'm afraid there's nothing in here about it. A lot of these pieces belonged to Lawrence Tulley, the duke's grandfather, who wasn't diligent about cataloguing his collection. If you're hoping this has any value of significance, I'm afraid it doesn't. The valuable pieces are either being retained by the family or sold to museums."

"No, it's not the value I'm interested in. It's the history."

"I'm sorry I can't be more helpful," Sophie says before walking off to speak to one of the sale attendants.

I turn back to the painting and check the price. One hundred pounds.

Fuck it. I'm splurging. Dad's going to have some questions when he gets the credit card bill, but my total haul isn't so extravagant. Besides, this is an academic pursuit. He'll understand.

For the drive to Jamie's estate, the mystery woman rides on

the seat next to me. I begin to wonder how, presumably, a Tulley family member gets put out with the old bedsheets and ill-advised fad wardrobe. What relegates a person to a yard sale folding table? At some point, she meant enough to someone to have her portrait painted. When did that change, and why? What betrayal or tragedy befalls a family already so entangled in scandal and strife to prompt the wholesale disposal of this woman?

"You better keep that thing in your room." Peering over his shoulder from the front seat, Lee scowls at the painting. "I don't like its eyes."

"Uh-oh, mate. She's heard you," Jamie warns, glancing at me in the rearview mirror as he drives. "Better keep your door locked while you're sleeping, Abbs."

"It's a painting, not a cursed doll," I grumble at them. "Unless I wake up tomorrow with gray hair, I'm sure it's harmless."

Lee faces the front. "That's what it wants you to think."

We approach a set of iron gates, then proceed through a tunnel of trees that opens to a long gravel driveway that rounds a fountain in front of a palatial Elizabethan manor. Tall windows reflect acres of manicured lawns as Jamie pulls up to the front door.

"Stop it," I blurt out, staring through the passenger window.

"We have stopped," he says, puzzling over me.

"You just, like, *live* here? Like it's a perfectly normal thing to do."

He smiles, at least a little charmed by my astonishment. "No, I live two doors down from your bedroom. My family lives here. Occasionally."

"Occasionally," I repeat as we get out of the car.

"There's the flat in London and summer home on the continent," he says with a British upper-crust poshness that has Lee rolling his eyes. "This here is nearly a relic. Kent Manor has been in the family since the Napoleonic Wars. The story goes our ancestor had some quarrel with the patriarch of the previous occupants. During the wars, the man lost three heirs to the fighting, a brother to sickness, and the aging patriarch himself was robbed and stabbed to death in London."

I look at Lee. "And you're worried about a painting?"

"In the end," Jamie continues, somewhat smug, "Kent offered to keep the man's widow comfortable until her death in exchange for assuming the responsibilities of the manor."

"How generous," I say, grinning.

He smirks. "Wasn't it." With his expensive sunglasses reflecting the sunlight, he leans against the side of his Jaguar. "We do get the occasional special guest. Elton John stayed here once."

He says it with such gravitas that I'm compelled to burst his bubble just for fun. "I met Elton once. My dad opened for him a few times during the Asian leg of his tour back in the day. He was huge in Korea."

Lee huffs. "Am I really the only gay man in England who doesn't know Elton John?"

At home that evening, I take my haul up to my room. The painting goes atop the dresser, and I sit back on my bed watching it watch me. Lee wasn't entirely wrong about her eyes. They're intelligent and perceptive. She knows you're there, wondering who she is, asking questions she won't answer. Who is she, and how did she end up an anonymous figure inside a frame, forgotten and discarded?

The grim thought sends an odd shiver running up my spine. I think that's what my dad feared most of all, what propelled him through his career: a persuasive phobia of obscurity. And it's what made him give it all up too. Fear of never knowing his daughter, of her not recognizing him. Memory controls us more than we realize.

"Souvenir?"

I jerk at the sound of his voice.

Jack leans against my doorframe in a pair of plaid pants. His hair's wet, and beads of water still cling to his bare chest. He smells like man soap. The scent fills my room in an instant—thick and humid—like I'm standing with him in the shower. A thought that runs rampant through my brain until he nods at the painting like snapping his fingers in my face to see if anyone's home.

"Who's the lass?"

"Yeah, uh, I don't know." I recover myself, hoping he doesn't pick up that every time he wanders half-naked into my field of view, I lose track of time and space. "We stopped at an estate sale. I picked it up more out of curiosity."

Jack bobs and weaves his head as he enters, examining the painting from different angles. "The eyes. I swear they're following me."

"Lee doesn't like her." I grin. "He thinks she's going to crawl out of there and end up standing over his bed with a butcher knife."

Jack shudders. "Thanks for the nightmares."

"I'm supposed to come up with a research project for one of my classes. Solve a mystery of sorts. I figure this qualifies."

He approaches the painting again. "She's a stunner, that one."

How absolutely typical that Hot Jack would have a crush on a painting I bring home. Eliza will love this.

"I want to find out who she is, but I'm not sure where to start."

With a shrug, he taps the corner of the painting. "Start with the artist."

I go to take a closer look. The signature is so subtle I hadn't noticed it before.

"What does that say?" I ask, squinting at the right-hand corner. "Dyce?"

"Looks like."

"What are the chances of locating one World War II–era painter named Dyce in the whole of England?"

"Guess you're about to find out." He steps back, still studying my new treasure. "Bizarre, isn't it? To put a portrait out on the front lawn and not say anything about who they are?"

"Part of her charm." Excitement begins building inside me, that same nerdy glee I feel every time I'm about to delve into a period of unknown history. "What could possibly have gotten her black-balled by a family like the Tulleys? Was she a misfit? A rebel? I don't know. And there's something about her expression. It's like she'd just swallowed a smirk, you know? She was up to something."

I glance at Jack to realize he's no longer contemplating the painting but transfixed on me.

"What?" I say self-consciously.

"Really turns you on, does it? This history stuff."

Oh boy. Somebody this good-looking isn't allowed to say the words *turned on* in my vicinity.

"It's kind of my passion," I confess.

He chuckles. "My ego would be massive if chicks were talking about me with that kind of passion."

For my own sanity, I turn the subject on him. "Aren't you passion-ate about something?"

"Rugby" is the instant reply.

I snort.

"—and sex."

My snort turns into a startled cough.

"Big fan of that," he adds with a faint smile.

I gulp. Is he flirting?

I busy myself by adjusting my side braid, which is coming undone after a long day out. Then I look up and swallow harder, because when my gaze was averted, he sort of snuck up on me and crept close enough that I can feel the heat from his skin on my cheek.

Like the girl in the painting, he has magnetic eyes too. Gaze-into-them-and-fall-in-his-arms eyes. Trip-over-my-own-two-feet eyes. I wonder what he's seeing in me, staring so intently.

"How about you, Abbs?" His voice has gone a bit raspy, almost mocking.

"How about me what?"

"What are your thoughts on sex?"

My breath catches.

Is he seriously standing here all nonchalant, asking me for my sex thoughts in clear defiance of house rules one through infinity?

"Um." I bite my lip and don't miss the way his gaze focuses on that. "Sex is...fun."

His mouth curves. "Can't disagree with that." Jack tips his head, pensive. "You popped your UK cherry yet?"

Oh my God. Did he really just say that?

"No. Why, are you offering?"

Oh my God. Did *I* really just say that?

My heart is beating triple time, the air so thick I can barely draw a breath. My lungs are burning.

"I think"—Jack watches me for a moment; then he visibly swallows and finishes—"I'd better head downstairs and prep dinner."

The scent of him lingers in my room well after he's gone. Taunting me.

9

After classes Monday afternoon, I make my first visit to Pembridge's historic Talbot Library. Although it only formally became part of the university in the late nineteenth century, the building itself has stood for more than six centuries. It was once a church, featuring Gothic windows and towering ceilings, polished stone floors and flying buttresses. The wooden shelves and railings are dark and smooth from generations of hands leaving them almost shiny, like river stones or a petrified branch on a beach. It's breathtaking. Seems almost preposterous I should belong here. Part of me expected to be tackled by security at the threshold.

And the smell.

Old books.

Paper and binding glue.

Embedded deep in the grain.

I haven't been this turned on since last Thursday when Jack's towel almost slipped as he padded past me down the hallway.

Passing the glossy wooden tables where students study in silence, I seek out a computer terminal to search the catalog for any references to an English painter named Dyce. To my surprise, I get a hit.

Franklin Astor Dyce.

But there's a snag. A big yellow RESTRICTED banner across the top of the result. The book I need is housed in the special collections archive. I'm not sure what that means in this instance or if it's even accessible. The listing does give me a room number, though. So I go hunting until I see the small placard above the doorway to a separate wing of the library. In front of that doorway is a circular help desk, inside which sits a stone-faced man with graying hair at his temples. He scowls at a table of girls hunched over open books and tablets.

I approach the desk. "Excuse me, sir?"

When he doesn't respond, I step around to his sight line.

"Sir? I had a question about a book."

His answering sigh and impatient expression suggest that part was obvious.

"I need to see this book." I slide him the piece of scratch paper I used to scribble down the decimal number. "It says it's restricted. How do I—"

Before I can finish, he pulls out a clipboard and shoves it in front of me. "Fill this out."

The simple form asks for name, student ID number, the title requested, and the reason. While I complete it, the man glowers at me with arms crossed.

"Guess they haven't gotten around to digitizing this process yet, huh?"

He doesn't appreciate my comment as he snatches the clipboard out from under the last *y* in my signature. The warden inside his fortress scrutinizes my form. Then his hawklike brown eyes lift to mine, and his intense examination somehow gets me feeling guilty, like I'm smuggling produce and livestock through customs. He's got cop stare.

"Go on then," he grumbles.

I look at the diverging hallways behind him with uncertainty.

The man jerks his head. "Take the number, pull the volume, you read it in one of the open booths, you put it back. Nothing leaves the archives."

"Right, thank you." It's then I notice the nameplate on the desk. "Mr. Baxley."

He huffs and looks away, unamused by my usually charming disposition. We're bound to be famous friends, the two of us.

The book I'm looking for is a huge leather-bound slab. I lug it to one of several small rooms with a tiny cubicle and chair. Within the study of the history of English portraiture is a collection of artists representing various eras and illustrations of their respective styles and artistic movements. In the early twentieth century, Franklin Astor Dyce painted for a number of prominent noble British families and was the preferred artist of the Tulleys—when they still held a place of privilege and admiration.

There are prints of some of his portraits, but none are my mystery woman.

I grumble in frustration, because now I'm back to the Tulleys being my only clue to her name and origin. Last night, I snapped a photo of the painting and attempted a long-shot reverse image search. No dice. (Pardon the pun.) Googling Tulleys alive during the 1920s to 1950s turned up several names but no pictures matching my woman. Some too old. A few too young. But that sweet spot of late teens to late twenties, which I estimate to be her age range, is a big blank spot for this anonymous figure.

At any rate, I snap a few photos of the relevant pages from the book before putting it back on its shelf. I wave to Mr. Baxley on my way out, though he pretends to ignore me.

Back at the computer, I find a few books related to the Tulleys and pull those from the general collection shelves to check out. One, however, requires another venture into the restricted archives.

"Hi," I say when I approach the warden's fortress. "It's me again."

Grumpily, he pushes his round-rimmed glasses up his nose, then slides the clipboard across the desk without making eye contact.

"I think we might be onto something with our digitizing idea," I continue, filling out another form. "Like a card scanner for students' IDs. Or a thumbprint reader."

I hand him back the clipboard with a smile. Stone-faced, he jerks his head to the corridor.

Yeah, he's softening to me.

I'm surprised it's taken this long, but when hopping on the Tube into the city a few days later, I finally encounter a busker on the way to the platform.

Strumming an acoustic guitar, he sings a rendition of the "heart is a windmill" song—as Jack calls it. He's got a nice voice and plays it well. Not an imitation of my dad but his own interpretation. I know Dad would appreciate it, so I pull out my phone, as several others have, to record a few seconds of his performance and then text it to my father. I drop a few quid in the bucket at the man's feet on my way to catch my train.

Celeste invited me to lunch today, and this is my first nervous foray into London proper to meet her at a Korean food place near her job. I thought the subway tunnels were crowded, but the short trip didn't prepare me for the frenetic crush that greets me as I ascend to street level. I'm practically trampled when I make the mistake of freezing at the top of the stairs. I don't decide to move in any direction so much as get dragged along in the wake of everyone else going about the afternoon rush.

It's loud. Louder than anything I'm used to back home. I've got my head bowed, trying to pull up walking directions on my phone. Celeste said to exit the Tube and head west, but I always forget my awful sense of direction until I end up miles from civilization staring at a vulture on a tree branch.

After circling the same block twice to figure out which way my dot is pointed on the map, I cross the street—narrowly missing being clipped by a cyclist—and get on the right route. It takes only a few minutes until the noise—cars, conversation, and music pouring out of restaurants and storefronts—starts to become almost comforting.

It has a strange insulating quality as my ears adjust and filter the sound to a dull hum.

The initial shock wears off. I start to notice the city through the bustle, its vibrancy. When I smell kimchi, I follow the scent to a neon sign of a green dragon and a cartoon cat figure in the window. Inside, Celeste sits at the counter in front of a woman at a smoking flattop grill.

"You found it," Celeste says by way of a greeting, standing at my arrival.

She's a lot taller in daylight. A slender, lithe figure in leggings and an oversize shirt of gauzy material over a tank top. Her curly black hair is thick and pouring over her shoulders.

"I ordered for us if that's all right," she adds.

"Yeah, I'll eat whatever. Thanks again for inviting me."

With a tentative smile, I sit down beside her and tuck my canvas bag at my feet.

"I reckon we were quite hard on you the other night." She sips a glass of sparkling water and watches me, and I realize she's waiting for me to participate in this conversation.

"I mean, yeah," I laugh. "A little."

She nods briskly. Celeste strikes me as the type who appreciates honesty. "Don't take it personally. We grill every newcomer just as hard. We're a tough lot, but we mean well."

"So you said you work around here?" I ask, changing the subject. "What do you do?"

"I teach ballet. Six- to ten-year-olds, mostly."

"I feel like I should have guessed that." It was either dancer or runway model. If she'd have said, like, administrative assistant, I would've been sorely disappointed. We all want incredible, unordinary people to fulfill our fantasies so we can live vicariously through them. "Do you still dance too?"

She responds with a noncommittal head tilt. "I always thought I'd dance professionally. It was my dream. The only thing I enjoyed. Our parents scrounged to send me to lessons, then ballet school."

"What happened?"

"I developed a chronic condition in my hip. I ignored the signs for about three years, until Mum finally forced me to see someone. The doctor said I could have surgery to correct the problem or keep dancing through the pain in the short term and risk permanent damage later. End up in a wheelchair by the time I'm thirty." She shrugs. "Wasn't much of a choice at that point."

"I'm so sorry," I say, clucking with sympathy. "That must've been devastating."

Celeste smiles wryly. "*Devastating* is an understatement. I was depressed for about a year. Inconsolable, really. Then my PT told me about a dance school her sister's daughter went to needing teachers. It was maybe another six months of being angry at the suggestion before I came around to the idea."

The woman at the grill puts down three baskets of Korean tacos and skewers with waffle fries in front of us. Between Celeste and her brother, eating with this family means bringing my appetite. Thankfully, no one's ever accused me of leaving food on my plate.

"And you enjoy it now? Teaching?"

"Oh, I love it. The kids are wonderful. I hadn't realized that ballet wasn't fun anymore. Before my surgery, I was obsessed, but I don't think I loved it the way I can now. Seeing them practice a new skill until they perfect it and how excited they get, even coming in to hang out with their friends. I'm happy when I leave work at the end of the day."

Her face takes on a calmness as she speaks. Serenity. I get it. It's like how the library is my happy place. We aren't complete until we've found our passion.

"How'd you get into ballet? Just pick it up one day, or...?"

"Our mum. She was a dancer before she had us. She's still quite active in the London arts world."

Her phone buzzes on the counter, and she glances at it. The spark that flares in her expression at the name on the screen gets me intrigued.

"Oooh. Who is Roberto?" I pry.

She licks her lips to smother a smile. "A good friend."

When I refuse to break eye contact while we each finish our taco, she caves to my curiosity.

"He's a benefactor of the dance school. A philanthropist of the arts, in fact. And quite a nice man."

"An older man, huh?"

"Forty-three in October."

"Wow. Much older then."

That's not at all what I expected. A gorgeous twenty-two-year-old like Celeste must have an avalanche of Instagram dudes filling her DMs.

"Don't mention it to Lee." She types out a quick text before sliding the phone in her purse. "He gets all bent out of shape about it."

"Secret's safe with me."

I bite into another taco, then douse my tongue with a gulp of water to put out the fire. I was not expecting such an aggressive level of heat.

"What about you?" she counters. "You have a boyfriend at home?"

"No boyfriend." I drink some more water. My tongue is numb. Not sure I can feel my teeth either.

"Fancy anyone? Any fit lads in your classes?" Whatever my face does, it makes Celeste put down her taco. "That's a yes. Who is he?"

"No one. I mean, there's a guy or two I think are attractive, but it's nothing. They're both off-limits anyway."

"Excellent! Forbidden love is the best kind." She pouts. "Come on. Give me something here."

I hesitate. Then I groan. "Promise you won't say anything to Lee?"

"Promise."

"Ugh. Fine. I might be lusting over a flatmate."

She gasps. "Don't you dare say Jamie!"

"What's wrong with Jamie?"

"Oh Lord, it's Jamie?"

"It's not. I'm just wondering what's wrong with him."

That gets me a snicker. "Oh, darling, we don't have that kind of time. So it's Jack then?"

I don't know whether it's the embarrassment or the spice flaming my cheeks. I reach for my glass in case it's the latter.

"Maybe," I say after taking a deep gulp of water. "I mean…he's hot. Don't you think?"

Her eyes sparkle. "I believe that's another understatement."

"What's his story?" I push, all pretenses of playing it cool now forgotten. "Dating wise, I mean. He never brings girls home, but I assume he's not celibate or anything."

"Um, no, he's not celibate." She laughs to herself.

I tense. "Oh. Are you two…?"

"What? No, no, nothing like that. I'm just saying—the boy gets around. I don't think he dates so much as fucks and runs. He probably doesn't bring women home to deter them from getting attached. Jackie doesn't seem like he's looking for attachments."

"Fucks and runs, huh?" I mull that over.

She lifts a brow. "I suppose the question is—what do you want from our dear Jack?"

I smother another groan. "Honestly, there's no point even talking about this. Like I said, he's off-limits. I got a very long lecture when I first arrived about the perils of sleeping with a flatmate."

"The Jamie rule," she confirms with a nod.

I laugh. "Exactly. Anyway, I think I'd better look elsewhere for romance. Or sex. Or both."

"Actually, that reminds me," she says. "I'm meant to go to a polo match in a couple weeks. Come with me. I promise a slew of eligible talent for your perusal."

I went to a water polo match once in high school, because Eliza's boyfriend was on the team. I was doing great until they all filed out of the locker rooms like a school of Speedo-wrapped penis fishes. I couldn't stop laughing. I don't know, it was some strange nervous response, leaving me in absolute hysterics on the bleachers. Eliza had her hands mashed over my mouth and was practically burying my head in her lap while moms and even the referee on the side of the pool with his little whistle in his mouth stared at me with irritation.

This probably won't be like that.

"I love horses" is for some reason the thing that comes out of my mouth. It's not a lie, but still.

Weirdo.

"Brilliant. Yvonne and Nate are coming too."

My face does the thing again. And Celeste gasps again.

"What?"

"You fancy Nate? He's the other forbidden apple?"

"No."

"Liar."

"I met him once."

My protest goes unacknowledged. "Oh, Yvonne would die."

"Better not tell her then. For her own safety." I say it as a joke. But also not. "And don't tell your brother about this one either."

Celeste bites her lip, staring at me with bright excited eyes. "I won't say a word. Swear it."

I want to believe her. But there's also a certain mischief about her general aura that leaves me apprehensive.

She tips her head pensively. "Guess that makes you the daddy's girl type, yeah? Falling for the bad boy musician."

Horror washes over me. "What? No."

I hadn't thought of it that way. It's not like I compare every dude with a guitar to my dad. If anything, I've avoided that whole scene because I have zero interest in getting sucked into a bad rip-off of my own origin story. Nate is the first musician I've ever been attracted to, truth be told.

"It's not like that," I insist.

Celeste's amused expression says she's not buying it.

I think harder on it and realize, well, maybe the bad boy part isn't so far off. I might not typically be drawn to musicians, but I will admit to a teeny fascination with the rough-around-the-edges type.

Girls just want to have fun after all.

So what's a little prosecco and polo?

10

Parents shouldn't have internet if they can't use it responsibly. They're fragile and can't be allowed to run wild on the mean streets of cyberspace. Case in point: my dad's downloaded every London news app to his phone and spends his mornings sending me articles and weather updates. I thought he had friends. And, like, hobbies. Instead, terrorizing me has become his full-time occupation.

> Dad: Three Arrested in Organized Crime Bust—BBC

> Me: I'll keep my eye out for Tony Soprano.

> Dad: The mob is no joke, kiddo.

> Me: I'm screenshotting this entire exchange and forwarding it to Dr. Wu.

Sitting on my bed after getting home from class, I've got my laptop open and am trying to do homework. It's slow going with my dad's nervous texting. It'd be endearing if I didn't have to worry about him spinning himself into a panic all alone on that ranch.

Dad: You're not commuting to school alone, right? Safer to travel in packs.

Me: Like the roaming wolves of the countryside.

Dad: I just want you to be safe.

Me: I know. Don't worry.

I remember the time in elementary school back in LA when a couple girls got into a fight at the bike racks and one of them got half her lip torn off after being slammed on the concrete. So far, London is far less intimidating.

With a tap on my door, Jamie pokes his head in. "We're ordering sushi for dinner. You in?"

"Sure, whatever you guys like."

He comes in and sits on the end of my bed. He's wearing fitted ripped jeans that probably cost more than my entire wardrobe and a salmon-colored polo that shows off his leanly muscled arms.

"You look nice," I tell him. "Do you have a date or something?"

"Nope. Just wanted to look pretty for you, darling."

"Stop flirting with me. I'm busy."

He chuckles. "Still getting to the bottom of the painting?"

"Trying to. Hey, maybe you can help. Tell me more about the Tulleys."

He sighs, settling further onto the bed. "That's a long and sordid tale."

"Go on," I prod.

"These days, they're pariahs. But like I told you before, a century ago they were quite cozy with the Crown."

"I read that sometime in the 1920s, there was speculation one of the queen's daughters might marry a Tulley heir."

"Would have been a natural fit," he says. "Certainly, the conversation would be had."

"What's really interesting is the Tulley line was nearly wiped out after World War II. The duke had three sons before he died." I scoot closer to Jamie and angle the laptop so he can see it. "This is Lawrence Tulley, the youngest son. He's the one who inherited the title."

"The youngest was the heir? Fascinating."

"Right?"

We study the image on the screen—a portrait done in oils, courtesy of good ol' Dyce. With his perfectly coiffed brown hair and cold smirk, Lawrence has a smugness about him that puts me off.

"And you know why that is? Because the oldest brother, Robert, disappeared." I click on another browser tab, showing him Robert Tulley's portrait. "Just walked out the door one day, never to be heard from again. And if you think that's bad? Meet William"—I open another image, this one of William Tulley—"the middle brother, who drowned at sea when the *Victoria* was lost on its Atlantic crossing during a storm. He was one of seven hundred passengers to not survive."

"Bloody hell. If that's not a curse."

I sigh. "With that said, I still have no idea if any of that is relevant to my mystery woman."

"Makes for a good story, though. I hope you figure it out. I'm invested now."

"Ahem," someone clears their throat.

Jamie and I glance toward my doorway, where Jack stands, shirtless as usual. His abs are insane. It's hard to look at them sometimes because they melt my brain.

And my panties.

"Well, don't you look cozy," he drawls. His amused smile doesn't quite meet his eyes. "Am I interrupting?"

"Abbey here was giving me a crash course on the Tulleys of yore."

"So what you're saying is you didn't place our dinner order."

"Forgive me, darling. I forget how cranky you get on an empty tummy." Jamie slides off my bed.

"Call me when dinner comes," I tell the guys. "I'll be up here working on this proposal till then."

After they leave, I open a fresh Word doc to start my research proposal. With a subject this rife with drama and intrigue, my assignment definitely won't be boring.

In class the following morning, we each take turns presenting our proposals for our professor. Beside me, Amelia cringes and sinks into her seat as we listen to the third student describe their intent to investigate the history of Brexit. Our professor, who hasn't twitched a muscle in several minutes, grows more violently quiet with each unoriginal rehash of the same topic.

For his part, the student standing at the front of the class seems suitably chastised as he squeamishly describes his research objectives, wishing desperately to burst into ash and float out the AC vent.

After he's concluded and rushed to cower in his seat, Professor Langford turns to address the class from front row center.

"Anyone else going to get up to talk about Brexit?"

Wisely, no one raises their hands.

"You have until Wednesday to propose any other subject or take a zero."

Thus commences a furious cloud of keyboard clicks as far more than three students begin googling other topics.

With a traumatized sigh, Langford asks for the next volunteer. Amelia confidently thrusts her hand in the air. A moment later, she holds court at the front of the room, telling us about the band of French prostitutes who, during the revolution, acted as spies and assassins for the cause of liberation. They were famous for their ferocity and violence, rumored to have worn pearl-like earrings and pendant jewelry carved from the teeth of their victims and even leather bracelets made of human flesh.

A visibly relieved Langford approves Amelia's proposal without question.

"That's fucked-up," I tell Amelia when she retakes her seat beside me.

"Isn't it gruesome?" She flips open a folder to show me paintings and illustrations depicting the antics of the killer prostitutes. "So my vibe."

I don't have anything quite so bloody, but when it's my turn to present, I try to paint a picture for my professor. Of a family a hairbreadth from the throne struck by tragedy, mystery, and scandal. An epic downfall of the rich and famous. And of a woman in a discarded portrait.

"There's no shortage of contemporary sources regarding the modern Tulleys," Langford says, considering my proposal.

I nod in agreement. The divorces, drug addicts, and assorted scandals are well-known tabloid fodder, I've discovered.

"Less so for the early twentieth century," she adds.

I project one of my photos of the painting for the class. As expected, no one has the slightest idea who she might be.

"She would have been important to have been painted by Dyce," muses the professor. "If you can authenticate the painting is indeed one of his."

Shit.

The possibility of a fake hadn't even occurred to me. I'm not sure if that would make my project more or less interesting. Still, the professor approves my proposal, and I know I'm in good shape regardless of whether I solve the mystery of the painting. Based on the several avenues for research—the missing Tulley, the drowned Tulley, and the family's fall from grace—something is bound to be worth writing about.

I think about it all day, spending my evening at the Talbot Library trying to track down as many books as possible that mention the Tulley clan. Not even the library warden can bring down my spirits. Mr. Baxley and I are old friends now. As in I chat his ear off and he stares back stone-faced. It's less a give-and-take friendship than a give-and-glare. He'll come around.

When I waltz through the door of the flat later, it's past eight o'clock and my stomach is growling with accusation. I always forget to eat when I'm at the library.

"Abbey! Babe! Get in here now!"

Lee's urgent declaration has me racing into the living room, only to skid to a stop at the sight of him. He's sprawled on the couch, a glass of red wine in one hand and a shoulder-length platinum blond wig on his head.

"Fancy," I tease. "What's the occasion?"

He hops into a standing position, his movements as graceful as those of his ballerina sister. "Where have you been? I've been sitting here in dire need of emotional support with nary a housemate in sight!"

I bite my lip to keep from laughing. Lee is melodramatic on a good day. Tonight it's next level.

"What happened?"

"Another George bites the dust."

Lee chugs half his glass, then sets it down on the coffee table and picks up the bottle of merlot. Next to the bottle are three empty wineglasses, which tells me he wasn't kidding about sitting around waiting for one or all of us to come home.

He quickly pours a full glass and hands it to me. "Drink."

"I haven't even eaten dinn—"

"Drink!"

Like a dutiful friend, I take a sip. "All right. So this is about New George?"

"Old George now. I broke it off. He was far too clingy." Lee drains the remainder of his glass and pours himself another.

"Is it really considered breaking up if you've been dating less than two weeks?"

"One would think," he huffs. "I sent a very lovely text telling him I didn't see things going anywhere, and this bloke wouldn't accept it! He showed up at my bio class today and ambushed me." Lee's eyes widen in horror. "Can you believe that? The nerve of this entitled boy! Forcing me to end things in person!"

My laughter spills out. "Oh, you poor thing." I reach out to pat him on the arm.

Although, in Lee's defense, demanding an in-person breakup from some random guy you met on a dating app and went out with a few times? That's bold, George.

"I'm emotionally exhausted," Lee announces, heaving a dramatic breath. "I stopped by the off-licence for several bottles of very bad merlot, made us a breakup playlist, and brought down my wigs. Shall we begin?"

And that's why, when Jack and Jamie stumble in from the pub a couple hours later, Lee and I are wearing matching pink wigs and dancing to Blondie's "Call Me" while singing along off-key and far too loud.

Did I mention I'm drinking on an empty stomach?

"What on earth?" Jamie looks from me to Lee, then glances at Jack. "You seeing this too, mate?"

"Oh, I am." Jack's blue eyes track our frenetic dance moves for a moment. Then he shrugs and says, "Right then. What're we drinking?"

11

OUR PARTY OF TWO TURNS INTO A PARTY OF FOUR AS OUR roommates crack open another bottle and proceed to empty it in five minutes flat. At some point, Jamie orders pizza, and we eat while the music plays and the wine flows. Lee forces us to play a game called "tell me a secret," which basically just entails him demanding to know private details about our lives and then pouting each time we don't want to spill the tea.

It's the most fun I've had in a long time. I love it here. I love these guys and this flat and the freedom—the *freedom*.

It's even more intoxicating than all the alcohol we're consuming.

Now it's nearing midnight, the table is littered with empty pizza boxes, and the wine's all gone. I'm curled up in the armchair, drunk and happy. Jamie's on one end of the couch. Lee's on the other, swiping on his phone. Jack's lying on the carpet, his head resting on a throw pillow as he watches soccer on TV.

"You know what, Abbs?" Jamie drawls from his perch.

"What, Jamie?" I play along.

"You're a cool bird."

That makes me smile. "Thank you."

"Thought you were sort of meek when you first showed up," he continues, his tone contemplative, words a bit slurred.

I'm miffed by that comment. "Meek?"

"Meek. Timid. Maybe a wee bit of a prude, yeah?" He's on a roll, too inebriated to realize I'm glaring at him. "But you're good fun. You've got banter."

"Thanks?" I'm still not sure if I'm angry he thought I was a prude.

"And you're fit," he adds, winking at me.

"*So* fit," Lee agrees, though his gaze remains glued to his phone. His swiping finger is busy, busy, busy. Grindr, I'm guessing.

"Abbs!" he suddenly exclaims. "Come here and see this bloke."

I go to the couch and settle between Jamie and Lee, leaning over the latter's phone. "Oh, he's cute." I admire the profile pic on the screen.

"Says here he's new to this app," Lee says, skimming the dude's bio. "Recently got out of a five-year relationship—"

"With a woman," I finish with a gasp. "Been questioning his sexuality for a while and wants to do some exploring to figure out if he's bi."

"Bi-curious lads are fun," Lee informs me.

"Scroll up?" When he does, my jaw falls open, and I swivel my gaze back to Lee. "His name is George? Are you kidding me?"

"Bi George," Jack supplies.

"Bi-*Curious* George," Jamie corrects.

There's a beat of silence and then we all hoot in laughter, because the moniker is utterly brilliant.

I watch as Lee swipes right on George. Instantly, the words *It's a Match!* pop up on the screen.

"Lovely." Satisfied, he turns to wink at me. "Third George's the charm, right?"

"Here's hoping."

"I shall keep you posted on our shagging progress," Lee promises.

"Please do."

Jack snickers from the carpet, his gaze still glued to the soccer—sorry, football match on TV.

On my other side, Jamie stretches his legs out and watches me curiously. "Right then. What about you? Have you shagged anyone here yet? Found yourself a fuckable lad at uni?"

From the corner of my eye, I notice Jack's gaze flit from the television to the couch.

"I'm not discussing my sex life with you," I answer primly.

"Why not?" Jamie protests. "I'll tell you all about mine if you'd like."

"No need. I already hear your sex life through the walls every other night."

He beams. "Thank you for noticing."

At that, Jack shakes with laughter. "Don't think she meant it as a compliment, mate."

I lock my gaze on Jack's. "What about *you*?" I challenge, mostly because he didn't come to my rescue when Jamie started grilling me. Let's see how *he* likes the hot seat. "Who are we *shagging* these days? Because I've yet to hear any sexy noises coming from your room."

And thank God for that. Otherwise, I'd probably be weeping silently in my cereal every morning.

"Jackie boy doesn't bring birds home," Jamie explains. "Sleepovers are a commitment."

"And you're anti-commitment?" I ask him.

"Commitment's fine," Jack answers vaguely. "I'm just not looking for a girlfriend right now."

"But you hook up." I don't know why I'm pressing him. Must be the wine.

"Yes." He sounds amused. "I hook up."

With who? I want to demand, but that's too nosy even for me.

"All right! Round two of tell me a secret," Lee announces, setting his phone down and topping up his merlot. "Abigail, you're up first."

"You know my name's not short for Abigail, right?"

He gasps. "Wait. It's not?"

"Nope. Just Abbey. Named after Abbey Road." I stick out my tongue. "There. That's your secret."

"That's not a secret," he retorts with his trademark pout. "We want something better."

Jamie nods. "Something dirty."

I roll my eyes at him. "Pass."

"Something mortifying then," Lee suggests. "Worst sexual experience."

"That's still a dirty one!"

Lee's stubborn as always. As well as very, very drunk. He waves his wineglass around so jovially I worry for our carpets. "Tell me a secret, Abigail!"

Since I'm equally drunk, I end up giving Lee what he wants and revealing an embarrassing secret.

"I slept with a guy in high school who told me one of my boobs was much bigger than the other, and now it's all I see when I look in the mirror."

Bad move, Abbey.

Suddenly, I have three dudes squinting at my chest. Even Jack has sat up to take a good look.

"Oh my God. Stop staring!" My cheeks are flaming.

"You brought that on yourself," Jack says.

He's not wrong. But still.

"I've got a bra on anyway," I grumble. "You can't see the difference unless I'm topless."

"I agree," Jamie says gravely. "You must take your top off so we can better assess."

I reach over to slug him in the arm. "You're the worst."

"Are you really insecure about it?" Lee asks in a serious voice. Not mock serious like Jamie's was but as if he's genuinely upset to hear I might feel self-conscious about any part of myself.

"God, yes," I confess. "I dated someone last year, and every time we got naked, I kept stressing about what he was thinking. Like, *I can't believe I'm having sex with the weird-boob girl.*"

"Trust me," Jack says roughly, his eyes locking with mine. "That's not what he was thinking."

My pulse quickens, and it takes some willpower to break the eye contact.

"Jackie's right," Jamie assures me. "Besides, I'd bet my entire trust fund you're being—how do I say it nicely—crazy."

Jack snorts.

"They can't be that disproportionate," Jamie adds, shrugging.

"He used the words *much bigger*. That implies a huge proportional discrepancy."

"Proportional discrepancy," he mimics. "Look at you, all articulate when you're sloshed."

"Let me see them," Lee orders, once again bringing the scorch of embarrassment to my face. "I'm the obvious candidate to judge the proportions, given that boobs do nothing for me. I promise I won't objectify you."

"Or...and hear me out...I don't show them to anyone."

"I'll do it," Jamie volunteers.

"No," everyone says in unison.

Lee gives me a sad look. "I can't live with myself knowing you feel ashamed of your own body. It can't be *that* glaring a difference, luv."

"It is," I insist.

And then, because I happen to suffer from must-always-be-right disease, I reach for the hem of my shirt.

I pause, turning to glare at the other two. "Don't you dare look or I'm smothering you both in your sleep."

I stand up and turn my back on everyone but Lee, who also rises. Then I take my shirt off and reach behind me to undo the clasp of my bra.

There's a choked noise, a cross between a curse and a groan.

I growl without turning around. "Don't you dare look, Jamie."

"Hey, that was Jack," he replies, sounding a bit smug.

Before I can second-guess myself, I toss the bra on the couch and give Lee a defiant stare. "Well?"

He stands in front of me, hands on hips, forehead creased in concentration, like he's a fashion designer examining a prototype on a mannequin.

"Which one is supposed to be bigger?" he finally asks.

"This one!" I point to my right breast, betrayed that he couldn't discern it right away.

He purses his lips and squints harder.

"See?" I challenge. "It's bigger, right?"

"I truly don't see it, babe. And you know me. I'd tell you if I did. I live and breathe the drama."

I can't argue with that. "You really don't think one is drastically bigger?"

"Not at all. But did you know you have a freckle under your left nipple?"

Jack starts to cough.

I snatch up my bra and shirt, throwing the latter on without bothering with the former. "All right. You've lost your breast privileges," I tell Lee, jabbing my finger in the air. "You took liberties. Freckle assessment wasn't on the table!"

He howls and walks over to sling his arm around me. "I love you, Abbs. You're the best flatmate I've ever had."

After that, the excitement dies down and we start cleaning up. Despite the fact it's one in the morning, Jamie announces he's going out after getting booty-called by a girl in Chelsea.

I swear, that guy has so much sex I'm surprised his penis still works.

"I'm going up to bed now," I say once we've collected all the wineglasses and trash.

"Me too." Jack joins me in the living room doorway.

"Night, darlings. I'm staying up a while longer to sext with George." Lee flops back onto the couch, engrossed by his phone within seconds.

Upstairs, Jack doesn't turn toward his room but follows me to mine.

I glance over my shoulder. "Can I help you?" Somehow I manage to sound nonchalant even though my pulse is racing again.

Why is Hot Jack coming to my bedroom at 1 a.m.?

"I'm walking you to your room," he says gruffly. "You drank a lot tonight."

"I'm fine."

"You just took your shirt off in front of Lee."

"So?"

Our eyes lock. There it is again—the surge of heat.

We have chemistry and I think we both know it, but I don't know what to do with it. There's that pesky house rule, for one. But also the fact that Jack is clearly determined not to make a move. And I'm not sure I want him to. It'll only complicate our living situation.

And yet I say, "Jack?"

"Hmm?" He's still watching me.

"Tell me a secret."

He's right. I drank too much.

I almost take it back, but now he's coming closer. Dragging a hand over the stubble on his jaw. His gaze sweeps over me. Rests briefly on my breasts, which are now perfectly outlined by my thin top thanks to my braless state. My stupid freckled nipples tighten the second they have his attention.

For a moment, I don't think he heard the question. But then that big broad body is mere inches away as he brings his lips close to my ear.

"A secret? Hmm. Well…" His breath tickles my hair. "When you took your top off downstairs…" His voice gets dangerously low. "It got me rock hard."

Oh my God.

Before I can even register that, he's gone, softly closing my door behind him.

12

THE THING ABOUT POLO IS, I DON'T KNOW ANYTHING ABOUT POLO.

Standing under a long white tent, I stare with fascination at the horses galloping around the pitch. With every crack of a mallet, I struggle to keep track of the ball. Like golf, I don't know how anyone follows the damn thing. All I see are hooves and sticks and flying tufts of dirt and grass. It's exciting, though. Energetic. Even if I don't understand the rules or exactly what I'm watching. Celeste tries her best to sum it up for me when she sees my eyes glaze over, explaining it's not too dissimilar to football, a comparison that makes even less sense until I realize she means soccer.

She was right about the scenery at least. There's no shortage of hot guys who've stepped off the covers of a fashion magazine in their crisp white button-downs, blazers, and perfect Amalfi Coast tans. A lot of tall, gorgeous women on their arms too.

"Who's that?" I ask, nodding at the raised platform where a small group of spectators watch the match.

"You certainly aim high, don't you?" She grins at me. "That's Prince James. The queen's sister's son."

I don't know what I expected a royal to look like in real life. Not that he should be adorned with medals and sashes or anything fancy, but he just looks so…average. A regular guy in a casual summer suit. Maybe because in England, the monarchy isn't surrounded by a dozen Secret Service agents in dark suits and sunglasses.

Still, I never thought I'd find myself at the same venue as a member of the royal family. Like it's a totally normal thing to do.

"I'm surprised he's showing his face in public," remarks Yvonne, who stands on the other side of Celeste. Nate was here a moment ago, though we barely said hello before Yvonne sent him off to get her a drink. "Only last week, he was all over the *Mail* getting into his car with that Alisha woman from Eurovision."

I lift a brow. "Isn't he married?"

"Exactly." Yvonne huffs. "And he had the nerve to deny it like we didn't all see it with our own eyes. He's a prick."

The girls turn their attention back to the match. I attempt to as well, but it isn't long before my vision once again becomes a blur of horse legs and mallets. I give up. Polo is the sport equivalent of gibberish.

I poke Celeste in the arm. "How are things going with Roberto?"

She slides her sunglasses down and follows as the teams charge past us down the field. "Yeah, good. He travels a lot, so he's out of town this week. These were his tickets to the match, actually."

"Thank him for me then. I'm not sure I'm following, but it's fun."

"Lee told me about your painting. Any luck identifying the mystery woman?"

"Yes, Abbey." Yvonne leans in. "I hear you've got a secret Tulley. Naughty lot, that family."

So I keep hearing. But most of the available information I've found on the Tulley clan is about its current members. My findings on the Tulleys of the WWII era thus far are limited to the duke and duchess, and there's very little about their children or extended family.

"I found a small art museum in Rye, where the artist is from," I tell the girls. "So I'm hoping they'll have more information about him and maybe his subjects. I'm taking the train out there tomorrow."

"Nate's from East Sussex," Yvonne says as he arrives with her champagne.

He hands her the flute, then drags a hand through his tousled hair. "What's that?"

"Abbey is hunting an artist in Rye. Weren't you headed that way to see your mum and dad tomorrow?"

He casts his gaze at me, and I'm suddenly self-conscious. About my outfit, my hair, and whether I'd worn enough sunscreen or turned a hideous shade of cooked while outdoors. The knee-length green dress I'd chosen for today seemed modest when I slipped it on, but when Nate's dark eyes rest briefly on my bare legs, I suddenly feel like it's way too short. Nate, meanwhile, manages effortless indifference, somehow pulling off wearing only a fitted T-shirt and jeans as if we're all ridiculous for trying so hard.

His hair falls across his face. It isn't eighties-rock-star long but not close-cropped either. Just deliciously messy and curling slightly at his nape. I become obsessed with the way a strand sticks to his eyelashes.

"You want a lift, Abbey?" he asks.

I'm not entirely sure I haven't hallucinated the offer until Celeste nudges me with her elbow. "Manners, darling."

I blush. "Yeah, sure." My tone is all *no big deal*. I get rides from gorgeous men on the regular. Nothing to see here. "If it's no bother."

"Not at all. I'll pick you up first thing." He pushes hair out of his eyes, then grabs his phone from his back pocket. "Give me your number. I'll text you when I'm on my way tomorrow."

My gaze flicks toward Yvonne, but she's gone back to watching the match, unfazed that her boyfriend asked for my number. I pose absolutely no threat to her.

She's got Nate fetching her champagne after all.

"Are you coming too?" I ask her.

The crowd suddenly erupts in cheers as someone apparently scores. Yvonne claps against her glass, careful not to jostle her drink, before glancing over at me.

"No, I've things to do," she says, smiling. "But good luck. I hope you find what you're looking for."

Okay, yeah, cool. A two-hour ride alone with Nate and his hair. That's fine. That's totally fine.

Shit.

I'm up and dressed early Sunday morning when I come downstairs. I received a text from Nate about fifteen minutes ago, informing me he'll be here in forty minutes. Which gives me another, oh, twenty-five minutes to battle my growing anxiety and hope it doesn't turn into a full-blown panic attack.

I know this isn't a date.

But it still sort of feels like one.

Jack is at the counter when I walk into the kitchen. "Morning," he greets me.

"Morning." I tentatively shuffle past him toward the pantry for some cereal and pretend he's not shirtless. That his biceps aren't rippling as he uses a wooden spoon to mix pancake batter.

It got me rock hard.

Those rough whispered words have been haunting me for more than a week now. They've also become the soundtrack to my Hot Jack fantasies, which I like to alternate with my Broody Nate fantasies. The number of orgasms I've had while thinking of those two might be a cause for concern.

As I pass him, I notice for the first time a scar on his back. Small and round, with jagged, weblike borders. Almost like a bullet wound.

"What is that?" I demand. "Were you shot?"

He half turns to see what I'm looking at, then glances over his shoulder at the scar, feeling it with his fingers. "That? No. I fell off a four-wheeler my sister was driving. Rolled into a ditch and was impaled on a branch."

"Wow, seriously?"

"Oh yeah. Now, this one. This one's from getting shot." Jack turns sideways to point out a faint mark above his hip. "My mate shot me point-blank with a paintball gun."

"A paintball did that?" The pink raised area is evidence of the torn skin that was once blown open.

He chuckles. "A hazelnut. He filled the paintball gun with them."

"A freaking hazelnut?" I'm at a loss. What is it with boys? Why don't they just freeze each other's underwear like normal people? "You need new friends, Jackie."

"I'll keep that in mind, Abbs. Go on then. Show me yours."

My heart does a stupid flip. "Um. Pardon me?"

Jack pours out some batter on the griddle before facing me again. "Your scars. I showed you mine. Fair's fair."

"I only have one." Shrugging, I throw my foot up on a stool, roll up my linen pant leg, and point to the pale, thin line just above my knee. "Summer camp. I came in too hot on the zip line and crash-landed. Found a nail poking out of the deck with my leg."

"Damn."

"I mean, it's no hazelnut bullet," I say with feigned modesty. "But I did have to get a tetanus shot, so…clearly that makes me tougher than you."

"A tetanus shot? Fuck, that's sexy."

"Isn't it?"

Jack pulls his first pancake off the griddle, then stirs the batter still in the bowl. As he pours out another one, some batter manages to splatter his chest.

"You gonna eat the pancakes or wear them?" I say with a taunt-ing grin.

I grab the dishrag beside the sink to wipe it off. I'm already engaged in the act by the time the message reaches my brain that wiping batter off Jack's bare chest has a vaguely sexual connotation, but I don't know how to escape it now as time slows while he watches me.

In the silence, I feel my pulse race in response to some intangible signal. I'm not sure which one of us is breathing hard. I think it's me. A vivid hallucination of running my hands over his warm flesh flashes in front of my eyes. His muscles quiver under my touch. Either I'm kidding myself, or he feels this *thing* too.

"Morning, you two," Lee announces as he and Jamie enter the kitchen.

Jolted from the moment, I drop the rag and step away from Jack. I'm hyperaware of my heartbeat.

"Watch out for that one," Jack says to the boys, turning back to his pancakes. "She's no respect for the house rules. Just groped me right out in the open."

"That so?" Lee arches an eyebrow at me.

"I knew she was trouble," Jamie says. "The redheads always are."

They have a good laugh at my expense while I go sit with my cereal, hoping my face doesn't look as red as it feels.

Thankfully, the door buzzes.

Jamie perks up. "We expecting someone?"

Nope, but I am.

"Later, boys." I drop my bowl in the sink with an eye right at Jack. "I'm heading to Rye with Nate for some research."

Jack's gaze narrows, but I'm already strolling out of the kitchen.

"Did she say Nate?" I hear Jamie demand.

I grab my bag from the hallway and slip on my shoes before heading out the door.

Outside, Nate is waiting at the curb. With his motorcycle.

Oh.

I pause on the sidewalk. It isn't fair, really. The sight of him leaning against the bike. Like, stop, dude. You were already hot. This is just overkill. A girl can only take so much.

"Morning," he says in that deep voice of his. It's not quite a smoker's voice—I've yet to see him smoke anything—but there's a slight rasp to it that makes certain parts of me tingle.

"Morning," I answer awkwardly.

He hands me a helmet. "Ready?"

Hesitant, I stare at the bike. "My dad would kill me if he knew I was on a motorcycle."

"Yeah?"

"He's hated the things ever since a bandmate of his died in a crash a few years ago. Made me promise never to ride one."

Which is maybe a lot to announce first thing in the morning to a guy doing me a favor.

"I'd never put you in danger," Nate says softly. "I'm a safe driver. Never even gotten a speed ticket." His earnestness sets me back. "Trust me?"

I can't imagine what reason I have to do so, but even though I barely know the guy, I feel safe with him.

"Yeah, of course." With that, I slide the helmet on.

I came here for an adventure after all.

He's got this faint smile as he watches me. Like he's in on a secret. I don't know how to read it or why it's directed at me, but I like it.

Nate helps me adjust the chin strap, then tucks a few strands of hair out of my eyes. The light brush of his fingers against my forehead leaves my throat dry. Then he gets on the bike and disengages the kickstand. I hop on behind him, my pulse quickening when Nate takes my wrist to wrap my arm around his waist.

"Hold on tight. It gets bumpy."

Leaning forward, I practically paste myself to his back. He's muscular beneath my arms. I feel his abdomen expand and contract as he balances our weight on the tires. The bike roars to life, and he puts it in gear. Then we're peeling off from the curb through the rushing air down the streets of Notting Hill.

Not long ago, my dad wouldn't let me go to my college classes without texting me every ten minutes. I was the only nineteen-year-old I knew with a curfew. But as much as I appreciate Dad's concerns, I can't live my life governed by his fears. This is the most impervious, indestructible time of my life.

If I don't take advantage of it now, I'll eventually end up an old woman with few scars but more regrets.

13

WE DON'T TALK DURING THE TWO-HOUR RIDE SOUTH, OUT OF THE suburbs and through the countryside to the coast. It's just the rumble of the machine between our legs and the wind across my face. The blur of green and smell of briny waters as we draw closer to the riverside village.

Nate slows as we drive along cobblestone streets lined by Tudor buildings. Rye is one of those adorable, picturesque English villages I imagined from movies and books. A collection of old houses beside quaint shops, centuries-old lampposts, and ivy climbing the walls.

We park along the curb a few blocks from the museum, and I pull out my phone to map the walk.

"If you have other stuff you need to do, I can entertain myself here for a while," I say, setting my helmet on the seat.

He pops out the kickstand and turns off the bike. "Wouldn't be a very good escort if I abandoned you in the middle of nowhere, now would I?"

The word *escort* exiting his mouth does weird things to me. His whole mouth does things to me, in fact. The curve of his lower lip when he talks. The flash of white teeth. I become stupidly entranced until he pulls his helmet off and runs his hand through his hair.

His hair.

"Well, okay then." I abruptly head for the sidewalk, because another second of staring at him and I'll become embarrassingly obvious.

"Lead the way." The soft chuckle tickling my back says he damn well knows I was checking him out.

The museum is in a small two-story building in the village center beside a café and used bookshop. Inside, white walls display framed portraits and muted landscapes. An older woman comes to greet us at the sound of the chime above the entrance.

"Good afternoon. Welcome." She's short and petite, wearing all black save for a colorful scarf hanging delicately over her slight shoulders. "I'm Marjorie, the curator here. What brings you in today?"

Her gaze lingers questioningly on Nate as he drifts away to look at the art. Admittedly, he stands out in a place like this, wearing a leather jacket over a simple T-shirt and lived-in jeans.

"My name's Abbey Bly," I tell her. "I'm a student in London, and I wondered if I might ask you about a painting by Franklin Dyce. I understand he's from Rye."

"Yes, of course." Her face lights up, giving the impression she doesn't receive many visitors. "We have several of his works here on display. I'm happy to help if I can."

I pull up a photo of the painting on my phone to show her. Marjorie slides her glasses from the top of her head to the bridge of her nose, then holds the phone closer to get a good look.

"Anything you could tell me would be helpful," I say hopefully.

"Without seeing the painting itself…" She continues to examine the image. "Yes, I'd say the color and composition are consistent with Dyce's portraiture. Come."

She leads me to a room off to the right. On the near wall are several portraits of ladies in postwar-style dresses and men in formal military uniforms.

"These are all Dyce. Let's see…" She studies them for a moment, then the photo again. "An educated guess would be between 1946 and 1952. A young woman of nobility wasn't wearing her hair like this much later than that."

"Any idea who she might be?" I try to temper my excitement.

Marjorie furrows her brow and zooms in on the face. "I'm sorry, no. Can I ask where you found this? If it is Dyce, I'm not aware of it."

"I bought the painting from an estate sale. It was owned by the Tulley family in Surrey."

"Yes, that would seem right." She beckons me with a wave to follow her to yet another small room of portraits. "These two are Tulleys. Donated after their deaths to the museum. Prewar."

My gaze eagerly sweeps over the paintings. These are the great-great-aunt and uncle of the three brothers. Great-aunt and uncle to the duke and duchess on the father's side.

"Painted not long before their deaths, in fact. As I understand it, they weren't particularly well-liked. Excellent artistic examples, however."

Hence they were donated. It seems tossing out portraits is a Tulley tradition.

"Would it be possible to find out if this is an authentic Dyce painting?" I ask her.

"Certainly, yes. If you'd like to forward me any other photographs you have, I can get you an answer. If further verification is required, we'll need to examine the painting itself. That is if you're able to send it to my contacts in London."

"Yes, for sure."

We return to her desk at the front of the museum where she hands me a business card. Nate is still wandering on his own. She casts a suspicious glance in his direction as he disappears around a corner.

"If the painting is authentic," she continues, "would you consider allowing the museum to display it? It likely isn't terribly valuable, I'm afraid."

"Picked it up for a hundred pounds," I agree.

Marjorie shakes her head. "That family would sell their own offspring if they could make a quid. In this case, Dyce isn't van Gogh, and the subject isn't Queen Margaret. But the museum would be proud to hang it. We would credit you, of course. From the collection of Abbey Bly."

I smile to myself. Right, as if I'm so sophisticated an art buyer as to have my own collection. Only if some IKEA and Anthropologie prints count as a *collection*.

"If you can help me, I suppose it's the least I could do for your time," I say.

I don't need the painting itself for my research. Anyway, it'd be pretty cool knowing that when I leave England, my name is written on a wall in a small southern village, forever connected to an artist and his infamous patrons.

***

Next door, Nate and I order lunch to go before driving south along the river's edge to a pebble beach where the river meets the ocean. There, a tiny black hut with a red roof stands alone on the shore.

The ocean here is breathtaking. Cool salt wind whips my hair around my face. Only the occasional seagull or lone pedestrian walking their dog interrupts the natural setting. On the concrete steps of the hut, we sit with our takeout containers of fish and chips.

"Find what you were looking for at the museum?" Nate asks.

"Maybe. The curator is authenticating the painting for me. Doesn't tell me who the woman is, but at least I'll know if I'm on the right trail or if it's back to square one. If it isn't a real Dyce, then she might not be a Tulley at all."

"Do you have any theories?"

"I do," I admit. "But I don't want to say just yet."

It's a bit weird, but I've become protective of her, this forgotten girl with no voice of her own. A man doesn't get discarded for reasons women often are. He barely gets a finger wag for a scandal that would otherwise brand a woman for life. I don't know yet what got her tossed outside on that table, but I don't like the idea of anyone speaking ill of her.

"What about you?" I shift the focus to Nate.

"Do I have a theory?"

"No. I mean, I feel bad. You had plans today, and I hijacked them. Weren't you supposed to visit your family?"

"If I'd wanted to, I would have."

The bitterness in his voice sets me back.

"Sorry," he murmurs, seeing my reaction. "That wasn't at you."

"I just thought, because Yvonne said…"

"It was Yvonne's idea. My mum got to her."

Nate stares out at the water. There's this distance about him that comes and goes. A tidal force that ebbs only a moment before rushing back in.

"You don't get along?" I ask.

He picks up a smooth bluish-black pebble and rubs it between his fingers. He's got great hands. Big, masculine. Musician's fingers. They're sexy as hell.

"Mum and I are fine," he finally says. "Most of the time."

"Things not great with your dad then?"

"No, not great." Letting out a long breath, he flicks the pebble away, then pops a fry into his mouth. He chews slowly before saying, "I'm not going to be good company if we stay on the topic."

"Right, sorry. My name's Abbey and I have trouble with boundaries," I say with an apologetic laugh.

That earns me a crooked grin. "Never apologize for being curious."

"Hmm. Okay. Then tell me about yourself. You were nice enough to bring me all the way out here, and I barely know you. Hell, I don't even know your last name."

"Mitchell." A fleeting smile appears before his brow furrows. "As for the rest, there isn't much to tell."

"I don't believe that."

He dodges, dipping a piece of fish into some tartar sauce before sliding it into his mouth.

"Where I come from," I say when he doesn't respond, "girls aren't supposed to accept rides from strange men on motorcycles. So you've gotta help me out here."

He capitulates. "All right then, Abbey. What would you like to know?"

"Hmm. Okay. You're a musician. Is that your dream?"

Nate smiles. "No, not at all. It was something I picked up as a kid out of boredom. Got good at it by accident."

That comes as a relief for some reason. I suddenly hear Celeste's voice in my head, teasing me about daddy complexes and bad-boy musicians.

"Okay, then what do you want to be when you grow up?"

He chuckles at the question. "I want to travel. And I think I'm a decent writer. If I could do both, travel and write about my experiences—that'd be all right."

"Well, that's unexpected. I didn't peg you for the Jack Kerouac type."

"Minus the drug abuse and alcoholism," he says dryly.

My gaze sweeps over his jaw, the beard growth shadowing it. His gaze is on the water again, dark eyes taking on a faraway glint.

"You're a romantic."

He glances over at me. "Are you having a laugh?"

"Not at all. I'm impressed, actually."

Nate has a depth and sincerity about him I hadn't expected. Far more than a bad boy on a motorcycle. I mean, I don't hate the motif. It suits him. But it's nice to know there's some meat on the bone.

"Any more questions?" There's a note of humor in his voice.

"Nah, I've grilled you enough."

"It was quite torturous."

I laugh and say, "Here—you get a free pass at retaliation. I give you permission to ask me anything. Whatever tickles your fancy."

The second the words exit my mouth, I realize how suggestive they sound.

But Nate doesn't go there. Entirely, anyway. He goes there, but in a PG manner.

"What's your story, Abbey? You have a man back home?"

"Oh. Um. No. I don't."

His lips curve slightly. "I see. So you left a trail of broken hearts in your wake, I presume? A rock star ex-boyfriend with a guitar, singing bad Gunner Bly covers outside your window? Telling you his heart is a windmill."

I blanch. "Definitely no. First of all, if anyone tried serenading me with my father's love songs, I'd hurl. And anyway, I've never been into musicians. Feels too close to home, you know?"

Nate watches me for a beat. Thoughtful. Then he nods. "I get it."

Shit. Was that a mistake? Did I basically just say, *I would never be interested in you because you play in a band*?

And does it really matter if that's how he took it? He's with Yvonne. He's not supposed to care whether some random American girl has the hots for him.

Not that I have the hots for him.

I don't.

Truly.

Like, just because he's insanely good-looking. And smart. Interesting. Enigmatic. Exudes a raw sex appeal that makes my knees weak…

None of that means I have the hots for him. *Get a grip, Abbey.*

"Go on. Tell me your life story then," Nate says, sipping his water bottle.

"It's short and uneventful," I warn him. "All the most interesting things about me happened to someone else."

"I don't believe that. You come off much older than nineteen. That doesn't happen on its own."

"Side effect of being a rock star's daughter. Trust me, it's not as glamorous as it sounds."

When his insistent stare begs me to elaborate, I sigh and unpack the short version.

"You want my story? Okay. It's being raised by nannies and microwaving SpaghettiOs for dinner. Reading about yourself in stories by people you've never met. Seeing pictures of your dad stumbling out of bars or getting arrested for another DUI plastered on the cover of a magazine. Celebrating a birthday in an empty house while he's playing to a packed stadium. I guess that stuff ages you."

I love my dad. We have a great relationship now, but there are just some things that, even after you've forgiven them, still linger in the blood. Especially when you're little. The earliest scars last the longest.

Nate looks at me, and for the life of me, I can't discern his expression.

"What?" I ask, self-consciously wiping at my mouth.

"You're nothing like I expected either."

"Don't believe everything you read," I joke. "I'm jaded beyond repair."

"I don't think you believe that."

"Oh, you know me so well now, huh?"

Nate's eyes lock with mine. "I'm starting to."

It begins again. The tickle in my gut. That feeling of numbness in my toes. I watch his eyelashes flutter against the wind, and if this isn't smitten, then the fish in this Styrofoam box has gone bad.

And I have no business feeling this way about another girl's boyfriend.

OCTOBER

14

I FEEL LIKE I HAVEN'T LEFT THIS LIBRARY IN WEEKS. NOT THAT I don't appreciate the atmosphere—it's the lack of progress in my research that's becoming tedious. Every day, every spare moment from the time I arrive on campus until I leave well after dark, I comb the shelves for one book that inevitably leads to another in an endless thread that never reaches a destination.

Tonight is no exception. It's nearing eight o'clock, and I've already been here for four hours. When my eyes are so tired I can barely read the words on the page, I take a break and step outside with a candy bar I stuck in my bag a week ago. It's only mostly melted.

The weather's changing. Now well into October, the autumn chill has settled in. The cold stone steps sting through my jeans as I sit down and check my phone to find missed texts from Celeste, Eliza, and my dad. I answer his first, assuring him I'm still alive and well. Then Celeste, who's taken an interest in my Tulley endeavor.

> Celeste: Roberto showed the picture around to some people he knows at the archive department of the BBC. No help there. Sorry.

> Me: Worth a try. Thank him again for me xx

Look at me, texting all British-like. Ending my texts with kisses has become a habit now.

> Celeste: I think I've got him hooked. He wants to meet with his friend who teaches in the history department at Cambridge. See if they can't find a name.

> Me: Sorry I've hijacked your boyfriend lol

> Celeste: This is better than telly. Speaking of which… I got drinks with Yvonne and Nate last night. He asked about you.

I don't know how to answer that, but I know bait when I see it.

> Celeste: That must have been some road trip you two took.

> Me: It was fine.

> Celeste: Right. You stick with that story.

Nate was a perfect gentleman during our visit to Rye. Nothing remotely scandalous or untoward occurred. Except in my head, where the scent of motor oil and warm engines reminds me of his broad chest beneath my palms as we traversed the country roads.

In the nearly two weeks since he brought me home to Notting Hill, I've found myself obsessing over the most random details about Nate. Like the tiny tears in his jeans. The frayed edges around his back pockets where the permanent outlines of his phone and wallet have become lighter than the rest of the fabric. How soft his T-shirt was. The small scar over his eyebrow. That gravelly tone to his voice.

I've entirely lost my mind.

But Celeste's not allowed to know that.

Eliza, on the other hand...

> Me: OMG has it really been a week since I messaged you?? I'm so sorry I've been out of touch. I live in the library now.

> Eliza: No worries. Just keeping my promise to check in when I haven't heard from you in a while. You know, making sure you weren't murdered in a dark alley during a Jack the Ripper walking tour.

> Me: That was oddly specific. (P.S. I'm still alive)

> Eliza: Speaking of Jacks. How's Hot Jack? Have you played bedroom rugby yet?

> Me: Nope. Lee's strict about his house rules.

And Jack's busy hooking up with anyone but me, I decide not to add. At least that's what I think he's doing. He hasn't been around much lately.

> Eliza: Boring. And you haven't met anyone else you like? In two months??

> Me: Well...

> Eliza: I knew it! Spill!

Me: I might have a second crush. Remember I told you about the guy who gave me a ride to Rye?

Eliza: Wasn't that weeks ago? Why didn't you say anything before?

Because I thought if I pretended the crush wasn't there, it would just go away. But it's still here.

Eliza: On a scale of 1–10, 1 being "I guess we can hold hands" and 10 being "take your penis out right now!" how hard are you crushing?

Me: Like a 7?

I'm lying. My attraction to Nate is at that visceral level where he simply breathes and I swoon.

Eliza: You slut.

Me: Would be an 8, but he's a bassist.

Eliza: Oh no. I suppose it was inevitable.

Me: What was?

Eliza: That you'd end up with a rocker. Seems like a natural fit.

Is it? There's nothing less appealing to me than Dad's former lifestyle.

Then again, Nate isn't interested in becoming a touring

musician, so really, there's no reason we shouldn't be able to make it work—

What part of "he has a girlfriend" don't you understand, Abbey?

Right. I need to stop acting as if I have any shot with him. He's with Yvonne. The end.

> Me: Gotta go. Still at the library.

I slide my phone in my pocket and head back inside. As always, Mr. Baxley sits at his information desk guarding the precious archives from us ne'er-do-wells and our greasy fingers. He scowls at me as I approach.

"Tell me something," I say. He's already slapping down the clipboard. "Anyone ever try ordering a pizza? Some tacos, maybe? For the sake of variety?"

He doesn't twitch a muscle. Perfectly still in his abject disdain as I fill out yet another request form.

"I'm going to crack you, Mr. Baxley. One of these days."

Unconvinced, he jerks his head to allow me access. As if I don't have a sleeping bag and mini fridge set up under a desk with my name on it by now.

And so the cycle begins again. I read, and a footnote sends me to yet another volume. Not an hour later, I'm back. An exasperated Mr. Baxley slides the clipboard in front of me without so much as a grumble under his breath.

"Is this really necessary?" I ask. "I'm already in there. I keep filling out the same information for the same reason. Why kill all these trees?"

He doesn't budge, so I scribble down a snarky response on the form in protest of this library's archaic and redundant regulations.

REASON FOR REQUEST:

I like books that start with the letter R.

The next time, I get more creative.

REASON FOR REQUEST: A HAIKU

The quest for knowledge
Is right at my fingertips.
Insert five words here.

The time after that, a personal approach.

REASON FOR REQUEST:

I knew this kid named Martin in the fourth grade who came from a super religious family. He showed up on Valentine's Day with cards for everyone in class—except me. It was very hurtful, Mr. Baxley. I cried when I got home, and my dad called Martin's mom and was like, "What the hell, lady? Teach your son some manners." She apologized profusely and put Martin on the phone to explain himself, and—get this, Mr. Baxley. Martin confessed that he left me out because his father told him redheads were created by the devil to lure weak men into the red pits of hell. I wonder what ever happened to Martin. His parents sent him to Catholic school the following year, where I assume gingers are forbidden from attending.
Oh, I am requesting this book for research purposes.

Pleased with my juvenile antics, I hand the clipboard back with a smile. "You don't have to be a slave to bureaucracy, Mr. Baxley. Fight the power."

Back at my desk, I get an email from Marjorie at the museum in Rye informing me that the painting is authentic. And while she's taken pains to exhaust every contact she has, no one recognizes the woman in the portrait.

Another dead end.

In frustration, I fling my pencil across the room. It lands with unsatisfying quiet.

Yes, I can continue my research project on the tragic Tulley brothers, but who was this girl? Who, damn it? How is it possible someone so connected to a prominent family can simply disappear from history but for this one painting? It's an infuriating mystery that loses its romance with every slammed door.

I've managed to chart a family tree for the modern Tulleys. They're all accounted for with names and photos, none even remotely resembling the woman. And no long-lost sisters or daughters either. I thought for sure that a hole would appear on a branch somewhere. A blank space where this woman would fit. But no. Nothing.

I think maybe the library and I need to go on a break, Ross and Rachel style. It's getting late, and I'm exhausted.

In a fit of desperation, I return to Mr. Baxley with my phone.

"Do you know this woman?" I push the phone at him to show him the photo. "The Tulley portrait artist Franklin Astor Dyce painted her sometime after World War II."

His typical grimace evaporates as he carefully peers at the photo, squinting behind his glasses. "I don't, I'm afraid."

I swallow another rush of frustration.

He continues to study the image, then sets my phone down. "But perhaps you might want to have a look"—with a pencil, he scribbles a decimal number on a slip of paper—"at this."

He hands it to me. Along with the damn clipboard.

Touché, Mr. Baxley.

But I suppose this is progress.

15

THE BOYS ARE HOSTING A PARTY TONIGHT, AND THE FLAT IS heaving with their friends and friends of friends. Strange faces that mostly look past me like I'm the child who's supposed to be at the neighbor's house for a sleepover so the big kids can play. I try to be social, and the guys do introduce me to everyone, but they get caught up in conversation that starts to box me out and I'm left drifting on the periphery. It isn't their fault, this outsider syndrome of mine. I don't blame them.

I've done the rounds. Now I'm tucked into a corner with a glass of wine watching from a distance. Truthfully, I'm preoccupied. Itchy and edgy. Disappointed.

Yeah, I can't pretend anymore that's not what I'm feeling. I'm disappointed.

Nate and Yvonne aren't here.

I shouldn't care. I keep telling myself not to. But ever since our road trip, I've become more impatient to see Nate again. Part of me had even thought he might make the effort to connect again (as friends, of course), but obviously I was mistaken.

I get it, though. Having a girlfriend is a pretty good reason why he hasn't made the effort.

And why I should banish the thought.

I'm not particularly close to Yvonne and feel no special loyalty to her. Still, sniping another woman's guy is a shit thing to do. It wouldn't win me any points with the rest of the group either, I'm sure.

Uh-huh, like it was even a remote possibility that you could steal him from her? the amused voice in my head inquires.

Ugh. This is ridiculous.

I've been here more than two months now. It's been fun, but it's time to stop letting myself entertain absurd scenarios of unrequited obsessions. Time to face the bitter truth.

And find another glass of wine to wash it down with.

When I enter the kitchen to get myself a refill, I spot one of Jack's rugby teammates digging around in the drawers.

"You live here, right?" he asks, glancing at me over one broad shoulder. He's clad in jeans and a striped polo shirt that stretches across his chest.

I really need to start paying more attention to rugby. The guy's stacked, with rugged good looks and playful eyes.

"Yup," I answer.

"Help me find the bottle opener?"

I open the dishwasher and pull it out of the utensil bin. "Jack threw it in there so people wouldn't run off with it."

"Outstanding." He pops the cap off his beer and raises the bottle to me. "Cheers."

We clink and drink.

"I'm Sam." He leans against the counter. "You're Abbey, yeah?"

"Yeah. Is there a sign on my back?"

"Jack talks about you."

"Oh." An embarrassed blush heats my face. "Don't believe a word of it."

"All good stuff. Promise." Sam's got a disarming smile and easy demeanor about him. "You're quite fit, you know. I see why he didn't mention that."

I laugh nervously because I don't know how to take that. "You just put it right out there, huh?"

Sam shrugs with a bright, tipsy grin. "Was that a bit cheeky?"

"Maybe a little. Please, don't let me stop you."

His grin widens as his gaze travels over me, lingering briefly on the bare skin revealed by my off-the-shoulder sweater. Despite Lee's best efforts to dress me tonight, I chose my own outfit. Oversize sweater, denim skirt, and black combat boots. Cute and casual. Even Lee grudgingly admitted I looked good when he saw me walk out of my room. I'm sure it pained him to do so.

Someone turns up the music in the living room. Not a song I'm familiar with, though I've been absorbing a lot of British rock lately.

"Shall we have a dance?" Sam asks.

Nashville Abbey would say no. She'd be too far out of her comfort zone and self-conscious about looking silly in front of a crowd.

London Abbey has a few drinks in her and needs something to chase away the idea of a guy out of reach. So I chug my wine and grab his hand, leading him to the living room, where others are crammed together.

For a few minutes, I let go of all my apprehensions and distractions. I let Sam pull me close as he presses his lips to my hair, uttering flirty words I don't entirely discern through the music and his accent. I just nod and smile, amused for the moment to go with it. There are worse ways to spend an evening and more destructive means of forgetting a guy.

Across the room, I notice Jack noticing me. His usual unbothered smile falters as he sizes up his friend. His eyes narrow. When Sam nuzzles the side of my neck, Jack walks away from his conversation to approach us.

"Oi, mate." He jabs Sam's shoulder. "You're slobbering on the girl."

"He's really not," I counter, still dancing in Sam's embrace.

"On my best behavior," Sam says, still grinning and unaffected. "Swear it."

"House meeting." Jack gives Sam a shove, and although Sam raises a curious eyebrow, he backs off.

"Thanks for the bottle opener," he tells me. With a wink, he retreats.

Jack takes his place, but with quite a bit more distance between us. That doesn't stop his addictive scent from gripping my senses. He always smells so fucking good, like soap and sandalwood with a hint of spice. He's wearing a soft gray sweater and black trousers that make his ass look delicious. (I know this because I confirmed it with my eyes. Multiple times.)

Propelled by the music, I continue to dance, defiant. After a beat, Jack begins to move too, probably because he feels awkward standing still.

"That was cute," I tell him. "Petty but cute."

"Go on," he says, sporting a scowl that's more endearing than threatening.

"No, it's cool. I get it. Don't want other kids playing with your toys. I'm sort of flattered."

He lifts a brow. "You think I'm jealous?"

"Sam already gave you up. He told me all about how you can't stop talking about me to the team. Like you're basically obsessed with me."

It's the wine talking. A lot of it. More than I realized until I remember I had a glass while we were cleaning up for the party. Then a glass while I was getting dressed. A glass for every time I resisted the urge to ask Celeste if Nate and Yvonne were coming.

And, well, they've kind of added up.

Jack grins at me. "I've never mentioned you once. Someone asked me earlier if you were a lost neighborhood child. I said no, that's the mouthy American who doesn't know how to put her dishes away."

"Uh-huh. That's why you practically threatened to fight your friend so you could cut in, right?"

"I was protecting him. He's very dumb and unsuspecting."

"Protecting him from what? I mean, worst I'll do is take him upstairs and fuck him. Seems like a sweet deal for Sam."

Oh my God.

I can't believe I just said that. And it isn't even true! I'm not the bring-a-total-stranger-upstairs-and-fuck-him kind of girl. Yet for some reason, wine always emboldens me when it comes to Jack.

I glimpse a spark of heat in his eyes before his features strain. "Don't think I've heard you say that before."

"Say what?"

"*Fuck.*"

My forehead wrinkles. "I say the word *fuck* all the time."

"Not in that context." He licks his lips. "So. Is that it? You want to fuck my mate, do you?"

"No," I stammer. "It was just a joke."

My heart's suddenly pounding louder than the bass line of the song, beating even faster when I realize we've managed to work ourselves closer together. His hands on my hips. Mine resting on his chest. A rapid rush of excited nervousness charges across every inch of my skin. I tip my head up at him to see his expression is slightly hazy. Eyelids heavy. I wonder if he feels it too or if it's just the alcohol crossing our wires.

It's the same exhilaration I felt the first time I saw Nate. Which is even more confusing, because the two of them are so diametrically different. Jack's easygoing. Quick with a laugh. Nate's more complicated. Intense and guarded.

I'm attracted to both of them.

And they're both equally out of reach.

"What're you looking at me like that for?" Jack peers down at me, searching my face.

"I don't know. You're just…you're impossible to read," I admit.

Just like that, his crystal blue eyes become shuttered. Proving my point.

"Am I?" he drawls.

"Yes. It's maddening sometimes."

"Yes, Abbey, I'm the maddening one."

"What's that supposed to mean?" I protest.

He shifts his gaze away. "Nothing."

"Jack." He can be so frustratingly confusing.

When he looks at me again, his blithe demeanor is back. "Ah, don't mind me tonight, Abbs. I've too much liquor in me. I talk nonsense when I'm drunk." His grin stretches wide. "And you'll be in for it when Lee catches you trying to grope me again."

My gaze drops to my hands, which are splayed over his pecs. His hands brush mine as I snatch them away and take a self-conscious step backward.

I'm not able to respond, as a commotion suddenly breaks out across the room. Everyone rushes to watch a couple of Jack's teammates scuffling in the hall. Not a fight but more a drunken wrestling match that bounces off the walls and clatters into the dining room.

Jack trudges after them, shouting at them to knock it off as knickknacks and photos tumble to the floor. I cross the threshold in time to see the guys crash into the dining table where the Dyce portrait is propped in a chair. I'd been taking more photos earlier and brought it down for better light.

Now I watch, helpless, as it falls under the feet of these two-hundred-and-thirty-pound clumsy buffalo.

"Oh no," I gasp.

"Enough!" Jack pries his friends apart while I lunge for the painting. "You've fucked it now. Dickheads."

I'm nearly hyperventilating as I lay the portrait on the table to inspect it. I promised it to a museum, for Pete's sake. Luckily, there doesn't appear to be any damage to the painting itself. The paper backing is torn, but that can be replaced.

A wave of relief crashes over me. Thank God.

"We're sorry, Abbey," one of the contrite men say.

"Yeah, we didn't see it there," the other chimes in with appropriately sad puppy eyes.

"What's the damage?" Jack comes up beside me.

"It's okay. Just this torn area—" I stop.

In the process of prying the tear open a bit further, I suddenly realize there's something hidden beneath the backing of the painting.

16

I PASSED OUT IN MY CLOTHES LAST NIGHT, MY HAND STILL CLUTCH-
ing the letter we found hidden in the painting. Now it's morning, and
I'm wide awake and dressed, although I still feel a little drunk as I
sit at the breakfast bar reading and rereading the sad, short goodbye.

*I'm sorry. I cannot marry you, my darling. I love you dearly, but
my destiny lies with him. Where he goes, my heart will always
follow.*

Forgive me.
—Josephine

The envelope it came in is old and yellowed, without a name or
anything else to suggest its intended recipient. Not even a date on
the letter itself. The epitaph itself sits lonely on the page. I've read
it dozens of times, and each word is no less gutting with repetition.

I've spent weeks imagining the life she must have led. The world
spiraling outside her window, ravaged by war, smoldering remnants
of a continent emerging from tyranny. What it must have meant
to be a young woman when the air raid sirens finally ceased, in a
country now left to mourn the dead and rebuild its soul. I can't even
fathom the resilience required. The bravery to endure.

Now I have a name for my mystery woman. Presumably anyway. Except the same questions remain.

Who was Josephine? What was her connection to the Tulley family, and why would they have a portrait painted of her?

And now another mystery presents itself: Who were the loves that pulled at her heart, and who ultimately lost her?

The questions gnaw at my brain all day. I spend hours on Google, each search a variation of the name Josephine and Tulley, each one leading to a dead end. I need better sources, which doesn't bode well for my resolution to temporarily break up with the Talbot Library. Guess I know what I'll be doing after class on Monday.

That night, I'm still obsessing over my latest discovery as the group ends up at the pub. Because not enough of us woke up with hangovers.

In the cultural exchange of the past few months, I have to admit I underestimated the commitment of the British to their drinking culture. It's as if the whole country joined a frat in college and decided to just do that forever until their livers failed them or it gave them superpowers. The superpower being they could drink even more.

"She married the rich one," Celeste declares from across the table.

"I think that's it," Jamie agrees. "You've not found a picture or mention of a woman that matches among the nobility of the time, so that seems to suggest she was of common birth. Marrying into the Tulley family was likely a step up."

As it's been for a few weeks now, the gang is enthralled with the latest update on the Josephine saga. Tonight, they're arguing over their theories of Josephine's letter.

"No, mates." Lee holds up a hand at Jamie when he dares to protest. "I'm telling you. She was bi. Josephine had a girlfriend. Talk about scandalous for that time, yeah? Why else would the Tulleys get rid of the painting?"

"If she married a Tulley," Jack says beside me, "why haven't you found any mention of her?"

Therein lies the rub. That, coupled with her ending up in my dining room, says this wasn't a happily ever after for anyone.

I chew on my lower lip, thinking it over. "Okay. So the duke and duchess had three sons. All of them would have been the right age at the right time to be the competing love interests. We know for certain that the heir, Lawrence, didn't marry a Josephine."

"And so there were two," Celeste finishes ominously.

I grin at her. "My guess is Josephine found herself in a love triangle with Robert and William and was finally made to choose between them. One brother died. Another disappeared. Compelling circumstances to erase her from the family tree."

"She killed him."

We all turn to Yvonne. It's the first thing she's said tonight since we sat down. She's had her head buried in her phone without Nate to entertain her.

Despite my promise to myself, I'd felt a jolt of excitement at the sight of Yvonne approaching us at the door when we arrived.

Followed by bitter disappointment when she said Nate wasn't coming.

"Killed who?" Lee asks, glancing over at her.

"The one who disappeared," Yvonne hypothesizes. "She'd already planned it before the one who died asked her to marry him. But that would have ruined her plans to run off with the first one's fortune, so she turned down the second and he left England with a broken heart, only to perish at sea. Thanks to her, the duke and duchess lost two out of three sons. Hence Josephine never made it to the family history."

It's not the worst theory. But not all that likely either.

"I think it's romantic," Celeste interjects. "Not the murder part."

"Romance is dead," Lee responds bitterly.

"Oh no, mate." Jamie throws his arm around Lee's shoulder. "We didn't like Third George?"

"It's Bi-Curious George," I correct, and Yvonne laughs.

"Brilliant," she says in approval.

Lee heaves a sigh. "No, just another same old George. He decided the cock wasn't for him. And now I'm once again left bereft without a soulmate in sight."

"Maybe if you stopped searching for your soulmate on a hookup app." Celeste aims a pointed glare at her twin.

"Oh God, no." He smirks. "I am exactly that bitch. Anyway, I've a date tomorrow."

"Long live romance." Jamie holds his glass up, then takes a drink.

Lee winks at me. "His name's George."

"Seriously?" I demand.

"No, but how wild would that be? This one's called Freddie. He claims to be a proper gentleman with a penchant for romance and spoiling his lovers."

"Nah, mate, he only used that *romance* line to get in your knickers," Jamie says, rolling his eyes.

"Jamie." Celeste tilts her head toward him. "Tell us, what's the most romantic thing you've done for a girlfriend?"

"Ha!" Jack smacks a hand on the table, rattling our drinks. "Lord Kent sends them home with a gift bag of tiny soaps and a photo of himself."

Jamie cracks a smile. "What he said."

Celeste waves them off. "You're both pigs. On our first date, Roberto got us into the National Gallery after hours and arranged for a screening of my favorite movie in the Sunley Room."

"What's your favorite movie?" I ask.

"*Center Stage*," she says like I should have known.

"That's not romance." Lee's pint glass is empty, so he helps himself to Jamie's. "Staying up all night until your partner vomits up their grandmother's gold cross pendant when you'd told them if they kept sucking on that thing, one day they'd swallow it—that's romance."

I cover my mouth when an involuntary gag reflex threatens to spew pinot grigio all over the table. "That's nasty."

"What about Nate?" Celeste asks Yvonne.

She sighs in answer. "He's not the romantic type."

"You mean he's never penned you a love song or recited poetry in your ear late at night?" Lee says mockingly.

"Afraid not." She smooths a hand over her sleek blond hair before reaching for her drink.

"Ever brought you flowers at least?" Celeste presses.

Yvonne shakes her head. "Not Nate's style."

It's awful, but a tiny, petty part of me is happy to hear Nate hasn't made any grand romantic gestures for Yvonne.

"Go on then." Jamie prods at Jack. "Your turn."

Jack shrugs. "Romance? Mate, I've never even brought a girl home. I think I gave one a carnation for Valentine's in primary school once."

I don't have anything to add to the romance discussion. My one "adult" relationship consisted mostly of hooking up in his dorm room between study breaks. Living at home with a scarily overprotective parent meant no sleepovers, and our dates were less romantic outings than group hangs at the movies or the grill on campus. I don't even remember if he got me a birthday present.

Later, on our way home, I'm yet again crammed in the back seat of a cab with Jack to one side and Jamie asleep on the other. We hit a pothole that doesn't rouse him from his content snoring.

"You really never brought a girl home?" I ask Jack, because I'm feeling bold and a bit tipsy. "Like ever?"

"Like ever," he imitates with a smile.

"But you dated, right?"

"Sure. Dated around in high school. And there was one girl I was steady with. It's a different thing, though, to take 'em home to Mum."

"Is what someone might say when they have commitment issues," I tease.

"You're not the first to say that."

"Can't imagine why."

He offers an adorable shrug that bumps my shoulder. "I'd have to be head over heels for someone to introduce them to Mum. I wouldn't put any woman through that level of cross-examination unless I thought she was the one."

I laugh. "Your mom's a tough critic, huh?"

"The toughest."

"Are you guys close?"

"Ay. She raised us by herself after Dad died." Jack's careful to keep his voice down for the sleeping Jamie, who I think might be drooling on my shoulder. "Five kids all on her own, and we weren't an easy lot, you know. Still aren't." A sheepish smile flashes in the passing streetlights.

"It's just my dad and me too. But I don't think I've been much trouble at all. It's disgusting how good I am at following the rules."

He snickers. "Let's not brag about that, shall we?"

"What about your siblings?" I ask curiously. "You said some of them were older? Are they married?"

"Shannon's eighteen, with a boyfriend I've a feeling she'll ditch after graduation. Oliver's a year younger than me and single. Charlie's twenty-three, so two years older. Also single. Noah's the oldest at twenty-five. He has a girlfriend—Bree. Ah, God, she's fucking awful. That's shitty of me to say, but she treats him like a pet. Everything he does. Like telling him what to eat, what to wear. He has to ask permission to have a beer."

"You're exaggerating."

"I'm not. Last Christmas, Mum handed him a piece of pie, and his girlfriend starts in on him about how he's put on a few pounds."

"That's terrible."

"Mind you, my brother has, like, six percent body fat. The bloke's lips have abs."

I laugh at the hint of jealousy in Jack's voice. The competition in that family must be on another level.

"Mum hates her."

I absorb all the information he gave me, realizing that despite having lived together for two months, this is the first time Jack has offered a more in-depth look at his family life. Before tonight, all I knew about him was that he has some siblings and likes rugby, going to the pub, and walking around shirtless. And that his favorite meal of the day is breakfast, or brekky as he calls it, which never fails to make me laugh.

Not that he told me his whole life story just now, but hey, it's something. The problem is it's whetted my appetite. I'm hungry for more.

Sadly, more talking is not in the cards for this cab ride. Jack leans closer, and suddenly there's another drunk man using my shoulder as a pillow.

"Wake me when we get there?" he mumbles.

"Sure," I say, ignoring the quickening of my pulse.

The feel of him draped on me, warm and muscular, is downright butterfly inducing.

Lee would not approve.

17

THE LEAVES ARE CHANGING IN KENSINGTON GARDENS. A CRISP breeze blows orange, yellow, and red across the sidewalks and into floating plumes turned up by the wake of morning rush-hour traffic. It's late October. All of London is drenched in black coats and puffer jackets on my walk to campus.

"What was that?" my dad demands on the phone. "Is someone honking at you?"

"No. It's just normal traffic noises, weirdo. I'm walking to class."

I sip my coffee (I've still not learned to appreciate tea) and dodge TV camera crews that are about to go live from outside an iron fence in the ongoing saga of the royal philanderer. Apparently, Prince James remains staunch in his refusal to own up to his affairs, despite two swimsuit models recently coming forward with claims they had a threesome with the prince at a drunken yacht party in Monte Carlo.

"Anyway. What's up?" I ask Dad.

It's a rhetorical question. Same thing that's always up.

"I haven't heard from you in a while." His disappointed voice has grown more insistent and accusatory over the last month or so.

"I know. I'm sorry. I'm eyeballs-deep in solving this mystery of the portrait. I spend all day in class, then the library, then homework. The time difference makes things a real bitch."

"Abbey."

He can't see me roll my eyes, but I'm sure he senses it. "Sorry."

"I told you, you can call any time."

"You say that, but you're going to be cranky if I wake you up at three a.m."

"The alternative makes me crankier," he argues. "In other words, I'd like to hear from my kid more than once or twice a month."

"I'm not that bad," I argue back. "Besides, we both know you'd like to hear from me more than once or twice a *day*."

"It's a father's prerogative."

"Yeah, nice try. It's a daughter's prerogative to have a life. Quote me on that and tell it to Dr. Wu at your next session."

"Cut your old man some slack," he says with that guilt trip tone that is way too effective. "I miss you, baby girl. This house is empty without you around."

"I wish I could come home for Thanksgiving, but I have a test that week. There's no way I can miss it."

"I know. It's fine."

The unhappiness in his voice gnaws at me. This is hard on him. More so than he anticipated maybe. I should probably be more sensitive to that.

"How about this?" I suggest. "We'll FaceTime for Thanksgiving dinner. I'll do a turkey and everything."

"That'd be real nice. I'd like that."

"It's a plan then."

We say goodbye as I reach campus and hustle to my first class. Amelia is already there when I take my usual seat. She can't wait to tell me about the newspaper article she found describing the unusual brutality of one of her research subjects.

"Fifty-seven lashes with a poisoned blade," she reads from the article she's managed to translate with her rough understanding of French and a language app. "Have you ever heard of anything so outrageous?"

"I'm impressed," I admit. "My arm would have gotten tired after thirty lashes, tops."

"I'm obsessed."

Amelia is in full-on homicidal girl crush territory. And I'm happy for her, I guess?

Today we're updating our professor on the progress of our research projects. In my case, I'm forced to report I've stalled on Josephine. But I can't dock myself a point for effort—I've exhausted myself on library research and endless internet searches through academic catalogs, running to ground every loose lead or obscure reference.

It's as if Josephine was scrubbed clean from history except for one painting released from a dusty attic. After weeks on this fruitless venture, I'd be lying if I said I wasn't at least a little disappointed in myself. Not to mention kicking myself for picking such a difficult and elusive subject. Why not another investigation of Jack the Ripper, the Solway Spaceman, or the Highgate Vampire? I could have saved myself all sorts of grief.

When it's my turn to present, Professor Langford picks up on my frustration and suggests I rededicate my efforts to further study of the brothers.

"There's a small museum and cemetery not far from the Tulley estate in Surrey," she tells me. "I'd suggest availing yourself of their assistance."

Huh. How'd I miss that? Especially after finding the gallery in Rye. I was so preoccupied with a connection to Josephine, I managed to ignore the obvious avenues on the family. Sorely missing a dose of perspective, it seems.

"Finding a primary source within the family would also be prudent," my professor adds.

I breathe out a sharp laugh before I realize she's serious. Primary sources are every historian's best resource, of course. In this case, that's not so easy. How the hell would I get the current duke and duchess to agree to an interview for some student's class project on their ancestors' personal tragedies and private embarrassments? Or even get close enough to ask?

Then I get a terrible idea.

After class, I give Jamie a call.

"Abbey, darling, settle an argument for me," he says instead of *hello*. "Should ketchup be consumed cold or at room temperature? We need an American perspective on this."

"You don't even eat ketchup."

"Of course not. There's nothing so hideous in all of creation," he says, because, Jamie. "But if one did…"

"Room temp. Obviously."

"Yeah, see," he says away from the phone. "She says you're barking, mate."

"Hey, so listen," I press. Jamie is a doll, but the boy is easily distracted.

"Right, sorry. What can I do for you?"

"I need a favor," I confess. "A big one. Any chance you could get me an introduction to someone connected to the Tulleys?"

"Oh." He chuckles. "Well, you don't make it easy on a bloke. This about the painting still?"

"Yeah. Bonus points if it's a member of the family."

"I see." There's a long pause with some indistinct chatter in the background mingled with the sounds of London traffic. Like me, he's on campus across town today. "For you, Abbs, I'll do my best. Give me some time."

"You're a peach," I say in relief.

If anyone can swing it, it's his lordship Jamie Kent.

"Tell me I'm your favorite roommate."

"My very best favorite."

That was easier than expected. Far from a done deal, however. In the event Jamie can't manage a connection, I'll need a fallback plan. As I'm typing some notes to myself on my phone, I receive a text.

My fingers freeze at the name on the screen.

> Nate: How's the hunt?

Holy shit.

I can't believe he's on my phone.

Like, the fucking nerve of this dude.

But also, I'm kind of okay with it.

Maybe more than okay.

I haven't heard from him in weeks. So long now that our road trip seems almost a hallucination. I'd even started to wonder if I was the reason he'd been absent from the usual group outings.

Now he slides into my texts all cool and casual. Typical. He's got that energy. The fleeting rogue, always asking forgiveness with a bashful smile and those brooding eyes. And we never say no because of course not. If their schtick didn't work, their species would've died out generations ago.

I'm tempted to answer immediately, but I stop myself.

The sensible thing to do is respond with a polite but succinct *yeah, good*. Whatever his motivations in contacting me now, they're definitely not the ones that I entertain in the whispering parts tucked way back in my own head. Reading more into a simple message says more about me than it does about him—or his intentions. The easiest way to let myself off the hook is not to lunge at it in the first place.

I, of course, do none of that.

> Me: If you want to give me a lift to a cemetery in Surrey, I can fill you in.

> Nate: Where are you now?

> Me: Albert Hall at Pembridge.

> Nate: Meet me out front in fifteen.

18

I BLOW OFF THE REST OF MY CLASSES FOR THE AFTERNOON TO HOP on the back of Nate's motorcycle. After only a few miles, the lash of colder air across my face reaches bone, and I cling to Nate for warmth and hug the body of the bike with my legs. It's all I can do to stop from shivering. At a stop sign, he notices my nearly frozen fingers and tucks my hands into the front pockets of his leather jacket.

"Better?" he says roughly.

"Much." My voice sounds odd to my ears. Somehow simultaneously too high and too throaty.

The more time I spend with him on this bike, the more I believe I'm starting to understand him. The freedom and impermanence of his nature, exposed to and at eye level with his surroundings. It takes a particular kind of person to own a bike. It's the difference between seeing a city from a tour bus and actually plunging yourself in its streets.

I get the sense that Nate's the type of guy who immerses himself in everything. He needs to feel the texture between his fingers, searching for that authentic something that makes the experience worth having, not content with the behind-the-glass view. It's in his aura, and I think it's that restless quality that I instinctively gravitate toward.

Streets narrow through thickening trees as we approach the

Tulley estate. Only about a mile down a winding road, past the iron gates, a small historic cemetery comes into view. There, an old stone church with its pocked exterior dripped in black from centuries of rain stands guard over the dead. Beside it is the modest brick museum with a painted wooden sign.

Nate pulls up alongside the building in the empty parking lot. Still straddling his bike, he takes my helmet, then brushes my hair out of my face as I stand.

"A little brisk, was it?"

"Didn't bother me," I lie. Because I don't want him to think I'm, what, uncool?

He smiles in return as he gets off the bike. I'm not sure if that's an approving look or because he knows I'm only putting on a brave face. Either way, I like that I get that out of him.

No one greets us when we walk inside on a gust of wind that throws dry leaves at our heels. The room is dark, save for soft amber pin lights over glass display cases and the open window shutters at the back of the room, casting harsh shadows.

"Hello?" I call out in search of anyone to help us.

"The lunch lull?" Nate says.

"Guess we beat the rush," I joke.

We wait another minute or so before losing patience and heading off to wander the exhibits on our own. My gaze absorbs every detail, an eagerness building deep in my belly. I'm on sensory overload in here. Everywhere I look, I see something that begs for my attention. Photos, newspaper articles, handwritten letters. Leather-bound journals open to dates of some significance. Pieces of personal artifacts. Jewelry and carved gifts from foreign dignitaries.

I let out a giddy sigh.

Nate looks over, an indecipherable glint in his eyes.

"What?" I say self-consciously.

"Nothing. Just…" His tongue comes out briefly to moisten his lower lip. "You should see yourself right now. Your whole face is lit up. Cheeks flushed. You look like you just…" He trails off, wrenching his gaze away.

"Like I just what?" I ask. Because I'm a masochist.

His eyes flick back to mine. Just for a moment. "Like you just had a good fuck."

I feel those words between my legs.

"Oh" is the only syllable I manage to utter through my dry throat.

All business now, he drifts toward the nearest display. "All right then. What are you hoping to find?"

I force my mind back on task. "Okay, so I found a note hidden in the backing of the portrait. It was written by a young woman named Josephine."

"The subject of the portrait, you reckon?"

"I think so. In the note, Josephine was telling someone she couldn't marry him because she was in love with someone else. There's a chance it's one or more of the Tulley brothers, but I need evidence to support the theory."

Nate and I drift around the room. There's an enormous family tree dating back centuries hanging on the far wall. On another wall, a painted coat of arms and a military uniform with medals and other regalia. All of it offers remarkable glimpses into the legacy of the Tulley family, but none of it is of importance to my investigation.

"What got you curious?" I ask suddenly. We're at opposite sides of the room, strolling past exhibits.

"Huh?"

When I glance over my shoulder, I catch him watching me. "You haven't been around much lately," I clarify. "I was surprised to hear from you today."

"Yeah." He turns back to the framed pictures on the wall, reading the printed labels beside deteriorating pieces of paper. "It occurred to me you don't have many ways to get around to conduct your research. Thought I'd be of service."

"I see. Purely academic interest then."

I scrutinize a gown in a standing glass case, which was purportedly worn by a Tulley at a royal wedding during the reign of William IV. I feel Nate's intermittent gaze at my back.

"As research assistants go, I'm moderately reliable," he drawls, then wanders off again.

He's a tough nut to crack. Stiff upper lip and all that. I can never quite tell if he's being flirtatiously obscure or politely evasive.

Or maybe I'm simply reading too much into this again. Nate doesn't go to college. He works nights as a bartender when he isn't playing gigs. So it's possible he has a lot of daylight time on his hands and not nearly enough ways to spend it. In that case, I'm a brief distraction between obligations.

Then again, Jack and Jamie aren't offering to drive me an hour into the country for homework.

"Take a look at this," Nate calls from another room.

I search for him until I find a hidden corridor tucked behind a bookcase. In the small room, a projector shows black-and-white newsreel footage of ships arriving at a port. Weary, huddled people in blankets disembark at the pier. On the adjacent wall are framed news articles, photographs, and two small oil portraits of a familiar figure.

"The *Victoria*," I breathe. "William, the middle brother, was lost at sea when the ship sank."

I've seen photographs of William Tulley before. In this context, however, surrounded by the footage of the disaster's aftermath and headlines from around the world that announced the tragedy, he feels more alive than a grainy image in a book.

He was a handsome young man in his midtwenties with soft, narrow features and a rebellious mustache, his gaze perpetually fixed toward the horizon. A wanderer's spirit.

"He was cute," I remark.

Nate's amused voice tickles the back of my head. "Was he now?"

"Sure. I mean, I totally would've tapped that," I say before remembering I'm not with Eliza but rather with a gorgeous Englishman.

That gets me a strangled laugh. "I reckon poor old Will would've been riddled with confusion if you hit on him using that phrase."

I start laughing too and affect a (not good) posh British accent. "Hullo, sir, I would like to tap you. Please, remove your britches." I turn to beam at Nate. "Hot, right?"

"So hot," he says solemnly.

I continue to study the *Victoria* materials, wondering why William Tulley ended up on this doomed ship. "You know what's wild? William wasn't even on the official passenger manifest. Wasn't scheduled to take the voyage. He was a last-minute addition to the crossing."

"How on earth do you know that?"

I smile smugly. "I'm a possessor of infinite knowledge, Nate. That's how you roll when you spend your entire life in the library."

"Should we brag about that? Truly?"

A laugh sputters out. "Fair critique. But it came up in my research. I tracked down the manifest, and his name wasn't on it. Instead there was a handwritten notation from someone at the shipping company saying Lord William Tulley would be joining them. They even cleared out a first-class cabin for him. Probably had to kick out some poor soul to make room for his lordship. Annoyingly, it doesn't say if he was traveling alone or not."

"But the fact that he boarded the ship at the last minute must mean something, right? Running away to America to nurse his broken heart."

"Or," I counter, "running away to America with the woman he stole from his brother."

"Also a possibility," Nate says unhelpfully before moving toward the next display.

A few moments later, he calls me over again.

"Over here."

He gestures for me to join him in front of a glass case. Inside, two pieces of paper lie side by side. The handwritten letter is addressed to William's mother, the duchess. Dated mere days before the *Victoria* embarked from England, the letter is written in black ink that has become faded over the decades. I lean in and squint to make out some of the text.

Rest assured, dear mother, we shall reconcile when we're both good and ready. Brothers cannot hate each other forever. This shall pass.

"He's talking about his relationship with Robert," I tell Nate, excitement surging through my blood. "That's the eldest brother who disappeared."

Some parts of the letter are difficult to read, so I pull out my phone and snap several pictures of the display case. I'll upload them to a photo editor later and play around with the exposure settings, see if I can make the words more palatable to the eyes. But the important thing is I was right.

William and Robert were estranged before William boarded that ship.

And while there's no mention of Josephine, this is the strongest indication yet of the rift between the sons that could explain Josephine's place in the story.

"What do you think it means?" Nate asks.

"I don't know. Nothing I've found so far suggests Josephine was on the ship. Did William leave England because she chose Robert? Or did she follow William to America and leave Robert behind?"

I've still found no clue as to how or why Robert disappeared. There are plenty of theories but none with any evidence I could hope to follow. As with everything in this mystery, each clue is another unanswered question.

Continuing our search, we come across a diary entry from the duchess. She describes her son Robert as the steadfast sort, a young man with an intense conviction and will but well-liked and admired by his peers.

William, in contrast, was never at peace to sit idle on the grounds of the estate. *His heart seeks exploration*, the duchess mused. He was most fulfilled when out on some new adventure, which was a difficult pill to swallow for a mother who wished to keep her sons close to her.

"Hello there."

The sudden appearance of a tall middle-aged man startles me.

"Sorry I didn't hear you sooner," he says, his expression rueful. "Afraid I fell asleep in the back after my lunch."

"That's all right," I answer. "I hope it's okay that we're in here. The door was open."

"Of course. All are welcome." He smiles. "Though we don't get many visitors if I'm being frank. Are you a student?"

"Yes, actually."

He nods, hunched under the low ceiling. He's lanky and brittle in a wool sweater and collared shirt. "That's about all who find a reason to come here these days. There's the ladies' bridge club on Sundays. And we do get the odd photo shoot. An episode of *Midsomer Mysteries* was filmed here once." That last tidbit brightens him right up.

"Well, that's something," I say with a smile. "May I ask a strange question?"

He beams at me. "I adore strange questions."

"Excellent." I gesture to the large portrait hanging on the wall behind Nate. "Do you have a theory about Robert Tulley? About what happened to him?"

"Ah." He thinks on it a moment. "Well, I can't say I know better than any who've attempted to answer that question before. However, Robert was a charming, honorable man who cared a great deal for his family. I suppose whatever occurred, it was quite extraordinary. I've often wondered if it was his kindness that did him in."

"How do you mean?" Nate asks.

"Loyal young man like that, perhaps too trusting of the world. There are any number of ways for someone to take advantage."

I purse my lips. "You believe he was killed then. Rather than ran away."

"Who'd run from all this?"

I take his meaning. The former glory. The wealth. The titles and privileges. It's an ironic metaphor, though, standing in this empty, dark little cottage surrounded by the faces of the dead. Sifting through the wilting remains of the Tulley legacy as their estate crumbles into scandal and bankruptcy.

"They're buried out there, you know. Nearly every one of them. If you'd like to visit."

My breath hitches. "Would that be okay?"

I'd been tempted when we first drove by, but it seemed uncouth. Cemetery tourism has always felt wrong to me.

"They sit there all alone otherwise," the man says soberly.

Nate and I make our way out to the cemetery and walk the rows of weathered headstones. The man at the museum gave us a map of the deceased, and we soon find Robert Tulley's empty grave. I stare at the eerie blank space where the date of death should be.

"My mother left me," I say.

Which is an awkward way to start a conversation, but the instinct to do so erupts from my mouth without permission.

"Sometimes she'll send a birthday postcard or something," I continue. "Mostly, though, she disappeared. Dropped me off at my dad's doorstep when I was two and fled without a backward look. I don't know where she is or what she's doing. When she dies, I might not even know."

"That's brutal." Nate's voice is low, somber. "I'm sorry."

"I guess what I'm trying to say is it's weird how context changes the story. History talks about Robert in these mysterious, tragic terms. But what about the people who knew him? The ones left behind. Did they feel abandoned? Discarded? Or if he left for love, why did he let his family forever grieve his loss without closure?"

Nate watches me with that inscrutable expression of his. "You're passionate about all this."

I shrug, hoping the heat flaming my face doesn't appear as obvious in the cooling late-afternoon air.

"Who doesn't love a good story? It's romantic, isn't it? Love and death and tragedy-torn families. Beats Instagram and reality TV or whatever bullshit."

Nate cracks a half smile that quickens my pulse. "Can't argue that."

We walk toward the next row, where I stop in front of another headstone. Lawrence is here as well. The youngest brother, whom the duchess described in her diary as a spoiled, petulant child. The books that mention Lawrence before he became the patriarch of the Tulley family labeled him an unserious, uncurious boy with no remarkable qualities. A boy who managed to be so unlike his brothers.

"If Robert hadn't disappeared and William hadn't died," I say, "Lawrence wouldn't have inherited the family's land and titles. He wouldn't have produced the descendants who humiliated the Tulley name and drove the estate into ruin. It's tragic."

"It's a very British story," Nate says wryly.

"I take it you aren't a monarchist."

He slides a dry glance at me. "No."

I step away from Lawrence's grave. As we continue exploring, Nate shoves his hands in the pockets of his worn jeans, his long legs moving in easy strides. He's got this completely unfazed aura to him. Unfettered. More than that, he gives off the vibe that he might take off at any moment. He's here with me now, but only because he chooses to be. Nothing or no one can capture him unless he lets them.

"Shall we head off then?" He glances at me.

"Sure, let's—" My gaze snags on a flash of color among the

greenery. "Actually, wait. Just one more thing," I tell him before dashing off.

I steal a handful of pink and orange flowers from a nearby bush and carry them to the grave of the duchess. Bending down, I carefully lay them on the weathered stone. I don't know what propels me. Maybe the fact that she lost so much. That we spent the afternoon combing through her private words. It feels wrong to trample through the family's dead without some gesture of appreciation.

As I stand with muddy prints on the knees of my jeans, Nate holds out a dark red flower I hadn't noticed him pick.

My heartbeat accelerates.

"What's this for?" I squeak, trying to talk through the surprised lump in my throat.

"Reminds me of your hair." He twirls the short stem between his long, callused fingers. "And I felt like it."

I bite my lip. Hard.

This is the guy who doesn't *do romance.*

Our fingers brush as I accept the flower from him, and my pulse kicks up another notch. Avoiding his eyes, I duck my head and smell the delicate petals.

"Abbey," he starts. Voice low.

I swallow. "Hmm?"

The distance between us has closed by inches, and when I look up, his face is hovering over me with dark come-hither bedroom eyes. The intensity is almost too much. I'm so hypnotized, in fact, that I barely notice we're getting closer and that my eyelids are drifting shut, until my phone buzzes in my pocket with such insistence that someone had better be dying.

We jerk apart as I pull my phone out to read the text.

> Jamie: You're meeting with Lord Benjamin Tulley tomorrow afternoon.

"Holy shit," I blurt out.

That startles Nate. "What's wrong?"

"No. Wow. I can't believe he did it. Jamie got me a meeting with Lord Tulley for my research."

"Ah. All right." His hands slip into his pockets again. "Shall we go?"

He turns away to head back to his bike.

I stare after him, uncertain. Talk about whiplash. I'm not sure I understand what was about to happen before Jamie's text, except that I'm nearly breathless when I type a reply.

> Me: Thank you! I owe you.
> How'd you manage that?

> Jamie: You're welcome, and yes, you do. He's a lad from school. Several years ahead of me but we've met a few times. Friends of friends. Try not to embarrass me, darling.

He follows that with a winking emoji.

Bless that boy.

It's good to have friends in high places. Particularly ones whose interruptions stop you—no, save you—from making the incredibly stupid mistake of kissing someone else's boyfriend.

19

As I heat up dinner leftovers later that evening, I try to stave off nausea thinking about all the ways I could make an ass of myself in front of Lord Tulley. Adding to the queasiness is my anxiety over Nate as my mind keeps replaying the incident at the museum.

I think he was about to kiss me.

No. I *know* he was.

And if he had, I think I would've kissed him back.

All right, fine. I *know* I would've kissed him back.

Which is very, very concerning, because that's not me. I'm not that girl. I don't tread on other women's territory, and I'm ashamed of myself for almost going there. At the same time, my clueless heart won't stop skipping like a giddy schoolgirl every time I imagine Nate's mouth on mine.

Speaking of mouths I want on mine, Jack walks into the kitchen.

In a red hoodie and faded jeans, he stands beside me and just scowls. He's clearly pissed about something yet refuses to voice it.

"Use your words," I urge.

He ignores my teasing grin. "You went to Surrey today."

"I did. I was checking out a museum my professor pointed me to."

The microwave beeps. I open the door to pull out my plate of steaming pad Thai. We ordered it yesterday from another one of

Lee's hidden finds. I swear, that boy knows all the best restaurants in this city.

"You went with Nate?"

"Yeah. So?"

There's a suspicious silence behind me.

"How'd he manage to fit you and Yvonne on that bike?"

The bite to his voice gives me pause. I slowly face him. "What's that for?"

"Hmm? What?" He plays dumb as we stand at opposite sides of the counter. "I just didn't know you two were such good friends."

"We're not." I frown. "Why do you look so mad? He gave me a ride to another museum. Nothing more."

"That's not why I'm mad."

"So you *are* mad. All right. Let's hear it."

Jack crosses his arms over his chest. "If you're going to be gone for hours, you need to call someone and let them know."

My mouth falls open. "I'm sorry—what?"

"You can't just take off gallivanting around the countryside without letting anybody know where you're going. That shit's dangerous, Abbs."

My anger fades. Now I'm trying not to laugh at him. His expression is cloudy with disapproval, and he has this tough-guy warrior stance going on that's sort of hot and adorable at the same time.

"Lee was worried," Jack finishes, awkwardly dropping his arms to his sides.

"Lee, huh? That's funny, because he didn't call me all evening. And when I texted him on my way home, he seemed more put off that I couldn't stop at the off-licence to pick up wine." I raise my eyebrows in challenge. "Didn't get a call from you either. You know, if you were so worried."

That gets me a glare. "Just keep us in the loop next time," he mutters before stalking out of the kitchen.

Then, just because I'm a smart-ass jerk, I set my plate on the counter and reach for my phone. I open the texting app that everyone in this country seems to prefer and start a new chat with Jack. It isn't until his profile image pops up that I realize he and I have never texted each other outside the group chat for all the roommates.

Jack's profile is a picture of him and a young blond I assume is his sister, Shannon, judging by the resemblance between them. I click on it and type a new message.

> Me: After dinner, I might take a walk to the café down the street to pick up some muffins for tomorrow morning. Just in case you come downstairs and find me missing. When I get back, I'll likely take a shower, so if my room is empty, it means I'm in the bathroom. No need to call the police. I repeat, don't call the police.

I get a middle finger emoji in response.

Laughing to myself, I send back a kissy face and then eat my dinner.

Later, while Jack and Jamie are at a rugby match and the pub, respectively, Lee stations himself in my bedroom so we can hammer out a "game plan" for my meeting with Lord Tulley tomorrow. I swear, Lee is more excited for this meeting than I am. He flings dresses at me with the verve of a major league pitcher, bouncing with enthusiasm.

"You need something sophisticated but flirty," Lee is saying, holding yet another garment in front of me.

"Why flirty?"

His features contort. "Babe, I'm not explaining the bits and bobs to you."

"I'm not trying to marry into the family. This is just a school assignment."

He whips another reject at the discard pile on my bed. Just about everything I own has been judged too hideous to be seen in public.

"What's that face?" He studies my reflection in the mirror.

"Huh? No face."

"Mm-hmm. So then you're *not* doubting my fashion expertise?"

"Not at all."

I'm not sure which of us is worse at this.

"Abbey. Luv. If you want to go poking around in this lad's family skeletons, you've got to ingratiate yourself to his masculine instincts."

"I'm sorry?"

Lee grabs my shoulders to press another dress to me as he appraises it in the mirror. "Get him to like you."

"You know, it's a little disheartening you think that requires so much underhanded calculation."

"Please," he scoffs. "I'm jealous. You're lucky I don't stuff you in a closet and go myself."

"I don't think it's going to be all that enthralling, to be honest."

"Are you mad?" Lee cocks his head at the next dress he holds up. "I'd claw eyes out to meet one of the infamous Tulleys in person. Ordinary people are so passé."

I roll my eyes. "You're such a snob."

"And?" He scrutinizes two dresses, holding them out. Then he pushes them in my hands. "Either of these will do. All right. Off I go. I've got to put on my mask. This complexion doesn't happen by accident."

I'm grinning to myself as he leaves. Lee is nothing if not entertaining. I hear him exchange a few words with Jack out in the hall, followed by the bathroom door shutting and Jack's heavy footsteps. I'm still considering my options between the dresses when Jack pokes his head in my room.

"Come to scold me again?" I ask mockingly.

He mocks me right back. "I don't know. Have you been a bad girl again?"

Oh God.

Hot Jack shouldn't be allowed to utter the words *bad girl*.

His gaze shifts to the two dresses I laid out on the bed. "The red one makes you look like a schoolteacher."

"How do you know?"

"You wore it, like, two weeks ago."

Did I? I don't remember. "In a good way, or…"

"Not the sexy kind." Jack invites himself in, his long stride eating up the space between us. The glassiness in his eyes and whiff of lager on his breath says he went out with the boys after his match.

Nearly every stitch of clothing I own has been tossed around my room, so I start putting things on hangers and folding the rest to place into drawers.

"How was the game?" I ask.

"We humiliated them. Their girlfriends will never be sexually attracted to them again."

"Oh. Pity."

Pushing fabric aside, he picks through the piles of clothes on my bed. "Got a date?"

"Jamie set up a meeting for me with Benjamin Tulley to ask him some questions for my research."

"He's good in a pinch, our Jamie. When'd that happen?"

"He texted me when Nate and I were in Surrey."

"Right. Your private chauffeur Nate."

"Stop making a thing out of it. I needed a lift and he offered."

"Twice."

I grab a stack of shirts and shove them in my drawer. It's my turn to avoid his gaze. "Is that a problem?"

I thought I'd kept my attraction to Nate well hidden for the most part. But if it's become obvious to Jack, chances are others have noticed too.

And if Jack believes I'm chasing another girl's boyfriend, what must he think of me?

Because he can't be jealous.

That'd be silly. Right?

"Do whatever you like, Abbs."

I catch him watching me in the mirror. "Next time I need a last-minute ride to the country, you'll be my first call."

"I like the blue one." He comes to stand behind me with the dress in his hand. Slowly, I turn to accept it. "It looks nice on you."

It's back again, that insistent desire I've tried to tamp down. The one that makes me wonder what his hair feels like between my fingers. The ache to run my hands across his chest. To have his touch against my skin. It sneaks up on me. Blindsided.

How does he *do* that?

And why can't I ever get a handle on what he's feeling? I can never tell if I'm imagining the chemistry between us. If it's just in his nature, his personality, to be flirtatious. Most of the time, I'm convinced that's the case. But then he goes and looks at me like *this*, and I start to doubt myself.

He steps closer.

"What are you doing, Jack?" I ask through a dry throat.

"Not doing anything, Abbey." But his eyes are gleaming with mischief and a few pints.

I gulp. "Lee wouldn't like knowing we're alone in here together."

"No," he agrees thickly. "I'm sure there's a house rule time limit on having boys in your room."

"If there isn't, then there should be."

A hint of a smile touches his lips. Then he licks them, and my heart rate triples. I'm not sure who moves first, but before I get a whole breath in, he's got my hips pressed against my dresser with both hands and his lips are centimeters from mine.

"This is a bad idea," Jack whispers.

"Terrible," I whisper back.

"Just want one taste," he mumbles, and then he kisses me.

His mouth is soft and warm as it covers mine, the slightest tang of English beer on his tongue. I grab two fistfuls of his shirt, twisting. Rising up on my toes to meet his kiss.

Who is this girl?

I don't recognize myself. It's like I'm watching from across the room, not entirely aware or in control. Jack flicks some instinctive switch in me, and my subconscious takes over.

He's not at all hurried or forceful. Rather, it's a slow, gentle exploration that makes my head go hazy. His tongue slicks over mine, caressing, teasing, then retreating so I have to chase it into his mouth with an anguished moan.

I'm falling into him, responding to his skillful touch, when suddenly he breaks the kiss and pulls back to leave me stunned and breathless.

Jack looks at me, silent, his expression impossible to discern.

"Yeah, I'm knackered. I'm off to bed," he mutters before strolling out of my room.

The blue dress lies in a puddle on the floor.

I blink in confusion. It's as though I imagined it. A blurry daydream staring into the glare of the sun, that moment when you're caught in a brilliant blinding light before your eyes adjust to the dull surroundings.

What the hell was that?

20

I'VE BEEN A DISASTER ALL DAY. POURED COFFEE IN MY CEREAL AND squeezed hand lotion onto my toothbrush. I didn't see Jack this morning, and I'm not sure if that made it better or worse. On my way to campus, I ran headlong into an angry Italian tourist because I was so distracted with replaying and reexamining the kiss that I didn't see her until I had a mouthful of her scarf.

Even now as I sit in class, I stare at my notes and realize I'd written the date three times but not a word of what the professor has said for the last forty minutes.

Who does that? Sneaks up on a girl to lay a kiss on her with no context and then saunters off to bed?

It's infuriating is what it is.

He's got some nerve.

Stop acting like you hated it.

Fine. I didn't hate the kiss. Not even a little bit.

But I had put the notion of Jack being an option out of my head. House rules and all. So what the hell do I do with these feelings he's implanted in me? And thanks to him avoiding me this morning, I have no clue how he feels about it either. Then again, what else is new? I never know what Jack's feeling.

Most likely, he'll completely brush this incident off. Crack some joke to the boys about how I jumped him while he was weak and inebriated. Laugh the whole thing off as a drunken gag. Which is why I should stop obsessing over it. I'm meeting Benjamin Tulley for lunch this afternoon, and I can't show up a hot mess. When class lets out, I pop into the restroom to fix my hair and makeup, then give myself a silent pep talk.

We will not embarrass ourselves in front of a lord.

We will not make Jamie look bad for getting us this meeting.

We absolutely will not show up with toilet paper stuck to our shoe.

Yeah. Good talk.

The restaurant where we're supposed to meet is in a hotel about two miles away. It's a trek, cutting through Hyde Park, but on a brisk October day, it's a pleasant walk. The Lanesborough is a gorgeous Greek revival building near the Wellington Arch. I'm certain I'm underdressed when two doormen in formal attire greet me at the entrance. Inside, I'm astounded at the opulence of shiny marble floors, tall columns, and ornate carved ceilings. I'm tempted to snap a few photos until I catch a man at the front desk watching me and think better of it.

"Excuse me," I say, approaching him. "Which way is the restaurant? I'm meeting someone."

"Your name?"

"Oh, uh, Abbey Bly—"

"Abbey," a brisk female voice says from behind me.

I turn to find a familiar brunette in a high-necked black dress approaching. I scan my brain trying to place her, then realize it's the woman from the Tulley sale. What was her name again? Sophia?

"Sophie Brown," she says, extending a hand. "We met several weeks ago. I'm Lord Tulley's assistant."

"Right. Sophie." I was close with the name. I lean in to shake her hand. "It's good to see you again. Are you joining us today?"

"I'm afraid not. I'm off to the office to pick up some paperwork. But Benjamin is here and waiting for you."

Sophie nods toward the front desk, and instantly there's another man at my side, dressed in three-piece formal attire like the desk clerk. With an outstretched arm, he beckons me to follow him.

I bid Sophie goodbye, and the man escorts me through the lobby and down a corridor into a breathtaking restaurant like I've only seen in movies. The decor is a Regency motif in soft shades of powder blue and gold, with tufted velvet furniture, crystal chandeliers, hand-painted wallpaper, and intricate scenes carved along the walls at the ceiling.

I'm ushered to a table where Lord Tulley is already seated, reading on his phone. I recognize him from the tabloid pictures online. He's slender and impeccably dressed in a navy suit and folded pocket square. Handsome too, in a specific British kind of way. I read that he's twenty-seven years old, but he looks much younger, like the college boys I pass on campus every day.

"Ms. Bly," the hotel employee says by way of introduction. Then he hastily departs.

"Abbey." Lord Tulley stands and greets me with an enthusiastic smile I don't anticipate. He's taller in person. "Quite pleased to meet you." He gestures to a chair for me to sit. "I'd be delighted if you called me Ben."

"All right. Ben. Thank you again for agreeing to meet with me. I know this is an odd request."

Immediately, waiters in white gloves arrive to put my napkin in my lap, fill my water glass, and apparently swap out most of the silverware. The entire choreography is a bit overwhelming and sets me off-balance. Ben watches me as if he notices none of it.

"My office receives two dozen interview requests a day. Never from a student, however. And an American at that. You certainly piqued my interest."

"I should probably start by saying I'm not here to embarrass you in any way. My interest is purely historical."

Ben smiles, cocking his head just so. "My mother's seen my bare backside on the front page of a tabloid. I'm not sure I'm capable of further embarrassment."

I smother a laugh. "Good point."

"We can relate in that regard, as I understand it."

Waiters arrive with an artful green salad that I hesitate to ruin by eating it. The kind of plate that would break Instagram and now I'm certain my dad's going to blow up my phone when he sees this credit card bill.

"I hope you don't mind," Ben says. "I took the liberty of ordering for us."

"Thank you. And I take it you looked me up."

"I do my homework as well," he says lightly.

He's charming. Approachable and disarming. Given what's been written about him in the British press, I'd prepared myself for a real prick. So far, he's quite gracious.

"It wasn't easy, of course. You haven't any social media that Sophie could find."

"No. I learned that lesson in high school. It's either completely toxic, full of people trying to get close to my dad, or trolled by sleazy celebrity press zooming in on pictures of a fourteen-year-old girl's cellulite. I cleansed myself of the hassle and never looked back."

"Well done." He barely glances away, and a waiter appears to pour two glasses of wine for us. Ben raises his at me. "To self-preservation."

"Cheers," I say, clinking his glass before taking a sip.

"Enjoy that. It's one of the last bottles the Tulley winery ever produced."

"Oh, I didn't know you were in the wine business."

"One of several ventures we've had to retire in the current"—he pauses to consider his words—"restructuring of our financial affairs."

"I'll savor it then."

"It's shit," he laughs with self-deprecating humor. "My great-grandfather understood even less about wine than he did finance. It's a metaphor, if you will, for the spectacular decline of the entire estate. Lawrence Tulley spent an outrageous fortune on some slick git to tell him to buy this thing or that. Spent another absurd fortune to procure it without the slightest notion of what he was doing. Then promptly ran it into the ground."

"Is that where you believe the slide began? With Lawrence?"

"Between you, me, and the flatware," he says, tapping the side of his nose. "Though my father isn't much better. Every few years, he'd come up with some fool scheme. Dad's an easy mark for bad investments and doomed business ventures. Plenty have attempted to make him see reason, but he's a stubborn old mule. I'm not convinced he's noticed they're selling the country house out from under him. He spends most of the year on his yacht in the Med or the chalet in the Alps. We've flats in London and all over the world that I doubt he's even seen since he was my age."

"I know the feeling. A few years ago, I was cleaning out my closet and found dolls I hadn't played with in years," I say, deadpan.

"Yes, quite," he answers with a chuckle. "You understand."

Ben's a good sport, not at all touchy about the reality of his family's situation. If anything, I get the sense he's frustrated by his lack of status to do anything to stop the bleeding. Not that he's living a frugal existence by any means. I think he'd be happy to rearrange the entire estate if allowed to. Modernize their portfolio and try to do something productive with what's left. As it is, by the time he inherits the title, it won't be much more than a piece of paper.

"You didn't come to hear a bitter posh lament his vanishing inheritance," he says then. "Please, the floor is yours. How can I be of service?"

The waiters clear our plates as we finish our salads. It allows me a moment to gather my thoughts and prime them with another sip of critically endangered wine.

"If you'll forgive the faux pas," I begin, "I was browsing the estate sale at your family's home in Surrey…"

He smiles wryly. "This isn't about my baby pictures, I hope."

"No. It's someone else's picture, actually. I'm interested in this portrait of a woman." I reach into my bag, then hand him a printout of a photo I took and a scanned copy of the letter. "I'm operating under the assumption that she is the Josephine from the letter. I found it hidden in the backing of the portrait."

Ben looks startled. "You bought this from the sale?"

I nod.

He examines the photo closely. "Interesting. Please, go on."

"Okay, well, I haven't managed to identify her or her relation to your family. Believe me, I exhausted so many other avenues before requesting this meeting. I've been to Franklin Astor Dyce's hometown in Rye, to the museum there. They assure me the work is authentic. I went back to the museum in Surrey. Spent hours scrounging through every archive in the Talbot Library."

"There isn't much you don't know about us at this point." Ben studies the letter. "You don't know who this letter was meant for?"

"No, but I have a theory. The curator at the Rye museum agreed to a time frame of late 1940s to early '50s, which is about the same time Robert Tulley disappeared and William Tulley died in the *Victoria* disaster."

"You believe this girl was involved with the brothers?"

"It's a stretch, maybe. I know. I haven't found a single reference to a woman who would match her age or description for this time period, though. Not if she's a relative or closely associated with the family. But why else would this portrait have sat in the house for so many decades if she wasn't connected to your family?"

"I've never seen it before. That's not itself remarkable."

"It's a long shot, but I hoped you might have some idea. Or at least give me a clue to follow. I'm at the end of my rope on this hunt."

Our main course arrives. A delicate piece of fish over veggies, the presentation so refined and immaculate I'm almost embarrassed it has to go in my stomach with my morning Cheerios.

"May I keep these?" he asks, gesturing to the photo and copied letter.

"Yes, of course."

"This is a bizarre sort of mystery. There isn't a reason I can think of the family would have commissioned a portrait if not to mark some formal occasion. A wedding or anniversary, certainly. A signifi-cant birthday. Still, it would only be done for a member of the family or close inner circle. I admit, your theory is intriguing."

"Do you know much about your great-grandfather's brothers?"

"Not as much as I should, I'm afraid. They died, Robert presumably, before Lawrence inherited the title. It's generally said the brothers weren't close. I do remember, years ago, there was a row about a documentary that wanted to explore the *Victoria* tragedy. Granddad forbid the family from participating. Over the years, there have been requests by someone or another investigating what happened to Robert. He was never interested in lending his time to that either."

"Like I said, it was a long shot." I've stopped getting my hopes up for a major breakthrough. Every minor step forward now comes in smaller increments. "I do appreciate your time in humoring me."

"Don't think you're getting away that easy." Ben pours the remnants of wine in our glasses. He waves off a waiter who lurches to save him the effort. "You have me well intrigued. I'm afraid I won't be satisfied until I know how the story ends."

"We might be waiting a long time."

The alcohol has seeped its way into my pores, heating my face with the warmth of a midafternoon buzz. I've never been day drunk before. And probably never will be again at this price point. So I take another gulp of wine, because I might as well enjoy myself.

"I'm not sure there are any leads left to pursue. You were sort of my last resort."

"Then we cannot in good conscience surrender the fight," he says with amused earnestness. "You've captured my curiosity, Abbey. I'd very much like to help you."

"Really? What do you suggest?"

"There are some boxes of old documents stashed away at one of our summer homes on the coast. I'll speak to my father about getting access. If he permits it, I'll have Sophie ship them to you. Can't promise there will be anything of relevance, but I've a hunch that if there's anything to be found, it'll be in there."

I don't even try to hide my excitement. "That'd be fantastic. Thank you. Anything at all about Robert, William, or a woman who could be Josephine would be so helpful."

I'm not sure why Ben gets such a bad rap in the press. Based on this lunch, I've found him delightful. He has no reason to accommodate my inquisition or waste his time entertaining my curiosity, yet he's been more than courteous. Friendly, even.

The check arrives. Ben places his hand over it when I try to steal a peek. I glimpse what looks like a total of four hundred pounds before he slides it away from me.

"Please. I'd be a dreadful host if I didn't treat. You've been a welcomed distraction to my day, Abbey."

"You're sure?" It's a feeble offer. Inside, I'm relieved. Dad would've lost his shit when he got the alert that I'd spent a fortune on lunch. "I feel bad I can't offer anything in return for your help. I've taken so much of your time."

"There is something you could do," he says, passing off the check to the waiter. "Let us finish our conversation. I'd be interested in what else you've learned about Josephine and my family's history. I'm to attend a ball for Princess Alexandra's engagement in a couple of weeks. I'd be delighted if you'd join me."

Holy shit.

"Wow. Um, thank you."

I foresee a frantic eruption of flying fabric in my future. Already picturing Lee propelled to next-level fashion monster.

"Feel free to bring a friend, of course. I know how the ladies are obsessed with royalty."

I wouldn't know.

Despite my indifference to the monarchy, though, I would never miss an opportunity for a good story. And this is one for the books. I just had lunch with a lord, and now I'm going to a royal ball.

How is this even my life?

21

CELESTE IS THE FIRST TO JUMP ON ME FOLLOWING MY LUNCH WITH Ben. She texts as I'm leaving the library later to ask how the meeting went. I make the mistake of mentioning the invitation to the ball, and by the time I get home that evening, her gentle requests to be my plus-one have graduated to outright violent threats.

> Celeste: No pressure, but if you don't bring me, I will find you in a dark alley.

> Me: Have you considered bribery?

"Abbey, that you, luv?" Lee calls from the kitchen as I kick off my shoes at the front door.

"Yes, dear."

"Get in here. Now."

The urgency in his voice is enough to make me sprint down the hall.

"What's wrong?" I find Lee sitting at the counter with his laptop open and his sister on the screen.

"You have a decision to make," he says, spinning on his stool to face me while clutching a cup of tea.

"Abbey, tell him he's too late," Celeste says on-screen. "You've already invited me to the ball."

"Bollocks. I'm obviously her favorite."

"Piss off," she snaps back. "You'd spend the whole night in the coat closet with the valet. You can do that anywhere."

"Jealous."

I try slipping away. The two of them seem content to argue among themselves. But Lee grabs the strap of my bag before I can make an escape. He has a deceptively long reach, that one.

"You're not getting away that easy, Abbey Bly."

"How about you two decide and let me know?" I suggest.

The stairs above our heads rattle seconds before Jack stalks into the kitchen. He's shirtless and has his earbuds in. And he doesn't so much as blink in my direction as he goes to the fridge and gulps down a protein shake before grabbing a bottle of water. I might as well be furniture when he turns and leaves out the front door, without the slightest acknowledgement of my existence.

I don't even get a chance to fumble over my words or smile awkwardly at the unresolved question of the kiss. He beats me to it with outright indifference.

Fuck, that's irritating. How do you walk right past someone you live with and pretend there isn't this enormous question mark hanging in the air?

Dick.

Earlier, I'd briefly entertained the idea of inviting Jack or Nate to the ball. But seeing as how we don't seem to be on speaking terms anymore, I guess Jack is out. And to be honest, it's probably not Nate's scene. I'm sure he'd rather throw himself off a bridge than be caught dead in a tux, schmoozing up royals and pretentious nobility. And I'm not sure Yvonne would appreciate it.

Besides, I wouldn't put it past Lee or his sister to have either of them tied up and chained to a radiator in the basement to eliminate the competition.

"Come on, Abbey," Celeste grumbles, her impatience plain her voice. "If you bring my brother, he'll ditch you the second you get there. You don't want to be left alone all night, do you, luv?"

Lee mutes his sister. "Babe, it's cute and all you two've become friends but plainly ridiculous not to invite your flatmate."

Celeste begins gesticulating wildly, silent. It doesn't take long for her to catch on and text me.

Celeste: Unmute me right now!

After I show Lee the message, he turns to the laptop camera and shoves his middle finger in the air. Their house must have been fun growing up.

"I promise not to abandon you," he says. "You've got to be my wingwoman. I'm trying to get wifed up to an earl or a baron. You wouldn't take that away from me, right?"

This sucks. A part of me would rather let them go together instead of me to avoid disappointing either one of them. Except I really want to go. And I can't very well stand up Lord Tulley.

I need to think about it.

"I'm going to take a bath," I tell them, then hurry upstairs before Lee can drag me back by my hair.

A few minutes later, I drop myself into a hot tub with the lights off, music on, and a book I'm reading for my English lit class on my phone.

It occurs to me after my toes begin to prune and the bubbles have almost dissipated that I should have given more credence to Lee's warning about the house rule. If I'd been more faithful to the one and only tenet of the flat, I wouldn't be staring down the possibility that Jack and I have irrevocably changed the dynamic not only of our relationship but all of us. Things were good here before. I don't want it to be awkward now.

When the water's gone lukewarm, I towel off and return to my room to put on pajamas. I'd considered going back to the library after dinner, but now I'm not in the mood. All my energy has been sapped by the descending fallout dropping in slow motion. I haven't been here even one whole semester, and I've already fucked it.

In bed, I continue my reading until there's a knock at my door.

"I haven't made up my mind yet," I call.

Jack opens the door to peer inside. "Hey."

"Oh." I sit up against my headboard. "Thought you were Lee."

"Can I come in for a minute?"

Well, damn. I'd just gotten all comfortable and sullen about not having this talk, and now I'm not sure if I'm prepared. Still, the waiting will be more excruciating.

"Sure."

He walks in, his tall frame encased in plaid pants and a faded black hoodie, blond hair damp as if he'd just had a shower. Droplets of water gather at his temples, one trickling down and falling onto his cheek. He wipes it away and closes the door behind him, then plasters himself against it as if trying to stand as far from me as possible.

I consider proposing he stand in the hallway making hand gestures, but his preoccupied expression says he wouldn't see the humor in it.

"What's up?" I prompt.

I slide out of bed and get up, because it feels weird lying under the covers while he remains upright. Like I'm a queen receiving her audience or something.

"I wanted to say I'm sorry," Jack starts, his voice gruff.

"Oh. Okay." Most of my irritation with him evaporates with that simple admission.

"For kissing you. That was stupid. I was drunk, but I can't blame it entirely on that. I don't know what went through my head before I did it." He pauses, then curses under his breath. "That's a lie. I know what I was thinking."

Just like that, my throat becomes arid. "What were you thinking?"

"You know what."

The air shifts, thickens with tension.

My teeth dig into my lip as I lift my gaze to his. "Do I?"

"There's something here." He gestures between us. "Been there for a while, no?"

Since the day I moved in, I almost say.

Instead, I remain silent. It's rare to get Jack talking. About anything substantive anyway. I'm afraid that if I speak, he'll stop, and I desperately want to hear what he has to say.

"I think you're bloody amazing." His gaze never leaves mine. "Smart. Gorgeous. You make me laugh." He licks his bottom lip. "Turn me on."

I can scarcely breathe now. "I turn you on?"

"Yes. Christ. There's nothing I want more right now than to throw you on that bed and smash your back out."

I blink. "I'm sorry, what? You want to—ohhhh." As usual, my cheeks burst into flames. "I take it that's more of that Aussie slang?"

His lips twitch with a slight grin. "I keep forgetting you don't get half the shit I'm saying. I'll say it clearer." His eyes become molten. "I want to fuck you."

My core clenches.

Do it, I want to beg.

"I want to be on my knees with my face between your legs."

Oh.

My.

God.

"I want to feel you squeezing my cock while I come inside you."

Yup. I'm dead. He's killed me and my vagina.

"All those things sound…nice," I manage to croak out, my voice shaky and lust drenched.

Jack's face clouds with regret. "But I can't. We can't."

The disappointment is so visceral and all-consuming I feel my entire body deflate.

"You're my flatmate. But more than that, I like to think we've become friends, ay?"

"Ay. I mean, yeah. Yes."

This is incredible. I had no idea it was possible to go from *ferally turned on* to *horrifically mortified* this fast. I drop my gaze to my socked feet, afraid he'll see my hurt and frustration.

"Abbs. No. Don't do that." He steps closer, touching my chin to tip it upward. "Look at me. I'm trying to do the right thing. We've a good arrangement here. Can't have this exploding in our faces, yeah? Lee and Jamie adore you. They'd kill me if I fucked this up for everyone."

"Who says you would?"

"I don't do relationships," he admits. "And you"—he blows out a breath—"you don't do one-night stands."

"Says who?" I counter, because I hate it when people tell me who I am.

He slants his head in challenge. "Do you?"

Goddamn it.

"No," I mutter. "I don't." I straighten my shoulders and muster a dismissive look that takes some effort. "Okay. I guess that's settled."

Jack shifts uneasily. "We can pretend it never happened then?"

"I've already forgotten about it."

"All right." He hesitates. "Good night."

Without another word, he leaves and closes the door behind him.

Yeah, I don't think I'm taking Jack to any royal shindig.

As if smelling blood in the water, Lee invites himself into my room and sprawls across the foot of my bed like he's posing for a boudoir photo session.

"What did Jackie want?" he demands suspiciously.

"Nothing, really. We were talking about midterms," I lie. "He might need some study help."

"Well, that's boring." Lee props up on his elbow and plants his head in his palm. "You didn't say earlier—how was lunch with Lord Tulley? Give me details. Don't spare anything."

"Can we do this tomorrow?" I ask with a yawn. I'm mentally exhausted.

He furrows his brow, sitting up. "You all right?"

"I've got a headache coming on."

"Say no more." Lee jumps up. "I'll bring you a cuppa and leave you be."

He's almost out the door when I call his name. He turns at the threshold.

I swallow a smile. "Better get your tux pressed."

He makes an ear-piercing noise like a chew toy exploding and dashes off.

I'm not stoked about breaking the news to Celeste, but I'm fairly sure she was only joking about leaving me for dead in an alley. Truth is, Lee's been a good friend since the night I arrived jet-lagged and confused at his doorstep. Seems only right I return the favor.

NOVEMBER

22

THERE'S A SMALL COHORT OF US WHO TEND TO OCCUPY THE SPECIAL archives section at the library. My first few days among their ranks, I received more than a few curious glances and suspicious glowers. Now on the back end of the semester, they've accepted me as one of their own. We nod at one another as we comb the stacks. Recognize the official dibs status of one another's desks and preferred reading nooks. It's a silly thing, yet coming in after class knowing I won't have to fight for a seat is a small reassurance that despite the chaos popping off at home, the library is still a safe and sacred retreat.

Even Mr. Baxley with his derisive scowl and militant adherence to archaic bureaucracy has become a welcome part of my routine.

In need of another book, I approach his fortress. He's got the clipboard of forms ready before I can pull out a pen.

REASON FOR REQUEST:

Vitamin D Deficiency.

He doesn't smile at my form, but I think he wants to.

There's only so much bland Tulley trivia I can parse in one sitting, however, before my vision goes blurry. After more than an hour, I take a break to brush up on my royal etiquette. I'd overlooked the need until Lee mentioned at breakfast that a side effect of this ball meant I had a lot of curtsying in my future and I'd better get some lunges in to strengthen those knees. Also, I'm not sure of my agility in heels. It's been a while since I went out in anything fancier than a pair of two-inch leather boots.

When I've had all the fun I can stand for one day, I return my books, wave at Mr. Baxley, and brave the blustery weather while slipping on my coat outside the library.

Winter is already beating against the door, and the city is quieter as the weather's turned. Everyone is huddled and hurried. No moms and nannies with strollers stopping for a chat. The summer sightseers are long gone. No more food trucks and sidewalk vendors. I know it gets old for the locals, but I enjoy the gloomy gray clouds and shadowy pall over the city on days like this. The daunting ominousness. It's the London I've always imagined in my head.

As I'm debating what to do about lunch, a text message pops up. From Nate.

Nate: Fancy some lunch?

I stare at the phone. The correct answer to that question is a resounding *no*. But I'm a glutton for heartache.

Me: Sure. I'm starving. Just leaving the library.

Nate: I'm about ten minutes away. Can I pick you up?

Again, the correct response is no. The worst possible thing for me to do right now is get on the back of his bike and plaster my body against his.

This time, I don't screw it up.

Me: I'll meet you. Sending you directions.

Nate: See you soon xx

Oh shit. He xx'd me. I think that's the first time he's ever done that.

Heart pounding, I scroll through our meager chat thread to make sure. Yup. He's never text kissed me before.

I remind myself that this means absolutely nothing and promptly push the thought out of my head.

I've been craving the Egyptian place down the street that Lee first took me to, so I head that way while texting Nate the location. By the time I'm seated and scarfing down flatbread, he walks in shaking the helmet head out of his hair. Dark jeans encase his long legs, and he's wearing a black Henley beneath his leather jacket. He's so fucking sexy it's nearly impossible not to stare. At least I'm not the only one—I notice two women at a table by the window overtly checking him out as he walks past.

"Thanks for waiting." He grins at my full tray of food.

I don't even pretend to be contrite. "You're welcome."

Nate places his order at the counter, then comes to sit with his drink while he waits. "I think Lee used to work here."

"Mm-hmm," I hum through a mouth full of bread. "We ate here my first day of class."

"How's that going?"

"What? School? It's fine."

He leans back in his chair, the epitome of cool. "What about your lass Josephine?"

"Is this why you invited me to lunch? You're dying to know about my research?"

He shrugs.

The waitress arrives to set his food down, momentarily interrupting us.

"Okay then. For the sake of conversation," I say once she's gone, "and not because I believe you have any genuine interest, I met with Ben Tulley, if you must know. He took me to an embarrassingly expensive lunch and invited me to a ball for Princess Alexandra's engagement."

Nate's expression flattens. "You being serious?"

"We shared the last bottle of white from his family's soon-to-be-sold winery."

I mean to imbue the statement with as much sarcastic haughtiness as I can portray, but I'm not sure it translates. If anything, Nate looks more troubled.

"You ought to be wary of that one." Nate stabs at his lunch like he's mad at it.

"Who? Ben?"

"That family is a black hole. You won't even know you've drifted too close until you can't escape."

"I appreciate the poetic advice. But as long as I'm still young and single, if some fancy guy wants to drag me around to his fancy parties, I'm going to take him up on it."

"As long as you're not foolish enough to fall for him."

The accusation stings a little. More so because I'm not sure he didn't mean it to.

"I could do worse." Like drunken Aussie rugby players who can't kiss a girl and mean it. "I didn't come all this way just for the libraries. So what's wrong with a little adventure? How many times in my life will I get to fall for a lord?"

In all honesty, Ben isn't really my type, not to mention eight years older than me. But it's more the principle of the thing. And the fact that Nate's dismissive attitude has poked my more combative instincts.

"If you want an adventure," he says roughly, "you could come with me this summer whilst I'm traveling."

I snort out a sarcastic laugh. "Right. Sure." It isn't a serious invitation and doesn't deserve a serious response. "Because you haven't had enough of hauling me all over southern England."

"I wouldn't offer if I minded." At that, Nate's dark eyes become abruptly intense.

His sudden bouts of earnestness give me whiplash. It's also honest, though. Maybe even endearing. He doesn't say much, but I know what he does say I can take at face value. It's refreshing.

I eye him pointedly. "You still haven't told me why you invited me to lunch."

Another shrug. Guys should get shock treatments as children to break them of such infuriating habits.

"Nate," I push.

He slowly chews his food, then swallows. "I don't know why I asked. Every now and then, I think about you. Wonder how you're getting on. New city and all."

Just when I thought I'd managed to get my heart rate under control around this man, he goes and says things like that.

"So you just wanted to check up on me?" I prompt, ignoring my thundering heartbeat.

"Yeah. Well, no. Bloody hell, I don't know." He sounds flustered. "You're an interesting paradox."

"I don't think anyone's ever called me a paradox before."

"You are." He shoves a hand through his messy hair. "Sometimes you come off as wiser than your years. Or maybe *worldly* is the better word. And then other times, you're young, inexperienced…" He drifts off.

I bristle. Inexperienced? I mean, he's not entirely wrong.

But he's not entirely right either.

He notices my expression and his lips curve slightly. "Like that. That look. Other women, older ones, would try to hide it. The insecurity. Not you, though. Your eyes reveal everything you're thinking and feeling."

"And yours reveal nothing," I counter.

"Yeah, I've heard that before."

I fix him with a defiant look. "Let's say it's true—I'm young, inexperienced, insecure at times, everything you just said. What of it?"

Something I can't interpret flickers in his expression. "Some men might be drawn to that. Triggers the urge to take care of you, protect you."

"Some men, huh?"

He doesn't respond.

Irritation flares inside me. "I swear, it's like pulling teeth with you guys. First Jack, now you."

"Jack?" he says sharply, and I immediately regret my slipup.

"Nothing. Forget it."

"Something going on with you two?"

"No. I don't know. I mean, he came home drunk and kissed me and then shoved me into the friend zone, so I don't know what the fuck, you know?"

"He came on to you?" Nate's tone takes on a dangerous edge.

"Not like that. It wasn't aggressive. He sort of sprang it on me and walked off." I laugh to myself. "Went to bed, actually."

I forget for a moment who I'm talking to. With the time difference between Eliza and me, I guess I've felt the shortage of outlets to get this stuff off my chest. I certainly can't talk to my roommates about it. Or Celeste, who'd just tell Lee. In my right mind, I wouldn't unload this information on Nate. But he's deceptively easy to talk to. He lulls me into complacency.

"Anyway, we had a chat and are going with *it never happened*," I finish awkwardly.

Nate has a way of penetrating me with a silent stare until I begin to question my entire existence.

"You seem bothered," I say to cut the unnerving quiet.

He shrugs. "Seems a shit thing for Jack to do. Especially to a friend."

I put my utensils down. "How about us? Are we friends?"

"Yes," he answers. Cautious now as he senses the shift in my demeanor.

"Because I hadn't decided whether I should bring it up, but since we're talking about friends kissing friends…I'm not trying to play the home-wrecker."

You could float a feather in the stillness of his expression. Unreadable, except that I've come to discern his flatness as a mask for turbulence and unease.

"I don't think I've asked you to," he says tightly.

"But you did try to kiss me. And don't say you were drunk, because the other guy beat you to it."

Only a twitch at the corner of his jaw gives away his discomfort.

When Nate responds, it's with slow, measured words. "There was an organic moment. It wasn't premeditated, and we didn't act on it."

"Because we were interrupted."

"It was a choice, wasn't it?"

I get it now. This is how he deflects.

"Tell me something," I say. "Or tell me to piss off if it's none of my business. But I've watched you two. Listened to the way she talks about you. And I can't for the life of me figure how you and Yvonne make sense."

Leaning back in his chair again, he pushes his plate aside to buy himself time to consider. "Why do any of us get together? We're all looking in other people for something missing in us."

I fall quiet, mulling over his response. It reminds me of that song about how love is trying to stitch ourselves back together with our ancient other halves, and every dysfunctional relationship is just us trying to force together two pieces that don't fit. Which is kind of true and also cereal box philosophy.

"What's she got that's filling that hole?" I ask slowly.

"Yvonne is uncomplicated. Independent. Low maintenance. It's that stability, I suppose, I'm attracted to." He pauses for a moment. "Although she's younger than I usually go for."

"She's twenty-two, no? And you're, what, twenty-four?"

He nods. "I tend to date older women."

"How much older?"

"Quite a bit older," he admits. "Mid to late thirties, typically. They're self-sufficient. Fully formed. Aren't tilting at this whim and that."

"Sounds more like a matter of effort than some romantic idea of your other half."

"Perhaps." Nate reaches up to run a hand through his hair. "The women I'm with don't have any expectations of me, Yvonne included. I appreciate that."

This might be the most unfiltered admission about himself I've managed to wrangle out of Nate since I met him. A rare glimpse under the skin of someone who's usually so enigmatic. He's not deceptive, exactly. More like vaguely elusive. It's both attractive and frustrating.

"You don't like her," he muses, eyeing me over the rim of his glass.

"That's not true at all. Honestly, I hardly know her. She's nice to me when I'm around. She seems outspoken. Witty. But I can't exactly call her a friend yet. Anyway, regardless of my feelings for her, I still respect the line in the sand," I say in a frank tone. "You're dating her. That makes you hers. I respect that, and I don't want to be dragged into a situation I don't belong in. So with that said, there can't be any more 'organic moments' between us. What happened at the cemetery was wrong, and I'd like to make sure it doesn't happen again."

Nate's face reverts to its default position: unreadable.

I wait for him to concur, to throw in his two cents, but all he does is offer a brisk nod.

"We're in agreement then." I stick out my hand across the table. "This is a strictly platonic situationship. Purely academic. You're practically my intern."

Finally, he cracks a smile. "Friends," he echoes, shaking my hand.

A thought occurs to me as we're standing to leave, making me falter.

"Do me a favor, would you, friend? Don't mention the Jack thing to anyone. It isn't worth upsetting the whole house over. Things will get complicated."

"My lips are sealed."

At the exit, it's Nate's turn to hesitate.

"So, ah, this friendship thing. Are friends allowed to text each other?"

My traitorous heart flips like it's competing for gold in Olympics gymnastics.

"Depends what," I answer.

"*Hello, how are ya? How's uni? Tell me about your research.* You know. Purely academic," he mimics, biting his lip like he's fighting a grin.

"Yeah…I guess that's okay." I bite my lip too, but for other reasons. "As long as we operate under my dad's golden rule: don't text anything you wouldn't want to see screenshotted and on the front page of the papers."

"That's a good rule."

Our gazes lock, and it takes some effort on my part to break the eye contact. I hastily reach for the door handle.

Nate beats me to it, holding the door open for me. "All right then, Abbey. I'll text you."

23

I've never liked shopping. Mostly because I despise trying on clothes. There's the violence of nonsensical sizing practices of fashion brands, but also this hygiene video we watched in sixth grade about body fluids, bacteria, and black lights that left me shaking in a cold sweat at my desk. To this day, I can't go into a changing room and squeeze my ass into a pair of jeans without thinking about every ass that's come before mine.

I am one hundred percent that chick in the restroom shooting people dirty looks in the mirror when they don't wash their hands.

Which is why I've put off the question of what to wear to the ball for weeks before finally mentioning it to my dad to ballpark what a reasonable spending limit might be. I left him a voicemail overnight and woke up to a text message with an address to a private atelier.

Lee has a prior engagement (and if I'm honest about it, I'm not sure I can handle his particular approach to styling me today), so I extend the olive branch to Celeste instead. She doesn't miss the opportunity to remind me I'm her sworn nemesis for not inviting her to the ball, but the chance to go on a dress binge is enough for her to declare a truce.

In the cab on the way to Celeste's flat, I get a text from my super platonic buddy Nate, who kept to his word and has been messaging me here and there over the past week.

Nate: Hello, how are ya. How's uni?

I bite my lip to keep from smiling. Damn him for being so charming.

Me: School's great. How's bassisting?

Nate: That's not a word.

Me: I'm a word creator. Sort of like a content creator, but with words.

Nate: You really didn't need to add the second part. I understood the concept of word creation without it.

We're not swimming in profound conversations, he and I, but we also both know it needs to remain that way.

I tuck my phone into my purse when Celeste slides into the back seat. It isn't until our cab pulls up in front of the building that I realize this excursion is on a whole other level.

"You're kidding," Celeste exclaims, stepping out of the car in downtown London. She gapes at the sign over the door of the nondescript old building. "*This* is the friend of your dad's?"

"I guess so."

Dad outdid himself this time.

"You're wearing Sue Li to a bloody royal ball," Celeste tells me, exasperated.

I might be fashion averse (according to her brother), but even I've heard of Sue Li. This designer has dressed everyone from Lady Gaga to Harry Styles to costumes for the Royal Opera House. A legit big deal.

Celeste sighs. "You realize I hate you, right?"

"If I let you borrow the dress, can we still be friends?"

With narrowed eyes, she speaks through her teeth. "Get the shoes too and I'll consider it."

The lobby is a loud, frenzied expression of colors and patterns reminiscent of the eclectic contrasting styles Sue Li is known for. Always toeing that line between genius and disaster. Chaos soup on fine china.

"Welcome." We're greeted by a towering woman who's close to seven feet even in flats, with neon green eyeshadow and a buzz cut. She looks between Celeste and me. "Abbey?"

"Nice to meet you," I say, feeling downright minuscule. "This is my friend Celeste."

"I'm Mori. I hear you need a dress."

"I do, but I have no idea what's appropriate. I've never done something like this before."

"Someone got herself invited to Alexandra's prewedding festivities," Celeste says with lingering venom.

"Sue filled us in." Mori gestures for us to follow her from the lobby toward a narrow staircase.

Upstairs, we're led to a wide-open space where mirrors and clothing racks line the white walls of painted brick.

"We've taken the liberty of selecting a few garments," Mori tell me.

Celeste and I are treated to champagne while two more assistants wheel out a rack of gowns in front of a dressing pedestal.

"We have a changing curtain," Mori says. "Or if you're not shy…"

This is why I at least had the good sense to put on matching bra and underwear.

"Lay it on me," I say, trying to pull off something akin to cool indifference. Because I totally belong and am no way in over my head with all this fancy shit.

"You're making the society pages now for sure," Celeste informs me as I get undressed and leave my clothes beside her on the velvet settee. "So much for a low profile."

"Think a veil is too much? Brits enjoy an audacious hat, right?"

"Not for evening," Mori's male assistant says sharply, unzipping the first dress from its hanger.

"No, yeah. It was a joke." Or I thought it was.

"Funny," he says, with a pained attempt at a smile that can't quite graduate from a sarcastic cringe. My humor is clearly lost on him. Which is awesome because now this dude is going to the pub later to tell the other fashion assistants about the gauche American.

Cool people don't get me.

The first dress is an architectural green number with asymmetrical polka dots hidden in the pleats of the skirt. With my hair, green is always the first place people go. And it's lovely, especially since it's the same shade of sea green as my eyes. But...

"It's eating you alive," Celeste says, her head cocked in the mirror, studying me.

"Right? If I was a foot taller, maybe." I turn, peering at myself over my shoulder to get a view of the back. "Not sure short people can pull off this much look."

Mori is still evaluating, pulling and tucking, when my phone rings on the settee next to Celeste. She sees *Dad* on the screen and hands it to me. His face pops up as I answer the FaceTime call.

"What do you think?" I say, holding the phone up to show him the dress. "First one."

"Green is always a great color on you," he answers, apparently on the back patio of our house around the fire pit. "I see you found the place okay."

"This is brilliant, Dad. Thank you."

"Thanks, Dad," Celeste calls.

I spin around to let her wave at the camera.

"Who's that with you? This one of the roommates?"

I suddenly get a seriously stupid idea. One of those sudden

instincts that takes hold of my better judgment and commandeers my mouth until I'm a helpless bystander trapped in my own body.

"Say hi to Jamie, Dad."

Celeste's eyes shoot to mine in alarmed confusion. Then like osmosis, she gets it.

It's a dastardly ruse, drawing her into my web of lies. I'm ashamed of myself as soon as the plot is underway.

"Sue's gonna take great care of you," Dad promises as I hand off the phone to Celeste so I can slip into the next dress.

"How do you know her?" Celeste asks him.

He chuckles. "Funny story. I ever tell you this one, Abbey?"

Three sets of hands pick and peck at me, getting me into this dress. "Don't think so."

"It was during the Gibson fire. Some Sony Music exec's Grammy party out in Malibu. I was about your age," he tells us. "Took home three awards that night and was feeling pretty invincible. The house is filled to the beams with rock stars, suits, and half-naked women. Music so loud they could probably hear us in Van Nuys. Then suddenly there's screaming, loud enough to drown out the music. People go from looking around to running aimlessly for the doors. Diving through windows. That's when we realize…"

"What?" Celeste says, nodding as I model the blue and yellow scoop-neck dress. "What was it?"

"We smelled the smoke. So we go outside, and the sky is bright red. Ash falling on our heads. The fire is maybe a hundred yards behind this house, coming up over the hills, and charging right for us. People are panicking, trampling each other to get out, find their cars. No one has their keys because the valet guys bolted at the first sirens, so now there's hundreds of keys scattered on the driveway. People start picking up random Porsche fobs."

Celeste is wide-eyed. "That's terrifying. What'd you do?"

This dress is nice, but it isn't tearing at my heart. It still feels a little avant-garde for a royal ball. Mori's crinkled eyebrow says

I'm not pulling it off. We peel me out of this one and on to the next.

"My buddy Scott finds us and shouts, 'We need to get outta here, man.' Only we're so trashed, we have no idea where we are or how we got there. So Bobby, he climbs up on the wall around the yard, and he says, 'Hey, the neighbor's got a pool.'"

"Seriously, Dad?"

Sometimes it's astonishing to think how improbable it was that my dad lived long enough to contribute to my creation at all.

"We hop the wall and dive in, watching the flames climb down the hill toward the house. Then this angry old Japanese lady comes out with her two huge angry dogs. She's shouting at us, like, 'Hey, you dumbasses. Get in my Range Rover if you want to live.'"

"Sue Li rescued you from a wildfire?" Celeste shakes her head in amazement. "Woman is literally a superhero."

"We spent the night on the beach with half of Malibu. Some billionaire had his yacht offshore waiting to ferry people if the flames jumped the road. People had their horses and goats and even some dude with a miniature zebra—all wading into the surf because the heat from the flames was so intense."

Celeste laughs. "No offense, Abbey, but your dad's a lunatic."

And I realize then, as I'm sliding into the third dress, why I'm lying to my father. Why I'm digging myself deeper into the hole that will eventually fill with water.

I want my own stories.

I want to wind up trapped in a death-defying predicament only to escape with some preposterous adventure.

To have no idea what's coming next and emerge on the other side by the skin of my teeth.

To flirt with danger and dance with the fates.

I've spent my life telling someone else's stories with no context of my own, borrowing life experiences that amount to an empty glass. And now I'm parched.

So that's why I maintain the lie. Because going home isn't an option. I love my life in London. I love my friends and my roommates and the possibilities in front of me. I can't go back to my dad's house and mac and cheese night.

Even if it means a painful conversation later, at least I'll have some memories.

I take the phone back to show Dad the dress that caught my eye even while it was still on the rack. It's red and white with severe angles but tailored in all the right places, as if it's been waiting all this time on its hanger for my body. Minus the foot and a half of extra fabric at the bottom.

"What do you think, Dad? I really like this one."

"You'll be a stunner in any of them. I know you'll have a great time. Jamie going with you?"

Celeste gives me the evil eye.

"Please, don't get her started again."

"Get whichever dress you like. If you need shoes or purses or any of that stuff, get that too. Sue owes me a favor," Dad says with a wink.

"Oh really?"

"Story for another time. Just be sure to say hi to Queen Margaret for me."

"Oh my God, Dad."

"What? We go way back, the queen and I. I played a private concert at the palace for the holidays one year, and we stayed up for hours eating cake, talking about James Brown and Billie Holiday. The old greats. Most people don't know, but Maggie has a great love for American rock 'n' roll."

Celeste is gaping at me. "I'm going to have to write a book after this."

"This is the one," Mori declares, studying my reflection in the mirror. She plays with my hair, pulling it off my shoulders to show off the neckline. "We can set you up with my jewelry, but I wouldn't throw too much else on it. The dress is doing the work. Let it."

A brief fantasy of myself plays in the mirror. I stand there for a moment, imagining this other person I could become. I'm looking at a blank page to write a new story. With the right dress and a ticket to a royal ball, anything can happen.

I smile at my reflection and say, "It's perfect."

24

There's a car waiting outside at seven o'clock sharp.

At 7:08, I'm standing impatiently at the front door in my dress and heels, purse dangling from my wrist, hair pinned and sprayed against a Category 4 hurricane. Lee scurries down the stairs, stops, remembers something else he forgot, and scurries back up the stairs for the fifth time.

"Is this some kind of manic ritual?" I ask Jamie, who leans against the staircase giving me an amused look.

"Two years ago, Celeste got him front-row Adele tickets for his birthday," he says, popping cashews in his mouth. "He missed the first hour of the show in a panic over a chin zit."

Jamie's midchew when a sneeze overtakes him and sends disgusting bits of snot and cashew in my direction.

"Oh my God, Jamie. You are horrific." I fret, making sure none of his bodily fluids got on my dress. Thankfully, no. "I've seen enough of your snot this past week to last a lifetime."

"Sorry." He swipes his sleeve over his runny nose, then sniffs a few times. "I told you, it's these bloody allergies."

The door opens and bumps me in the back, almost plastering me to the wall. Behind it, Jack walks in, oblivious to me or the weak resistance my body puts up against his forceful entrance.

"You know there's some rude-looking bloke outside with a black car?"

Jamie gives him a nod. "Other side, mate."

Jack takes the hint and peeks behind the open door to find me and my whole getup smooshed against the wall.

"What are you doing back there?"

"Just hanging out," I answer sarcastically.

"Okay, I'm ready." Lee comes galloping down the stairs in a sapphire tux. "For real this time."

"Sure you've not left some stray nose hairs untrimmed?" Jamie mocks him with a smirk, popping another cashew.

Lee strides past to slide his feet into a pair of patent leather shoes. "I would never."

"You look different," Jack says quietly while Jamie and Lee banter. His blue eyes drift over my dress, which, admittedly, is doing most of the work. "I mean nice. You look really nice."

"Thank you."

In the weeks since we (translation: he) agreed to pretend the kiss never happened, things have gone back to normal between us. Sort of. My body still hasn't gotten the message from my brain that Jack and I are strictly relegated to the platonic sphere. My nerves still respond to every small compliment. Stupid things like his shoulder brushing mine trigger a response.

"Here, take a picture." Lee shoves his phone at Jack and wedges himself in beside me to pose for the camera. "Next time you see me, I'll be calling from a yacht in Amalfi with my new rich boyfriend."

"I hope all your dreams come true," Jamie says, stepping in to adjust Lee's bow tie.

"Thanks, luv." Lee grabs his phone from Jack and glances at the time. "Right. Enough dawdling. My future husband could be getting away."

"Keep an eye on this one, would you?" Jack nods toward me as he speaks to Lee. "Try to keep her out of trouble. She's liable to topple the monarchy."

I mock glare at him. "I would never. Not on purpose anyway."

"Don't wait up." Lee takes my arm and escorts us out the door to the impatient driver waiting at the curb. Once we're on our way, my date lets out a deep sigh. "I might actually shit myself."

I glance over with a grin. "Cranberry."

"What?"

"If either of us is in crisis or just wants to get the hell out of there for some reason, we say *cranberry*. That's our escape word."

"Good plan. I like that. And if one of us needs to ditch the other—"

"*Grapefruit*."

"Got it."

He spends the rest of the drive reminding me of the customs and protocols regarding the royal receiving line and how to behave if I should stumble my way into encountering royalty in the wild while at this event. Mostly, we're relying on not leaving me unsupervised. When all else fails, do what everyone else does.

Not far from Notting Hill, we encounter the traffic jam of limos and town cars lining up to enter the gates of Kensington Palace. Spectators and photographers press against the police barricades. TV news crews are set up to capture the arrivals. Lee rolls down the window a couple inches to peer up at the helicopters hovering overhead.

"This isn't real," I mutter to myself.

"A little nip for the nerves?" He produces a flask from his breast pocket.

I shake my head. I'd be hurling before we even stepped out of the car.

When I was little, maybe a year or two after my mom left me at Dad's doorstep, he brought me to the People's Choice Awards. I think someone on his PR team got it in their heads to create a sort of debut, introducing his daughter to the press and casting him as the good father. There are pictures of me in my tiny pink dress and too much makeup, posing with celebrities I wouldn't recognize unless they were on Nickelodeon. What I remember most is lots of standing, being horribly bored, and waking up in the back of a limo with Dad's publicist watching *True Blood* on her iPad while he was inside at some party until the sun came up.

This probably won't be like that.

What seems like an hour later, we arrive at the front of the line, where we're ushered from our car into the palace. We follow the traffic through the immaculate halls, security checks, formalities, and finally into the ballroom where hundreds of elegant guests mingle with glasses of champagne and hors d'oeuvres. Up on the raised stage, a ten-piece orchestra plays instrumental covers of contemporary pop songs. I feel small under the tall mural ceiling, towering oil portraits, and priceless tapestries.

"Pinch me," Lee whispers.

I give him a little squeeze on his forearm.

"I can't believe we're here. My mum and dad couldn't even imagine." Lee is in total awe as he absorbs the extravagance of it all. "Celeste may never speak to me again."

"Sorry."

He winks at me. "Worth it."

On my first walk to campus after arriving in London, a man on the street handed me a brochure about tours of Kensington. Now I'm here, on the other side of the velvet ropes, spying Elton John in the crowd. I can't help thinking my dad would already have attracted an audience if he were here. A guitar materializing out of thin air as they begged him for a song. Not because he's famous—he just has that energy. Every room coalesces, shrinks around Gunner Bly. Magnetism.

Me, I feel myself shrinking. Retreating into this costume, blending into the scenery. Unaware how I got here and certain I don't belong.

Then Lee jabs his elbow into my arm. "That one there? Parked her Rolls-Royce through the front door of a sweets shop last year."

He gives a surreptitious nod over his shoulder. "That bloke?" He directs my attention across the room. "He's a descendent of Napoleon and was briefly the governor of a small town in Sweden until they found out he'd been importing horse meat and passing it off as elk in a kickback scheme."

"Abbey?" Benjamin Tulley manages to sneak up on us, dressed to the nines in a tailored tux. Charming as ever, he takes my hand, brings it to his lips, and leaves a polite kiss atop my knuckles. "That dress is stunning, if I may."

"Yeah, you know…" I swing the skirt around a little because how often will I get the chance to sashay in my life? "Just something I had lying around."

"I've no doubt." Ben lingers on me with the same cheeky grin I first saw at our lunch that disarmed me so thoroughly. Then his gaze flicks to Lee. "Ben," he says, introducing himself.

"Lee. Thanks for the invite, mate."

"Yes, you're quite welcome." Ben's inflection is somewhat terse. His posture stiffens. "Pleased to meet a friend of Abbey's."

He doesn't sound so pleased. That English stiff upper lip is so rigid it might crack right off his face.

"Tell us, yeah? That lad there." Lee homes in on a skinny blond guy who resembles a young David Beckham. "Is that really Colin Hartness?"

Ben looks over. "The Olympic boxer? Yes, I believe it is. He's a good friend of Prince John's from the army."

"Right." Lee straightens his jacket, then leans in to kiss my cheek. "Don't wait for me, luv."

He's off without pause to slip himself into the conversation surrounding Hartness, leaving Ben and me in his dust.

"My roommate," I explain. "I was threatened with bodily harm if I didn't bring him. Now I'm wondering what I've set loose on this unsuspecting party."

"Ah, I see. I was afraid I'd become the third wheel."

Ben closes the gap between us as he accepts two glasses of champagne from a passing tray to hand one to me.

I hold back a laugh that Ben thought Lee and I were a *thing*.

"No, it's not like that. Lee has greater ambitions. He plans to marry up. Tonight, if possible."

At that, Ben's wry smile returns. "I'm rooting for him."

One sip of the champagne almost knocks me on my ass. It's as if I've never tasted the stuff until now. Everything before it was swill. Swamp water. I'm only bathing in this from now on. Pouring it on my cereal. Boiling my pasta in it. Transfusing my blood with it. I finally understand the fascination with the stuff.

"Good?" Ben prompts.

"You people have been holding out on us. No wonder the French invented guillotines."

He laughs, shaking his head. "A Yank isn't inside the palace ten minutes before she's plotting a violent revolution."

"Start planning your escape routes," I say with a smile.

"Before we lose our heads then, shall we have a dance?"

He extends his arm to me.

This is one of those moments. When you're entirely present and aware of the memories you're making. A moment you'll never have a second chance at, so best to squeeze the most from it.

"Love to."

25

BEN ESCORTS ME TO THE DANCE FLOOR, PASSING OFF OUR champagne glasses to a waiter. Vaguely familiar faces and attractive people with perfect posture dance to the orchestral arrangement of a twenty-year-old soft rock song. He clasps my hand delicately in his and places his other at a polite height on my back. I imagine the sixty-year-old dance teacher who smacked his hands with a ruler until he was as light as a butterfly.

"You're making a face," he says, watching me.

"I've never danced like this. Not well anyway." This is miles beyond a prom sway.

His brown eyes soften. "You're doing fine."

"Let's make a deal? I won't lock the doors and set the curtains on fire if you can manage to keep me from embarrassing myself."

He breathes out a laugh. "I will venture to do my best. For Britain."

After a verse or two, I start to get the hang of it. Ben's a good dancer. Effortless. By the second song, I've forgotten to feel self-conscious while Ben narrates the gossip about the other guests. The British reality TV star who went to school with the bridegroom and whose father is now dating her ex-boyfriend. The queen's second cousin, whose husband, it was recently revealed, spent the last three summers on a German billionaire's private sex island.

"We're all either on the brink of bankruptcy, sex scandal, or both," Ben says with self-deprecating humor.

"All I did last night was wash my hair and watch TV. A scandal might be a nice change of pace."

"Please, you're welcome to meet with my lawyers next Thursday if you like. Perhaps you can explain to me why I'm paying them so much to tell me I'm broke."

A while later, Lee finds us on the dance floor. His eyes are wide and bright, whatever news he's harboring practically tearing past his lips. "Can I borrow her?"

Ben steps back. "By all means. I'll see if I can't locate the lavatory. There are nearly eighty, I'm told."

Lee takes Ben's place, hugging me close as he wraps his arm around my waist and sets a quicker rhythm to his step. He's buzzing with energy.

"Having fun?" I tease.

"I'm in love."

"That was quick. Have you and Colin set a date yet?"

Lee recoils. "The boxer? God no. I'm in love with Eric."

"Poor Colin. He was cute."

"And we shared a beautiful moment in one of the eighty bathrooms. But I can't listen to that accent for the rest of my life. And then, my dear Abbey, I met Eric," he says with a yearning that is almost lewd. "His family builds yachts."

"It's everything you've always wanted."

"Like, okay, I know I sound like a shallow bitch. He does have other qualities. He likes jazz and nature documentaries."

Neither of which I've ever seen Lee express an interest in. "Whatever makes you happy."

"What about you?" he asks as we rock back and forth in our little circle of the dance floor. "Shall I start calling you Lady Tulley?"

"Definitely not. I mean, Ben's great company. But this isn't a date. It's practically a business meeting."

Lee raises one eyebrow.

"What?"

"Hey, I'm thrilled to mooch off your new friendship. Don't get me wrong. I'm just saying, men like that don't bring beautiful young women to a bloody palace for what is essentially a homework assignment."

"I hear what you're saying. And in any other case, I'd say you're right. But I think he's genuinely interested in discovering more about his family. He's invested in the mystery."

"Maybe. If not, you shout *cranberry*, and I'll pull a fire alarm."

Ben returns then with two fresh glasses of champagne. "If I could interrupt for a moment, Abbey, there's someone I'd like you to meet. Come along too, Lee, if you'd like."

As I accept the champagne he hands me, Ben sniffs, rubbing at his nose. Man, autumn allergies in England are no joke. Jamie's been snotting all over the house for the last week. I guess he's not the only one.

"Up for a little mingling?" I ask Lee, offering him my arm.

"Always."

Well into an endless spring of champagne, I've loosened up enough to start enjoying myself. Ben introduces us to some friends of his, nobility and a couple of British television presenters I pretend to recognize, because there's nothing more awkward than telling a celebrity you've never heard of them. Lee charms them all. He's entirely in his element, telling jokes and flirting his ass off. Still, his gaze drifts back to Eric, whom he leaves us to find when Ben invites me to dance again after dinner.

"Was it worth it?" Ben asks. He leads me around the dance floor as the orchestra plays a ballad.

"Tonight? Absolutely. I'll never forget it."

"These things become tedious after a while. More an obligation than an occasion." He gazes down at me. "I think you've salvaged the evening for me."

"Glad I could help."

The first strains of the violins hit my ears as they start up the next song. I recognize it in three notes and stifle a groan. Ben smiles at the embarrassment blooming red on my face.

"I know this one. What's the line?" He narrows his eyes, recalling, while at the same time searching my face for the answer. "Something about windmills."

I decide to play coy. "Never heard of it."

"I'm quite sure the room would entertain a serenade if you'd fancy stepping up to the mic," he says, having fun at my expense.

"My singing is actually banned by the Geneva Conventions." I break away to escape the dance floor, but Ben is too quick, catching me.

"Don't go. The chorus is the best part."

I hold up my empty champagne glass. "I need a refill."

He relents, following me as I attempt to place myself in the path of a roving champagne tray. Ben has more success, easily snagging glasses for both of us.

"As it happens," he says, "I do have news for you."

"You've been holding out on me," I accuse. "What'd you find?"

"Why don't we find somewhere a little more private to chat about it?" Ben offers me his arm. "Let's get some air, shall we?"

We weave our way through the perilous ballroom full of dress trains and protruding ceremonial swords hanging off the hips of men in military uniform. Ben brings us to a secluded alcove just outside the ballroom. The halls here are quiet and otherwise empty.

"I found letters sent from a private investigator Lawrence hired to find Robert a few years after his disappearance," Ben reveals, looking quite pleased with himself. "Though he couldn't say for certain, there was some suspicion Robert might have fled to Ireland to live under an assumed name."

I gasp. "He didn't die. I knew it."

"After interviewing people close to Robert, the investigator believed he left to avoid an arranged marriage with one of the royal princesses. Allegedly, he was in love with someone else."

"It's Josephine. Has to be." My mind races with possibilities. This is fantastic news. "But that still doesn't tell us if she went to Ireland with Robert or with William on the *Victoria*."

"Rather romantic either way, no?"

"I think it's tragic. In one scenario, she might have boarded that ship imagining a new life in America with the man she loved, who was giving up everything to be with her, only to perish in a horrible disaster. In the best case, she escaped with Robert, but forever exiled. Not an easy way to live."

"There's romance in tragedy, don't you think? The two are inextricably entwined. What is romance, love, without the threat of imminent ruin? We give our souls to another person when surely the only possible end is sorrow. For one of us at least."

"Sure, I guess. The inevitable end of life is death. But saying this fact makes all of existence inherently tragic is a gloomy way to look at it," I point out. "Does an ounce of salt in a pound of sugar spoil the whole cake? I don't think that's true."

Ben watches me with an odd sort of expression, closing the gap between us by a few inches.

I bite my lip at his nearness. "What?"

"You're quite passionate." His voice is soft.

"Is that a nice way of saying *overbearing*?" I laugh. "Sorry. I get a little intense sometimes."

"Not at all. It's infectious. In a good way. It's why I was so enthralled the first time we met. You won me over."

He leans in farther, tilting his head. Just a fraction.

My knees become a bit wobbly, both from his nearness and the copious amount of champagne I consumed tonight. Ben notices me sway and reaches out to place a hand on my hip.

I feel the warmth of his palm even through my dress.

"Steady," he says. "We don't want you tripping and ruining that beautiful dress."

I swallow through my dry mouth while my heart gallops in my chest like a skittish horse. Or maybe it's not nerves but excitement. I can't deny that Ben Tulley is growing on me. He's charming as hell, with a wry humor I appreciate.

And didn't I come to London for adventure, to have my own stories to tell?

Well, right now, it seems I'm at the part of the fairy tale where the prince wants to kiss me at the ball.

"Your lips are exquisite." Ben's gaze focuses on my mouth. "That color you're wearing is hypnotizing."

"Oh, I'm not wearing any lipstick. Just a bit of plain gloss."

That summons a low noise from his throat. "Bloody hell, Abbey Bly. I don't think you've any idea your effect on people."

He draws me closer, brings his mouth to mine and—

"Lord Tulley!" comes a shrill voice.

We break apart before our lips manage to connect.

Almost immediately, I'm hit with a gust of relief. Because as magical as this evening has been, I'm not the girl who makes out with older men at royal balls. Celeste might jump all over the opportunity, but she's also perfectly content dating forty-year-olds. Not that Ben is forty. Twenty-seven certainly isn't ancient. But he's got almost a decade of experience on me. And while I prefer to take things very slow, Ben strikes me as a man who likes to move fast.

So when his executive assistant marches up to us on impossibly high stilettos, I'm happy for the interruption.

"Abbey, hello." Sophie greets me with a tight smile.

She's wearing a stunning navy-blue satin gown, her dark hair arranged in a complicated-looking twist at the nape of her neck. Everything about her appearance is utterly effortless. Even though she's not part of the nobility, she looks like she belongs among them, whereas I feel awkwardly out of place.

"Hi," I say, fidgeting with the diamond tennis bracelet around my wrist, a loaner from Sue Li. "It's good to see you again."

"Yes, likewise," she answers in a sharp tone that tells me she's lying through her teeth. She turns to Ben with an equally sharp expression. "I'm afraid I need to steal you away, Benjamin. Lord Fulton has been looking for you. He would like a word."

"That blowhard never limits himself to one word. I've never met anyone who drones on and on like our dear Lord Fulton."

"Nevertheless," Sophie says brusquely, "he has requested an audience."

The look she gives him is rife with warning. I don't blame her. I mean, she literally just stopped her boss from kissing a college student. Her mind is probably still running over all the salacious tabloid headlines they almost woke up to tomorrow morning.

After a beat, Ben relents. "Then I suppose I shall grant it."

She reaches for his arm, but he stops her by waving a hand.

"A moment, please," he tells her before shifting his attention to me. "To wrap up our discussion—I didn't have time to review all the papers, but my staff is boxing them up and having them sent back to the city. I'll do my best to go through the rest and contact you if I find anything of note. Perhaps we can meet again for dinner then."

"Sure," I say lightly, making a pointed effort to avoid Sophie's hard gaze.

"I have a business trip to Ibiza next month. I'll be away for an extended period. After that, however, I'd love to catch up."

"Sounds great. I look forward to it." I finally find the courage to meet Sophie's gaze. "I'd better go find my flatmate."

As I make my hasty escape, I hear their hushed voices at my back. Sophie tries to speak quietly, but the acoustics in this place are phenomenal. No wonder my father enjoyed playing here so much.

"She's a teenager, you bloody fool," Sophie is hissing at the lord.

"Mind your tone," he snaps back.

"Benjamin—"

"No. Enough. I allow you many liberties, but you mustn't forget who the boss is, my dear."

Hoo boy.

I walk faster, praying I don't trip and fall flat on my ass.

I think we're at the part of the evening where I plaster myself to Lee's side before I start an international incident.

The last I see of Lee, he kisses me on the cheek, whispering "Grapefruit," before climbing into a limo with Eric. Ben and some of his friends talk about an after-party as the ball winds down and the guests thin out, but I'm exhausted and ready to nurse my blisters with an ice pack. Besides, I don't think Sophie would approve of a "teenager" partying the night away with her employer.

Ben offers me his car to take me home but can't manage to find his phone and is maybe a bit too inebriated to handle the logistics. Instead, I slip away when he goes to the bathroom. The nice man at the arrival loop outside gets me a cab.

The house is empty when I return to Notting Hill and peel myself out of my dress and into some pajamas. I pull my hair down, wipe off my makeup, and sit on the couch to watch some late-night TV. The red, angry outlines of my shoes are still scored into my feet.

One of those cringey "dating" hotline commercials comes on, which prompts a thought about what Jack is up to tonight. Out on a date maybe.

I heave myself off the couch and pretend the thought of Jack hooking up with someone else doesn't make me want to burn down a small village.

As I'm contemplating scrounging for leftovers in the fridge, I get a text.

Nate: You up?

26

It's past midnight. According to Eliza, that places us in booty-call territory. But Nate also happens to be a bartender, so if he was working tonight, he might just be getting off shift.

My fingers are a bit shaky as I type a response.

> Me: Yes. Just got home.

> Nate: Can I stop by?

> Me: Sure, the guys are out.

> Nate: See you in a few.

I don't know what possessed me to add that second part. What does it matter that I'm here alone? Or why Nate would need to know that?

My head's a mess.

Still, I brush my teeth, fix my hair, and throw on some jeans and a T-shirt before Nate knocks on the door. Unhappiness creases his handsome features, so I bring him up to my room when he says we need to talk.

"Sorry for the late hour," he starts gruffly. "I came straight from work."

"I figured. What's up?"

Wary, I sit in my desk chair while he paces the floor, running his hands through his hair in a sort of agitated ritual. His black trousers and snug black tee, combined with the dark stubble shadowing his strong jaw, lend him an air of danger. This guy radiates sex appeal.

"Am I imagining this?" He glances at me, pausing for a second before resuming his path across my room.

"This being…?"

"You and me. What's happening between us."

Oh.

"I text you more than I text Yvonne," he mutters when I don't respond. "What does that mean?"

"I don't know that I can answer that."

"You're five years younger than me. That's too young, isn't it?"

This is more emotion than I've seen from him ever. Though he's still guarded, this display seems like a culmination of long-lingering frustration.

"Too young for what?"

"You know what."

"Yeah, okay." I feel myself blushing. We're past the point of playing dumb, I guess. "I'm not sure what to say. I'm sort of in a tough spot here. I mean…Yvonne."

"Right. Exactly." Nate turns away. Paces a few more steps. "Theoretically, though. If we're being hypothetical."

I get to my feet. His nervous energy has become contagious as I start to wander the room.

"Do I like you? Is that what you came here to find out?"

He answers with a heated stare.

"Sure, I guess I have a crush."

In my defense, I think it's the half-dozen glasses of champagne that glossed my lips enough to let the admission slip out.

I pause at the foot of my bed. "Or did. But we talked about this."

Nate approaches me. "Right."

"Because you have a girlfriend."

He moves closer. "Right."

"We agreed."

Until he's standing right in front of me. "We did."

Reaching for me, Nate places his warm palm against my cheek. His face hovers above mine as my breath catches. He's so good-looking it makes my heart pound.

I want to reach for him. To grab him as if to say, *Hurry up already. If you want me, take me. Put me out of my misery.*

But I don't.

"We can't do this, Nate."

I break away, crossing the room to put some necessary distance between us. I can't trust myself in his proximity, because I do want this. Him. I have since the moment I saw him under the cheap stage lights of that pub. But crushing on a taken guy is one thing. It's harmless.

Acting on that crush is not.

"I'm sorry. I don't want to be that girl."

His voice is low, tortured. "I'm not in love with Yvonne."

That doesn't make it any better. If anything, it might be worse.

"You're still with her." Irritation colors my voice. This guy is so frustrating. "As long as that's the case, I don't want to be in the middle of it."

Nate is temptation on a heaping plate of mischief, and I see no other way to remove that temptation than to take myself out of the situation. Even if that means losing a friend.

Because really, how is it friendship if we only end up trying to make out with each other at every encounter?

He conveys his own frustration by raking a hand through his hair. "You want me to choose," he says flatly.

"No. I don't want you to do anything. I'm just telling you how it is. Nothing's changed—I'm not interested in poaching another woman's boyfriend. And honestly? I'm not interested in hooking up with someone who's playing two girls at the same time."

He doesn't respond. Like the kid in the back of the class who tries to disappear when the teacher calls on him. Nate the escape artist. Which is all the more reason not to waste a thought on the man trying to have it both ways.

Finally, a ragged breath slips out of his mouth. "I'm not trying to play you, Abbey. Yvonne and I, our relationship is casual. And if there's something here, between you and I, shouldn't we figure that out?"

The lure is so strong it's like being pulled by a magnet. I suddenly picture my arms around his waist on the back of his motorcycle as we ride off somewhere no one can find us. Hidden away, it'd be so easy to be selfish.

But that's not who I am.

"No, we shouldn't. Because it's a shitty thing you're doing to her. My advice, as a friend: figure out what you want. Don't drag her along only to hurt her later." I shake my head at him. "And I don't think we should text anymore. Not even about the weather."

"Abbey."

"Time to go, Nate."

This isn't at all the encounter I expected, but I'm too tired to hold his hand through his crisis of the heart. I like Nate. I'm attracted to him. But I don't like being a wedge in the lives of people I barely know, and the last thing I want is to be anyone's side piece or fallback plan. I deserve better.

> Celeste: Fancy some breakfast?

I wake up the next morning to a growling stomach and a breakfast offer. Yet to my relief, I don't feel hungover. After all the champagne I drank last night, I thought I'd be suffering from nausea and a pounding headache.

I don't know if it's a good thing or a bad thing that Britain's drinking culture seems to be agreeing with me.

Since I'm utterly famished, I text Celeste back and we agree to meet at a tiny café a few blocks from the flat. After a quick shower, I head out on foot, surprised by the warm-ish temperature and lack of rain. It's a clear, brisk November day.

The café is packed when I walk up. There's a line outside to get in, but Celeste messages telling me to come inside. When I enter, I do a quick scan of the crowd until I spot Celeste's gorgeous head in a small booth across the room. I'm already talking as I approach her.

"I'm so happy you texted. I don't think I've ever been this hungry before in—" I stop when I notice Yvonne sitting on the other side of the booth. "Oh. Hey, Yvonne. I didn't see you there."

Awesome. A little warning would've been nice.

I mask my unease. Because really, Celeste couldn't have known that Yvonne is the last person I'd want to see this morning.

"Morning, darling." Celeste scoots closer to the wall to make room for me beside her. She's wearing a red sweater and a checkered silk scarf, looking (as always) like a supermodel ballerina.

Yvonne, on the other hand, is actually dressed sort of casual today. No chic outfit or perfectly done hair, just a loose long-sleeved shirt and a white headband pulling her short blond hair away from her makeup-free face. She's still gorgeous, of course, but more approachable today.

"So. Heard you had quite the night," Yvonne remarks in that crisp intonation of hers.

I falter.

Fuck.

Did Nate tell her he came by my flat last night? Why would—

"Snogging lords at royal balls now, are we?" Celeste pipes up.

I swallow my relief. "Oh." Then I frown at them. "Wait. Who said I made out with him? I didn't."

"My brother. He texted about an hour ago and informed me he was marrying a yachtsman and that you're poised to be the future Lady Tulley."

I sigh. "Of course he did."

A harried-looking waiter comes over to take our orders, even though we've barely had time to glance at our menus. He stands there tapping his foot impatiently and murdering us in his head while we scramble to pick something. This place is so busy I have a feeling they want their customers in and out like some human assembly line.

Once he's gone, I fill the girls in about the ball, making it clear I didn't snog anyone.

"I mean, at one point, I think he was about to kiss me," I do confess. "But his assistant interrupted."

"His handler, you mean," Celeste says dryly. "That poor woman. I reckon a large part of her job description is ensuring the young lord's trousers remain zipped."

"Aw, Ben's not that bad," I argue, reaching for the cup of coffee another frazzled waiter suddenly drops in front of me. I thank him before continuing. "I think Ben's caddish reputation has been grossly overexaggerated."

"Sorry, Abbey, but that reputation is well earned," Yvonne warns, her expression serious. "He's an absolute cad. In the tabloids every other day, caught up in some debauchery or another."

I shrug. "As the daughter of a man who was in the tabloids his entire life, I have it on good authority that half the shit those rags write about people is false."

"Fair point." Celeste wraps her fingers around her coffee cup. "But Yvonne's not wrong—the Tulleys and debauchery go hand in hand. I'm thrilled you had a good time, though." She gives me a grudging look. "And I suppose it was right of you to take Lee. He's not stopped gushing about it."

"I don't think he even came home last night. At least I didn't hear him come in."

Our food arrives in record speed, and I forget my manners as I practically inhale my avocado on toast. The two of them are far more restrained, Celeste daintily spreading jam on her toast while Yvonne picks at a poached egg.

"What did you end up doing last night?" I ask Celeste between mouthfuls of food.

"Roberto stopped by mine for a quiet dinner. He brought the most exquisite white wine, and we got drunk and shagged on the living room floor."

Yvonne's eyebrows fly up. "Are you serious! Our prudish Roberto had a shag somewhere other than a bed?"

"Mental, right?"

I wash down my toast with some coffee, laughing at Celeste. "You never mentioned Roberto was a prude. Is he actually?"

I still haven't had the pleasure of meeting her forty-three-year-old lover-slash-philanthropist. Lee says Celeste likes to keep her boyfriends to herself. She's never even brought one home to their parents, according to him.

"He's...reserved," she finally answers. "Vanilla, I suppose."

Yvonne snorts. "You suppose?"

"All right, all right. He's very set in his ways," Celeste says, grinning. "He prefers missionary position—always in a bed—and blow jobs only while lying down to receive them. And he doesn't make a sound during either act. It's quite unnerving."

"Nate isn't very vocal either, particularly during blow jobs," Yvonne says with a shrug. "It's not that unusual."

I feel a stab of jealousy at the thought of her on her knees in front of Nate.

Immediately followed by a sharp prick of guilt at the memory that this woman's boyfriend was in my room last night asking if there was "something" between us.

The nausea I didn't experience this morning now makes an appearance. I gulp down some more coffee and hope neither of them comments on my sudden mood shift.

Luckily, we can't loiter in the café long. We've barely taken our last bites before the waiter marches over with the bill and practically orders us to leave. We part ways on the sidewalk, and I walk home trying to remind myself that I haven't crossed any lines with Nate.

I flat out told him I wasn't interested in playing home-wrecker. I told him to stop texting me. Hopefully he respects that. Like, stop torturing me with your brooding bad-boy-ness, dude. Just keep having silent sex and receiving silent blow jobs from your girlfriend and leave me out of it.

Back at the flat, I run into Jamie in the upstairs hallway.

"Hey. Jamie. Question," I say. "Do you make noise when you get a blow job?"

"Heaps of noise," he confirms. "Would you like a demonstration?"

"Ew. No."

I hear him chuckling as he heads downstairs.

I spend the rest of the day catching up on my favorite TV shows, then eat an early dinner with Jamie, because Jack is out with his rugby friends, and Lee still hasn't come home. I don't know if I should be worried Lee is chained up in a bathtub somewhere because Lord Eric stole his kidney, but every time I text him, he assures me he's fine. Or rather, he's in heaven, according to the latest assurance.

It's weird having Lee gone all weekend, though. I didn't realize what a huge presence in my life he's become. He's my best friend here.

Around noon on Sunday, I'm still in my lazy clothes, reading in bed, when two soft knocks sound on my door.

"Abbs?" Jack's voice.

"Yeah?"

He comes in, wearing jeans and a black long-sleeve that hugs his broad chest. "How about a drive?"

I wrinkle my forehead. "A drive?"

"Yeah. Out to the country. I borrowed my mate's car. It's a junker, so I figure he won't notice a few dents."

"You borrowed a car for me?"

"Heard you chatting with Jamie yesterday about renting a car so you could practice driving, and it reminded me I promised you we'd go." He shrugs. "I'd rather you went with me than Jamie. I feel like I've a better shot at keeping you alive. So?"

A slow, hesitant smile spreads across my face. "Really?"

"If you'd like."

I perk right up. He's been promising me a chance to practice driving on the other side of the road for months. I'd given up on it happening.

"Oh my God. Of course I'd like!" I put the laptop back on the nightstand. "Let's go for a drive."

Jack flashes that grin that makes me all gooey inside. "I'll meet you downstairs."

27

When we pull away from the curb ten minutes later, I experience a moment of hesitation, because this could be a long and uncomfortable trip in silence if Jack and I can't figure out anything to say to each other. Our conversations come in fits and starts lately. I'd never give Lee the satisfaction, but he was right. Tempting the boundaries of the roommate relationship is inevitably going to affect your friendship. Hence house rule number one and only.

I'm racking my brain for neutral subjects that can't possibly veer into dangerous territory when he breaks the ice first.

"Talked to my brother Charlie yesterday. Noah had a fight with his girlfriend."

"The girlfriend we don't like?"

"Bree. Noah's been crashing at Charlie's place since the fight."

I grin. "Your mom must be popping champagne."

"Charlie took his phone while he was sleeping and blocked Bree's number," Jack adds, laughing. "He was going to delete all the photos of her from his Instagram, but Noah caught him."

"Know what you need to do?"

He glances at me from the corner of his eye as he merges onto the highway. "What?"

"You guys need to get someone else in there ASAP to distract Noah. Make him remember what life was like before her."

"A new girl. Someone hotter and not batshit crazy."

"Even better if she's an old crush. Maybe the one that got away. Nothing turns the head like nostalgia."

"I'll pass that along to the team," Jack says in amusement. "Shannon will love playing matchmaker."

"How's the rest of the Campbell clan?" I ask. "Last week, you were saying your brother Oliver's got that surfing tournament, right?"

"Yeah. He was worried he wouldn't come up with the entrance fee, and then, uh"—Jack focuses on a car up ahead—"some sponsor hit him up out of nowhere and gave him the rest of the money to enter. They're going to cover travel and hotel too. Mum was relieved. She always feels like shit when she can't afford to help out."

"Aw, that sucks."

"Yeah." His voice roughens. "We aren't exactly swimming in cash. Money was always tight when I was growing up. Even when Dad was alive, there wasn't much to go around."

"I imagine it wouldn't be easy with five kids."

"No, not easy. But they tried. And Mum's still doing her best."

The rest of the drive isn't at all awkward. We chat about his family and my dad. My classes and his rugby schedule. Being with Jack comes so naturally. We just vibe.

About ninety minutes south of London, he pulls the beat-up old car over on a dirt shoulder in the middle of nowhere to let me get behind the wheel. Out here, it's nothing but two-lane country roads covered in fallen leaves. Miles of brown hills and stone walls.

Now in the passenger seat, he watches me as I adjust the mirrors. "Remember," he says. "The red sign with the word *stop* on it—"

"Accelerate to eighty-eight miles per hour and ram it."

Jack tightens his seat belt. "Just try to keep it between the lines and don't run into anything."

Truth is I'm a little nervous, so I keep my speed under the limit while I get the hang of feeling like I'm driving in reverse. To distract himself from the creeping terror evident on his face, Jack hums to the radio. Until there's a slight miscommunication at the four-way stop.

"The one to the right goes first," he says. But it's too late. My foot is already pressing the gas. "No, to the right! The right."

I mash the brakes, sending us both jolting forward. We end up nose-to-nose with another car in the middle of the intersection. The other guy starts laying on his adorable English horn.

"I'm sorry," I say breathlessly. "I thought we got there first."

"Oh, Christ. This was a bad idea." Jack covers his eyes and sinks into the seat until we've cleared the intersection.

"Come on. Aren't you going to tell me this isn't half as scary as the time you bare-knuckle boxed a kangaroo when you were seven?"

He shoots me a disapproving scowl. "I regret this already."

If he didn't then, he certainly does when I nearly kill us attempting to navigate my first roundabout.

"For fuck's sake, woman." Jack braces his hands against the dash, slamming his foot into the floorboard like he could take control from the passenger seat. "Are you aiming for the other cars?"

Nervous laughter jumps from my chest when we narrowly escape unscathed. "Whoops."

"Fucking Americans." The lives that have flashed before his eyes are stripped from his soul and expelled in one relieved exhale. "You're bloody fucked in the head."

"What? I'm not doing it on purpose. They're the ones driving on the wrong side of the road."

After a while, he's clearly resigned himself to his fate, because the near misses barely faze him. He even relaxes enough to tell me a story about the time his brothers left him adrift at sea for nearly an hour because Jack had told their mom about their secret stash of cigarettes.

"How old were you?"

"Twelve, I think," he answers, as if it's a normal part of growing up. Abandoned at sea, learning to ride a bike, just the usual.

"And they left you to tread water in the middle of the ocean?" I'm gaping at him.

"No, I had my boogie board. Noah's friend took their parents' boat out, and we were all swimming, hanging out. I was floating on my board with a line tied to the stern. Before I know what's happening, they throw the line and take off. Do a few laps around me, right? Expecting me to beg or cry. I was like, *fuck off, I'll paddle home.* So they left me."

"No offense, but your brothers kind of suck."

He shrugs, a grin stretching his lips. "Sometimes. I think they'd like you, though. You'd fit in well with that lot."

I feign a casual tone. "That right?"

"Yeah." He laughs. "You're all completely mad."

We stop off in a small village to grab a bite to eat. At a table by the window, I watch the foot traffic and the old man at the bus bench feeding the crows. A shopkeeper from the convenience store argues with him, shooing the birds away from his door with a newspaper. Undaunted, the old man tosses nuts on the ground from his paper lunch bag.

"What about Josephine?" Jack asks, digging into his roast beef sandwich.

I sigh glumly. "Well, I'd hoped Ben's suggestion that Robert might have been living in Ireland would give me something more to go on. It's such an important clue. But I haven't found any new information. If the Ireland thread is true, then his secret's stayed safe all this time."

"Is that it? A dead end?"

"I still have to turn in something for my assignment, so I've got no choice but to move on to researching the other Tulleys at this point. Unless Ben comes back with anything new, I think Josephine will stay out of reach."

The painting is now at the museum in Rye, courtesy of the Abbey Bly collection, but it mocks me in my memory, this ever-present smirking mystery amused at my feeble attempts to unravel its secrets. A total pain in the ass in fact.

"Speaking of Ben Tulley." Jack's casual tone is betrayed by the tensing of his jaw. "How was the ball?"

"It was fun. I'm glad I went, but I wouldn't want to do that every weekend, you know? After the shine of the famous people and nobility wears off, it ends up being just another stuffy party in shoes that hurt your feet."

"He didn't..." Jack stops, then changes course. "You don't get a bad feeling about that guy? Tulley?"

"No, why?"

"People say things."

"Not everything people say is true."

He frowns. "There's pictures of him doing wild shit all over the internet."

I lift an eyebrow. "Why don't you just ask what you really want to ask? Am I hooking up with Lord Tulley, right?"

"That's not what I wanted to ask," he says stubbornly.

"Uh-huh. Sure."

He's staunch in his protests. "It's not. That family is a bunch of black sheep. I was making sure he didn't try anything."

"And if he did?"

Jack narrows his eyes. "Did he?"

I burst out laughing. "Oh my God. Just fucking ask, Jack."

"None of my business."

He's so infuriating sometimes. And in my exasperation, I straighten my shoulders and give him a smug look. "Since you're dying to know—we did almost kiss, but we got interrupted."

His jaw ticks.

"What? No lecture?"

"Do you want one?" he asks.

"Not particularly, no. Because I didn't do anything wrong." I push the rest of my sandwich away, my appetite gone.

"Tulley is almost a decade older than you. You realize that, right?"

"Yes, Jack. I can count."

He studies me for a long beat before wiping his hands and tossing the balled-up napkin on his plate. "Ready to get out of here?"

"Sure." I swipe the car keys from the table as he reaches for them. "But I'm driving."

He scoffs, practically chasing me out the door. "The hell you are. I've too much to live for."

In the tiny parking lot, I dangle the keys in front of him. "You want these? I'll give them back if you tell the truth."

"About what?"

"What do you care if there's something happening with me and Ben Tulley? Seriously, Jack. Why do you care so much?"

28

I LEAN AGAINST THE DRIVER'S SIDE OF THE CAR AS I WAIT FOR HIM to answer. He takes his sweet-ass time, fighting it till the bitter end before sighing in surrender.

"I'm just protective, that's all."

There's that word again. *Protective.* Nate said something similar when we had lunch that day, admitting I trigger a protective instinct in him. Do I really do that? And why? I always thought I came off as independent and strong, not as a damsel in distress. I wonder what it is they're both seeing that I'm not.

"You worry me sometimes, all right? You're not the girl who goes around kissing blokes a decade older."

"Maybe I am." I flash him a defiant look. "Women date older men all the time. Celeste's boyfriend is forty-three."

"You're not Celeste."

The flicker of concern in his eyes unleashes a rush of frustration that comes out in the form of a strangled groan.

"Then who am I? Because sometimes I have no goddamn idea. Don't you get it? That's why I'm here! It's clichéd as fuck, but I came to London to find myself. I want to have adventures. I want to kiss lords. And I don't need a lecture or a protector. I already have my father clinging to my leg to stop me from leaving the house. Don't be like that too. If you want to protect someone, go shadow Lee for a day or something. I don't need it."

His lips twitch at that.

"What?" I demand.

Jack leans against the car beside me, sliding his hands in the pockets of his coat. Then he turns a fraction to face me. "You're cute when you're angry."

"I'm not angry."

"Still cute."

It starts again. The nervous static in my fingertips. The flutters in my belly. Half my attention becomes consumed with my own breathing because suddenly it sounds too loud between my ears. This energy that builds in the space between us is so obvious it practically manifests in colors and strands of light. I hate that I feel this way around him and I miss it when it's gone.

"Don't say stuff like that if you don't mean it," I warn.

He blinks innocently. "What'd I do?"

"Seriously?" He's impossible. "You're doing this on purpose, right? To get a rise out of me?"

"Why would I do that?"

Jack's got this thing he does with his face. Smirking at his own mischief. It if wasn't so hot, I'd smack him upside the head. Charming guys who know they're charming are the worst.

"Cut it out," I order.

"Your nose sort of twitches and your lips curl up when you're mad," he says. "I like it."

"Yeah, well, don't." But I can't keep a straight face, and it only encourages him. "You're incorrigible, you know that?"

"Is that bad?"

"Yes." No. "I hate it." I really don't. "It's awful."

His grin grows wider. "You're a terrible liar."

And I realize in that moment why I like being around him so much. Jack brings out my silly, ridiculous, playful side. He makes me feel young. I mean, I *am* young. I know that. But I very rarely feel it.

By the age of five, I was a little adult, attending awards shows with my dad and learning fast that I was the mature one in our parent/child relationship. And then suddenly I wasn't. Dad retired, and then *he* became the adult, and out of nowhere, my life became sheltered. He wasn't—and still isn't—keen on me going out, partying, dating. Since the second I hit adolescence, he's been projecting his fear and regrets over his checkered past and questionable lifestyle choices onto me.

So no. It's rare for me to experience all those youthful, carefree feelings other girls my age take for granted. Jack brings that out in me. Our friendship is fun, and I feel giddy when we're together.

And inevitably that always seems to trigger a rush of need that now rises inside me.

I look up at his hazy blue eyes and know he's feeling it too. He's not drunk this time either.

Jack stares back at me in an infinite moment of anticipation that expands like a bubble of time as it engulfs us. I know before it happens that I'm going to regret this. And I don't care.

I kiss him.

On my terms. Because I feel like it, and whatever he tells himself later, he means it in this moment. He returns the kiss with intent. Hurried and insistent. As if he knows I've waited weeks for a second chance at this.

He makes a low, rumbling sound and deepens the kiss.

I melt against him. My hands climb his broad shoulders to pull him closer. He presses me against the passenger door, his tongue slicking over mine.

"You drive me mad," he mumbles before hungrily kissing me again.

I feel him hard against my pelvis and can't stop myself from rocking my lower body. Just slightly, but it's enough to summon a groan from his throat. I swallow the husky sound with another frantic, greedy kiss, needing to feel his tongue touching mine again, teasing me into oblivion.

Kissing Jack feels like the most natural thing in the world.

But it's over too quickly.

"Fuck." He pulls back, biting his lip. "I've no bloody willpower around you."

"Is that such a bad thing?" My heartbeat is still so erratic, my knees weak.

"Christ, I don't even know anymore." His voice sounds hoarse. "No, I do know. Nothing's changed, Abbs."

"Meaning?"

"Meaning I'm still shit at relationships. Meaning I still don't want to jeopardize things between us. I count you as one of my closest friends. I don't want to lose that."

"Who says you would?"

There's a trace of self-deprecation in his answering laugh. "That's what always happens. When you're with a woman, suddenly there's a whole new set of standards you gotta meet. And I never meet them." Before I can delve any deeper into that response, he adds, "Besides, we already established we don't want to ruin the dynamic of the house, right?"

There he goes, speaking on my behalf again. But the rational part of me knows he's right. If we got together, the house dynamic would be shot to hell. It'd be too convenient. Dating a guy who sleeps thirty feet away starts to look like shacking up pretty quick. Which turns into practically married even quicker. And that's got *quick, fiery end* written all over it.

At least that's what I tell myself as I stand here in the face of yet another rejection from Jack Campbell.

"Right," I say, brushing it off with laugh. "We'd be married and divorced in six weeks. Tops."

"Right. Lawyers are so expensive these days."

"It'd be an ugly custody battle. I'd obviously get Lee and the house."

"Of course." Jack unlocks the door, and we get in the car.

"You'd get Jamie," I continue as he starts the engine. "But splitting up the kids is always tough on their development."

"We have to think of the children."

That's how we talk ourselves right back into the friend zone.

There's a suspicious creature in the window when we get home close to suppertime. Walking up the sidewalk, I spot a blur of orange before the curtains sway. I glance at Jack to check that I'm not hallucinating. His dark-blond eyebrows shoot up, confirming he saw it too. As we let ourselves in the door, the blur scurries across the foyer.

"What is that?" demands Jack. "A ferret?"

"I don't think ferrets are orange."

We kick off our shoes and hang our coats, then creep into the living room.

"Anyone home?" Jack calls.

No answer.

I walk around with slow steps, peering under the furniture. Under the sofa, two glowing eyes shine back at me. The creature's body is crouched in the shadows.

"I see it." I get on all fours, plaster myself to the floor.

"I wouldn't do that." Lee appears in the doorway behind us.

After being MIA all weekend, it's a relief to hear his voice. When I glance over my shoulder at him, the first thing I see is the bandages on his hands.

"He's quite feral," Lee warns.

"Let me grab a broom," Jack says. "I'll get it out of here."

"What? No. He isn't a stray. I adopted him. His name's Hugh."

"Seriously, mate? Are you mental?"

Still lying on the rug in front of the sofa, I try to coax Hugh the semi-feral cat out from underneath. He stares at me, unblinking.

"Give him a chance. The girl at the shelter said he just needs time to acclimate to his surroundings."

"Mate, you're boggled if you think that thing's staying."

The front door opens, and now Jamie is standing in the clump at the threshold of the living room, watching me silently wrestle this cat in a battle of will. I've never felt so disrespected than engaging a cat in a staring contest.

"What's happening here?" Jamie asks curiously.

"He's gone and gotten a damned cat," Jack snaps. He's fully pissed, and it's a strange phenomenon.

"Really? When did we talk about taking on a pet?"

"Exactly," Jack growls.

"Right, I know I should've asked first," Lee speaks up, uncharacteristically sheepish. "It was sort of a spontaneous thing."

"What?" Jack demands. "You got lost and wandered into an animal shelter? Mate, come on. That thing can't stay."

Jamie comes to kneel beside me at the sofa. "Not so friendly, is it?"

I turn to grin at him. "Misunderstood, maybe."

"One of my aunts is a cat lady. She says as soon as you stop paying attention to them, they get interested."

"Hmm. Okay. Let me try that."

We hop to our feet, and I proceed to take a seat on the sofa, pulling my legs up.

"I can't bring him back to the shelter," Lee says as he and Jack continue to argue over Hugh's fate. "Give him a chance."

"I don't care where you take him. You can't dump an animal on the rest of us without asking."

Jamie rejoins the argument. "Seriously, mate."

"I just don't get why you'd bring home a cat," I chime in, not in accusation but genuine curiosity.

"Oh, bloody hell. I know what this is." Understanding suddenly dawns on Jack's face, summoning a loud curse from his lips. He turns to glare at Lee. "Let me guess. You're dating someone new, and your new beau happens to like cats, yeah?"

I wrinkle my forehead. "Wait. This is about the lord from the ball?"

"Oh, mate. You didn't." Jamie tosses his hands up and dumps himself into the armchair. "You couldn't just buy him some flowers, for fuck's sake?"

"This is what he does," Jack explains to me while still glowering at Lee. "Celeste says he's—what does she call it again?"

"Boyfriend chameleon," supplies Jamie.

"That's it. He gets smitten with a bloke and takes on his interests. Last year, he dated a guy who raised poisonous snakes. Before that, it was the semipro extreme sports guy."

Jamie starts to laugh. "Ah, right. Hey, Lee, whatever happened to that BMX bike you spent two thousand pounds on?"

"Kindly fuck off, Jamie," Lee says cheerfully.

Oh dear. I swallow a laugh. "It's good to explore different interests, I guess. But how did we end up with this cat?"

"Yes, Lee, how?" Jack says sarcastically.

Cornered, Lee starts talking very fast. "I admit it was a bit rash. We were in bed last night—"

Jamie scoffs. "Of course."

"And Eric said he was flying to France next weekend for a cat show. He's into pedigrees and certain breeds and the like. He has a whole, I don't know what you'd call it, *stable* of show cats. They win money, if you can believe that. It's massive. And, well, I wanted a trip to Paris. So I might have said I was into cats as well. And then before I knew it, I'd spun an elaborate story about our cat Hugh and spent all day going to every shelter in the city looking for something that could pass for a red mackerel Persian."

"That's not a fish, mate. It's a cat," Jack barks at him.

Lee rolls his eyes, exasperated. "It's a kind of cat."

"Am I mental? A mackerel is a fish, right?"

The boys proceed to go at it again over our fish cat, just as Hugh emerges from under the sofa to jump into my lap. The long-haired ball of fur curls up, tail over its eyes, and makes itself quite at home.

"Jamie," I hiss. "It worked!"

"Don't get too attached," he cautions. "We're not keeping it."

"We're keeping it," Lee insists.

"Lee, mate," Jack grumbles. "Let's be reasonable here."

The guys are still bickering over Hugh's fate when the cat and I head upstairs to take a nap before dinner.

29

A FEW DAYS LATER, I'M BACK IN THE LIBRARY. FOR THE FIRST TIME IN A long time, I'm working on a paper that isn't about Josephine or those damned interminable Tulleys, and it's a nice palate cleanser. Just a standard literary theory and criticism essay I can otherwise do in my sleep.

From my seat near the entrance to the archives and Mr. Baxley's fortress, I spy him approaching me out of the corner of my eye.

Stiffly, as if afraid to be seen speaking to me, he stands beside the table.

"Was my typing too loud?" I ask with a grin.

"You'll not be requesting access to the special sections today?"

I don't think I've ever witnessed someone fail so hard at trying to act casual.

I set my laptop aside. "So you did miss me."

"Am I to conclude you've completed your research then?"

He looks like he's in pain, like the effort of engaging in human contact is almost too agonizing to endure. I worry for his health if he attempts to keep this up. It's sort of sweet, though. I had no idea he cared so much.

"Not really, no. Without more clues to chase down, I don't think there's anything else in this building that can help me."

"Is that right?" The mask slips, an expression of concern overtaking his usual scowl of contempt. "That's unfortunate."

With my foot, I push out a chair for him to join me.

Several beats tick by.

Just when I've given up, Mr. Baxley sits down. While still letting me know with his eyes drifting elsewhere that he's only half interested in this conversation.

"I was able to find out that Robert and William Tulley were at odds right before the *Victoria* sinking," I tell him. "I don't know about what, but the hidden letter from Josephine about being torn between two men would absolutely be a motive for a falling-out between the brothers. I still have no idea if William was alone when he boarded the ship, as he was added to the passenger list at the last minute. I managed to locate the office where all the records for the Northern Star Line are archived—that's the shipping company that owned the *Victoria*. A clerk there is trying to track down any documents related to the ship that haven't been donated to museums. Maybe those will shed light on whether Josephine was ever on that boat."

"And the eldest Tulley?"

"There's speculation that Robert's disappearance was him running off to Ireland under an assumed name. Whether that was to hide his new bride or to escape the loss of his love to his own brother, who knows? Or maybe," I say and offer a wry smile, "I've concocted this entire story in my head and none of it has anything to do with anything."

"I see" is his enigmatic response.

"If I had a shrink, they'd tell me I'm projecting, right? Two elusive men fighting over the same woman. A little art imitating life?"

Mr. Baxley responds with a questioning look.

"Okay, so there's these guys. And they both say they're into me. But they don't want to be with me. Or can't. Depending on what you believe."

I have no earthly right unloading on this poor man. Except that I have few other people to unleash my thoughts on, and once I get going, the release is so satisfying I can't stop midstream.

"But then how much can they really like me, right? I mean, if you want something bad enough, you give up the family titles and fortune to move to Ireland and change your name. You cross an ocean with nothing but the clothes on your back. You definitely don't kiss her and then say, 'Let's just be friends.' That's a dick move."

Mr. Baxley stares at me. He all but shrinks behind his glasses, his chin receding into his neck. A man inexplicably pinned to his chair despite every fiber of his being screaming to run from this oversharing girl.

"I didn't get off the plane looking to date my way through London, you know? A love interest wasn't anywhere on my list of priorities. And now I have two. And they're both so wishy-washy my head is spinning." I heave a dramatic sigh, not unlike one Lee would bestow on someone. "But this is my fate now, I guess. To be desired but not enough. An ornament on a shelf they want to pull down and play with when it's convenient. These men. What did a girl ever do to deserve them, Mr. Baxley?"

My phone buzzes on the table.

> Nate: We need to talk.

"See?" I flash the phone at Mr. Baxley, who sits flustered and unmoving across the table. I'm not sure he's breathing. "This shit. Sorry. But seriously, what do we have to talk about? You have a girlfriend, bro."

I tap out a quick response.

> Me: No we don't.

Mr. Baxley clears his throat and hastily rises to his feet. "Yes, well. Good luck with your research."

Men.

> Nate: Please?

> Me: You still have a girlfriend, and
> that's a deal-breaker for me.

I might be attracted to Nate, but my self-esteem isn't so battered that I'm going to be that girl. Especially not for the bass player with the soulful eyes. I'm no one's cliché.

The phone buzzes again.

I'm about to chuck it across the room when I realize this text is from Ben Tulley. It's the first time he's made contact since the ball, although he did mention business abroad. I figured he'd be in touch if or when he had news. It seems now he does.

> Ben: Abbey, darling. I brought some
> homework along while I've been in Ibiza
> and found a few things that should prove
> useful. I've taken the liberty of having
> them shipped ahead of me. Sophie will be
> reaching out xx

Within seconds, a second message pops up from an unfamiliar number.

> Unknown: This is Sophie Brown, Lord
> Tulley's assistant. Expect a package this
> evening by courier. Should be delivered
> in the next hour or so. Please contact me if
> you've not received it by 8 p.m.

The news fills me with a jolt of renewed vigor. Without Josephine to keep my mind occupied, I've been left to wallow in my own dissatisfaction.

I wasn't aware how much I needed to solve the puzzle of Josephine until now, and not only for a grade. So I rush to pack up my things and run out of the library to catch the Tube home. Standing in the train car, jittery for a fix, I know I'm addicted. Right when I think I've cleansed the mystery from my system, the itch rears its head. Despite the numerous disappointments, Josephine is still the most satisfying part of my life these days.

When I get home, I'm met with the warm smell of tikka masala and what sounds like a live stadium inside our house. I drop my stuff in the foyer and follow the uproar to find Lee at the stove with most of Jack's rugby team crammed in our kitchen. The last time they were all here, they nearly tore the place down to the studs.

"Hey!" they shout as I walk in.

A chant like a garbled English drinking song I can't decipher goes around the room. After these boys have had a few drinks in them, I can't understand a word they say.

"Gentlemen," I say in greeting. "Save me some?"

"Make room, you lot." Jack shoves biceps to clear the way for me at the counter. "All right, Abbs?"

"Yeah, good. Thanks."

His smile still does me in. The glint in his eye that I swear is just for me. In other words, that thing he prefers to ignore but can't deny when we kiss. Call it inherent chemistry, I guess.

It's infuriating.

"They were about to start chewing on the doorjambs." Lee flits about the kitchen in his apron. Mixing bowls, cutting boards, and spice jars cover every inch of surface space. "I swear I saw one of them with a paper towel roll between his teeth."

"They were this close to cooking that damn cat." Jack laughs.

"What do you say, dollface?" One of Jack's teammates with a nasty red welt under his eye sidles up beside me. "Make us a sandwich while we're waiting. Some roast beef on rye? Or sourdough if you've got it."

The guys get a good chuckle at my expense.

"You ever find a girl that works on, marry her," I advise him.

"He tried," another one says. "But his mum's already married to his dad."

They go on like that until Lee fixes me a plate of food that I take into the living room to get a little elbow room and wait for my package.

I've just finished eating when the doorbell rings. I waste no time jumping off the couch to answer the door. The young man on the stoop asks me to sign for the heavy cardboard box, which I drag inside and then force Lee to carry upstairs for me.

In my room, we find Hugh snuggled up on my bed against my pillows.

Lee barely glances at his cat. "Let me know if you need anything else, babe," he says absently. "I'll be in the loo getting ready for my date with Eric."

"Sorry, bud," I tell Hugh, who's staring at the empty doorway. "You're simply not a priority for him."

Lee's entirely lost interest in the cat after barely a week. If the Lord of Cats asks, however, Hugh is the light of Lee's life. The reason for being.

Poor thing.

I grab a pair of scissors from my desk drawer to crack into this box. Inside is a lidded file box containing loose pages, folders, and yellow envelopes. At first, it's all nonsense. Fragments of stuff I don't understand. I pull everything out and start making piles based on names and dates, trying to apply some order to it all.

A bound ledger is the last thing at the bottom of the box. It appears to be an accounting of household expenses for the year, dated 1951. Something the head of the Tulleys' house staff would have kept, containing weekly entries for the butcher and florist, that sort of thing. I skim the rows until I find the names of staff with their weekly salaries.

And there, on line nineteen, is Josephine.

I'm in utter disbelief to see her there on the page.

"Lee!" I holler at the doorway. "Lee, get in here!"

He comes barreling in a few seconds later, a green hydration mask slathered on his face and worry flickering in his eyes.

"What's wrong?" He glances around my bedroom until his betrayed gaze lands on Hugh. "What did you do to her, you bloody demon!"

I can't help but laugh. "I'm good. Hugh only likes to assault you. But check this out!" I thrust out the ledger. "I found her! Her name is Josephine Farnham! She was a maid to the duchess."

"Brilliant." He looks genuinely pleased. Everyone in the house has been invested in this mystery from the start. "And what of her fate?"

"Well, I haven't figured that part out yet. But at least we have confirmation that she was connected to the Tulleys."

"The young maid who caught the eye of two young lords," Lee says dramatically. "I adore it. I'll be telling Eric all about this on our date tonight. Speaking of which…this mask won't be removing itself."

With that, he bounds off.

I spend the next several hours meticulously combing through every scrap of paper in the box. And it's a veritable treasure trove. I feel like one of those people who open abandoned storage lockers and find gold pirate coins and furniture that belonged to Marie Antoinette.

There's a letter from the duchess to Robert, which in not so subtle language tells him to get his shit together. He's supposed to marry a princess, and she isn't interested in his objections or preoccupations with the maid. If it becomes necessary, she threatens to fire Josephine and send her to work elsewhere.

Deeper in the stacks, I locate a black-and-white photograph of the household staff posed in front of the estate in Surrey. It's grainy and worn with the years, but a close examination finds the tall thin woman with dark hair and fragile cheekbones at the end of the second row. And either I'm imagining it, or she's sporting a tiny smirk of mischief.

It's Josephine. I'm sure of it. But not quite the same Josephine from the Dyce portrait. That one was distracted, sad almost. This girl in the staff photo has a lot more life in her.

I flip over the photograph and glimpse the date. It was taken a little more than a year before the *Victoria* sinking. Had Josephine fallen for either lord at this point? Maybe just one, and that's why she's so happy? New love and all. And then, by the time she posed for Dyce, she was entangled in a full-blown love triangle and riddled with turmoil?

So many questions.

Hugh paws at me from the bed while I sit on the floor. He starts tugging strands of my hair with his claws, tapping at my shoulder. I absently rub his ear while perusing pages until I find an invoice signed by William Tulley.

In the matter of a portrait commission, he agrees to pay Franklin Astor Dyce three hundred pounds.

Finally, proof.

This *has* to be Josephine's portrait. It would be way too big a coincidence to believe Robert had fallen in love with some other maid at the same time William commissioned a portrait that wasn't my painting.

I am now fairly confident in saying that Robert and William both had the hots for Josephine.

"So which one did she choose?" I ask Hugh.

The cat blinks at me, bored.

Damn it. This mystery is maddening.

Would William have hidden Josephine's rejection letter in the painting after she eloped to Ireland with Robert?

Or was she lost at sea among the victims of the *Victoria*, leaving

Robert with nothing but a brief parting note and the forgotten portrait?

I don't get the chance to let my mind muse over the possibilities, because the doorbell rings. Twice. Then a third time. A couple hours ago, I heard the stampede that was the boys going out for the night, so I haul myself up and head downstairs.

I open the front door to find Nate standing under the porch light.

30

"YOU KNOW, THERE'S A FINE LINE BETWEEN PERSISTENCE AND desperation," I tell Nate, who sits on the corner of my desk.

I keep a safe distance by leaning against my bedroom door. Just in case I decide this whole conversation is a bad idea and need to make a quick getaway.

Still, no amount of distance can stop me from noticing how stupidly good he looks. And he doesn't even try that hard. Showing up in a dark hooded sweatshirt and ripped jeans, his hair tousled from the ride here on his motorcycle. Slight shadow of stubble along his jaw. It's like the less men care, the sexier they look.

He nods wryly. "I'll be mindful of that."

"I meant what I said. We don't have anything to talk about. Nothing's changed."

"I broke up with Yvonne."

I meet his eyes, startled. "Okay, well, that's new."

A hint of a smile curves his lips.

"Why?" I ask, trying to play it cool.

"I wasn't in love with her."

"I'm not in love with crepes, but I've eaten more of them in the last week than I have in my entire life."

"I'm sorry?"

I have no idea why I said that. "Why now? I mean, you waited this long. What changed your mind?"

"You did."

And just like that, my heartbeat is dangerously out of control.

Nate runs a hand through his hair. "Couldn't keep seeing her while I was thinking about you. I was waiting for that feeling to go away. It didn't."

"Did you tell her why?"

Anxiety tickles my stomach. Yvonne and I are barely acquaintances, but she is Celeste's friend, and that complicates things.

"You mean did your name come up? No. I don't need to give her someone to blame. It isn't about that."

I take a breath. "Then maybe you can tell me what it is about. Because I'm having a hard time understanding."

He smiles faintly. "Why do I fancy you, you mean?"

"Yes. Feel free to be specific."

"You're making this rather difficult."

"Good. You kind of deserve it."

He does this smirking head tilt that I hate and adore in equal measure because I want to know what's happening inside his head when he does it. Desperately.

Nate goes quiet as he considers my request, eyeing me with that penetrating gaze that's excited and unnerved me since the night we first met. I half expect him to wriggle his way free of the topic. But then he surprises me.

"Because you're funny in a completely unpretentious way. You aren't impressed with yourself at all."

My teeth grab at the inside of my cheek to hide a shy smile. "That's a good start."

He begins a circuitous approach toward me. First stopping at my dresser to appraise the debris from my pockets and other knick-knacks. Then my nightstand, with my headphones and books. He inspects the contents of the document box spread on the floor.

"You're curious," he continues.

"As in strange?"

"As in inquisitive. I despise the uninterested."

The statement just further adds to my mystification that he and Yvonne ever found themselves in a conversation long enough to learn each other's names. The sex must have been amazing.

"What?" Nate asks roughly. "What are you thinking about?"

"Sex."

"Oh." He closes in on me.

"Academically." I dodge him, crossing the room to the small window bench.

"Of course."

Tired of stalking me around the room, he sits at the foot of my bed.

"Don't take that to mean I'm not interested in hearing more compliments."

He's a good sport, laughing huskily. "To be honest, I thought you were fit the first night we met."

"That's ridiculous."

My nerves go a bit haywire, losing their composure. It's like that startled feeling when you're about to fall but both feet haven't left the ground yet. On my window bench, I pull my knees up to my chest because if I don't hang on to my legs, they're going to carry me over to that bed, and then I can't be held responsible for my actions.

Nate scrutinizes me with a narrowed gaze. "It's okay to feel this."

"What does that mean?"

"It means…" He stands and strides toward me. Takes a seat beside me. "You'd rather make jokes than be present."

I swallow hard, my head a bit foggy with the slightest scent of motor oil that follows him. It's the dumbest thing but I can't get enough of it.

"Because I don't know how we do this," I confess.

I also don't have a filter where it comes to Nate. Not now anyway.

He's overwhelming. My entire body is scrambling to cope with the effects of him, both excited and terrified of where we go from here.

"Are you afraid of me?"

Yes, I almost say out loud. I'm afraid of letting myself fall for him. Of making a terrible mistake. I'm afraid of the untethered, unknowable next.

I bite my lip and say, "No. Well, maybe a little."

"Should I go?"

I shake my head. If he leaves now, I'll lose my nerve. And then spend the rest of my life wondering what would have happened if I'd worked up the courage to not overthink it. To take a leap and find out what's on the other side.

"You haven't said if I'm making an ass of myself here." Nate inspects the ink stains on my fingers from rummaging through the box of papers. He softly drags his fingertips across mine. "You've got me at a disadvantage."

I'm not sure that's true.

"Not a total ass, no," I answer, smiling.

The simmering anticipation is too much to tolerate sitting still. I get to my feet only to have Nate catch my hand. When I spin around, he captures my hips and presses me to the wall.

"Last time we were here..." he says.

"Things were a little different."

The heat in his eyes is unmistakable. So is the hard ridge straining against his zipper.

"I want you," he says roughly. "But it's your decision."

There'll be consequences, I know this. The only uncertainty is the magnitude of the fallout.

But right now, I can't bring myself to care.

Instead, I run my finger through the soft strands of hair at the nape of his neck as I pull him toward me to place my lips against his.

When we kiss, something inside me snaps open. A sort of delirious haste to grab for as much as I can get. Nate's thumbs push under my shirt to touch bare skin, and I forget everything but wanting to feel more of him. I strain into his hands, begging him to feel his way across my body. I'm not interested in a slow burn. I want to chase the high. Burn it down to the quick.

Nate breaks away just long enough to peel off his sweatshirt and toss it to the floor. I get one fleeting glimpse of his smooth muscular chest, and then his mouth is on mine again as he hikes my thigh up around his hip. He's hard between my legs. A jolt of heat sizzles through me. My hands travel the planes of his shoulders, down his back, over every ridge of lean muscle. Memorizing him.

I want him. More than I thought I could when I imagined what having him would feel like. The hunger catches me off guard, this ravaging, insatiable need to consume every exhilarating ounce of pleasure from him. When his mouth explores my neck, I'm already impatient for his lips to travel lower. A noise escapes me, urging him to satisfy the desire burrowing through me. I reach down and yank my shirt off.

Nate lifts his head. He bites his lip at the sight of me, then reaches back to unhook my bra.

I'm uneasy for a moment at being exposed, struck with that ingrained hesitation of being naked in front of someone for the first time. I try not to think about my right boob and that jerk in high school who informed me it was bigger than the left one, but the insecurity is there.

Until Nate licks his lips with lust in his heavy-lidded eyes and mumbles, "Fuck, Abbey. You're beautiful."

My self-consciousness fades with each admiring look, each whispered compliment. My fears are displaced by the heat of his palms cupping my breasts, the sensation of his thumbs brushing over my nipples.

My eyelids flutter closed, and my head falls back against the wall while he tastes one beaded nipple. Then the other.

His tongue does me in. Lights my nerves on fire. I'm hardly

aware of anything else until his hand slips into my jeans to feel how wet I am. A sound that comes from deep in his chest ripples through my body as his fingers caress me, making me unsteady on my feet.

"You're shaking," he whispers, traveling back up my neck with those dangerous lips.

"I don't think I can stand up if you keep doing that."

"Good."

He pulls his hand free to unbutton my jeans and tug them down my legs. Then he walks me back toward my bed and lays me down as he covers me with his body.

He dips his hand into my underwear and kisses me, sliding his tongue against mine while his finger presses inside me. My hips arch off the bed and I push against his hand, seeking more.

"What do you need to come?" he asks against my lips.

Rather than answer aloud, I tangle my hands in his hair and bring his head back to my breasts. He takes the hint and returns his attention to licking my nipple, tugging on it with his teeth while two fingers slide inside me. I don't want it to end. This taut, tangled anticipation. I'm half-mad and losing control, and soon my muscles clench around him and my breath catches.

I writhe beneath him as I find my release, eyelids shut tight against the waves of pulsing warmth. He kisses me deeply before I feel his jeans slip down to our feet and I open my eyes to watch him stroke himself before putting on a condom.

Nate drags his hungry gaze down my naked body. "Nice," he rasps.

"It isn't polite to stare."

He chuckles. "I'm not that polite."

As if I'd argue the point, he pushes my legs apart to sit forward and drag his erection over my wet core. I bite down hard on my lower lip, absolutely besieged by lust. He teases me, enjoying it while I wait in searing anticipation. When I'm close to chewing through my lip, he finally relents and presses forward to fill me. The sensation is a mixture of relief and a new insistent ache. He goes slow at first. Gentle. Letting me adjust to him. Then deeper, thrusting with greater intent.

I whimper.

"Good?" he murmurs, locks of hair falling onto his forehead.

"So good."

At that he throws one of my legs over his hip, withdraws slowly, then drives forward again. We kiss as I take more of him in this position. It's almost too much, my muscles contracting around him. Grabbing his back and dragging my fingertips down his warm, damp skin is all I can do to anchor myself as he thrusts.

"You have no idea how much I've wanted this," he says before kissing me again. Deep and greedy.

I spent more time than I'd like to admit imagining what sex with Nate would be like. A night like this when he would show up at my door in the middle of the night. I pictured him as slow and reserved. In all our time together, he's been guarded, always so careful not to give too much away.

Tonight, I feel like I'm meeting him again for the first time. The person he conceals inside has broken free. This Nate is passionate and in control, hungry for me and not afraid to say it.

His frantic heartbeat thumps against my chest as he moves inside me. His soft groans tickle my skin. Every inch of me is hypersensitive to the slightest touch. His lips across my collarbone. His tongue on my breasts. His fingers biting into the back of my thigh as he lifts my leg to open me further.

"I'm close," Nate mumbles into my neck. It's more a question than a statement.

Knowing I'm the one who brought him to the edge sends a thrill shooting through me. It's a powerful feeling, having a man at your mercy.

I glide my hands down his back to squeeze his butt. "What do you need to come?"

I echo his earlier words with a breathy sigh and a half smirk, eliciting another groan from him.

"Just you," he says, and then he sits back on his heels, spreading me in front of him.

It's intense and erotic the way he watches me take his dick. He pushes hair off his forehead as his thrusts become quick and deliberate, as his gaze becomes hazy and a hoarse noise passes his lips.

"Kiss me while you come," I whisper, my fingernails digging into his thigh as he fucks me harder.

With a groan of approval, he bends over to capture my mouth just as a shudder overtakes his body. He reaches his orgasm, pressed deep inside me. After a few deep exhales, he brushes one last kiss over my mouth and collapses beside me.

We lie there after he's disposed of the condom, still catching our breath. Eyes closed, I try to catalog every sensation and keep them present in my memory. Nate pulls me to rest my head on his chest while he idly drags his fingers through my tousled hair.

"Are you all right?"

His gruff voice jolts me from my thoughts. "Of course," I assure him. "Why wouldn't I be?"

"You got quiet on me. Pensive." He laughs, a bit uneasy. "Usually that means a woman is second-guessing herself and trying to figure out how to have the talk."

"The talk?"

"*What are we, what is this*, that sort of thing."

"Oh. Don't worry. I wasn't going to cross-examine you."

"Excellent. Because I don't think I can answer what this is yet. My head's barely wrapped around the fact that I'm in your bed right now. Let's see where it goes, yeah? Save the talk for another day."

I can't help but laugh. "Wow, you were really worried I was going to grill you, huh? It's fine. I don't expect any of that right now."

"Are you sure?" There's a lingering note of concern.

I rise on my elbow to grin at him. "Here, let me make it easy for you, Nate. We're not exclusive, we're not in a relationship, et cetera et cetera."

"For what it's worth, I don't sleep around," he tells me, and I believe him. "I barely have time to eat supper most days."

Which is why he liked being with Yvonne, I realize, but I don't say it out loud. I think it's true, though. Yvonne is independent, busy with school. She was happy to let him come and go as he pleased. Hell, she didn't even expect a single romantic gesture from him.

I'm not sure how long I'd be okay with an arrangement like that, but for now, Nate is right. I have no intention to rush anything, especially when my mind is still foggy from all the kisses I've shared with Jack. I think about my infuriating roommate almost as often as I think about Nate. Which is a total mindfuck.

"It's all good," I reassure him. "I'm not making any wedding scrapbooks yet. Let's check in, say, in a few weeks and see where we are then. Sound good?"

"Sounds perfect."

I lift an eyebrow. "But that means you can't turn into a jealous maniac when I'm dating up a storm, going through men like mints. Nonexclusive Abbey is dangerous."

"Uh-huh, I bet she is."

I snuggle close to him again, breathing in the faint scent of spice and exhaust.

"What do you think you'll do when your next term at uni ends?" he asks. "Go back to America?"

"I guess so. That's the plan anyway. My program is only for the year."

"Could you apply to stay?"

"Doubt it. It's a competitive program."

"Somewhere else abroad then?"

"I hadn't thought about it." I've been so preoccupied with Josephine and keeping up in my classes, I haven't looked much beyond this semester.

"Travel suits you, I reckon," he teases. "I have a hard time picturing you sitting still in Tennessee."

"It has its charms. You'd like Nashville. Ton of places to catch live music."

He lets out a breath. "I can't wait to get out of London for a while. If I spend too much time in this city, it starts to do my head in."

"If you had your way, nothing holding you back, where would you go?" I draw patterns across his chest and trace the lines of his abdomen.

"Everywhere."

I smile against his shoulder. "That's a lot of places."

"When I was a teenager, I thought it was just my shit home life, right, that made me so determined to get out. I came to the city thinking I was escaping, but then I got here and that feeling didn't go away."

"What is it, you think? Something more than wanderlust and curiosity?"

Nate thinks it over for a beat. "Fear, if I'm honest. I've always had this terror that I'll run out of time to see it all. That I'm wasting my life. Like I'm being chased."

"I get that," I admit. "It's hard not to look at my dad and think, well, shit, I'm the same age he was when he was first touring the world to sellout crowds. Shaking hands with the prime minister of Japan or whatever. He once went to a rave with Eminem after some awards show and woke up in a whole other state. I wouldn't know where to even begin on finding a rave, let alone attending one. I'm over here spending all night on the floor digging through property deeds and family letters."

"Oh, is that what that is?" Chuckling, he gestures to the paper piles strewn on the floor.

"Yeah. Ben sent over some old documents he found." A laugh pops up. "And I'm embarrassed to admit opening that box was almost as big of a turn-on as what we just did."

He snickers. "I don't know if I should feel offended."

"I said *almost*," I protest. "Seriously, though. I was beyond excited to go through these documents."

"Discovery is its own reward." He flashes a crooked grin when I look up at him with a raised eyebrow. "I might have read that under a juice cap once."

"I enjoy the research. It's exciting, in a way. But it isn't playing a concert on a glacier in Norway or trekking a volcano in Iceland."

"Can't you do both?"

"I'm not sure Indiana Jones is a real job people pay you for."

"Then what do you want to be when you grow up?"

I hesitate. I always dread this question because it seems so final once you vocalize an answer. You speak it, and it's like signing a contract in blood. A path is set, and it gets harder to deviate from it.

"I've toyed with the idea of getting my PhD. Teaching at a university maybe. But then I worry I'm giving up any chance at adventure if I burrow down in a stuffy basement office with my books. I'm still young, right? There's still time to become an astronaut. Or James Cameron."

"Can't you do both?" he challenges again.

"James Cameron in space? He's probably already bought the rights."

Nate laughs. "Adventure. Whatever that looks like to you. All I'm saying is I'd be on the road right now if I had the cash. Seems like you've got more than enough to take off anywhere you'd want to go."

"Try telling that to my dad. He still gets anxious when I ride in cars with people he doesn't know. Letting me move to London was a months-long argument, so I'm not sure telling him I want to spend three months backpacking across South America would go over well. Could put him in an early grave."

"Take some advice," Nate says, sweeping a few strands of hair off my face. "Don't spend what little time we have making everyone else happy at your own expense. You're the only one who will live with your regrets."

"Can I ask about your family?" I hedge.

He tilts his head down, questioning.

"The last time you mentioned them, you didn't want to talk about it. On the beach in Rye."

"There isn't much to say. I'm not unique by any means." Nate laces his fingers through mine, rubbing his thumb across the back of my hand. He lets out a long exhale. "Dad liked to knock me around. Just a mean old bastard who told himself he was making me tougher."

My heart clenches for him.

"Mum kept her head down and preferred to not get involved. Till one day he took a swing and I swung back. We don't talk anymore, me and him. She's always on me about not visiting, but most of the time, I'd rather swallow glass."

"I'm sorry."

"Don't be." He kisses my hair, pulling me tighter to drape my leg over his hip. "I don't pity myself. You shouldn't either. We've all got shit. Mine's not special."

I've never had this before—lying in bed with a man, talking about the real stuff. Our plans and baggage. This is what adult relationships look like, I guess. When you stop worrying about getting caught sneaking a boy in after curfew and instead muse about your lost childhoods. Sad as it sounds, it feels like growing up.

"Bollocks. I didn't mean to wreck the mood," he says. "I'm not being great company."

"Nah. I like your company."

I absently trail my fingertips down his shoulders, across his chest. When I reach his abdomen, he sucks in a jagged breath while gripping my ass. Just that small sensation reignites the warmth that pulses through my core and twists my stomach.

"Actually, I take it back. You're terrible company," I say in an impish tone. "I require cheering up. ASAP."

"I might have a few ideas about that."

Suddenly, he pulls me on top of him to straddle his hips. I feel him grow hard beneath me. The thrill of what I can do to him, how his body responds to mine, is a potent hit of adrenaline to my system.

And I'm dangerously close to developing a taste for it.

In the morning, I expect to wake alone to a text or note on my night-stand. Instead, I find Nate sprawled out across one side of my bed, his naked body a whole meal.

As much as I'd love to go there, I need to get him out of here before the whole house wakes up and this becomes a discussion. Frankly, I'm happy to put that off as long as possible.

He rouses as I peel myself out from under the covers.

"Morning," he mumbles, squinting against the sun and rubbing his eyes. It's hot and adorable at the same time, and it takes all my willpower not to jump on his dick.

"Morning. Not to be rude, but if you don't want an interrogation on your way out, you better hop to."

He flashes me a sly grin. "Are you kicking me out of bed?"

"You're cute, but yes."

On a groggy exhale, he climbs off the mattress to gather his clothes.

"To be clear, we're on speaking terms again," he says as he gets dressed, eyeing me over his shoulder. "Yes?"

"Definitely yes." I push him toward the door with a hurried kiss. "I'll text you later."

Looking endearingly dejected, he pulls on his shoes while I peek my head into the hallway to make sure the coast is clear. I don't hear anyone moving around, so I wave him on to make a dash for the stairs.

But just as he reaches the end of the hall, a creak breaks the silence. A door opens and Nate comes face-to-face with Jack.

They stop, both startled to encounter the other. Jack looks at him with confusion for a moment before his eyes slide past Nate to find me standing in my doorway. I watch as his expression morphs to understanding. His shoulders fall.

"All right, mate?" Jack says with a nod to Nate.

"All right, yeah."

Jack doesn't meet my eyes again as he goes into his bathroom and shuts the door. Nate shoots an uncertain glance back at me before he takes the stairs.

Fucking brilliant.

DECEMBER

31

For the past couple weeks, our encounters have been confined to Netflix and Nate's sofa. Which suits me fine, because Jack is still giving me the cold shoulder at home, and I have no intention of advertising my situation with Nate to the rest of the house. Better it stays uncomfortably between the three of us for now.

But tonight, after we've ordered Thai food, eaten it in bed, and then burned off the calories thanks to another bed activity, I'm finally starting to feel a little stir-crazy.

"Shall we go for a ride?" Nate suggests as he pulls a T-shirt over his bare chest. Clearly I'm not the only one with ants in my pants.

"Now?" I glance at the clock on his nightstand. It's late. 12:25 a.m. But I'm feeling energized after our naked time. "You know what? Sure."

"That's my girl."

I know he doesn't mean anything serious by that, but the words *my girl* leaving Nate's sexy mouth send a thrill skittering up my spine.

He shrugs into his jacket and shoves a black wool hat over his messy hair while I put on my coat, scarf, and gloves.

Outside Nate's three-story building, the street is teeming with Saturday night pedestrians leaving the bars and pubs, most of which stop pouring between eleven and midnight. But there's a club at the end of Nate's block that stays open till 3:00 a.m., so his neck of the woods tends to be more lively past midnight.

Nate hands me a helmet as he throws his leg over his motorcycle and starts the engine.

Climbing on the bike behind him, I lock my arms tight around his waist and brace for the frigid wind as he pulls out onto the street. With no destination in mind, we cruise the lit London streets until the colors recede and the way grows inky black. I feel like I'm in a nineties teen drama. The hour grows later and later as the motorcycle flies through the city streets. At some point, shiny condos give way to warehouses and boarded-up buildings, and as Nate slows at an approaching intersection, the faint sound of drum and bass greets my ears.

"Where's that music coming from?" I demand.

"No idea," he calls back. "Shall we find out?"

"Absolutely."

And that's how we find ourselves chasing a drumbeat, straining our ears and keeping our eyes out for the source of the music. It's two thirty in the morning, and I'm wide awake, riding on a motorcycle with my own personal British bad boy. It's surreal. Unforgettable.

At a corner with no street sign, the bass line is practically vibrating in the pavement below the bike. Or maybe that's the bike vibrating. But Nate seems to think he's found our music venue. He turns into a gravel industrial park, drives past broken windows and shipping containers, behind one of the buildings, and then the warehouse comes into view. The lot in front of it is packed with parked cars, scooters, and motorcycles.

"What is this place? A club?"

Nate shuts off the engine, then sets the bike on its kickstand. "You're in luck. I do believe we've stumbled upon a rave."

"Holy shit. Really?"

Excited, I climb off the motorcycle, removing my helmet. I give my head a vigorous shake to de-helmet my hair, until the long red strands cascade freely over my shoulders. When I'm done, I find Nate watching me with heat in his eyes.

"What?" I say.

"You've no idea how hot that was, do you?"

I feel myself blushing. Every time he looks at me, it completely does me in. Makes me feel desirable. Exposed.

"You ever been to one of these?" I ask him, trying to quell the rising sexual tension between us. We're in public, for Pete's sake.

"Not in years. Reckon I'm overdue an all-nighter at a rave. Shall we have a look?"

"Let's do it."

We walk toward the entrance of the warehouse, where a huge, beefy bouncer informs us the cover charge is twenty quid each. Nate peels some bills from his wallet, hands them over, and then we're inside, greeted by a blast of EDM and utter darkness.

I search for his hand and hold it tight, expecting something to jump out at me as we find ourselves traversing a long pitch-black tunnel. Instead, the tunnel opens to a cavernous room with projected images on the walls, floor, and low ceiling. It's a seemingly random splash of colors and images. A kaleidoscope of lights assaults my eyes as we're thrust into the belly of the warehouse amid hundreds, if not thousands, of bodies and thumping music. Lights spray over our heads and move color in all directions. I can hear the live drums, guitars, and electric violin, but I can't see the stage over the bobbing heads.

"Oh my God," I shout in Nate's ear. "This is amazing!"

His answering grin tells me the shock and awe on my face are obvious.

"Dance with me," I beg him. I shove my phone and little card wallet in the back pocket of my jeans, then unbutton my coat and grab for Nate's hand.

I don't peg Nate for the dancing type, but he indulges me. Our coats come off, tossed into some dark alcove that I hope we'll be able to find again later. We're close and sweaty and touching everywhere when we make our way into the crowd. We dance for so long I feel light-headed and deprived of oxygen.

"It suits you," he says against my hair as we dance, his hands skimming down my back and resting on my ass.

"What?"

"Freedom."

No one pays any attention when he leans in to kiss me. Deep and hungry. His fingers bite into my overheated flesh as his tongue explores my mouth. I'm breathless. Helpless to stop the lust and excitement and giddy joy that runs rampant in my blood.

I break the kiss and peer up at him.

"I wish I could suck you off right here on the dance floor," I find myself confessing.

Nashville Abbey would never have voiced such a filthy thought, but Nate's resulting groan tells me how much he likes the idea.

"Bloody hell," he growls when I reach between us and teasingly run my hand over his groin. "Don't start something we can't finish, baby."

I think it's the first time he's called me that.

And the first time I've felt like I truly hold power over a man. Not in a malevolent way but that feminine power of seduction, persuasion. The thrilling sense that I could bring him to his knees with one touch, one heated look. It's an incredible rush.

When we finally emerge into the damp early dawn, I almost don't remember who I am. It's like walking out of a dark movie theater into the blinding sun where you aren't a rebel space pilot.

"That was incredible." Leaning against his motorcycle, I pause to catch my breath.

"Didn't realize I had a little exhibitionist on my hands," he says with smoldering eyes.

"Didn't realize I had those tendencies," I answer mischievously.

"Let's go back to mine?" Nate cages me against his bike with his arms on either side of me, kissing my neck.

I beg off the suggestion. "Do you mind dropping me off at my place instead? I'm gross. I need a shower."

And I'm about ready to collapse. I don't know how my dad kept up with stuff like this for twenty years. It never occurred to me how exhausting all those exploits must have been. Guess that's why they invented cocaine.

"You can shower at my place," he says with a crooked grin. "We could shower together."

As tempting as that is, I just want to collapse into my pillows and sleep for a week. "Next time."

"Tease."

He hands me the coat I blessedly didn't lose at the rave, and we settle in for the ride home. Nothing's ever felt more refreshing than the cold morning air blowing across my skin as we make our way back to Notting Hill. This early, there are hardly any cars on the road. London is relatively quiet, shining with dew and sparkling in the sunlight. The perfect beautiful end to an extraordinary night.

Or it would have been, if not for Jack stepping out the front door when Nate drops me off at the house. He's shirtless in a pair of jogging pants and sneakers. Pauses only long enough to spot Nate at the curb over my shoulder, then puts in his earbuds, hardly acknowledging my existence before passing me to jog down the sidewalk.

"Call me later," I tell Nate, planting a quick kiss on his cheek.

"Abbey."

"Yeah?" I stop halfway up the stoop, turning to find Nate watching me with contemplative eyes.

"You're bloody fantastic."

The compliment comes out of nowhere and makes my heart skip a beat.

"Oh. Thanks." I give him a broad smile. "And thank you for tonight. I'll never forget it."

I duck into the house, still feeling myself blushing as I hurry up the stairs. After a shower, I put myself to bed tangled in knots again. As wonderful as last night was, it's not enough to distract me from the thickening tension between me and Jack. I'm not sure yet what I'm going to do about it, but I know the status quo is unsustainable.

Later, Nate calls me as promised. I'm reading at the kitchen counter when my phone lights up, so I mark my page and answer, smiling when his husky voice fills my ear.

"I've good news and bad news," he says in lieu of greeting. "Which would you like to hear first?"

"Bad, obviously."

He chuckles. "Forever the optimist."

"Or am I saving the best for last?" I counter.

"No. You're just a cynic."

"How dare you." I trace my finger along the spine of my book. It's about famous boat disasters, but so far, the information about the *Victoria* sinking has been bare bones. "All right, tell me the bad part."

"I'm off to Dublin tomorrow evening for ten days. The band booked a gig at a three-day winter festival over there, so we're making a lads' trip out of it."

"This sounds like good news," I point out.

"You won't see my dashing face for nearly two weeks. I reckon you'll be devastated."

"Hilarious. You're fucking hilarious." But I'm smiling to myself. Laid-back, jokey Nate is a rare treat. "Seriously, though, that's good news. Sucks you'll be gone for so long, but booking a festival is great."

"Pays great too. Which is the good news. Thanks to this gig, I'll be able to squeeze in a short trip to Budapest in the spring."

"Nice. And your work's okay with you taking ten days off?"

"My bandmate's wife owns the bar. One of the perks of the job."

"Ah. Lucky." I shift the phone to my other ear. "Make sure to send me a gazillion pics from Dublin. I've never been. But my dad has some pretty wild stories about hanging out with Bono at an Irish charity event they did together."

Even as I say the words, my spirits sink slightly. There I go again, living vicariously through my father.

"Yes, but has your dad ever spontaneously hunted down a rave at three in the morning and danced all night with the hottest bloke in London?"

"This new conceited side? I'm digging it, Nate. Keep it up."

But not only did he succeed in cheering me up, he also proved how well he's beginning to know me. That he understands how vital it is for Abbey Bly to live a life separate from Gunner Bly's.

His laughter tickles my ear. "I'll try. And I'll be sure to send plenty of photos from Dublin." There's a telling pause, then, "I'm going to miss you."

My heart does a somersault. "I'll miss you too."

32

THE HOUSE FEELS TOO SMALL WHEN JACK AND I AREN'T SPEAKING. Navigating becomes treacherous, especially when neither of us want Lee or Jamie to pick up on the tension. I come down from my room later that afternoon to rummage for lunch, careful to poke my head around the corner to check the kitchen is clear before I enter. All I see is Jamie sitting at the counter with a sandwich. I'm spreading mustard on bread when Jack strides in, then halts. He stands there, indecisive, for so long that Jamie looks up from his phone.

"All right, mate?"

"Huh?"

"You need something?"

"No, uh…" Jack glances around, then strides back out. "Forgot what I was looking for."

I pile turkey on my sandwich and nurture the stab of hurt that feeds my anger. For the life of me, I can't see where Jack gets off pinning any of this on me. I was just here, minding my own business, when he got it in his head to kiss me that first time. I don't accept responsibility for the consequences of his regrets, and it's unfair to lay them at my feet. I refuse to entertain his tantrums. For fuck's sake, I'm the youngest one in the house.

"Weird one, that Jackie," Jamie says. "He seem strange to you lately?"

"I really wouldn't know," I lie.

The path of least resistance is to stay in my room and avoid awkward confrontations altogether. So for the rest of the day, I busy myself with homework and scrutinizing the documents Ben left me. It does little to plug the drain of energy and emotion that saps me as the day wears on. When I can't stand these four walls anymore, I take a walk to a café a couple blocks over to grab a quick bite for dinner.

Venturing through the neighborhood alone, exploring, has become one of my favorite activities since moving here. I've grown adept at writing internal storylines for myself, imagining new personas and narrating the lives of people I observe. Today's the first time I've felt lonely while doing it.

Nate texts as I'm about to get in the shower, sending me a picture of his hotel room with the caption: Wish you were here with me. Naked, of course.

Of course, I type back, then set the phone down on the vanity, grinning to myself as I step under the hot spray.

After a long shower, I wipe the steam off the mirror and study my flushed, naked body, wondering what it is that Nate sees.

Everything about me feels average. Average weight, height, boob size, face. My best feature is probably my hair—it's long and thick, a dark shade of red that Eliza always says reminds her of autumn at night. I guess I don't mind my lips either. They're naturally red and fuller than most.

But I'm not a supermodel. I shouldn't have lords trying to kiss me. I shouldn't have Nate constantly aching for me. Hot Jacks kissing me left and right.

It sounds like I'm standing around admiring myself naked and humblebragging, but I'm genuinely bothered as I study my reflection. This is my first foray out in the wild, away from my father. I'm not experienced. I'm not worldly like Celeste or confident like Yvonne. I wish I knew how people viewed me but at the same time know I shouldn't care.

I head to my bedroom, where I dress and then get cozy under a blanket with my boat disaster book. After a few chapters, I put myself to bed early.

I'm not sure how long I've been lying in the dark with my eyes open when I hear a soft knock at my door. I know it's Jack, because I heard Lee and Jamie leaving for the pub.

"Yeah?"

A splinter of light from the hallway moves across my wall.

"Hey, sorry." A shirtless Jack wearing only his pajama pants pokes his head in. "I didn't realize you were asleep."

Bitterness stings my cheeks. "I'm not."

"I can leave."

"It's fine."

"Can we have a chat?"

Whether it's the regretful pitch of his voice or the exhaustion of keeping up the silent treatment, I don't have it in me to send him off. I'm too tired to fight him anymore.

"Come in," I tell him.

He's hesitant as he enters. Then he stands in the middle of the room waiting on me to decide how we do this. The room's got a chill to it because Lee is militant about the boiler temperature, so I don't particularly want to get out of my warm bed. Finally, I scoot to one side and pat the space beside me.

Jack takes up most of the bed, the mattress dipping toward him. Other than the diffused moonlight that slants across the floor, the room is black. We both lie on our backs, me under the covers, him on top of them. I pick at the buttons of the duvet cover, waiting for him to speak and listening to the soft groans and various ticks the house makes when we're still.

"I wanted to apologize," he finally says. "I've been, ah, avoiding you."

"Oh my God, really?"

"I take it you've noticed." Jack pauses. "You do my head in, if I'm honest," he confesses with a smile in his voice.

"Don't even start."

"What I mean is I don't think my mind's been right since you got here."

"Sure it hasn't been longer than that?" I'm only half joking. Jack's been a confounding enigma from the start. If there's any rhyme or reason in his behavior, that math is beyond me.

He nudges me with his elbow. "I'm trying to be serious."

"Right, okay. Serious." He can't see me, but I put on a stern face. "Okay, go."

"I've had a thing for you since the day we met."

"Have you been drinking?"

"Abbey."

"Just checking."

He exhales loudly. "I deserve that."

Yes. He does.

"I mean it, though. I wanted you the moment I met you."

"You mean the moment you found me in the kitchen my first morning here, looking like a deer in headlights?"

"Yes," he says simply. "You didn't feel it?"

I bite my lip. Because I did feel it. The attraction was there from the get-go. Potent. Alive. It was the same way with Nate.

"I felt it." *I still do*, I almost confess. "But I'm not playing these games with you anymore."

"I'm not trying to play games, Abbs. Thing is I'm not good at this. I know how to get women into bed. I know how to fuck them."

"No, you're doing amazing, sweetie."

He coughs out a sharp laugh. "I mean, it's all the other stuff. The intimacy part. Talking about feelings and the—"

"Serious stuff."

"Right. I'm shit at that part. Nothing comes out right." He throws his arms behind his head. "Guess it scares me a little too. Caring enough to mess it up. I don't know how to open up to people like that. I'm not quite sure how else to explain it."

"I think I understand."

I've seen how dejected he gets watching his favorite teams lose a rugby match on TV. How he spends half the game pacing the kitchen because he wants to know what's happening but can't bear to witness it. Too invested in the outcome. It makes him anxious.

"We're all afraid of getting hurt," I add. "Of not being good enough. If this stuff were easy, there wouldn't be reality dating shows, right?"

"True," he says, rolling over to face me.

This kind of vulnerability from Jack does a lot to break down the wall of hostility that's built up between us. It's hard to hold a grudge when he's enduring such obvious discomfort to let me understand him better. A little effort goes a long way with me. I don't expect perfection, just honesty. In fact, far above abs, good hair, and nice eyes, it's the most attractive quality in a guy. Someone who knows who he is and is honest with himself and me. It's something I could work on too, if I'm being fair.

"I'm jealous, all right?" Jack suddenly says, his features straining. He sounds tortured. "The idea of him touching you…fucking you… it's making me bloody mental."

My pulse takes off. "Oh."

"I meant what I said when I took you driving—I don't want to lose you as a friend." He curses under his breath. "But I also can't keep pretending I'm all right with just friendship. That I don't want more."

I suck in a breath. "Do you? Want more?"

After a long moment, he nods.

"Oh. Okay. Wow."

I never thought I'd ever hear these words from Jack. He's been so skilled at keeping me at an emotional distance that now that he's baring his soul to me, my brain can't quite comprehend it.

"So where does that leave us?" he asks.

I see only the vague outline of his face, though I feel the warmth of his body beside mine. The instinct to be closer to him, to touch him, tugs at me.

"Well, I don't think we're fighting anymore," I say.

"Should I let you go back to sleep?" His voice is husky.

My heart beats even faster. "I'll never be able to fall asleep now."

"Should I stay then?"

The darkness makes me bold. I reach out for him, lightly stroking the stubble along his jaw. "Yes. If you want to."

"I want to."

There's a moment of silent deliberation between us. So loud it makes my ears ring. I want him to kiss me. I would take the lead, but I'm afraid he'll push me away again.

Then Jack lifts the side of the duvet and slides beneath it. He takes hold of my waist and pulls me closer.

"We'll get this right eventually," he says gruffly.

I'm not sure which part he's referring to until his hand slides down to cup the back of my knee and hitch my leg over his hip. He threads his fingers through my hair, bringing my face closer. His nose grazes mine. Then his forehead. Searching for each other in the shadows, until finally our lips touch. The gentle warmth seeps through my limbs and burns in my blood, his tongue coaxing me to forget any lingering apprehensions.

Consequences are for daylight.

The kiss is gentle at first. Tentative. But it doesn't stay that way for long. I grab the back of his neck, softly dragging my nails over him. Jack skims his hand up my thigh and palms my ass, pressing me against him. I feel his erection between my legs. The sensation spurs a rush of unchecked desire, urging me to grind against him, which elicits a muffled groan that tickles my lips. His fingers bite into my flesh.

"Want you so damn bad," he whispers before burying his face in my neck, kissing my heated flesh. His lips leave flames of need in their wake. I'm on fire.

"Touch me," I whisper back, hearing the pleading note in my voice. I'm desperate to feel more of him, to ease this ache that's stalked me for months.

Jack slips a hand under my T-shirt to squeeze my breast and run his thumb over my nipple. My teeth scrape his bottom lip as we kiss again. His hands are big and rough and make me feel delicate, almost breakable, under their exploration. His muscles tug and tighten as I trace their lines, wanting to know more of him.

He pushes my shirt up, and I sit so he can pull it over my head. Instantly, he fills both palms with my breasts and hums in approval.

"They're perfect," he says solemnly. "Even the much bigger one."

A laugh chokes out. "Asshole."

With a laugh, he squeezes gently, his thumbs sweeping over my nipples. "You've nothing to worry about. Your tits are bloody mind-blowing. Perfection."

Then he lowers his mouth to one breast and sucks the peaked tip, eliciting a jolt of pleasure that sizzles from my nipple to my clit. God, he's good at that. His palm travels my stomach, my ribs, setting every nerve humming, until he slides his fingers between my thighs.

"I want to make you come," he says, his voice thick.

My answer is a soft sigh that transforms into a choked moan when Jack's hand dips inside my underwear. A shudder travels down my spine at the sweet sensation of him cupping my core, then swiping his thumb over my clit. He massages me for a moment before penetrating me with first one, then a second finger.

"Perfect," he whispers again, and I see his eyes gleaming in the darkness. "Knew you'd feel like this."

I bite my lip. "Like what?"

"Tight." He withdraws both fingers. "Soft." He pushes them back in, making me gasp. "Wet."

He's driving me wild. I lie on my back with Jack hovering above me, kissing my lips, my neck, licking at my exposed breasts while he fingers me. I hold my breath and cling to his shoulders to ground myself.

Teetering on the edge of collapse, I writhe against his hand. He feels so good, but I'm greedy. I need more. His dick is hard against my thigh, and it's...large. I knew he'd be big, but the proof of it, that long, thick ridge, makes my core throb. I want him inside me.

When I reach to pull down his pants, he stops my hand. I search for his eyes in the dark, but instead of an answer, I feel him remove his hand and pull me half on top of him.

Jack's the one on his back now, gently tugging my body up until I feel his stiff erection flush with my core. He guides my hips, thrusting up against me. The fact that we're still clothed is both torturous and exhilarating. He could strip me down if he wanted to, but he's choosing to tease us, to take it slow.

The friction is intense. It continues to stoke the building tension. Jack's breathing becomes haggard as I slide back and forth, reaching for relief, feeling him throb beneath me. His fingers dig into my hips. His face is buried at my neck, tongue tasting my overheated skin.

"I'm almost there." My voice comes out in a breathy desperate rush as I lose my rhythm and my muscles tighten.

"Really?" I hear the satisfied smile in his voice. "That was fast."

"Are you complaining?"

"No, just didn't realize I was this good."

"Cocky jerk."

I lightly punch him on the shoulder, but he retaliates by thrusting upward so his dick grinds my clit. I gasp with pleasure.

"Oh my God. More," I beg.

Chuckling, he flips me on my back and positions himself between my legs, covering my body. We kiss, our tongues tangling, as he brings me to orgasm. Panting and sated.

"Ah *fuck*," he suddenly chokes out. His hips move faster, and now I feel him shaking against me. "I'm gonna come."

He sounds almost startled by that, and even as the aftershocks of orgasm continue to tremble through me, I wrap my legs around his waist to keep our lower bodies locked.

Jack groans as he finds release, his face in the crook of my neck, his broad body shuddering for several moments before going still.

We lie there, catching our breath. My heart is pounding.

"That hasn't happened to me since I was fourteen years old," Jack says with a weak laugh. He doesn't sound embarrassed, though. Only sated.

"You must really like me then."

It's meant as a joke, but his response is emphatic, loaded with intensity. "I think I do."

He kisses my cheek, my temple. Draws his fingers across my forehead to brush away the sweaty strands. He tells me he'll be right back and leaves to clean himself up, then tiptoes in minutes later to slip back under the covers and pull me into his embrace.

As his muscular arms wrap around me, the implications of what we've done rush through my brain. What does tonight represent for us? With our recent history, I'm not about to assume his intentions.

And what do I do about Nate now? After our first time, Nate went out of his way to make sure I knew we weren't officially together. And since I'd place us firmly in the situationship category, I feel only the barest amount of guilt as I lie here in Jack's arms. It's mostly confusion, not guilt, that's muddling my brain.

"So what now?" he asks as if reading my mind.

"I'm not sure," I say softly. "But what I do know is you can't shut down anymore whenever it starts to feel serious or overwhelming or uncomfortable. We're friends first, right?"

"Right."

"That means you have to make an effort to talk to me." I twist my head to offer a teasing smile. "Use your words, okay?"

"I will," he promises.

"Good. Now, what about me?"

"What about you?"

"It's a two-way street. What can I do better? Other than not forgetting to do the dishes and the shopping."

Jack chuckles. "There's nothing to do better. I like everything about you."

"Come on. Pick a complaint. Give me something to work on."

He pauses. "I don't know… Patience, maybe?"

As someone capable of sitting in a library for eight hours straight without so much as a pee break, I think patience is a skill I've nearly mastered. But I wait for him to elaborate.

"Don't write me off if I can't say the right thing at the right moment. I won't shut down, but give me more than five seconds to collect my thoughts, ay?"

"Deal."

"Anything else we need to discuss?" Jack teases.

"Yes, actually." As awkward as it is, I force myself to bring it up. "I'm not going to stop seeing Nate."

He pauses again, then says, "Okay."

"Really?"

"I've pushed you away too many times. Of course you don't trust me yet. You don't trust this." He tightens his arms around me. "Reckon I've my work cut out for me. I'm up to task, though."

I smile in the darkness. I think I like this new, candid Jack.

A lot.

33

I HAVEN'T FELT MY OWN BUTT CHEEKS SINCE HALFTIME AS I SIT IN the stands clinging to a cup of hot coffee. After nearly an hour, I'm still not sure I understand any more about rugby than I did when I sat down. With that said, I do enjoy watching Jack run around throwing guys to the ground. Something about hearing the other team's groans of agony every time he muscles their faces into the dirt gets me kind of excited. I didn't know I could like sports so much.

So far, I've gathered that rugby is an amalgamation of soccer and football rules. Although every time I think I've gotten the gist of the game, some guy goes off and does something ridiculous like kicking the ball through the uprights in the middle of play or puts a guy on his shoulders to snatch a ball out of the air, and I'm entirely lost again. There have been almost a dozen offside calls in this match, and for the life of me, I still can't discern what that is. To me, it still looks like a bunch of beefy dudes running around in a free-for-all.

Fortunately, Jack's team is winning. He has a tendency to be a grump otherwise.

After last night's illicit activities, Jack was up early this morning, as usual. Which is probably for the best—it would have caused the house to activate DEFCON 1 if he'd been spotted creeping out of my room. The only thing that could've given us away to Lee or Jamie occurred during breakfast, when Jack was eager that I catch his game today. But I'd been promising to attend a game for months now and had rescheduled numerous times, so other than a smirk from Lee, I don't think any suspicions were raised.

It's fascinating to witness this other side of Jack. The feral, violent side. It's easy to see why every time the opposing team picks up the ball, they run anywhere but toward Jack. He's got the eyes of a carnivorous animal. Ready to chew throats and snap bones. Even among other rugby players, he's a big guy. He has at least ten pounds and three inches on most of them.

He's got a generous amount of inches other places too...

Head out of the gutter, Abbey.

Right. The occasional X-rated flash of memory from last night tickles my mind, and I adjust in my seat and wash it back down with another scalding sip of coffee.

In the dying seconds of the game, Jack's team wrestles the ball out of a dogpile of bodies and charges up the field, passing the ball backward to one player, then the next as they run forward. One guy is about to be tackled when he launches the ball into the air, and it happens to fall to Jack, who tucks it to his chest and bashes through one tackle and another, never leaving his feet. He's surprisingly fast for such a tall guy and manages to stay just out of reach of the last blockers as he dives forward to score.

I shoot up from my seat, spilling coffee as I scream his name. He hops to his feet, covered in mud. His teammates pile on him in celebration.

After the game, I hang out in the stands near the benches until Jack returns from the changing room to find me. He looks like a different person after a shower and a change of clothes. All fresh and new and devastatingly handsome with the glow of exertion.

"How was that?" he drawls, leaning against the cement barrier wall that divides the bleachers from the field.

"Not bad." I give him a coy shrug. "That bit at the end there was cool."

An unabashed grin colors his expression. "Yeah, you liked that?"

"It was okay."

"See me tackle that bloke to the ground?"

"I did. He looked quite put out."

"Bloody right."

Jack picks me up and lifts me over the wall to set me on the grass. There's a ball sitting beside the player bench.

Grinning, he picks it up and tosses it at me. "How 'bout we have a go?"

"Trust me. You don't want any of this." I juggle the ball, goading him with my eyes.

He stalks me toward the field. "Oh, you think you're dangerous?"

"Bet your ass."

"Shall I teach the rules before you go pro?"

"What's so complicated about hitting people and running with the ball?"

He cocks his head at me, stopping at the edge of the field. "What's this line called?"

"The sideline."

"The touchline. And when you put the ball down in that box down there?" he says, referring to the space drawn like a football end zone.

"A touchdown?"

"A try."

"Score or score not," I correct, tossing the ball to him. "There is no try."

"Here." He walks me to a hash mark on the field and hands me the ball back. "Give it a go."

"Go at what?"

Jack nods at the uprights. "Go on. Have a penalty kick."

I snort. "Easy."

Of course, I have no idea what I'm doing, but I line up my shot the way I watched the guys do in the game. I hold the ball out and take my best swing at it. I barely graze the thing, and Jack has to catch me from falling on my ass.

He busts out laughing. "Your form could use some work."

Despite my first attempt, he takes the time to teach me about the rules and terminology as we toss the ball around. He'd make a good coach actually, with his patience to explain things in terms I understand. And he's a good sport while he takes my occasional ribbing.

"All right, let's have it." He puts the ball on the ground between us. "All you've got to do is grab it before I do."

"And then what?"

"If you manage to be quicker than me?" A devilish smirk meets my question, and he gets in a sort of football stance over the ball. "Well, you could try kicking it through the goalposts again. Though I wouldn't recommend it."

"Watch it, Jackie boy."

"You can run it, or you can kick it into touch, as long as it hits the ground at least once first."

I crouch over the ball to mimic his stance. "Get ready to eat my dust."

"I'm not going to go easy on you," he warns. "Hope you can get grass stains out of that jacket."

We square up. I let Jack count us down. Then when he opens his mouth to say, "*One*," I snatch the ball first and dart past him before he realizes what's happened.

His hands make a glancing swipe at my coattails, but I'm already gone, sprinting as fast as my feet will carry me. The distance to the try line is much farther away than it looked a moment ago. My lungs are burning in the frigid air as I chance a look over my shoulder— just as Jack wraps a muscular arm around my waist and tackles me to the ground.

I land with a thud, and the ball pops out of my hands.

"You lousy cheat," he growls, marveling at me.

"If you're not cheating, you're not trying," I cough out.

"I can't believe it. I don't even know who you are anymore."

"I'm not the real Abbey." I prop myself up on my elbows to catch my breath. "I'm her evil twin. I stuffed her in a suitcase and shoved her in the back of the closet."

"Actually, that'd explain a lot."

I shove at his shoulder, but he pins me back to the ground and leans in, pressing his lips to mine. His tongue pushes past the seams of my lips, and the next thing I know, he's kissing me senseless. I forget myself and tangle my hands in his hair, wrapping my legs around him.

"I really like this Jack," I say between hungry kisses. "You know, the one who wants me so bad he devours me on the rugby pitch."

"Already told you—I've wanted to devour you from day one." Jack's face hovers over mine. He chuckles. "I thought it was obvious how much I fancied you."

"Honestly, no. I mean, sure, you kissed me twice, but you also ran away screaming both times."

"I did not scream."

"Still ran, though."

"But I came to my senses, didn't I? And I did fancy you." His lips caress mine before he lifts his head, offering a sheepish smile. "You said you didn't like it when I was acting overprotective, but being protective is a sign I care. Like when my mate was pawing you at the party and I broke it up?"

"Ha! I knew you interrupted us out of jealousy."

"Wasn't only jealousy. Sam's got a rep for rooting and running."

"Rooting?"

"Fucking," he clarifies.

"Oh my God. Stop being so Australian and speak English!" I grin up at him. "Okay. So you were protecting me from Sam. And Nate, apparently. Isn't that right, Mr. *If you're going to be out all day, call your flatmates*? Then there was Ben Tulley... Am I missing anyone?"

"I just don't want to see you get hurt. Whether it's your heart"—he lightly touches my chest, and a hot shiver rolls through me—"or, you know, getting yourself killed by driving on the wrong side of the road."

"The right side," I correct.

But I'm smiling. I reach up and touch his cheek, sweeping my fingers along the stubble dotting his jawline.

"I like how you care," I say shyly.

A screech suddenly tears through the stadium.

"You can't be here," a voice chides over the loudspeaker. "Hurry it up, you two."

Jack shoots a middle finger over his shoulder as his mouth brushes mine in another kiss.

"You rebel," I tease against his lips.

After one last peck, he quickly lifts me to my feet. "Not really. In fact, we better get the hell out of here. Coach'll have my head."

We make a run for it, sprinting out through the player tunnel like the cops are chasing us.

———————

An hour later, we're at a pub with Jack's teammates to celebrate their win, but I beg off early because I have a bunch of course readings I need to get off my plate. Besides, the rugby boys are noisier than a marching band and a bit much when they're drunk. So I leave him with his friends and slide into an Uber.

Halfway to Notting Hill, I get a text from Nate.

Despite having spent the entire day with Jack, my heart still skips a beat seeing Nate's name on my phone. Knowing he's thinking about me.

> Nate: Popped into the library at Trinity
> College today to photograph it for you. The
> boys thought I'd gone mad.

Several pictures pop up in succession, each one making me drool. Oh sweet Lord. This library. It's perfection. Heaven. I actually feel a tingling between my legs.

> Me: I have never been more turned on in my life.

Nate: Yeah? Hold on. I got more.

Three more pics appear. One is a close-up of a page from the Book of Kells. The other two are panoramic shots of the Long Room.

> Me: Stop. Please. I'm in an Uber and I don't think he'll appreciate me moaning out loud.

Nate: Getting you that hot, yeah? One sec.
Got another for you.

When the next image appears, I give a sharp intake of breath. Which draws the attention of my driver.

"All right back there?"

"Fine," I reply through the mound of cotton now stuffed in my mouth.

I can scarcely breathe. Nate just sent a picture of his long bassist fingers curled around the very obvious bulge in his faded jeans.

> Me: OMG. That's a dick pic!

Nate: Nah. It's dick pic adjacent. At best.

Nate: You're welcome.

> Me: Cheeky boy.

> Nate: Gotta go. Sound check in 20 minutes.

> Me: Break a leg at the show later.

Biting my lip, I set my phone on the seat beside me. It occurs to me that I went from making out with Jack on the rugby field to flirting with Nate via text in the span of two hours.

This is…not good.

I never understood how some girls could date more than one guy at once. But now…I think I get it.

Jack and Nate are so different, yet they each complement me completely. Jack's become one of my best friends. He makes me laugh and we have fun doing even ordinary, mundane things together. With Jack, everything is easy. But Nate… Nate draws a raw passion out of me I've never experienced with anyone else. He's spontaneous and unencumbered and possesses a sense of adventure that calls to that same instinct in me.

But I can't be with both of them.

Right?

Come on, Abbey.

Okay, fine. I can't have them both. Eventually I'll need to make a choice.

The problem is I genuinely don't know who I'd pick.

34

With only a couple weeks left in the semester before holiday break, I've become a near permanent resident in the library. My Tulley research project isn't due until the end of spring term, so that's resting on the back burner for now, a fact that's caused me to dodge various invitations to meet up with Ben Tulley, who's apparently back from Ibiza. Between writing essays and studying for exams, I can't squeeze a single extraneous distraction into my schedule. Well, except for Jack, who's been proving to be the best kind of distraction.

At first, our hookups were this little secret we carried around the house, acknowledged in winks and lingering glances. But then, when we weren't found out, we started to test the boundaries of what we could get away with. Sneaking off to make out while Lee and Jamie sit unaware in the next room. Stealing a kiss or two when no one else is home. Quietly fooling around in my room after everyone's gone to bed.

We're still treading well clear of that hard red line, never going past third base. Somehow, without speaking about it, we both seem to understand that actually having sex would irreparably change the dynamic. If we take that next step and it ends badly, there'd be no way we would both stay under the same roof. I know I couldn't stand it.

And as much as I enjoy cavorting like bandits around the house, there's still a persistent voice that tells me I need to figure out what I want. Sooner rather than later. Even though Jack knows about Nate, and Nate doesn't want to be exclusive, it isn't fair to anyone involved to try playing the neutral party between two guys. Least of all myself. I don't have it in me to protect my heart, the longer I let myself entertain the possibilities with both Nate and Jack.

After the holidays. By then, I'll have had time to clear my head and get some perspective.

And *then* I'll decide.

"After the holidays," I assure myself.

"And what shall be transpiring after the holidays?" comes Mr. Baxley's crisp not-interested-but-totally-absolutely-interested voice.

I grin as the bespectacled man settles across from me at my study table.

This has become our routine, reluctant as he likes to appear. I come in at my usual time to my usual table, spread out my study materials, and send him a wave. For a few minutes, he grumpily ignores me. Then he eventually gets up for his tea break and strolls up to my table to glance at my work on his way back with a steaming mug. He'll brusquely ask about my Tulley research (or some such thing as a pretext to start a conversation), and I will happily update him until it inevitably turns into a recitation of my recent love life dramas.

Despite the disinterest he portrays behind his flat expression and smudged glasses, he stands and listens. Sometimes sits. But he never walks away.

Once or twice, I've extracted a personal detail or two from the man, and I've learned that he's single and lives alone. Well, not entirely alone. He had a cat who died last week, a detail I managed to pry out of him after noticing he'd looked particularly distressed.

"I'll choose between Nate and Jack," I clarify. "Just pick one and date him. *Only* him." A groan lodges in my throat. "Who do you think I should pick?"

Mr. Baxley sips his tea. "I cannot provide that answer for you, Ms. Bly."

"Coward."

He arches a brow. "Oh, I've no doubt in my mind as to which gentleman you will select."

"Wait, really? You know who I'm going to choose?"

"Of course. It's quite obvious." His expression is mildly smug as he takes another sip.

"Oh my God. Tell me," I order.

"Absolutely not. I feel a duty not to become involved in the love quarrels of university girls."

My jaw falls open. "You traitor. I thought we were best friends. Oh, hey, I forgot—I promised you a picture of Hugh."

I scroll through my photo album until I find a shot where our cat doesn't look satanic and slide the phone across the table. Adjusting his glasses on the bridge of his nose, Mr. Baxley peers at the screen and nods in approval.

"Very handsome feline. That coat is marvelous."

"It's a pain in the ass is what it is. He sheds like crazy, which has Lee furiously vacuuming the house twice a day. I try to tell him it's hopeless, but he's determined to beat back the encroachment."

"It helps if you brush them," Mr. Baxley says, admiring the photo.

"I'm probably the only one who could get close enough. Hugh tolerates me okay, but he's declared open war on the rest of the house. Lee's entirely abandoned him at this point. Threatened to toss him on the street the other day when he stepped in one of Hugh's cold hair balls he'd coughed up overnight."

"The brushing will help with that too," Mr. Baxley informs me, regaining his aura of superiority. "They make certain food and treats that can decrease hair balls. It's important he get sufficient moisture content in his food as well as fresh water."

And then, as I sit there agape, he proceeds to share a plethora of cat-rearing resources with me, going on about general cat maintenance and using more words than I've heard him speak all semester.

It appears I've found Mr. Baxley's true passion.

After the library, I swing by the pub to grab a drink with Celeste for happy hour. It's a big crowd for a weekday, but we manage to snag a couple stools at the corner of the bar and order some chardonnay.

"I'm knackered," she says, slumping against the bar. "Last night, I was up till four in the morning reading for a two-hundred question exam only to realize I read the wrong book." She takes a swig of wine and wipes her mouth. "Please, Abbey. If you value our friendship, stab me through the eye with the stem of this glass."

I hoot out a laugh. Celeste is clearly at her wit's end, her untouchable composure long since abandoned. It's a condition we're all suffering from with the semester coming to an end.

"You're brilliant," I remind her. I don't think she's seen less than ninety percent on an assignment since coloring inside the lines and writing her own name. "Chin up. It's almost over."

She takes another big gulp and waves for the bartender to top her up. "I'll remember you abandoned me in my time of need."

"Speaking of which, we're getting everyone together for a small dinner at the house on Friday before we all scatter for the holidays. Nothing fancy. Just some takeout and drinks."

She pouts. "Are you truly going back to America for the whole winter break?"

"Yup."

"Come back early. You can spend a few days with me and Lee at our parents'. They'd love to meet you."

"I would, but my dad is really looking forward to having me home."

I'm excited to be home too. This is the longest Dad and I have spent apart since I was little. I'd been in such a rush to get out on my own, it didn't occur to me I'd reach the point when watching football and cheesy holiday movies on the couch together is my idea of a perfect evening.

Besides, putting an ocean between myself and Nate and Jack is the best recipe I have for getting some perspective on everything.

I'm too close to the situation. To them. I'm too addicted to Nate's adventurous, mysterious ways and Jack's cocky grins and rampant sex appeal. And I feel guilty for being addicted to them both.

To make matters worse (or better, whichever way you want to look at it), I don't know if this is solely about sex anymore. With either of them. Nate's still in Dublin, but we text frequently throughout the day, exchanging more than just flirtatious words and pictures.

And Jack is being extra affectionate. Stealing me away for clandestine kisses at every opportunity. Watching TV with me even when I know he hates my shows. It's sweet and demonstrates effort on his part.

To show some reciprocation, I decide to cook dinner for the flat when I get home from meeting Celeste. Well, I reheat some takeout and make a salad. But still. It's the thought that counts.

"Is this when you tell me you've been joyriding in my car and tore the mirror off?" Jamie inquires during dinner, swirling his third glass of wine.

"Would this get me off the hook if I did?" I ask sweetly.

"Certainly not."

"Then no, that mirror's always looked like that."

"I can't get over these cucumbers." Lee holds up a piece out of his salad. "It's like each one is its own little adventure into avant-garde."

"Hey." I point my butter knife at him. "When you're making dinner, you can cut your veggies any way you like. Besides, they're mostly all the same shape."

"That is not a shape known to science. Did you have to wrestle it out of the cat's mouth?"

Jack all but licks his plate clean and sits back with his arms resting on his abdomen. "You aren't about to tell us you're dying, right?"

"Afraid not. I'll be back to leaving dishes in the sink for a long time to come." I glance at Lee. "How come you didn't invite Eric? I told you he was welcome to join us."

Lee is aghast. "And have him lay eyes on the demon cat? He'll take one look at him and know he's not a show cat."

"Is that why you never bring him over? You're ashamed of our cat?"

"I, personally, loathe our cat," Jamie says glumly.

Jack nods. "Don't we all, mate."

"I like him," I argue.

And so begins probably the hundredth discussion we've had regarding Hugh. Although the orange demon truly has grown on me, I don't know if this living arrangement is sustainable. Poor Jamie has even reduced his nightly conquests to biweekly romps due to Hugh scratching outside his door every time he's trying to have sex.

Luckily, Hugh seems to have respect for the other sexy things happening in the flat. Jack has snuck into my bedroom almost every night this week, and Hugh hasn't made a single sound, thank God.

Around eleven thirty, I get a text.

Jack: Is the coast clear?

Me: Yes, but stay where you are. I'm coming to you.

Tonight, I'm switching things up. I rise from the bed and try not to jostle Hugh, who slits one eye open, then goes back to sleep at the foot of my mattress. A minute later, I'm skulking like a thief in the night toward Jack's room.

"Plot twist," he whispers when I crawl into his bed after closing and locking the door. "To what do I owe this honor?"

"Hugh's snoring."

Laughing, Jack slides his fingers through my hair and tugs my head toward him so he can kiss me. The moment our lips touch, he makes a low, tortured sound.

"What's wrong?" I whisper.

"I miss kissing you."

"You've kissed me, like, a dozen times already today," I remind him, biting my lip to keep from laughing.

"I know. I'm saying I miss kissing you when I'm not kissing you."

"By that logic, you'd have to be kissing me twenty-four seven in order to never miss it."

His warm breath tickles my lips. "Oh no, having your tongue in my mouth all day and night? The horror."

Our mouths collide again, and I can't deny he has a point—I much prefer it when his tongue is touching mine than when it's not.

In no time at all, our kisses go from sweet and lazy to breathless and greedy. When Jack tries to slip his hand between my thighs, I swat him away.

"What, I'm not allowed to touch you?" He narrows his eyes in outrage.

"I'm on a lady hiatus," I confess. "It started this morning."

I expect to see disappointment on his face, but all he does is kiss me again. "All good. Gives me more time to impress you with my make-out skills." His lips brush mine. "What do you think? Five gold stars or six?"

"Out of ten?"

"Out of five," he growls.

"Oh, in that case…" I pretend to think it over, which earns me the nip of his teeth on the side of my throat. "So violent," I chide. "Know what that means?"

He rolls onto his back, smiling. "What does that mean?" he prompts, playing along.

"It means you have to lie there and not make a single sound while I dispense your punishment."

"Punishment?" he echoes with a snort. "Abbey, luv, we both know you've not a single menacing bone in your—"

He curses wildly when I cup his package over his sweatpants.

I smirk at him. "What part of *don't make a single sound* didn't you understand?"

Before he can answer, I tug his pants down, swallowing a moan when his erection springs up. He's always so ready for me. Hard and eager. And my body always responds to it, heat pooling between my legs, inner muscles tightening with the need to clamp around him.

While Jack watches me through hooded eyes, I crawl my way down his long, toned body and curl my hand around his thick shaft.

"Still waiting for that punishment," he taunts.

"Making you wait is part of the torture."

I give him a firm squeeze, and he jerks on the bed.

Grinning, I lower my head and curl my tongue around his tip. This time, his answering jerk is accompanied by a strangled expletive.

I look up and find him eyeing me with anticipation. His broad chest rises on a ragged inhale.

"You okay?" I flick up an eyebrow.

"I will be once you stop teasing."

"Oh, Jack, *luv*. I'm definitely not going to stop teasing."

I keep my word, proceeding to torment him with long, languid licks and too-short sucks that soon have him squirming in agony. Each time I look up, more beads of sweat dot his forehead. His facial muscles grow more taut, as if it's a physical struggle to maintain his control. And each time I release his hard length, he thrusts his hips, desperately seeking my mouth.

"Ask me nicely," I mumble as I swirl my tongue.

"Ask you what?" he croaks out.

"To make you come."

I tighten the suction of my lips and bring him nearly halfway down my throat.

"Holy bloody Christ." His hips snap up again. "Goddamn fucking *hell*. Why are you so fucking good at that?"

I have no idea. I didn't think I was anything special. But reducing Jack to a panting, cursing, shaking mess says otherwise.

"Make me come," he pleads hoarsely, one hand moving down to cup my head. His fingers thread through my hair. "Please."

I can barely contain the smile threatening to crack my face in half. I decide to have mercy on him. I give him what he wants, working him with my lips, tongue, and fist until he's cursing again.

"I'm coming," he groans.

His thrusts become erratic as he spills into my mouth and—

A knock raps on the door.

"Jackie, darling, you all right in there?"

35

JACK AND I FREEZE AT THE SOUND OF LEE'S VOICE.

Well, as much as we *can* freeze with Jack still shuddering from release and my mouth still working him.

"Fine," Jack grunts at the locked door. "I'm all good, mate—" He groans again. My attempt to release him causes him to push his dick back in. "Don't stop," he whispers. "Suck it dry."

Oh my God.

If I'd known earlier how deliciously dirty Jack was, I would have tried to get him naked much sooner.

My heart is pounding as I continue to stroke and suck him through his orgasm.

"Babe…" Behind the door, Lee's muffled voice takes on a note of amusement. "Are we having a wank?"

"Something like that," Jack growls, his body finally going still.

When I peer up, I see the haze of satisfaction darkening his blue eyes.

There's a pause, followed by a gasp.

"Do you have a bird in there? Oh my God!"

"Pipe down," Jack chastises our roommate while one corner of his mouth lifts in a grin. "Abbey's asleep down the hall."

I smother a wave of laughter and rest my cheek against Jack's rock-hard thigh. His fingers are still in my hair, stroking gently.

"I expect details tomorrow morning," Lee orders. "Understood?"

"Go away, mate," Jack says instead, his voice firm.

Once Lee's footsteps retreat, I sit up and demurely wipe my mouth. "You're going to be interrogated tomorrow," I warn Jack. "Like, waterboarding levels of grilling."

"Worth it." He tugs me toward him to plant a kiss on my cheek.

I nestle closer, reaching for the soft fleece throw at the foot of his bed. I pull it over us and rest my head on his shoulder.

"Wish you could spend the night in my bed," he says.

"Lee wakes me up with a cup of coffee every morning. He'll legit call the cops if he finds my bed made and me missing."

"At least stay till I fall asleep then?"

My heart melts against my rib cage. He keeps lowering his guard around me and it's…exhilarating. It's a weird thing, Jack's inner defense system. It's not the same as Nate's guarded nature, which is a result of Nate not trusting other people. Jack doesn't trust *himself*. I'm not sure why that is, but it's becoming clearer the more time we spend together.

The mattress suddenly vibrates, tickling my leg, and I reach down to find the source.

"It's your phone. Here," I say, passing it to him.

Jack checks the notification and there's no mistaking the way his entire body tenses.

"Everything okay?" I ask.

"All good." With a quick motion, he swipes the notification away. "Just an email."

Something about his vague answer raises my own guard. "Who's emailing so late?"

Jack leans over to set his phone on the nightstand, then wraps his arm around me again. "Mate from school. He's a night owl."

It doesn't sound like a lie, but it also kind of does. I decide not to push, because at the end of the day, it isn't really my business. We're not exclusive, and I'm not his girlfriend.

I push my rising unease away and force myself to focus on snuggling and pillow talk.

"You heard from your brothers lately? Any update on the evil Bree?"

"They're still broken up, far as I know." He sounds pleased. "Shannon says she and Mum went out for a secret celebration dinner."

"Dude. No wonder you're too scared to bring women home. They really hated this one, huh?"

"Oh yeah." His hand moves over my shoulder in an absent-minded caress. "They're protective is all. We're a tight-knit clan. Always looking out for one another."

"Honestly, that sounds wonderful. Being an only child is lonely. And I didn't even get to grow up with both parents. Dad and I are close, but sometimes I wonder what it would've been like to have a mom and dad in the same house, maybe a couple of siblings."

"It's nice," Jack admits. "Chaotic, certainly. But nice."

"How old were you when your dad died?"

"Six. Things got rough after he passed. Real bloody rough. Noah became the man of the house at the ripe old age of ten. Shannon was only a toddler."

"I can't even imagine how difficult that must have been for your mom."

"It was bad for a while. There's a decent welfare system in Sydney, but not the best. Other family members tried to help out, but they weren't exactly wealthy themselves. By the time I was thirteen, I was working three jobs. Two under the table for cash."

"That does sound rough." I squeeze his hand in sympathy.

"Yeah." He speaks in a faraway tone now. "Never really got to be normal like other lads. I mean, of course, we partied. Raised hell when we got the chance. But keeping the family afloat came first. Helping Mum out was more important than anything else. Girls, parties. None of that mattered."

Curiosity tugs at me. "What about the girl you were dating in high school? You said it was a steady thing."

He hesitates.

"Sorry. You don't have to talk about that if you don't want."

"No, it's fine." He shrugs. "There was one girlfriend. Lara. She was fantastic. And I..." I feel his chest dip as he swallows. "I let her down, over and over again."

I suddenly remember something he'd said the day we went for that drive. About how there are standards you need to meet when you're in a relationship. How he's never been able to meet them.

"Is that why you think you're bad at relationships?" I sit up with a slight frown.

"I was a shit boyfriend. I stood her up on her birthday."

"Seriously?"

"It wasn't intentional. I was supposed to get off early at the surf shop where I worked to take her out, but two of my coworkers called in sick, and the manager said he'd pay me overtime to stay. I figured I'd make it up to Lara, but she wasn't having it." He laughs without much humor. "I tell you, I've never had a verbal beatdown like that." The laughter fades as he bites his lower lip. "She said I was the most selfish person she'd ever met."

"You had to work. It's not like you ditched her on her birthday to go joyriding or kangaroo hunting or whatever it is you Australians do down there."

"I could've said no to my manager. I didn't."

"Your family needed you."

"So did Lara. It was her birthday, for fuck's sake. Anyway, that was one sin among many. I made heaps of promises to her that I didn't keep."

I reach for his hand, lacing our fingers. "You had responsibilities. If she couldn't understand that, that's on her, not you."

"Either way, I hurt her. Badly." Regret flickers through his expression. "It felt like shit, hurting somebody I cared about."

"And you're scared you'll do it again?"

"Sort of, I suppose."

I rub the inside of his palm with my thumb. "Want to know a secret? You will."

"I will what?"

"You're going to hurt someone again."

He looks startled. "What?"

"You are," I say simply. "We all are. I'm sure I'm going to hurt many people during my lifetime. Not maliciously. Or maybe, sometimes, it might be malicious. Maybe I'll say something in anger that I'll regret afterward. But it's going to happen. Human beings are wired to hurt each other."

"Well, aren't you depressing," Jack says with a smile.

"But you know what else humans are wired for? Forgiveness. So yeah, you'll probably hurt someone again the way you hurt Lara. But if you're lucky, they'll forgive you."

"Bloody hell, Abbs. Why do you have to be so…"

"Amazing?" I supply, waggling my eyebrows.

I'm joking and expect him to respond in kind. Instead, he pulls me into his arms and lays a deep, blistering kiss on me.

"Yes," he agrees when we break apart. "Amazing."

"Jackie boy had a bird over last night," are the first words to exit Lee's mouth when I saunter into the kitchen the next morning.

Man, he's such a gossipy snitch.

At the breakfast bar, Jack eats his pancakes and ignores Lee's announcement, but I notice the way his broad shoulders tense.

"Holy shit," I exclaim, conveying the appropriate amount of shock and awe. "Wow." I raise one eyebrow at Jack. "She must be really special if you invited her here."

He bites his lip, slowly meeting my gaze. "She might be."

My heart almost bursts in my chest.

Oh no.

I'm catching feelings.

Okay, that ship sailed a long time ago, I have to amend.

But before this moment, those were basic-level feelings. The I-really-like-you tier of emotion.

This is the next tier. I've officially graduated to that floaty, happy cloud between the two *L* words.

God. I'm in over my head.

Luckily, Lee distracts me from my troubled thoughts by grilling Jack with the kind of steely determination rivaled only by the KGB. To his credit, Jack holds his ground, but Lee is still badgering him when I duck out of the kitchen after breakfast.

I get ready for school, gathering all my research notes for the Tulley project, which I'm supposed to update Professor Langford on this morning.

Speaking of the Tulleys, a text pops up as I'm zipping my school bag.

> Sophie: Abbey, Sophie Brown here.

> Me: I know. I saved your contact info :) What's up?

> Sophie: I need to arrange to ship that box of documents to my office. Benjamin's father has agreed to donate some of the documents to the museum in Surrey. Benjamin said you already made copies and have no need for the originals anymore, correct?

> Me: Yes, that's correct. Are you in the office this morning? I can drop the box off before class if you'd like. Saves you the shipping costs.

She doesn't seem enthused at the prospect of seeing me in person, but Ben's office is literally around the corner from the building that houses my morning classes. We agree to meet before my first class, and I grab Ben Tulley's box and leave the house a few minutes later.

Lee and I take the Tube together. I'm worried he'll want to gossip about Jack's new lady love, but he simply chatters on about Eric and the weekend trip they're taking to some spa in Paris. They're getting hot and heavy, those two. I like seeing Lee happy.

A short while later, Sophie meets me in the lobby of Ben's office, a converted three-story town house with a nondescript white exterior. There's a lift, but we're only going to the second floor, so Sophie gestures for us to take the stairs. Despite wearing high heels, she ascends the steps like she's walking on air, while I struggle to carry the box and at the same time try to keep the strap of my messenger bag secure on my shoulder.

"How is the research going?" she asks.

"Not well," I admit, hating the reminder. The Josephine portion of my project has completely stalled, leading me to a maddening dead end.

Upstairs, there's a large reception area and a pair of mahogany doors leading to what I assume is Ben's office. Beyond the doors, I glimpse a commanding desk, built-in bookshelves, plush chairs, and expensive carpeting. A second office is tucked off to the side of the waiting area, and it's there that Sophie takes me. This space is smaller but actually appears lived in, whereas Ben's office looks like a room in a model home that nobody uses. All for show.

Something suddenly occurs to me. "What does a lord do?" I blurt out.

"I'm sorry?"

"For work, I mean. I know Ben's father is the one who runs the estate and all that, but what exactly is Ben's job? What does he do?"

"Not much" is the muttered response.

"What?" I glance over in surprise.

"I said, 'So much,'" Sophie repeats, a wan smile firmly in place.

I call bullshit. She totally said *not much*. And that note of disdain wasn't missed either. Methinks someone doesn't like their boss.

"Lord Tulley runs a nonprofit," she explains, taking the box from my hands to set it on her desk. "As well as sits on the board of two foundations."

"Oh. Okay. That does sound like a lot." I gesture to the box. "Please thank him again for letting me dig through all this stuff. It's helped so much."

"Are you any closer to solving your mystery? Benjamin filled me in on the Josephine saga."

"Nope. Dead end. All I know is she was a maid who was probably involved in a love triangle with two Tulley brothers. I have no idea what happened to her." I give a hopeful look. "Ben is traveling again, right? The last time we spoke, he mentioned there might be more documents in the cache at their Ibiza house."

Her expression hardens again at the mention of Ben. "I'm sure he'll reach out if he discovers anything else of use."

I fidget with the strap of my bag. "Okay, great. Anyway. I should be going."

"Yes. I'm afraid I must also be off."

We leave her office and head back for the stairs. It's awkward again, and I find myself making dreaded small talk to fill the uncomfortable void.

"Any big holiday plans?"

Sophie spares me a brief look before continuing her descent. "I'll be spending Christmas with my dad, as I usually do."

"Oh, me too." I offer a tentative smile. "He's basically my only family."

At that, her face softens. "I'm in a similar situation."

"Does your father live in the city?"

"No. He's in an assisted living facility thirty minutes south."

"Oh. I'm sorry. Is he sick?"

"Early-onset Alzheimer's." Sorrow creases her features. "He's fifty-three. The symptoms started in his late forties." Her voice catches just slightly. "He's aged so much these past five years. Almost unrecognizable now."

"I'm sorry," I say again, my heart aching for the pain I see in her eyes. "That must be really difficult for you."

We emerge from the stairwell and enter the airy lobby.

"It's not the most pleasant of circumstances," she admits. "But I'm grateful he's well cared for. The facility he's in is the best in the entire country."

"That free health care has its perks, I suppose."

She gives a derisive laugh. "Oh, darling. Our health care system is good but not that good. I pay for private care out of pocket. It's a substantial amount, but as with you, my father is my only family. I refuse to put him in a government-run place."

I don't blame her. I would only want the best for my dad too.

"I'm sorry," I say for what feels like the hundredth time. "I didn't mean to bring up such a sensitive subject."

"You didn't know."

At the door, we hesitate again. The truth is I like her. She's elegant and interesting and clearly very intelligent. The kind of woman I would like to be friends with.

So I feel compelled to say, "About the ball…"

A frown touches Sophie's lips. "What of it?"

"I know what you must think of me. I mean, you found me and your boss in a, um, compromising position. But you should know, I was grateful for the interruption. I drank a lot of champagne that night. Seemed like a good idea at the time to let a lord kiss me at a royal ball, but I'm glad it didn't happen."

Skepticism flits across her face. "Are you?"

"Yes," I say truthfully. "I got caught up in the moment. But I'm not interested in Ben that way. Besides, I already have my hands full with my own love triangle."

"Is that right?" I think I see a twinkle of humor in her eyes.

"Yes." I groan. "But that's a story for another time. I'm going to be late for class."

"Right then." She holds the door open for me.

"Please let me know if Ben discovers any more secret Tulley papers that might be useful, because I could really use another breakthrough. Although at this point, I'm going to need a miracle to solve this mystery."

My breakthrough comes later that day and from the unlikeliest source.

On my walk back to campus after lunch, I get a call from a London number I don't recognize. To my amazement, it's Mr. Baxley.

"I found your number in the student registration," he says, answering my obvious question. "I wanted to inform you I have some pertinent information regarding your research."

I suck in a gust of frigid air. "Really?"

"I took it upon myself to conduct some further study, during which I managed to locate a living descendent of Josephine Farnham."

Excitement courses through me. "Here? In London? That's incredible."

"She's called Ruby Farnham. She indicated she has some documents you might find useful, and she's willing to speak with you. If you'd like to come by the library, I can give you her contact information."

Holy shit. This is fantastic. If anyone can put the final pieces together and hopefully tell me what became of Josephine, it'll be her living relatives.

"Mr. Baxley, you're truly a credit to your profession," I blurt out, my voice ringing with gratitude. "Thank you. You've saved my life."

"Yes, well." He clears his throat to mask his characteristic discomfort. "Don't leave me waiting all evening."

As we're hanging up, I get a text from Nate, which drags me right back down to earth. He's back from Dublin and wants to meet up.

Immediately, a pang of guilt twists my gut. I think about what I was doing last night and with whom, and that tight, uncomfortable sensation intensifies.

My generation is constantly being told to embrace sexual empowerment. Love the way you want to love. Fuck who you want to fuck. Get married or have casual sex. Be polyamorous or monogamous or ethically nonmonogamous. I constantly hear these terms being thrown around, and I *want* to be that unfettered person, the one who doesn't feel guilty about dating multiple people.

But I don't think I am.

36

Several days later, I'm able to set an appointment with Josephine's grandniece Ruby, who lives in a village about an hour north of London. I don't know why I'm more nervous about this meeting than any of my previous research outings, but I've been messing with my hair in the mirror for twenty minutes, and all I've managed to do is leave clumps of red on the bathroom floor. Finally I say to hell with it and wrap it up in a bun.

I'm getting my bag together and checking to make sure I've got the right address in my phone when Jack strides into my room.

"Where you off to?" he says, shirtless and still sweaty from his run.

"Going to interview that woman about Josephine."

"You need a ride? I can ask Jamie to borrow his car."

"The Jag? He would never. Anyway, I'm good."

Jack wrinkles his forehead. "You said it was out in Tonwell? You're not taking the train all the way out there?"

"No, I got a ride. But thank you."

He follows me downstairs, watching as I put on my shoes and grab my coat. I had hoped to slip out of here while he was in the shower, but no such luck.

"What, Ben Tulley send you another limo?"

He's mostly kidding when he peeks through the curtains to look out the front window. The smile fades when instead he sees Nate leaning on his motorcycle at the curb.

"Ah. Got it."

"I won't be late." I try to keep my voice light, but the tightness of Jack's jaw is impossible to mistake. "I mentioned my appointment and he offered."

And I wanted to see him, but I don't say that part out loud. It's true, though. I've missed Nate.

If this were an easy decision, I'd have made it already.

My phone buzzes in my pocket. I don't have to look to know it's Nate asking if I'm ready to go. For all our sakes, I don't answer it.

Jack leans against the door, still watching me.

I bite my lip. "I'll be back in a few hours."

"All right."

He takes a step toward me.

"Jack—"

He has me up against the wall before I can blink. His lips find my neck, planting hot, hungry kisses along the tendons there. My knees wobble as Jack's hand drifts down my stomach toward the juncture of my thighs.

I gasp when he cups me over my jeans, the heat of his palm sending a sizzle of pleasure to my clit.

His mouth moves close to my ear. "I'm going to sneak into your room tonight, Abbey," he rasps. "And I'm going to eat your pussy all goddamn night."

Oh. My. God.

Then he smiles. "I want you to think about that when you're with him today."

My heartbeat is dangerously unstable. With a little smirk, Jack withdraws his hand and wanders toward the stairs.

Outside, I'm still struggling to banish Jack's threat—or rather promise—from my mind when Nate greets me with his crooked grin. "You weren't thinking of standing me up?"

Just that small inflection in his voice, the way he shoves his hair out of his eyes, throws me headlong back into the blender of conflicted feelings. Ten seconds ago, my heart was pounding for Jack. Now it's careening for Nate. This is not good.

"Not a chance. Just some house business."

Nate isn't shy about tilting my chin up to kiss me. A deep I-haven't-seen-you-in-weeks kiss that wakes up every nerve and gets me thinking about blowing off this whole trip to head straight to his place.

"Hi," I say, breathless when he releases me.

Nate smirks, satisfied with himself. "Hi." Then he helps me put on my helmet and pushes stray strands of hair off my face to slide a pair of goggles on me too. "You'll want these. Too cold without them. Your eyes will freeze right in their sockets."

I fit them on. "How do I look?"

"Brilliant."

Feeling the bike rumble beneath me as we tear through the streets of London never gets old. Even the freezing air doesn't bother me, arms wrapped tight around Nate's waist. The ride reminds me of what I love about this city. The architecture and culture. The distinct neighborhoods with their particular rhythms. I love our ranch in Nashville, but there's nothing quite like London.

In Tonwell, we take it slow through the cobblestone streets to a small cottage just beyond the village center. A petite woman in her late forties comes to greet us at the door.

"Well, you certainly do make an entrance," she says after introductions are made. She's in drab overalls with black stains at the knees and her graying hair tied up in a bandanna. She pulls off a pair of brown work gloves and waves us in. "Come on in and get warm. I'll put on some tea."

We follow her inside and take a seat at her kitchen table.

"Sorry I'm in such a state," she says as she fills a kettle. "I've got chickens."

Out the window, I notice a garden in her backyard and a wooden structure I assume must be her chicken coop.

"Thank you for agreeing to meet with me," I say gratefully. "I realize it's a strange request."

"Oh, I'm delighted." Ruby puts out a plate of cookies, which Nate gratefully helps himself to. "I haven't got much family left, so your call gave me an excuse to spend some time getting to know my ancestors." She gestures across her kitchen to a box on the floor. "That's them. Go on and help yourself. Jo was a fascinating girl. Wish I'd had the chance to meet her."

"Do you know what happened to her?" I ask, unable to hide my eagerness. "Where she ended up?"

"Can't say, I'm afraid. My grandfather Matthew was Josephine's younger brother. From what I gathered, Matthew was still a young boy when Josephine and their sister, Evelyn, went to work for the Tulleys. They didn't see so much of each other after that. That wasn't unusual, you know. When you staffed a family like that, you more or less gave up your own. You sent money in a letter every week, maybe popped in a couple times a year, but for the most part, it was goodbye."

When the kettle starts whistling, Ruby pours our tea and sets the cups down at the table.

"Milk and sugar?" she offers.

"Please."

"None for me, thanks," Nate says, hauling the box over and lifting it into the empty chair between us.

"How did you come into all this?" I reach into the box to pull out some of the letters bundled and tied together.

"From my mum, who passed two summers back. It's been in my attic since I cleared her place out after that."

"I'm sorry for your loss."

She nods at that. "I emailed my cousin this week asking her to check her own attic, so perhaps we'll come across more documents that could prove useful for you. As it stands, this is all we have. Our family history mostly evaporated after the war. Displaced. What bits we have are scattered, so it was good to realize I had this. I had just assumed it was bank statements and credit card bills."

Ruby sits with us for a while, telling us more about herself and her family and what little she recalls of her grandfather, Josephine's brother, growing up. She pulls out some artifacts she found of interest and helps provide some context for the names and relations. Like a letter to Josephine's mother in which she confesses she's fallen in love.

"Oh my God, listen to this." I'm practically bouncing in my chair as I read parts of the letter aloud. "'He is the most generous man. He adores me. And he treats me as his equal, Mother, as if he's proud to have me by his side.'" I skim the next couple paragraphs and gasp. "Oooh, and this: 'His mother does not approve. It has caused a strain on his family.'"

Nate's answering laugh is wry. "How very unhelpful. Her description of this great love is interchangeable with either Tulley brother."

"Ugh. Right? Would it have killed her to spell it out for us?" I groan in annoyance, which summons a chortle from Ruby. "'Dear Mother, I love Robert. Yours truly, Josephine.' Or 'Dear Mother, William rocks my world. Your loving daughter, Josephine.'" I grumble. "Women, amirite?"

Nate looks like he's trying not to double over in laughter.

"Is she always this entertaining?" Ruby asks him.

"Oh yes. Certainly." Winking at me, he reaches over to squeeze my hand.

I flash him a smile before moving on to another letter. This one also fails to mention the name of Josephine's lover, but one line stands out to me. This time, I don't read it out loud.

Oh, Mother, I feel dreadfully guilty for my part in this. Yet my

heart led me here, and don't you remember? You once told me that
the heart never leads us astray.

The guilt is a reference to her predicament, I assume. The part
about your heart never leading you astray is what sticks with me,
though.

Is that true? Does your heart always lead you where you're
supposed to be in the end? If so, I wish mine would point me in the
right direction already. Jack or Nate. Take your pick, heart.

Spending the next hour poring over Ruby's documents, a
comprehensive picture of Josephine Farnham begins to form in my
mind. The young maid was an intelligent, mischievous, and adventurous woman full of passion and curiosity. Her letters to her mother
reveal that she went into service for the Tulleys hoping it would
expose her to new people and experiences. And I suppose it did.
Eventually. But mostly, it left her stifled. In one letter, she confesses
she is desperate for a change but reliant on the income. In a later
letter, it's obvious her reason for staying now has more to do with the
man she loves than her salary.

Ruby allows me to take photographs of her archives, which I'll
include in my final project. Despite not having an answer about
which Tulley brother Josephine picked, I feel an odd sense of resolution. A strange confidence that whoever Josephine ended up with, it
was the right choice.

The heart never leads us astray.

After taking up more than enough of Ruby's time, she sends us
off with a loaf of homemade bread, and we return to Notting Hill
at dusk. Outside the house, we linger on the sidewalk for a while,
neither of us in a hurry to say goodbye for the night.

"I close tonight," Nate says, hands tucked into my back pockets
as he leans against his bike. "But if you wanted to come over after."

I shake my head regretfully. "I'm planning to be fast asleep by
then. It's a school night, you know."

"Right. Fair enough. As long as you're not avoiding me."

"If I am," I say, fidgeting with his belt loops, "I'm doing a terrible job."

Before he releases me, Nate captures my lips with his. His tongue slips past them, sensual and full of reminders. I get caught up in their lure until he pulls away with a parting kiss to my forehead.

"I'll text you," he says.

I back up as he puts on his helmet and starts his motorcycle, smiling faintly before he peels off the curb toward the waning purple horizon.

The moment he's gone and I walk toward the house, the guilt sets in. I know Jack's home, and he'll have heard us drive up.

I'm really not cut out for juggling two guys. Yes, neither of them asked to be exclusive, but I know I can't keep it up much longer.

Either way, something's gotta give.

JANUARY

37

I'm back in London by the first week of January and already missing my dad back home in Nashville. I hadn't realized how much dumb things like my favorite cereal bowl and the scent of the fabric softener were emotional triggers. Or hanging out in the living room with Dad watching *The Grinch* and *Home Alone* on TV with popcorn and hot chocolate. It was harder to say goodbye this time. Turns out I'm more of a daddy's girl than I wanted to admit. For his part, Dad was a trooper. He kept the teary heartstring tugging to a minimum. Hardly mentioned the number of pedestrian fatalities in the UK at all.

Going home was the recharge I needed to get my head on straight and chase away the dreary gray clouds. Still, coming back to Notting Hill was a relief after the long flight. There's something about walking in on Lee yelling at the boys about burning dinner that my soul needed while I was away.

Now, on the last Sunday before classes start, Jack and I are cozy on the couch while he watches a rugby game on TV and I get a head start on next semester's reading assignments.

"See that one there?" he asks, tapping my leg. He's got his arm draped over my lap as I sit with my back leaning against him.

I half glance up from my book. "Hmm?"

"His dad scored four tries in a single game for the All Backs in the World Cup."

"Mmm."

"Literally ran over an English player like the bloke was a bunch of daisies in a field. Mowed him right over."

"Mmm."

Jack pinches my hip. "You listening to me?"

"No," I say, lifting my head from my book to smile at him. "But you keep going if it makes you happy."

"You're a bit of a shit, you know that?"

"A bit."

As if defending my honor, Hugh jumps up from the back of the couch to bite at Jack's ear.

Hugh does this. Randomly attacks the boys. I think it's just his way of trying to play and get their attention, but the guys are all living in fear of mortal danger. It was up to Jamie to care for him during the break, and if the scars on his arms are any indication, the poor guy has PTSD.

"Christ, you demon," Jack hisses, cupping his reddened ear. "That damn mad thing is trying to kill me."

"Better be nice to me then."

"I'm always nice." He leans down to kiss me, but we jerk apart when we hear the front door open and then Jamie appears.

"Right." Jamie tosses his coat and scarf on the armchair, then picks up my legs to sit at the end of the couch and drape my feet over his lap. "What's for dinner then? I'm famished."

He isn't the least bit fazed by me and Jack being a little snuggly on the couch. So far, we've managed to keep the more blatant displays under the radar, too paranoid to chance anything more.

"Text Lee," Jack says. "See if he wants Chinese."

As he pulls his hand away to be less conspicuous, his finger-tips brush across the bare skin of my stomach under the hem of my sweater. Lee is far more suspicious than Jamie, and if he walks through the door, we don't want to be too flagrant.

It's these small exchanges that keep my head in a fog. The small expressions of his desire. It does a number on me. Everyone loves a secret, and I can't deny there's something exhilarating about sneaking around. All the excitement of being naughty without the guilt of hurting anyone. Good wholesome trouble.

But it does get old. I mean, isn't this why I left Nashville? To get some autonomy. Freedom. To make out with a guy anywhere I see fit, not lurking in the shadows and laundry rooms of my own house, listening for approaching footsteps. How much different is this than sneaking a boy through my window after curfew?

It only illustrates the crux of my predicament. Jack and I aren't really together if we're hiding it from our roommates. And because we haven't broached the subject, I haven't made a decision about Nate either. It's probably a good thing Nate was in Portugal over the holidays, sparing me the anxiety of seeing them both.

When we spoke about it in Nashville (or rather, when I agonized over it for hours and she listened while probably drowning in boredom), Eliza was convinced the answer would become clear to me after some time away. But I'm more torn than before I left.

When I'm with Jack, it feels right.

And when I'm with Nate, it also feels right.

Awesome.

———————

I'm still obsessing over it the next day when I meet Celeste for lunch. She treats us to a fancy café where I find her sporting a new designer bag and a blinding diamond and emerald bracelet.

"Someone had a good holiday," I tease as the waiter pours our sparkling water.

"Armond" is her explanation. "He's the one who hosted the New Year's party Phillipa dragged me to."

"Ah, of course. Yacht Party Armond."

She covers her bashful smile with a sip of water. "He's a patron

of the national ballet company and on the board of several philan-
thropic arts organizations."

"What happened to Roberto?"

Celeste snorts. "Some actress. I guess it slipped his mind to
mention her before ringing me from Geneva to say he wouldn't be
stopping by for dinner with the family."

"Ouch. That's harsh."

"His loss." She brushes her hair back, the bracelet glinting in the
sunlight. "No way she's as flexible as I am."

I almost cough up my water. "Jesus, Celeste."

"What about you? Indulge in any hometown flings while you
were away?"

"Nope. Dad and I hung out mostly. He was a little clingy. But it
was nice to get some bonding time, just the two of us."

"Come on. You must give me something, darling."

"Really—"

"Don't lie to me," she insists. "Your cheeks are doing that pink
glowy thing. Either you're pregnant or…"

"Definitely not."

"So explain yourself."

It's impossible to win a staring contest with Celeste. She'd
sooner hold me at knifepoint in a crowded restaurant than let me
change the subject, so I relent. If only because I could use the advice.

"I seem to have gotten myself stuck in a bit of a triangle," I
confess.

Her face lights up. "I love those."

"Your brother won't."

"Oh God. Tell me it isn't Jamie."

"What? No. Jack."

"Oh. Right, that makes sense."

"It does?"

"Sure. We discussed this ages ago, remember? He's so fit. If you
weren't living with him, I'd have set you two up."

Her remark gets me wondering where Jack and I would be by now if we weren't roommates. Would this be a relationship? Exclusive? Bring me home to Mum? From the guy who doesn't do long-term commitments, it's hard to picture that changing.

"I'm impressed by your stealth," she says. "Lee is a bloodhound for those kinds of shenanigans. You two must be pretty clever for him not to have noticed."

"Assuming he hasn't."

"Trust me. He wouldn't keep it to himself."

Fair point.

"So who's the third point in this triangle? Have we been galivanting about the city with a certain Lord Tulley?"

I crack a smile. "Absolutely not." Though the truth is harder to get out. "It's, ah, Nate."

Celeste rocks back in her chair. "Oh."

Yeah, I expected that.

"He and I sort of hooked up. After he broke up with Yvonne," I quickly qualify.

"She's still in bits over him, you know."

Guilt pricks at my gut. "Really?"

"I tried to get her out of her flat during the holidays, but she wasn't having it. I think she's been in the same pair of sweats every night for a month."

"I had no idea she was so into him. Like am I crazy, because they never seemed…"

"That's just how she is. Yvonne was mad about him. She's devastated."

Well, now I feel like shit.

But…ugh. How much loyalty do I even owe Yvonne? I don't know her at all. We're not friends, and she hasn't gone out of her way to try to change that.

"Should I…" I trail off, biting my lip.

"Take her to coffee and tell her you charmed her boyfriend out from under her?" Celeste supplies. "No. I can't picture her reacting well to that. Best to keep that information to yourself."

I study Celeste's face, but her expression is unreadable. "Are you going to tell her?" If I should be sleeping with one eye open, I'd like to know.

"I don't want to be in the middle of it."

To be honest, neither do I.

Celeste sighs. "And if I'm being entirely truthful, it was quite obvious to everyone but Yvonne that Nate wasn't in love with her." She pauses. "So who do we like more? Nate or Jack?"

"That's the thing. If I knew, I wouldn't be in this mess. Physically, they're both attractive, so there's no clear winner there. Personality-wise… well, Jack's fun, you know? Easy. We can be silly together. Nate makes me feel more grown-up. He's challenging. Adventurous."

"Can't get much different than those two." She flashes a cheeky grin. "Who's the better shag?"

My cheeks heat up. "They're both very skilled in the sexy-times department."

"Well, this is a real conundrum then."

"I know." I blow out a frazzled breath. "And then, on the other hand, I don't know if there's a point in obsessing over any of this. Nate hasn't once asked me to be exclusive. And there's Jack, who said he was going to prove to me that he's serious after jerking me around a few times. I promised him I'd be patient, but he still hasn't made his intentions clear, so I don't know what this is. What we are."

My frustrated groan echoes between us.

"Piece of advice." She holds out her glass to the waiter when he comes by to top us up. "You're a beautiful, powerful, intelligent woman. You don't have time for silly little boys who can't make up their minds. Why should you settle for just one, be forced to choose, when you don't even know what you're choosing?"

She's not wrong. Neither of them has told me what they want out of this. A girlfriend? A friend with benefits? A fleeting fling?

How can I choose between them when I don't even know what they want?

Those questions haunt me for the rest of the evening, making it difficult to concentrate on the assigned reading for my European history class. It doesn't help that both Jack and Nate text within seconds of each other.

> Jack: Match is over. We murdered them. Grabbing a bite and pints with the lads at the Red Fiddle if you fancy joining us. If not, I'll sneak into your room later?

> Nate: Come over to mine? I'll be off early tonight. Around ten.

I groan out loud. God. Why can't I just choose already? I don't want to be sitting here trying to decide which guy I'd like to fool around with tonight. That's not me.

When I see Ben Tulley's name light up my phone screen, I answer on the first ring, desperate for an effective distraction.

"Abbey, darling. How are you?"

"Excellent. How's the weather in Ibiza?"

"Sweltering. And quite past its expiration. I'm home now. Back in dreary London."

"My condolences."

"One can't linger long in air he can't see. Lest we lose our stamina."

"I'll try to remember that. So. To what do I owe this honor, Lord Tulley?"

He chuckles. "I'm calling because I've some boxes here cluttering my drawing room and I wondered if you might fancy a peek inside."

My spirits are promptly bolstered. "You remembered," I say happily. "I was worried you might forget them in Ibiza."

"And miss hearing the delight in your voice? Of course not. So, fancy that peek?"

"I do believe I would," I answer, glad he can't see the huge dorky smile on my face.

"Brilliant. I'll send my car 'round."

I take a quick shower and get dressed, twisting my damp hair in a bun. I throw on some jeans and a T-shirt. But like my nicest T-shirt. I don't want to be pretentiously overdressed for a glorified study session, but I also don't want the doorman at Ben's flat to lock me out and call the cops.

"Hey." Lee pops in and throws himself on my bed while I'm picking out matching socks. "What do you say we go out to eat? Jamie's gnawing on his arm down there, and I don't feel like cooking."

"Can't. I've got plans."

"Oh? Do you have pics?"

I grin. "Not those kinds of plans. Ben's back in town, and he has some boxes for me to snoop through."

Lee jerks upright. "At his flat?"

"Uh-huh."

"Alone?"

"Are you asking to chaperone?" I inquire, rolling my eyes.

"Should I?"

I throw him a look. "It's not a date. I haven't even spoken to him in weeks."

"But he's back and you're his first call."

The suspicion clouding Lee's face makes me laugh. "I sincerely doubt that's how it happened."

If anything, after a month on the Spanish coast, I'm sure he's quite exhausted of female attention. Even the Energizer Bunny has to change out his batteries every now and then.

"Look, babe." Lee crosses his legs, meeting me with his serious face. "That Tulley reputation is well earned. It isn't all idle gossip."

"I know that. Ben's the first one to admit his family has its skeletons."

"Yes. And he isn't above reproach."

Who among us, right?

"Whatever he gets up to in his off hours is his business," I say, shrugging. "I'm not writing his memoir."

"No, you're just running over to his flat. In the middle of the night. Alone."

It sounds sinister when he says it like that.

"Not the middle of the night," I point out. "It's only eight."

"Abbey, luv." Lee uses the tone he reserves for when Jamie does something stupid. "Eric and I have talked about our dear Lord Tulley."

"Of course you have. Your boyfriend is a gossip," I remind him. Gossiping is the only thing Lord Eric enjoys more than his fussy show cats and the tall fussy man sitting on my bed.

"Maybe. Doesn't make him wrong. And he had some troubling things to say about Ben's not-so-private predilections."

"So what, he has a red room? Don't all you posh Brits?"

Lee sighs. "I mean…at his age, there's only one reason he gives attention to a college girl."

"First, he's twenty-seven, not thirty-five. And second, ouch, okay?"

"Look at me," my roommate says, reaching out to clasp my hands. "As a friend, I'm trying to save you from yourself."

My expression softens. "I appreciate your concern, but it's entirely misplaced. Yes, Ben and I got a little flirty at the royal ball, but that was ages ago. That ship has sailed. He's not a love interest. He's barely a friend. More like an academic benefactor. I'm going over there to look through some boxes, take some pictures, and that's it."

Lee drops my hands. I gather my bag off the floor and swipe my keys from the nightstand.

"I'll grab something to eat while I'm out," I tell him.

"Hey," he says before I leave. "I'll keep my ringer on. Call or text if you need anything."

When I arrive at Ben's penthouse, he greets me looking like he just stepped off a yacht. Sporting a tan and salt-sprayed hair. A linen shirt with the sleeves rolled up. Barefoot in khaki pants. He's like an ad in *Vogue* for sunglasses or a six-figure watch.

"Hope you don't mind," I say, carrying a paper bag into his stainless-steel chef's kitchen. "I asked your driver to stop on the way for some takeout."

He swirls a tumbler of dark amber liquor, watching me set cartons on the marble countertop. "You're quite a peculiar girl."

"I get that a lot."

"It's working for you," he says, lifting his glass to salute me. "Keep it up."

"Should we eat first, or we can nosh while we go through the boxes?"

"I admire your industriousness, but let's have a drink first." Ben pulls a bottle of white out of the wine fridge under the counter, then finds a corkscrew. "The boxes have been waiting half a century. They're not going anywhere."

I consider refusing, but I can't deny that putting down some of Ben's absurdly expensive wine sounds more appetizing than paper cuts at the moment.

"All right." I hold my hand out for the glass. "Hit me."

"That's the spirit." He passes me a generous pour and we clink glasses. "I do admire Americans and your appreciation for procrastination."

"Why do I feel like that's an insult?"

His answer is a wink as he sips his drink. He pops open a carton of food, becoming more agreeable to it once he's smelled the arresting aromas of the Vietnamese place I passed on the way here.

"Speaking of which," he says, "a few friends did invite themselves over when they found out I was back in the city."

Oh.

"Trust me, they're a lovely lot. Just don't let them give you invest-ment advice." He laughs.

"I didn't mean to intrude. If you've got other plans, I can come back another time. Or just take the boxes with me and arrange with Sophie to ship them back—"

"No, no. I'm not chasing you out. Far from it." Ben downs his drink and pours himself another. "I prefer to conduct business with friends. And as we embark on this adventure of discovery together, I should like us to be friends."

"Okay." Though I'm not sure how a party is conducive to the task at hand. I'm starting to feel a bit duped.

"Oh dear," he says. "I've gone and done something dreadful, haven't I?" Ben watches me with amused concern. "Please, darling. You mustn't be afraid of a bit of fun. Life is always throwing unexpected surprises at us."

My stomach sinks as I watch Ben reach into his pants pocket and pull out a small capped vial of white powder.

He flashes me a cheeky smile. "You really must give yourself permission to relish the chaos."

38

From the first bump of blow, Ben's lost to me.

I don't have time to consider an exit strategy before his penthouse is crawling with posh society's dirty secrets snorting powder off the coffee table and slathering themselves in expensive champagne. They're all quite pleased with themselves, sloshing about, cackling indecipherably.

I've got a headache.

"No, wait," some leggy brunette shouts at me. She nearly falls off the arm of the sofa before the gentleman nearest her grabs the front of her satin dress to rip her back from gravity's grip. She points a bony finger at my face. "I've placed you."

If she mentions the "heart is a windmill" song, I might knock myself over the head with a sixteenth-century bookend.

The finger wags and the alcohol runs away with her accent that turns to mud in her mouth. "I know you, tricky girl."

"Melissa, darling, freshen yourself up." The gentleman offers her his wrist with a line of cocaine on it.

She takes the bump while still talking to me. "You're the ginger who wore the Sue Li to the royal engagement."

"And she was stunning." Beside me, Ben hasn't lifted his arm from my shoulder since the circus rode into town. "A showstopper head to toe."

I tried excusing myself to the kitchen for a glass of water, but he only tightened his grip and ordered one of his fawning friends to pour me another glass of wine. I left that in a potted plant somewhere ages ago. For some reason, he'd unbuttoned his linen shirt at some point, and I've been trying not to look at his bare chest and the dusting of dark hair between his pecs. He's hairier than I would've thought.

"My God, I'd never recognize you," another handsome lizard draped over the sofa exclaims, all but licking his tumbler of scotch dry.

"I saw the takeout containers in the kitchen," a gorgeous blond says between giggles. "I thought she was the delivery girl." Then her eyes flick to mine. "Bless the dear girl."

"Are you incognito?" the first gentleman asks. "Benjamin, I didn't know it was to be a costume party."

"And you know what's even wilder?" Ben boasts to his friends. "Guess who Abbey's dear old dad happens to be—Gunner Bly."

"You're shitting us!" the blond cries. "Truly?"

Right. I think I've been a good sport, but I'm all tapped out on fun for the night. I'm clearly never getting a look at those boxes, so my time is wasted here.

"Benjamin, dear," I say with only a hint of mocking, waiting until he blearily meets my gaze. "I really need to get home."

"Of course. Where are my manners?" He pulls out his phone to quickly type something, then pockets it again. "My concierge will bring a car 'round. He'll let me know when it's arrived."

"I can wait downstairs."

"I don't think she likes our company." Melissa pouts.

"Not me," the lizard answers. His boyish eyes look up but fail to focus. "Surely, not me?"

"Nonsense." Ben's hand slips down my shoulder to rest at my hip. "I'll not have you sitting in the lobby like—"

"The delivery girl!" the blond exclaims. She hoists her glass in the air, spilling wine on the carpet.

Ten minutes later, the car doesn't materialize. Twenty minutes later, still no car, and Ben's wandering hands can't seem to keep themselves above the equator. Meanwhile, he keeps finding new people to stumble their way over with a new glass of wine to try shoving in my hand or a creative new attempt to get their thumbnail under my nose.

I move to pry myself free of Ben's grasp.

"Where are you sneaking off to now?" he teases.

"Calling an Uber."

I'm all out of fucks to give.

"Don't be cross with me." Ben rips my phone out of my hand. He tosses it to the brunette. "Babe, tell her I'm not awful."

A bolt of anger surges through me. Is he serious right now?

"It's bad luck to lie under a new moon." Melissa laughs in return, tossing my phone off to the blond.

"She's a witch," the blond one squeals. "Burn her!" She dips her fingers into her glass and flicks the wet tips at the other woman.

The gentleman and the lizard then take turns tossing my phone over my head while I try snatching it out of the air. Eventually I give up and throw a drink on one of them.

"No. Now come on," Ben interjects as his friend indignantly wipes champagne off his face. "Bad form, Abbey."

I don't give a shit. I grab my phone and dart for the bathroom before anyone can get a hand on me. I hear a knock just as I lock the door and throw my back against it for good measure.

There isn't much battery life left, and the nearest Uber is thirty minutes away. I suddenly hate Friday nights in London. The first tremors of panic start rippling in my stomach. I check every rideshare in the city for a quicker way home. No luck.

Damn it.

They're pounding on the door now, and I'm not sure I can stay in here another five minutes before Ben finds a key or a battering ram. In desperation, I type out a quick SOS, then check off a bunch of names in my contacts list and send it off in the hopes someone on that list will come for me. In the meantime, I sink to the floor, pressed up against the door, feet braced, prepared to fight to the death against the coked-out horde.

Somehow, of all the escapades I envisioned for myself, I never imagined when I moved to London that I'd be holed up in a British lord's powder room above the city, his rabid scavengers clawing at my back.

I'm pretty sure this is precisely what my father pictured. Dr. Wu will have to medicate him if Dad ever finds out about this.

"Abbey, I'm sorry," Ben pleads after a couple minutes. "We were only having a bit of fun. We're terrible, I know. Come out and let us apologize. No harm done, right? Be a good sport."

It goes on like that, every few minutes or so. Until they bore of me, and I hear the muffled laughter of them taking to mocking me instead.

Then, a new commotion.

Shouting.

Doors slamming.

A glass breaks.

I hear my name echoing through the penthouse, followed by a forceful knock at my back.

"Abbey, you in there? Let me in."

Relief hits me like a tidal wave. "Jamie? Is that you?"

I scramble to my feet and open the door for Jamie, who slips inside and slams it shut behind him. He grabs me by both shoulders and meets my eyes with his frantic gaze.

"All right, Abbs?"

"Yeah, good." I suck in a deep breath as what's just occurred solidifies in my mind. "You got my message? That was quick."

"We were at a pub nearby." He gives me a once-over, scanning me from head to toe. "What do you say we get out of here?"

Outwardly, he's calm. Entirely unruffled. But I suspect that's for my benefit.

It's working.

I swallow in relief. "Sounds good."

He takes my hand and leads me toward the living room, where I spot Lee first. Poor guy looks distraught and lets out a held breath once our eyes lock.

Then there's Jack, who doesn't notice me as he badgers Ben.

Fuck.

My stomach drops at the sight of him. I have a feeling I'm in for a long lecture tonight.

"Oi, I don't want to hear it, mate," Jack's growling at my captor.

"I'd kindly ask you to take your hands off me."

"If I mean to put hands on you, asking nice ain't about to stop me."

"I don't know what she's told you, but she's grossly exaggerated the situation."

Ben's gaze slides to mine as he watches me and Jamie cross the room toward the exit.

"That's my flatmate there," Jack says, looking more ferociously dangerous than he ever has on the rugby pitch. "If she says you even looked at her sideways, I reckon you and I will see each other again real soon. Count on that, mate."

The circus titter from the corner like a pack of mischievous sideshow clowns who've set a trap for an unsuspecting audience member coming down the aisle. They're all quite proud of their chaos.

"Come," Jamie urges, tugging me along. "Let's get out of here."

Jack isn't long behind us as we ride the elevator down.

In the lobby, security and the doorman eye us warily when what they should actually do is call the damn cops. But I imagine Ben pulls this shit so often they're probably used to it. They watch us leave, Jack staring them down the whole way.

"Nice tenants you got here," he calls darkly as we're walking outside.

Once we're on the sidewalk, I finally take a deep breath. The winter chill cools my lungs, and when I exhale, it's a faint white cloud.

"Did I not?" Lee snaps at me. "Literally, did I not?"

"Leave her be," Jamie says gently while typing something on his phone. "She doesn't need us telling her what for. She knows."

Jack's still clenching his fists when he finally looks at me. "Are you all right?"

I give a quick nod. "Fine."

"Car will be here in ten," Jamie tells me, tucking his phone away. "Hired us a private service."

Jack continues to scrutinize me. "You're sure he didn't hurt you?"

"He didn't. And I'm sorry, okay? I was wrong. You guys were right. He's a creep, and I didn't see it."

"What in the hell were you thinking?" Satisfied I haven't been maimed or worse, Jack's anger homes in on me. "You out of your bloody mind going in there alone?"

"Too right," Lee drops in.

"Shut it, mate. You didn't stop her."

"I should have locked her in our bathroom then?" Lee shoots back.

"Yes."

"He never gave me any hint," I say in my own defense. "I mean, he'd always been perfectly polite before."

Jack snorts. "Of course he was. If his type were bastards from the off..."

"Abbey," a familiar voice calls from behind me.

I turn, startled to see Nate jogging toward us up the sidewalk. He's wearing jeans and a black hoodie beneath a leather jacket, his hair windblown and his expression awash with worry.

"Oh, for fuck's sake," I hear Jack mutter.

"I saw your message," Nate says when he reaches our group. "What happened?"

"The fire's out," I assure him.

Although now I'm completely embarrassed by the ruckus I've caused, forcing everyone I know to come running to my rescue.

"Ben Tulley had her captive in his bathroom," Lee informs him.

"He what?" Nate's gaze jumps from me to the boys. Then those dark eyes turn bright with anger. "You lads let her go up there alone? Are you mental?"

"Right, mate." Jack steps between us. "Thanks for coming. It's sorted. Piss off."

"Hey, wait." I try to interject but Jamie pulls me back.

"I'd rather hear that from her," Nate says. He doesn't shrink from Jack's challenge, holding his ground. "Abbey?"

"We've got her," Jack retorts. "You've no part to play here."

"That's not your decision."

"You're embarrassing yourself, mate. It's pathetic."

"What's pathetic is this bloke in front of me who won't let the lady speak for herself."

Brow furrowed, Lee looks between Jack and Nate. "I don't understand all the hostility." His frown deepens as his gaze flits toward me for clarification.

I bite my lip and stare at my feet. Fuck. This is not the time for any of this to play out.

"She told you she was fine," Jack is saying.

"No, *you* told me she was fine, you wanker."

"What is happening right now, you two?" Jamie demands, blinking in confusion.

They both ignore him.

"Keep talking shit and I will put you down, ay?" Jack's shoulders hunch with barely restrained tension.

Nate gets right up in Jack's face. At six feet, he's about four inches shorter and yet looks equally formidable. "You want to throw a punch, let's have it. I'm not bothered by huffing and puffing."

"Nope." I throw myself between them. "I'm talking now, okay?

And I say both of you need to back off. Thank you very much for coming. I really appreciate that you came to help me, but I'm good now. So please, put your tape measures away and leave me out of it."

"Leave you out of it?" Nate echoes dryly. "I'm not going anywhere until I know you're all right, luv. I was worried sick when I got your text."

As if finally getting the memo, Lee gasps.

Fuck. I know that gasp.

"Are you together?" he exclaims, his head shifting from me to Nate. "Tell me you're not together."

Jamie's gaze flies to mine. "You're with Nate?"

I feel my cheeks heat up. "I…"

"You're with Nate?" Jamie repeats as if his brain is stuck in neutral.

"Come off it, yeah?" Jack mutters, impatient. "Let's just get Abbey home."

"You knew?" Lee swivels toward Jack, accusation in his voice.

"Yeah, mate, I knew," he snaps back. "Now can we please—"

"Abbey," a voice suddenly shouts, and we all glance toward the entrance of Ben's building.

Ben Tulley himself comes stumbling out the front doors, hair rumpled, the two flaps of his open shirt fluttering in the wind.

"Abbey," he calls unhappily. Stumbling toward us, he extends his arm to beckon me. "Please, come back upstairs. Give me a chance to apologize proper, yeah?"

Ben is about eight feet away from me when the flashbulb goes off.

"Abbey!" someone else yells. "Abbey, give a smile!"

My forehead grooves as I look around in confusion.

Then I spot him. The photographer.

No. That's too generous a term.

He's a vulture. Paparazzi. I grew up with those bloodthirsty vultures circling my father each time he left the house. I'd recognize them anywhere.

Another flashbulb goes off. Then another.

Deep dread crawls up my spine. Ben has stopped in his tracks, his expression going stricken when he realizes his picture is being taken.

"Abbey!"

Flash.

"Does Gunner know about you and Lord Tulley?"

Flash. Flash.

"Abbey! C'mon, darling, smile!"

Feeling the color drain from my face, I grab Lee's arm and dig my fingernails into it. "Get me out of here," I beg. "Please."

Luckily, the car Jamie hired is pulling up to the curb.

Lee snaps to action. "Get in," he commands. "Jamie, let's go, mate."

Jamie throws his coat over my shoulders and helps me into the car, with Lee sliding in beside us.

"Notting Hill," Jamie tells the driver.

It isn't until we're speeding off that I realize we'd left Jack and Nate there.

But I'm too shaken to care right now.

39

THERE ARE A PRECIOUS FEW SECONDS OF BLISSFUL IGNORANCE BEFORE the memories of last night present themselves forward. It wasn't a dream. I am the girl who spent the evening barricaded in Lord Tulley's bathroom. I'll never show myself among noble society again.

Can't say I'm too bummed about that bit.

Downstairs, I prepare myself to take a ribbing from the guys as I walk into the kitchen for breakfast. Having all night to stew about it, I'm sure Lee has a few more I-told-you-sos to get out of his system, not to mention a thorough interrogation about my relationship with Nate. He was so upset about my secret keeping that he went back to the pub after we got home last night, where I'm sure he griped about me to some poor bartender trapped behind the bar.

"Morning." I sit at the breakfast bar beside Jamie. He gives me a shoulder squeeze while Lee remains mute, sipping his tea like I'm not there.

Jack pushes eggs and sausage on a plate for me. "Morning," he murmurs to me, watching Lee from the corner of his eye.

"Everything okay?" I ask warily. "I know last night was a bit chaotic, but—"

"House meeting!" Lee interrupts, shooting to his feet.

"What?"

Arms crossed, he looms over us with a hard glare. "We're having a house meeting, Abigail. Right now."

"Oh. Okay."

He's still pissed at me. Clearly.

"I'll be nice. I'll permit you to choose what we address first." He bares his teeth at me in a feral smile. "What shall it be? Your sordid love affair with our friend Nate or the fact that you placed yourself in danger last night despite numerous objections from yours truly?"

"I figured we'd start with your I-told-you-so," I answer. "Because that's what you really want to say, isn't it?"

Before he can murder me for my insolence, the doorbell rings.

"To be continued," Lee growls before stomping off.

A moment later, there's some commotion at the front door before a stunned Lee comes chasing after an angry Yvonne. She's wearing a black peacoat that flaps around the knees of her dark-blue skinny jeans as she marches toward me.

"Bitch!" she hisses at me. "You must think I'm so stupid. Have a good laugh, did you?"

A queasy pretzel knots up my stomach. "Yvonne, I don't—"

"Do not even try to play dumb! I heard that one"—she nods toward Lee—"going on at the pub all about you and Nate. You going to lie straight to my face?"

Lee blanches. The repentant flicker in his horrified eyes tells me he feels bad about gossiping.

Yvonne curls the fingers of both hands around the top of Jamie's empty chair. Her knuckles are nearly white. "I'm a complete mug, aren't I? Try to be nice and the first thing you do is stab me in the back. Fucking slag."

"Hey." Jack shoves back from the counter and stands. "That's enough. You don't get to come storming into my house and yelling at my roommates because your boyfriend dumped you. Take it out on him."

I swallow the lump of regret in my throat. "Yvonne, I don't know what you heard, but I'm sorry," I say sincerely. "I swear nothing happened until after you broke up."

"Do I look fucking mental? All those trips driving you all over the bloody country. You did this on purpose. You bitch."

"No, you need to go." Jack approaches her, pointing the way out. "I'm not having it."

I try again to apologize to her. "I really am sorry. Honestly, Nate and I only got together after—"

"I don't want to hear it," she snaps at me, livid and red-faced. "You're a cow and a bad person, and you can fuck right off!"

At that, she stalks out of the flat and slams the door behind her, leaving us all stuttering to catch our breath.

I'm still trying to make sense of what happened when Jack rounds on me. "Seriously, Abbey?"

I blink. "What?"

"You and Nate are, what, a couple now?"

"No. I never said that."

"You told her you 'got together'—"

"Yes, got together. Hooked up. Whatever." Embarrassment creeps up my neck as my dirty laundry is aired to the entire house. "Which you already knew about, Jack."

"Yes," Lee interjects, his voice tight. "Let's discuss that, shall we? How is it that Jackie knew all about this torrid love affair while the rest of us were kept in the dark?"

Jack ignores him, glaring at me. "You still think Nate is a good guy? After all this?"

"All what? Yvonne showed up pissed because she found out I see Nate sometimes," I retort. "How is that Nate's fault? He broke up with her before he and I so much as kissed."

"How can you be so naive? You just saw her. Does that look like a woman who was let down gently? Nate doesn't care about anyone. Certainly not you."

I don't know if Jack's specifically trying to hurt me with that remark, but it stings just the same.

"But you do?" I shoot back. "You care about me *so* much you never once asked me to stop seeing him. Right, Jack?"

Lee suddenly gasps.

No. Oh God, no. Not again.

"Hang on," Lee orders, glancing between the two of us. "Are you two…"

Jamie crosses his arms. "That's what it sounds like."

For fuck's sake.

"We had one rule!" Lee shouts. "To avoid exactly this kind of ugly shit."

"Would you fuck off with your rules?" Jack snaps.

Lee spins on me. "You betrayed me."

My jaw drops. "What?"

"We're supposed to tell each other everything, and you've been sneaking around with not one but *two* blokes? Unacceptable!"

The doorbell rings again.

"For fuck's sake!" Lee screeches. "Can these people not let us finish one bloody house meeting!"

Unlike him, I'm overcome with relief at the interruption. That is, as long as it's not Yvonne coming back for a second go at me.

This time, I answer it myself, desperate to place some physical distance between myself and my angry roommates. When I open the door, I'm startled to find Sophie Brown on the front stoop.

"Sophie, hey—"

"Abbey, thank God." To my shock, she grabs both my hands and searches my face urgently. "Are you all right? Please tell me he didn't harm you."

It takes me a second to realize she means Ben.

"What? No. He didn't." I squeeze her trembling hands. "I promise."

"Truly?"

"Truly. The worst he did was snort a ton of cocaine and mock me for not wanting to get trashed with his friends."

Relief and disgust war in Sophie's eyes. "You've no idea how relieved I am."

"How did you know what happened?"

"Ben rang this morning." She looks annoyed. "He has the dreadful habit of doing that. Behaving in the most atrocious manner and then ringing me afterward to warn me of the potential repercussions."

I gesture for her to enter. "Why don't you come in? It's freezing out there."

"Oh. Yes. All right then."

She steps into the front hall, where she removes her long fitted winter coat. Beneath it, she looks chic in black slacks and a red sweater.

"I need to leave for class soon, but I've got about an hour. Would you like a cup of tea?" I offer as I hang up her coat.

"Yes, thank you."

I deposit Sophie in the living room and duck into the kitchen to prepare her tea and pour myself another cup of coffee.

Jamie has gone upstairs, but Lee and Jack are still there, so I give them a contrite look and lower my voice. "Can we please just table everything for now? I don't want any drama in front of Sophie."

Jack nods tightly. Lee glowers at me before heading for the stairs. I know they're not happy with me right now, but it's not like I planned to get trapped in Ben's flat and then have my romantic life explode like a grenade in all our faces.

I return with Sophie's tea on a little ceramic tray because I know how picky Brits can be about preparing it themselves. Thanking me, she pours some milk into the steaming cup and adds one teaspoon of sugar.

She uses the small spoon to stir her tea. "I tendered my resignation before I came here."

I stare at her in surprise. "You did? Why?"

"Because I can't do it anymore," she says simply. "Work for that vile man."

My eyebrows shoot up. Whoa. I got the sense she didn't like him, but it's obvious her feelings for Ben go beyond disgust. It sounds like she truly despises him.

"I never wanted this job," Sophie confesses. She sips her tea, hands shaking slightly. "My father worked for the duke—Ben's father, Andrew—for thirty years."

"He did?"

She nods. "My grandfather had connections with the Tulleys and was able to secure a job with them for my father. Dad started as a driver, but Andrew quickly took a liking to him. My dad is—was—a boisterous, outgoing man. Everyone was drawn to him. Nowadays, he's not as vibrant." Sadness flickers in her eyes. "He and Andrew grew close, friends even, and eventually Dad became his private secretary. Seemed only natural that when Benjamin required his own assistant, my father recommended me for the position. I was twenty-two when I began working for the Tulleys."

"Was Ben easier to work with at the start?"

"God, no." She laughs derisively. "He's an absolute wreck of a man. Scandals follow him everywhere. I needed money, however, to pay my way through uni. I was planning to leave his employment once I graduated, but then Dad got sick. It happened so fast."

My heart squeezes.

"When I told you I pay out of pocket for my father's housing, what I mean is my terms of employment pay for it. The Tulleys have a deep fondness for my dad, so the duke was more than happy to renegotiate my contract with his son to include provisions for my father's care."

"That was kind of him," I say.

She sets down her cup, guilt creasing her face. "I want you to know—I've never been asked to cover up any criminal or illegal behavior. I've never witnessed him lay a hand on a woman or do anything untoward sexually. But I've flushed his drugs and tucked him in the back seats of cars after causing some scene or another at a club or party. I've cleaned up his messes because if I didn't, I wouldn't be able to keep my father where he is."

"I get it," I say, completely sincere. "I would do the same for my dad."

Sophie gives a firm shake of her head. "But no more. Benjamin has conducted himself in reprehensible ways before, but he went too far last night. He said he locked you in the loo?" She looks horrified now.

I reassure her. "No, I locked myself in. They didn't want me to go, so I needed to escape in order to try and call a cab."

"But they took your phone?" she prompts. "He mentioned something about that as well."

I nod, my pulse quickening when I remember the panic I'd felt after Ben and his friends wouldn't let me leave.

Noting my response, Sophie's eyes flash. "And who is to say what would have happened if you hadn't gone to the bathroom, Abbey? Ben might not be a sexual aggressor, but I don't know about his mates. He doesn't fraternize with the most upstanding of citizens. He put you in a dangerous position last night."

"No, I put myself in it. But I understand what you're saying. And I don't excuse Ben's behavior. I'm not too thrilled with him at the moment either."

"I can't work for a man like that." Her tone is bleak. Laced with unhappiness.

"But what about your dad?"

"I will need to find other arrangements for him, I'm afraid."

That makes me sick to my stomach. As touching as it is that she's resigning because of what Ben did to me, she has to think about her family. Her dad needs to come first here.

"This isn't only about you," Sophie says as if reading my mind. "It has been a long time coming. You asked me what he does, remember? And I responded that he 'runs' his nonprofit. That was a lie. *I* run it. I do all the work and receive none of the recognition. Meanwhile, Benjamin makes mess after mess, and I'm forced to clean up after him." She shakes her head. "No more. I don't want this to be my life. And I know Dad wouldn't want it to be either. He liked and respected Andrew Tulley, but Ben doesn't take after his father. The duke isn't the brightest of men, but he's not self-destructive."

"Ben must take after Lawrence," I say dryly.

"It appears so." She sets her cup on the tray. "Anyway. I wanted to apologize again for his behavior."

"It's not your apology to give."

"Nonetheless. I am sorry." Sophie rises from the sofa. "I should be off. Thank you for the tea, Abbey."

"You're welcome here any time. And I really appreciate that you stopped by."

Once Sophie is gone and I've shut the front door, I turn around to find Lee standing right in front of me.

I jerk in surprise. "Jesus, where did you come from?"

"I'm a ninja." Lee glares at me. "House meeting."

I throw up my hand. "No. We'll have to save it for tonight. I need to get ready for school." When he opens his mouth to object, I hurry on. "Please. This has already been the busiest morning I've ever had, and it's not even nine."

"Fine. Tonight," Lee mutters.

I brush past him and charge upstairs, closing my bedroom door behind me. I lean against it and take a breath. Trying to absorb everything that occurred in the span of forty frickin' minutes.

At the memory of Yvonne's ambush, I release a heavy breath and realize I should probably give Nate a heads-up about what went down. When I grab my phone from the desk, I find a couple missed texts from him, sent while I was chatting with Sophie. I ignore those and send my own.

Me: Yvonne came by.

He responds a few minutes later.

Nate: What for?

Me: A chat.

Nate: Dare I ask?

Me: She stopped just short of flipping the dining room table. After calling me a cow.

Nate: Whoa. I'm sorry. Wouldn't have thought her capable of that.

Me: All good. I held my ground.

Nate: Sure you're all right?

Me: I'm fine. And to answer your earlier questions, I'm fine after last night too. I should've listened to you about Ben. He ended up being a creep.

Nate: I'm glad you came to your senses, but I'm sorry it had to happen the way it did. That bloody prick, not letting you leave his flat. I'd like to pay him a visit.

> Me: Don't. It's over. I don't even want to think about that guy anymore.

> Nate: I'm working tonight, but I'd like to see you. Come over around 10?

> Me: Yeah. That sounds good. See you later xx

When I go downstairs, Lee and Jamie have already left for class, but Jack lingers at the front door. We eye each other for a moment. Then he holds out his arms without a word and I step into them.

He wraps those muscular arms around me in a tight hug. "Sorry I snapped at you in the kitchen."

I hug him back. "It's all right. Tensions were running high."

"You okay?" he asks, his breath tickling my forehead as he presses a kiss atop it. "It's been a bloody mad morning."

"Tell me about it." I tip my face up, and suddenly his lips are on mine.

"I was so fucking worried about you last night," he says hoarsely.

I touch his cheek, giving it a reassuring stroke. "I know. And I never got the chance to thank you for coming to my rescue."

Jack kisses me again, deep and earnest.

And I realize I can't keep doing this. Seeing them both. I just made plans to meet Nate later tonight, and now I'm standing here kissing Jack.

It's time to make a choice. I know that. But I also can't help thinking about everything Celeste said yesterday, how I don't even know what I'm choosing.

Sure, they both offer me hot kisses and sexy words, but what they're sorely lacking in providing is clarity. I want to know where I stand with them. Where they truly see things going with me.

I think it's time I find out.

40

AFTER CLASSES, I SPEND MOST OF THE AFTERNOON IN THE LIBRARY, alternating between doing research and updating Mr. Baxley about the chaos of yesterday. He's horrified by Ben Tulley's behavior and chastises me for going to the penthouse by myself, which adds another name to the long list of people I've been lectured by.

Later, I manage to escape the dreaded house meeting because Lee ends up going for dinner with Lord Eric. And since Jack has an evening match that finishes after nine, I also manage to avoid any awkward moments with him about the fact that I'm seeing Nate tonight. Which means I'm able to leave the house undetected when I slip out the door.

After we slept together for the first time back in November, I assured Nate we didn't need to have "the talk." That I'd check in after a few weeks to see where we stood. But now it's been more than a few weeks, and I still don't know where we stand.

I have a plan in mind when I show up at his flat. I'd spent all day forming the words in my head.

And it all goes to shit the moment he kisses me hello.

"Was worried you might try avoiding me," he mumbles against my mouth. "After the Yvonne thing."

"Not your fault," I mumble back. "She's got a good reason."

He's mind-altering. A quick drug that hits the bloodstream and seizes control of my senses. It doesn't take much. The slightest taste. I'm barely through the door before his hands are climbing my ribs and we're halfway to his bed.

"Sorry I couldn't be there," he says between kisses.

"I don't think it would have helped."

His tongue touches mine. The scent of his skin fogs my senses. I've got his belt loops between my fingers, grabbing for his zipper before my better judgment snaps me back to the mission at hand.

"Wait," I say, breaking away from his kiss. "I wanted to talk to you about something."

He dips his head to kiss me again. "Talk away."

Laughing, I shrug out of his arms. "Yeah, not when you're distracting me with kisses."

Nate offers a cheeky grin. "All right. I won't kiss you for two minutes. Your time starts now."

"Where is this going?" I blurt out.

He blinks in surprise. "What?"

"Sorry. I should have segued into that better." I shrug sheepishly. "Basically, I think it's time we have the talk."

His hands fall to his sides. "Where's this coming from? What did Yvonne say to you?"

"Nothing. This has nothing to do with her. I'm asking for myself." My breath comes out in a slow exhale. "What do you want from me, Nate?"

"I'm not asking anything of you." He steps back to lean against the footboard of his bed, the top button of his jeans undone. "I like you the way you are."

I nod slowly, my gaze taking in our surroundings. Nate's apartment is sparse, with minimal furniture and the bare necessities. No more than four plates or forks. A single couch. Two chairs at his kitchen table. A bass guitar and amp in the corner. By the door, his leather jacket, helmet, keys, and backpack hang ready for an escape at a moment's notice. If he took off for good, there'd be hardly anything here to attest he'd ever existed. He would go from a memory to a figment of my imagination in an instant.

"You know what I mean," I say quietly. "I want to know where this is going."

"You're asking if I want to be your boyfriend," he says with far less enthusiasm than someone who's excited about the idea.

That stings a little. "Essentially, yes. Or if not now, is that stop coming up on this road?"

Nate lets out a sigh that never precedes a quick and decisive yes.

"I just got out of a relationship. And I'm sincerely sorry you've been dragged into the mess of it. But, Abbey, I can't say right now what I want out of this. I'm not looking to jump right back into a commitment yet."

Whatever disappointment he reads on my face, it prompts him to approach me, taking me by the waist.

"I'm enjoying our time together the way we are," he says, his voice rough. "Why do we have to make these decisions right now? Summer will be here before we know it, and I don't want to leave you with false promises before I hit the road. Can't we feel it out? Let it happen organically?"

Under different circumstances, nothing he's saying would be unreasonable. I mean, if we never met the right people at the wrong time, rom-coms wouldn't exist. Nate's not a bad guy for knowing himself and his own limitations.

But I also know mine.

"I'm sorry. No." I step out of his grasp, hanging my head. "I like you. A lot. Honestly, it would only take a little nudge to make me fall for you," I admit. "So yeah, I can't let myself become any more attached to someone who might take off without warning one day and leave me behind. Not knowing when or if he'll be back or if he'll still want me."

"Abbey—" he tries to interject.

"I'm not built for that kind of uncertainty, Nate. My heart can't take it."

"So that's it then? You're done?" His expression becomes strained. Unhappy. "*We're* done?"

I ignore the wild stinging behind my eyelids. "I think we have to be. I'm sorry."

With a sad smile, I kiss him on the cheek and shake my head when he asks me to stay. I take one last look at his rugged exterior and intense dark eyes. Then I go to the door, pieces of me dropping like bread crumbs as I walk away from him.

It's just past eleven when I walk through the front door, my heart bruised and battered, the unbearable weight of it making my feet drag. I didn't think it would hurt so bad, saying goodbye to Nate. But at least now I have my answer.

It was never going anywhere.

Doomed from the start.

"Abbs? Is that you?"

I swallow a curse at the sound of Lee's voice. Damn it. Why is he home? Why couldn't he spend the night with Eric and give me a reprieve? After a morning from hell and a night of heartbreak, I want to be left alone.

But when I peer through the doorway, I find not only Lee but all three of my flatmates congregated in the living room, wearing matching grave expressions.

"I'm sorry, you guys, I can't deal with a house meeting right now," I say wearily. "This has been the longest day of my life."

"Trust me, this is a critical chat." Lee chews on his lip, appearing genuinely concerned.

Jack nods. "It's not good, Abbs."

"Don't freak out," Jamie warns.

"Are you kidding?" A sick feeling washes over me. "How can I not freak out? You all look like you just found out a meteor is headed for Earth. What the hell is going on now?"

Without a word, Lee places his phone in my hand.

I peer down at the screen and gasp at the headline.

GUNNER BLY'S TEENAGE DAUGHTER SPOTTED AT TULLEY'S LONDON LOVE NEST!

Photos from last night assault my eyes as I keep scrolling. Me on the curb arguing with my flatmates. A disheveled Ben, his chest bare beneath his open shirt, lunging toward me. He looks like he crawled out of an opium den. I look rough myself. Flushed and agitated.

"Are you okay?" Jack says. Softly. Like he's afraid the slightest tremor might set off an explosion.

The breach of my privacy is the least of my worries. I'm staring down much bigger problems now.

My dad is going to freak when he sees this.

"This is not good," I say weakly.

"Can you contact them to take the pictures down?" Lee frets.

Jamie laughs. "Yes, because that's a thing tabloids do."

"They're paparazzi. I can't stop them from taking photos of me on a public street." I moan, handing back the phone. "Fuck. *Fuck*! He's going to kill me. He's legit going to kill me. With his bare hands."

"Maybe—"

The doorbell rings, and Lee shrieks in frustration.

"Make it stop! Can we not be left alone today!"

"This *is* getting rather ridiculous," Jamie remarks as he wanders into the hall to answer the door.

Two seconds later, a familiar male voice fills the flat.

"Where is she? Where is my daughter?"

I freeze. Oh my God.

I'm done for.

Deceased.

Scatter my ashes.

41

My father stumbles into the living room and skids to a stop a second later. When our gazes meet, I'm genuinely concerned about his appearance. He's beyond frazzled, eyes rimmed red from exhaustion, hair messy and unruly as he rakes a hand through it. He's wearing wrinkled jeans and an old band sweatshirt. Not a Gunner Bly one. Aerosmith. It's faded and worn, one of his favorites.

The air is thick with tension, pouring off him in palpable waves. Dad's suspicious gaze travels around the room.

It briefly rests on me.

Then Lee. Jack. Jamie.

Then returns to me.

"Oh, hello," Lee says, gawking at the middle-aged rocker standing in our living room.

Dad ignores him. "Who the fuck are these people, Abbey?" he demands.

I swallow the lump of fear in my throat. "Um. They're my roommates."

Silence crashes over us.

Endless hear-a-pin-drop silence.

Chest rising as he slowly inhales, Dad stares at me for an eternity and a half. Then he speaks in a low, deadly voice.

"I'd like a moment alone with my daughter."

The guys remain frozen in place.

He barks, "Get lost!" and they scatter like rats fleeing a sinking ship. I don't think Lee even puts on his shoes. The front door slams behind them.

"Dad—" I start.

"Sit," he orders, pointing at the dining table.

I scramble for a chair and try again. "Dad—"

"No. Don't say a word, kid. Not a word."

We sit at opposite ends of the table, my hands so clammy I have to wipe them on the front of my pants. The silence drags on again. It's unbearable. But it also gives me plenty of time to consider how we got here. All the opportunities I had to tell him the truth about my living situation but choked on my words, because the lie was easier to live with than the consequences.

I did this to myself.

"You saw the photos in the tabloids," I finally say. This time, he doesn't cut me off.

"Yes." His jaw is tight.

"But how are you here now? They were literally only published an hour ago."

"Some asshole from the *Daily Star* emailed my publicist at five o'clock this morning asking for a comment to go with the story."

My eyebrows shoot up. "Man, they work fast. The vultures were hungry."

"Eleanor knows to contact me at any hour if it pertains to my kid," Dad says flatly. "She texted me the photos they sent her. I took one look and booked a flight out."

He looks haggard. Half a day of traveling does a number on anyone, but I suspect the tired wrinkles around his eyes and limp posture are evidence of the shock it gave him to see his daughter plastered in the pages of a magazine, photographed with random men, including a notorious British lord.

This was a difficult transition for him, my year abroad. And now that he's discovered I've been lying to him, it justifies all his fears.

I knew better. I anticipated this very moment but convinced myself I could prevent the inevitable. Or at least delay it long enough to enjoy myself in the meantime.

Unfortunately, I never did come up with a plan for when it all blew up in my face.

"Okay," I start. "That headline is bad, but I promise you, it's not as bad as it looks—"

"Yeah, let's circle back on that one," Dad interrupts. He pushes hair off his forehead and searches my face. "First and foremost—who are those boys, these roommates?"

"They're exactly who they said they were in their emails. Lee, Jack, and Jamie." I bite my lip. "Only difference is they're not girls."

"Did you know this from the beginning?"

"No. I swear I didn't. I truly thought I was rooming with women. I promise."

He exhales, dropping his elbows to his knees. "You lied to me, Abbey. And not just once. This was a pretty elaborate scheme. I wouldn't have thought you could be so conniving."

Hearing him say that hurts more than I expected. It's like a dull knife stabbing at my chest. I hate disappointing my dad. Even worse, there's genuine pain in his eyes. It guts me.

"I panicked." It's the truth. The best one I have. "I got here in the middle of the night, and Lee opened the door, only Lee's a guy, and oh, Jackie and Jamie are guys too, and now what the hell am I going to do?"

"Call me. You tell me and we figure it out. I could have gotten you an apartment somewhere."

"I slept on it. I was convinced that in the morning, I would call you. Go to a hotel or whatever. But honestly, I figured you'd freak out and put me back on a plane."

"Give me a little credit," he says, wounded.

"Then I woke up and met them all downstairs for breakfast. We hit it off right away. I swear, it was like we'd known each other for years. It felt like home, and by the time we were done eating, I didn't want to leave."

"You could have trusted me enough to listen."

I can see how much it hurts him that I thought so little of his willingness to hear me out. That I expected him to be so harsh without a chance to plead my case. And I realize how unfair it was to decide what he'd say before he had a chance.

"Then once I decided not to tell you, it got complicated. I kept having to tell bigger lies to cover for the first one." It's hard to speak past the lump of guilt jammed in my throat.

"I think that's the part I'm having the most trouble with." There's anger in his tone, though he doesn't raise his voice. Looking back on those lies, I'm ashamed I found them so easy to live with. "It wasn't just one mistake. You tricked me over and over again. Who was the girl from the dress studio?"

"Celeste." I hang my hand shamefully. "Lee's twin sister."

"Fuck's sake, Abbey."

"I know. I'm sorry. Like so, so sorry. I know what I did was horrid, and I do regret it. I've been regretting it for months. I wanted to tell you, but I didn't know how to admit to everything I'd done. I was afraid."

"Was it worth it?"

That's a loaded question. And it pains me that a big part of me still thinks it was. I know now that I might have convinced him to let me stay. Even keep living in the house. Or maybe the last several months have softened him and I was right all along. Maybe he would've snatched me home in an instant. Either way, while I'm sorry for lying to him, I don't regret my time here.

"I shouldn't have lied. But separate from that, I do love it here. The neighborhood. My school. This house. And I know I can't exactly claim independence and keep asking you to sign tuition and rent checks, but I'd really like to finish out the year if you'll let me. I love my school, Dad. The Talbot Library is the greatest place on earth." Tears well up in my eyes. "I don't want to leave."

"I'm not here to drag you home, Abbs."

I blink through the burn of tears. "No?"

"No. I came so I could look you in the eye while you explained that headline, those pictures. But I get it now." His voice is heavy with remorse. "I lived a full life before I even turned twenty-five, one with packed tour buses and endless party favors. I didn't want that lifestyle to ever get you in its clutches. And meanwhile, you're over here begging me to keep going to school because you love the *library*." He starts to laugh, deep and raspy. "Not sure why I was so worried."

"I mean, that headline in the *Star* wasn't exactly something to *not* worry about."

"Yes. And I think we've circled back. Care to explain?"

"I told you about Lord Tulley, remember? He lent me those papers for my research project about his family." Bitterness coats my throat. "And then he sort of used them as a ruse to get me over to his penthouse."

Dad's eyes flash.

"No, nothing like that. He was having a party. Seems like Ben just wants everyone to get coked up and drunk with him. Makes him feel better about being a degenerate, I guess." I hurry on. "I didn't, by the way. Do drugs. I had one glass of wine before I realized I didn't want to be there. I called my roommates, and they came and got me."

I think back to last night, how the guys dropped everything to bail me out. They'd thought nothing of bursting into Ben's building, forcing their way past the doorman, and kicking down Ben's door because I needed help. Nobody can say they don't care.

When it counted, they were all there for me.

"The paps caught us when Ben was coming out to try to convince me to return to the party."

"So your roommates got you?"

"Yeah. They're good people, Dad. They've been good to me." I shrug. "We're a family."

"I see." He nods slowly. "So. What now?"

"Now…well, I promise to never lie to you again." I rethink that. "Okay, no. I can't promise not to tell a fib or two. But I'll never lie to you about something of this magnitude again."

His lips twitch. "I'll take it."

I smile. "Shake on it?"

We reach across the table to shake, and the moment his strong hand encloses mine, it feels like a load has been lifted off my chest.

"Come on," he says, tugging me to my feet. "How about we go out to eat? I'm starved."

"Might be kind of late to get a table anywhere," I point out. "But there are some takeout places that are open late. Or there's the pub if you're up for it. But first let me rescue the guys. I'm pretty sure they're hunkered down on the stoop without their coats and shoes."

I'm not wrong. I hear their muffled voices when I approach the front door. I fling it open to find them shivering under the porch light, rubbing their hands together in the cold like a trio of street urchins in a Dickens novel.

"You can come in now," I say, unable to smother my smile.

"We would've gone somewhere, but neither of us had shoes," Lee says repentantly, gesturing to his socks and Jamie's bare feet. "And Jackie boy forgot to put on a shirt again."

Jack glances at me. "Everything okay?"

I nod. "Good. We worked it all out."

We trudge back inside, where Dad greets the guys with narrowed eyes. Then he sighs and sticks out his hand. "I'm Gunner," he says.

Lee stares at him. "Oh, we know."

Jamie's the first to shake his hand, followed by Jack, then Lee. After the introductions, Dad purses his lips for a moment before extending an olive branch.

"I thought I might treat us all to dinner."

"I'm game," Jamie says instantly. He's always hungry.

Lee checks his watch. "I think Molly's is still serving food."

"Or I can get us a table at Soho House," Dad suggests.

"Right." An excited Lee snatches his coat off the hook on the wall. "Let's go."

"Wait," Jamie says. "I need to change my shirt." He smacks Jack's arm. "You need to put one on. Something clean, please. Don't embarrass us."

"What's Soho House?" I pipe up.

Lee and Jamie both shoot me a glare like I should be ashamed for asking.

"Somewhere we can get a bite without too much attention," Dad says. "You'll like it, kiddo. They do a great grilled cheese."

A dumbfounded Lee gawks at him. "It's an A-list only members club for actors and musicians and the like," he explains to me. "Very swank."

I sigh. "Dad, you don't have to make a fuss—"

Before I can even finish, Lee smothers me with his hand over my face. "She's delirious. Please, make a fuss."

"Abbs," Jamie shouts from upstairs. "Can you steam my shirt?"

"Look what you've done," I tell my father. "I hope they have a midnight menu."

———————

Our late-night dinner is not nearly as awkward as I expect, even with Dad asking the guys a mountain of questions. I suspect he wants to feel them out, give them the business or whatever, but by the time we're ready to head home, the four of them have become fast friends.

"Abbs, we're off," Lee says when I return from the ladies' room. "Dad is tired."

"Really? You're on a dad-name basis with him now?"

"Let me have this, Abigail," he hisses in my ear. "Give me a superstar for a second father, and I'll forgive you for hiding all your romances from me."

"Deal."

We exchange a grin, and I loop my arms around Lee in a tight hug. Emotion floods my chest as it occurs to me how much I've come to value his friendship. Today was brutal, tonight even worse. My heart still aches from my goodbye with Nate, yet one hug from Lee Clarke soothes some of that sting.

"What was that for?" he demands when I release him.

"Just an I-really-appreciate-our-friendship hug."

"Right then." He's rolling his eyes but at the same time beaming.

It's 1 a.m. when the five of us return to the flat so Dad can grab his suitcase. Despite all the guys offering up their own rooms for him, he's decided to stay at a boutique hotel nearby. You can retire the rock star but not the rock star's penchant for expensive hotel rooms and thousand-thread-count sheets.

"I'll grab you an Uber," I tell him, pulling out my phone in the front hall. "At this hour, it shouldn't take long at all to get one."

"Thanks, baby girl. Just gonna use the john and then I'll be out of your hair."

Lee stops my father at the stairs. "Thank you so much for dinner, sir. It was lovely."

"Quite," Jamie agrees. "Glad you'll be sticking around for a few days, Mr. Bly."

"I already told you guys, call me Gunner." With an exasperated smile, Dad bounds off to use the bathroom.

"I'm gonna grab a shower." Jack pauses on the bottom step, his gaze finding mine. He lowers his voice, which is futile since Lee is standing right there and isn't polite enough to pretend he's not listening. "Can we chat before bed?"

I nod, because I know we do need to talk.

As Jack heads upstairs, I turn to Lee and Jamie, giving them a grateful smile. "Thanks for being such good sports. You didn't have to stay up so late on a school night for him."

"Are you mental? It was bloody awesome," Lee declares, shaking his head.

"I'm sorry, did you just say *awesome*?" My surprise turns to suspicion when I remember my dad said it a bunch of times at dinner. Looks like Lee has a new role model.

"I meant *brilliant*," he growls before stomping to the kitchen. "Fancy a cuppa?" he calls over his shoulder.

"Yes, thanks," Jamie says, trailing after him.

I hear a plaintive meow from the top of the stairs and spot Hugh peeking around the corner. When I call his name, our grumpy cat turns and saunters off.

Rolling my eyes, I go upstairs to find him. I swear, if I didn't remember to pay attention to Hugh, the damned thing would be starved for affection. The Lord of Cats would not approve of Lee's stone heart when it comes to our dear pet.

At the top of the landing, I hear low voices wafting out of Jack's open door. I grin, hoping Dad hasn't cornered Jack to interrogate him. I should probably throw him a lifeline.

"No, I'm happy we got a chance to talk alone," Jack is saying.

I near the door, ready to interfere and protect Jack from a dad lecture, when my father responds with, "Thank you for not mentioning it to Abbey."

I stop.

Thank you for not mentioning it to Abbey?

Not mentioning *what* to Abbey?

Unease tightens my chest. I creep closer, no longer eager to interrupt them.

"Of course" is Jack's answer. "I am a bit confused, though. Did you truly not know I was a bloke?"

My father's laughter sounds muffled. Maybe because my heart

is now thundering like a cattle stampede from the anger coursing in my blood.

Either I'm imagining things, or the two of them...*know* each other.

"Had no idea," Dad says. "Gonna have to reread those emails now—"

Emails?

"—to figure out how the hell I could've missed it. I saw that profile picture and thought you were the blond girl."

Jack chuckles. "That's my sister."

"Well, regardless of the mistaken identity, I do appreciate you looking out for my daughter."

"It was no problem, really. Although—"

Jack's next words stop me cold.

"—I do wish you'd let me return the money."

42

I feel sick.

Weak.

The last time I felt this winded, it was after I got tackled by that behemoth Ruth Caskill during a game of field hockey junior year of high school. Only this isn't a game. This is the implosion, the ultimate betrayal, of two relationships that meant the world to me.

My father paid Jack to "look out for me."

He fucking *paid* him.

Actual money.

"That's totally unnecessary, kid. I'm the one who reached out to you in the first place. You don't need to return a cent—"

I burst into Jack's room, shoving the open door with such force it slams against the wall with a deafening *bang*.

Both men jerk in shock.

"Abbs?" Dad looks at me in confusion.

But Jack…Jack knows I heard every word. His face pales the moment he sees mine, broad shoulders dropping.

I stare at them both, my breathing so shallow I start to feel light-headed.

Somehow, I muster a semicalm tone and not a shriek of outrage. "What money is he talking about, Dad?"

My father briefly closes his eyes.

"What the hell is going on?" I push. "You two know each other?"

When Dad's eyelids flick open, I glimpse the unmistakable hue of guilt.

"Not quite," he answers in a strained voice. "I didn't know Jack here was a man."

"But you had contact with him before I left for London?"

"Not before." There's a pause. "I emailed him the day after you left."

My bottom lip starts trembling. I'm so angry I'm about to cry. I suck in a breath, my gaze shifting between them. They exchange a quick, frantic look as if waiting for the other to jump in with an explanation for me, but neither of them speak.

I release the breath, my entire body quavering. "One of you'd better fucking start talking."

"Language," Dad chides.

"No. Fuck that." Another bolt of fury sizzles up my throat and clamps around so tight, my next words exit in a strangled growl. "You've both been lying to me for months?"

Jack finally speaks. "That's not how it was." He scrubs a hand over his forehead, gaze averted. "I got an email from your dad on your second day here."

"Just an introduction," Dad takes over, hurrying to explain.

"Where did you even get Jack's email?" I ask suspiciously.

"It was on the housing listing. You emailed me the details, remember? I saved all the contact info."

I nod, remembering that the house-share ad *did* list Jack's email on the contact line. I'd emailed that address first, receiving a one-line response saying Lee was handling the details and giving me a number to text instead. Looks like Dad just kept on chatting with "Jackie."

"It's not a big deal," my father says, trying to downplay it. "I told him it was your first time traveling alone and living abroad. Asked him to watch out for you. Keep you out of trouble."

"And offered to pay him for his babysitting services?" My sarcasm can't be controlled.

"Abbey." Dad looks wounded. "It wasn't babysitting. I only wanted to make sure you were being looked after."

"He paid you," I say to Jack, seeking confirmation.

After a beat, Jack nods.

"How much?"

He mumbles something under his breath.

"What was that?"

"Paid my rent for the year," Jack repeats. He looks as sick as I feel.

My stomach churns. I gulp down the bile coating my throat.

I nod a couple times before turning back to my father. "What, you didn't feel like offering to pay everyone's rent? Just *Jackie's*?" I say the name mockingly.

"He offered," Jack says quietly. "I told him Lee and Jamie would never accept any payment. They're both loaded."

"But you, oh, *you* were happy to take my father's money."

He bites his lip. "I didn't know you, Abbey. Seemed like an easy gig. All I had to do was make sure you were staying out of trouble."

My eyes burn. No. No, I will not cry. So what if I thought Jack was spending time with me because he liked me and just found out it was because my dad was paying him?

I. Will. Not. Cry.

I swallow repeatedly. My throat is tight with tears I refuse to cry. "I see. So our friendship was a 'gig.'"

"No, of course not," he says quickly.

"Stop talking, Jack," I whisper. "Just stop."

I draw another breath. My lungs hurt from the oxygen I'm trying to force into them.

I coldly address my father. "You are such a hypocrite. You sat there in my dining room tonight telling me how conniving I was! I groveled and apologized while you chastised me about lying to you, and turns out you're a liar too! An even bigger one. You made me believe I was free."

"Abbey." He blanches. "You're not my prisoner."

I ignore the denial. "You couldn't even let me make my own mistakes. You have so little trust and faith in me, you had to insinuate yourself into my story, my adventure. My"—my voice catches—"friendships. You…"

It happens.

The tears start to fall.

Which means I'm not only gutted and enraged, I'm also mortified. I swipe at my wet cheeks with the sleeve of my sweater.

"Okay." I take another breath. Give my face another aggressive wipe. "I can't talk to either one of you right now. It's late and I'm exhausted, and if we do this now, I'm going to say a lot of things I'll regret. So please." I can't even look at my father as I say, "Just go to your hotel."

"Kiddo—"

"Go, Dad. Please. We can deal with this in the morning."

I can't look at Jack either. It hurts too much. So I turn on my heel and stiffly exit his bedroom. I find Lee in the hall, wearing his silk pajama pants, and a shirtless Jamie standing at his open doorway. Their faces are stricken. I don't know how much they heard, but I wasn't trying to be quiet about it, so I assume they got the gist of it.

"I'm going to bed," I say flatly, then walk into my bedroom.

Whispers sound from the hallway. The soft thud of footsteps near my room. I scowl at the closed door. Swear to God, if Jack or my dad are out there… But then the voices fade and footsteps echo on the stairs.

I hear the front door close. I hear the lock engage.

Then footsteps again, and this time, they *do* stop outside my door.

"Abbs," Jack says softly. "Can I come in? Please."

I wanted to wait until morning, but I realize there's no way I'm going to sleep tonight. Not with so many unanswered questions gnawing at my brain.

I open the door and am nearly knocked off my feet by the wave of raw emotion rippling in Jack's blue eyes.

He enters without a word. I stand at the foot of my bed. He leans against the door.

The silence is excruciating. Bitterness rising in my throat, I stare at him, this guy I believed to be my friend.

No, much more than a friend.

I was falling for him.

Jack drags a hand through his blond hair before his arm drops to his side. "I'm sorry," he says simply.

"Show me the emails."

My request startles him. He furrows his brow. "What?"

"Show me the fucking emails, Jack."

He flinches at my sharp tone. My harsh expletive.

"If you stand any chance of me understanding this, then I need to see the emails."

"Okay. Okay." He lets out a ragged breath and pulls his phone from his pocket.

As he hurriedly swipes a finger over the screen, silence once again fills the room. Even Hugh has decided not to intrude. There's not a meow to be heard from our aggressively vocal feline. The cat lies in the center of my bed, giving Jack the shifty eyes.

Finally, Jack passes me the phone.

I swallow my nausea and read the first email in the thread.

It's from Bly_Guy@gmail.com, my dad's throwaway account, the one he gives acquaintances or uses to sign up for online newsletters. He introduces himself as "Abbey's father" and, proving he wasn't lying to me before, informs "Jackie" that this is the first time his daughter is traveling alone, and gee, it would *really* ease his mind if "you guys could watch out for my daughter." Stick close to her for the first little while.

Then comes the embarrassing part. He says he "totally gets" how it might cramp their style or feel like a "chore," so he's happy to pay them for this arduous task. He'll cover all their rent for the year, how does that sound? "Easy gig, right?"

Again, I'm a gig.

A fucking gig.

He signs it *Mr. Bly.* I don't blame him for that. Fame isn't always something one wants to advertise.

Particularly when you're trying to hire a covert nanny for your hapless daughter.

But who's bitter?

"Abbs," Jack starts.

I silence him with a withering glare, then continue to scroll.

In his reply, J.Campbell@gmail.com is quick to assure my father that it's no problem, of course Jackie will look out for Mr. Bly's little girl.

Someone kill me now, please.

I exhale slowly and force myself to keep reading. Jack jokes that Lee and Jamie don't need the extra cash; they've already paid their rent in full for the year. Trust him, Dad's money is wasted on those two.

Dad responds that he'd still like to show his gratitude for Jackie's kind assistance. What's Jackie's PayPal address? He's going to cover Jackie's rent for the year. "Not taking no for an answer!"

Jackie, my kind, amazing roommate, doesn't put up a fight. "Mr. Bly, this is beyond generous."

In that same email, Jack tells Dad he has a rugby match that night and won't be able to respond to any emails until the following day.

Dad's response is so absurd that hysteria-laced laughter bubbles out of my mouth.

"For fuck's sake," I mutter to Jack before reading aloud. "'Wow, it's so impressive you play rugby! Such a rough sport. And female rugby players? They're an especially tough breed.'" I stare at Jack in disbelief. "And in your reply, you just agree that female rugby players are hard-core!"

"I thought he meant in general. I didn't realize he thought *I* was the female rugby player," Jack sighs.

Oh my God. These two dumbasses.

It would almost be funny if not for the fact that they were corresponding behind my back. Treating me like a child who needed help tying her shoelaces. Like a sheltered little girl who couldn't be trusted to live her own life.

Anger ricochets through me as I remember Jack's behavior in those early weeks. All those times I thought he was being sweet and protective. Worrying when I was out for hours in Surrey. Taking me driving because he didn't trust Jamie to do it. Protecting me from his friend Sam and Nate and Ben Tulley.

He didn't care about *me*. He only cared about giving my father his money's worth.

The burn of betrayal sears my throat, throbbing with the lump of emotion already jammed in there.

"I can't believe you took his money," I choke out, and now I'm crying again, my cheeks soaked with tears. I *am* a child. A fucking fool.

"I didn't know you," he says, a desperate note creeping into his voice. "And I don't come from wealth like the rest of you. I wasn't kidding about Lee and Jamie paying their rent in full for the year. Meanwhile I'm taking my mother's money when she can barely afford her own mortgage. I saw an easy opportunity and I took it."

I blink rapidly, trying to control my overflowing emotions. "I don't even blame you for that, Jack. You're right—I come from a place of privilege. I don't know what it's like to barely make ends meet. What I blame you for is keeping it a secret from me. You could have told me."

He hangs his head in shame. "I didn't know how to. I knew you'd be livid."

"No shit."

"At the beginning, it didn't feel like a big deal. I just kept an eye on you. Made sure you didn't get too sloshed at the pub, you weren't partying too hard, that sort of stuff."

"So a babysitter."

"No. Yes. Maybe at the beginning. But it didn't take long to realize how bloody amazing you are. I liked you right away—"

"Not as much as you liked my dad's money," I cut in bitterly.

"—and I justified it by reminding myself it's what I'd do for any other mate. Just happened I was getting paid for it this time. But the more I got to know you, the more wrong it felt accepting money from your father." Swallowing, he gestures to his phone. "Read the last email."

"No. I'm done reading."

He implores me with his eyes. "Please. It's one email. I sent it after we went driving. The second time we kissed."

I set my jaw. "Yes. I remember. You kissed me back and then pulled away, pretending you wanted to preserve our friendship—"

"I wasn't pretending."

"—when it turns out you just felt guilty for accepting blood money from my father. Right? Isn't that why you kept running away every time we kissed?"

"Please," he says. "Just read it."

After a moment of reluctance, I force myself to look at the screen.

Mr. Bly, as generous as you've been, I don't feel comfortable accepting any more rent payments from you. I consider Abbey a good friend, and I promise you I'll watch out for her regardless. I'd also like to return the funds you've already transferred, though I do need some time to pay those back.

Dad's response is typical. He tells him in no uncertain terms he won't accept any money Jack tries to pay back.

"Abbey," Jack pleads.

I lift my gaze from his phone.

"Doesn't that count for something?"

A sharp laugh slips out. I toss the phone back. "You want me to congratulate you for finding your conscience?"

He rubs his forehead, visibly tired. Anguished. "No. I..." He trails off.

I drop down on the edge of my bed as I think back to the past five, nearly six months. I didn't suspect for one second that Jack had been in contact with my *father*.

It's so humiliating.

No, it's…

"It's infantilizing," I mumble. "Do you realize how shitty this makes me feel? I knew my father didn't consider me an adult, but you… I thought you saw me as…" My throat tightens to the point of pain. "As a woman." I make a strangled noise. "But I was just a little kid you had to babysit."

"No," he insists. "That's not true at all."

More pieces start falling into place. "It all makes sense now. This is why you were keeping a distance at the start. Why you're still keeping a distance."

"There's no distance. I feel closer to you than nearly anyone else in my life," Jack says in a soft voice.

I go on as if he hasn't spoken. Because I don't believe him. I don't believe anything anymore.

"That's why you haven't asked me to stop seeing Nate. Why you haven't brought up the what-are-we subject. It's your way of keeping me at arm's length." I shake my head at my own foolishness. "I see that now. You told me you weren't the commitment type, but I didn't listen. That's on me."

"Please," he says, scrambling. "Let me fix this, Abbs."

"There's no need. This arrangement, the one with my father and now the one with me, has run its course."

"It hasn't. I can fix it."

He reaches for me, but I jump off the bed.

"I want to go to bed now, Jack. Just leave."

"Please—"

"No." With a trembling hand, I hold open my bedroom door. "We're done here."

He's reluctant to move, searching my expression for resolve.

When he sees no room for further argument, he steps toward the doorway.

"I'm sorry," he says roughly. "I never, ever meant to hurt you."

The lump obstructing my throat makes it difficult to speak. "We were bound to end up here. Better now than later, right?"

At that, I shut the door and sink into my bed. A moment later, Hugh leaps on top of me and does a few laps before curling at my feet. Feeling utterly numb, I watch the branches outside my window shudder in the wind for a while, replaying the careening avalanche of a night that has just fallen on my head.

The devastation is spectacular.

43

I skip my morning classes the next day and go to my father's hotel instead, where the concierge fawns and fusses over me like I'm the celebrity. The man even rides the elevator to the penthouse with me, then presents me to my father as if I'm a visiting dignitary and not the dude's daughter.

We don't say a word as we wait for the sycophantic gentleman to leave. Once he does, my father's polite expression collapses into itself, and he lets out an unsteady breath.

"Let's sit," he says.

"Fine." My tone isn't harsh but resigned. Yet he flinches all the same.

We settle on opposite ends of the plush love seat in the living area of his expensive suite. Across the room is a gleaming grand piano, on top of which sit an empty wineglass and two open bottles of red. The bench is pulled out, several pages of sheet music arranged on the piano shelf. I glimpse smudged notations done in pencil.

"Were you writing music?" I turn to him in surprise.

He nods. "Couldn't sleep. Stayed up all night working on a new song."

"Please don't tell me you're unretiring."

"Nah. I think I'll record it, though. Give it to you for your birthday this weekend."

My heart clenches. Damn it. Why does he have to say stuff like that? It makes it impossible to stay mad at him.

"You know when you first came to live with me, I used to sit and watch you sleep for hours?" Dad confesses. "Just fascinated that you were real. And terrified that I wouldn't know how to keep you alive. How to keep you happy and safe…"

He drifts off for a moment, donning a faraway expression.

"I know it might not have felt like it when I was touring, when you were left alone with your nannies, but you were the most precious thing to me. I'd lie awake every night while I was on tour thinking about all the ways I could screw you up."

"But you didn't screw me up," I point out.

"Because I made a conscious effort not to. Other parents, I'd see them let their twelve-year-old try a sip of wine. Drop their tweens off at the mall and let them roam around alone for hours. Let their teenagers get wasted, smoke pot. I thought they were nuts. Didn't they realize what kids do in malls? When I was sixteen, I got a BJ from my bandmate's sister in a goddamn dressing room."

"Ew, Dad. Gross. Next-level TMI." I'm cringing hard.

"I'm just saying, I knew all about trouble. I've seen girls your age strung out on God knows what, trying to sleep with anyone even remotely connected to some rock star or celebrity."

I know we're both thinking of my own mother when he says that. It's no secret Nancy slept with a few of Dad's roadies before she gained access to Gunner Bly. And although he's never confirmed it, the tabloids claim my father had a paternity test done before gaining custody of me. Normally I don't buy what they're selling, but I'm inclined to believe that story is true.

"I refused to let you go down that path," he says simply. "And I suppose that made me more protective than other parents."

"You suppose?" I can't stop the sarcastic snort that pops out.

"I was petrified when you got accepted to the Pembridge program," he admits. "I didn't know how to deal with the fear that

I wouldn't be there to protect you, and I guess I thought if I had a proxy over there, across the pond, it would save me some sleepless nights. It came from a good place, kid. Last night, you accused me of not having trust or faith in you. That's not true at all. It's the rest of the world I don't trust. Not you. Never you."

"You have no idea how humiliating it is, what you did. I thought you were finally allowing me some independence, and instead you were checking up on me behind my back."

"I'm sorry. It was wrong. What I did was wrong."

"I've waited my whole life to start living." My voice cracks. "Having my own stories and adventures, not just retelling yours."

Guilt creases his rugged features.

"There isn't much downside to being Gunner Bly's daughter, but it is a little chilly in your shadow. All I've ever wanted was some space to be my own person."

Dad curses under his breath. "Christ, kid. That one cuts deep. I didn't realize you felt that way."

"I don't want you to feel bad. It's not your fault that you are who you are." I sigh. "But it's time you allowed me to be who *I* am."

"And I promise to do that going forward. I promise to stop filling your head with all my stories and leave some space there for your own. Loosen the reins if you will."

"Thank you."

Silence falls between us, but I'm no longer stewing in anger or resentment. It's not possible to stay angry with my dad. Because I know he means it when he says it's coming from a good place. It would be one thing if his controlling nature stemmed from a need for power, to exert authority over his child like some toxic parents do. Dad's protectiveness comes from love and fear. How can I really hold that against him?

"Can you forgive me for going behind your back?" he asks hopefully.

"Of course I can. I don't love what you did, but I understand why. So we're good. We're okay." I search his still-anxious gaze. "*Are we okay?*"

"Baby girl." He scoots closer and slings one arm around me. "We're always okay. Yeah, I might be here right now because you wound up in the tabloids, but I don't care about that. I'm just glad I get to spend time with my daughter. And gratified to know she's happy and healthy and has good friends beside her. That's all I want for you, Abbey. I'm not here to ruin your life."

"I'd never think that." My eyes suddenly feel hot, stinging. "I'm so fortunate to be your kid. It's just you and me, big guy. No matter what."

He pulls me into a hug as he sniffs away the tears. I blink away a couple of my own, squeezing him tight. I have a great dad. I really do. And I've probably spent way too much time not appreciating how good I've had it.

He releases me and offers a contrite look. "I should add—I'm sorry I dragged your roommate into all this. I hope you two can work things out. He seemed like a good dude."

Just like that, I stiffen. "He accepted *payment* from you. To be my friend."

The reminder sends the burn of embarrassment to my throat.

"Before he even knew you," Dad points out. "And for what it's worth, he did try to return the money."

"I don't care," I say emphatically. "He breached my trust. How am I supposed to forgive that?"

"You just forgave me…"

"Yeah, because you're my father. He's my—" I stop abruptly.

Dad latches on to that. "I knew there had to be one," he sighs.

"Jack and I aren't dating."

"Are you sure about that?"

"We're not," I insist.

"But?"

"I thought maybe we were headed in that direction." Hesitation has me rubbing my temples. "But it's complicated, because there's someone else I like too."

"Someone else? Are you trying to give me a heart attack? How many guys are you dating, kiddo?"

God, this is awkward. And also oddly cathartic.

"Only one other guy. Nate. A friend of theirs. He says he likes me but can't be tied down. And he's a bassist."

Dad furrows his brow as if he's unsure whether to be disappointed he didn't raise me better or feel at fault that I'd be foolish enough to fall for a musician.

"Sounds like you have your hands full."

"It's been a struggle," I say, laughing at myself. "But don't worry, because it looks like it's over with both of them."

His eyes crinkle at the corners as a grin breaks free. "I don't know how bad I actually feel about that. I mean, I know this sucks for you, but it sure makes my job easier."

"The real sucky part is I might be in love with both of them."

"You're not."

"Um. Okay."

My baffled expression summons a chuckle from him. "Listen to me, kid. I know you've got a lot of love to give. Being *in* love, though, that's a whole different thing. The heart knows there's always just one."

"Really? When's it going to tell me?"

"You gotta listen. If you're in love with one of them, it's been telling you."

I don't know if that's true.

Or maybe it's proof I've never been in love with either one of them.

Dad sticks around for three days to spend time with me. I skip the classes I deem unimportant and squeeze the rest in between lunches and outings with my father.

But three jam-packed days of tourist activities also means the paps are staked out in front of the house at all hours to snap shots of Gunner Bly. He's still staying at the hotel, but the second he was spotted visiting me in Notting Hill, it was all over. We were besieged.

Lee is on cloud nine. Bouncing with joy every time a new photo pops up on Insta or some celebrity blog. Jamie's car parked on the curb. Our trash bins. Jack sweaty and shirtless. Lee in his pajamas. Me coming in and out of the house. It's typical paparazzi fodder and intrusive as hell, but Lee has ordered me to let the little people bask in the glow of celebrity. By little people, he means himself of course.

Last night over dinner, Jamie said there's an army of women salivating over Jack's shirtless pics on Twitter, which triggered an unwanted pang of jealousy followed by a jolt of angry self-reproach that I still care enough to feel jealous. Jack and I haven't spoken since the night I learned the truth, despite his attempts to get me alone. I've brushed him off every time, using my dad's visit as an excuse.

Really, though, I can't put my heart through another rehashing of Jack's betrayal.

On our last night, Dad takes me back to Soho House. Just me and him in a private dining room to celebrate my twentieth birthday. I make him promise not to tell Lee or the others, because I don't want them making a big deal out of it. Maybe if Jack and I were on better terms, I'd be down for a roommate hangout or even a small party, but right now it's too much of a hassle.

When our personal server brings out a huge slice of chocolate truffle cake with one lit candle on it, I smile at my father, the tears welling up.

"Happy birthday, baby girl."

"Thanks, big guy."

I blink away the tears and blow out my candle. The waiter discreetly places a second slice in front of Dad, then camouflages into the background.

"I get it now," Dad says as he watches me devour the cake.

"Get what?" I ask through a mouthful of truffle goodness.

"Why you needed to leave me."

The frank words and slightly sorrowful way he voices them send an arrow of pain to my heart.

"Dad—" I start to object.

"No, I understand, kiddo," he presses on. "I see it now. Thanks to me, your knowledge of the world before you moved here was… *secondhand*, I think is a good word for it. But how could you ever learn to take care of yourself, stand on your own two feet, if I didn't let you start living?"

"I think I'm getting there. The standing-on-my-own-two-feet part."

And I think I've done well. I left my safe, secure bubble in Nashville and entered a whole new world. I navigated a new city. Discovered the real struggles that come with having roommates. I made friends, real friends, who aren't part of my father's social circle or sealed in the same enclave of rich, rural Tennessee.

"Granted, I also made a ton of mistakes," I confess, reaching for my water glass. "Lied to you. Got tangled up in a love triangle. Naively fell victim to a scoundrel like Ben Tulley."

"You've made mistakes," he agrees. "That just means you're doing it right. The living part."

The rest of the evening passes way too fast, and before I know it, it's midnight and I'm on my front stoop, hugging my father goodbye. With a final wave, he slides into the back seat of a town car and is whisked off to the airport.

A rush of sadness washes over me as I step inside and make my way upstairs. When I enter my room, I find Jack leaning against my dresser.

I stiffen, my chest instantly going tight with emotion. A knot of anger and sadness. A deep stab of hurt.

"What are you doing in here?" I mutter, staring at my feet.

"I know you're still mad at me, but…am I at least allowed to say happy birthday?"

My head swings in his direction. "Who told you?"

"I overheard your dad talking to someone on the phone about the kind of birthday cake to serve at your dinner." Jack holds my gaze. "I get why you didn't want to make a fuss. I mean, Lee, right? But I'm glad you had a good birthday."

He takes a step forward, arms coming up slightly as if he's going to hug me.

"Don't," I warn.

But he walks to the doorway instead, where he pauses for several seconds, his expression growing more and more tormented.

"What can I do to earn your trust back?" he asks.

Sadness washes over me. "I don't know."

"Then it's over? Just like that?"

"It? What exactly was *it*, Jack? Were we together? Were we ever even headed for a relationship? Because the way I see it, you didn't care that I was seeing Nate—"

"I cared," he interjects.

"—and you didn't define anything. And now I know why. Because it wasn't real."

"It was real, Abbey." His voice is husky.

"I don't know if I believe that."

"Then let me prove it to you."

"I…" I blink to keep the tears at bay. "I can't. You're asking if we can go back to that relationship place when I don't even know if we can fix the friendship part."

He gives me a pained look. "Don't say that. We *are* friends. That hasn't changed."

"Go, Jack. Please. I need space. I've barely had a minute alone to sit with this since I found out the truth. So just let me be, okay?"

He exhales. "If that's what you want."

"It is."

"Okay." He steps toward the doorway, then glances over his broad shoulder, his blue eyes veiled. "Happy birthday, Abbs."

After he's gone, I lie on my bed and stare up at the ceiling. With a cranky wail, Hugh jumps up beside me and proceeds to swipe at strands of my hair while I do my best to ignore the agony clamped around my heart.

It serves me right that I'm lying here alone with an obstinate cat that's one tantrum away from chewing my throat out and making its nest in my entrails. A girl should know better than to hang her hopes on a man.

Or two, for that matter.

FEBRUARY

44

Nate: I hate this. I miss talking to you. I miss everything about you.

Me: I'm sorry.

Nate: You don't miss me? Not even a little bit?

Me: You know I do. But we're not seeing each other anymore, and I can't be your friend right now. Not while I still have feelings for you.

———————

Jack: Lee wants to know what you want for dinner.

Me: Then he can text me himself.

45

Jack: So that's it, we're going to keep tiptoeing around each other like this?

Me: I'm not tiptoeing. I'm just living my life.

Jack: Living your life avoiding me.

Jack: I get it. I deserve it.

Me: Don't put this on me. You're the one who's up every morning before everyone and out the door, then back after everyone's gone to bed or secluding yourself in your room.

Jack: Really. So if I tried to talk to you at home or sit with you, you'd allow it?

Me: Wouldn't you have to email my father first and ask if he'd allow it?

Me: What, no response?

Me: That's what I thought, Jack.

46

Jack: I hate this. I miss you.

Nate: I miss you.

Nate: Can't stop thinking about you, Abbey.

Nate: Are you just going to keep leaving me on read?

Me: If you keep texting things like that, then yeah. My heart can't take it.

Nate: I'm sorry. I'll stop.

MARCH

47

FEBRUARY SLIPPED THROUGH MY FINGERS. MARCH SNUCK UP ON
me while my back was turned. Then before I know it, spring break
is a week away, stalking me through the tall grass. I wanted to have
my Tulley paper done before the break, and it mostly is. I just wish
I had a resolution for Josephine. A proper ending other than "Who
the hell knows what happened next?"

But I'm at a dead end.

Amelia and I are peer editing for each other, and she'd lamented
about Josephine's unknown fate in the margins of my paper when
she sent it back last night. Her research tome on the killer prostitute
gang was brilliant, of course. Mine still feels unfinished.

Fortunately, on Monday morning, I receive two encouraging
emails.

The first is from the clerk at the Northern Star Line, now called
Global Cruise Initiatives. His name is Steve, and he was supposed
to be hunting any relevant documents connected to the *Victoria*. It's
been months with no word from him, so I assumed that was another
dead end. But he surprises me, writing to say he's attached some
digital copies of the original passenger manifest as well as documents
pertaining to insurance payouts for survivors of the disaster. The
latter isn't too helpful, given that it's confirmed William Tulley died
on the ship, but the former would go great in my appendix.

The second development comes from Ruby Farnham. Her email pops up as I'm meeting Celeste outside a tiny diner near her campus. We're squeezing in a quick lunch today between classes.

"Hello, darling," she greets me.

As we walk inside, I attempt to read the email and remove my coat at the same time.

"Anyone ever tell you you're an atrocious multitasker?" Celeste inquires politely after I wind up tangled in my sleeve with my phone lost somewhere in the bowels of my coat.

I manage to fish it out and grin at her. "Sorry. I was eager to read this email."

"I can tell. Who is it from?"

"Ruby Farnham. Josephine's grandniece."

After we slide into the cramped booth, I give the email a quick skim, but it's not as earth-shattering as I'd hoped. No smoking gun that says which Tulley brother Josephine picked or what her fate was. Rather, Ruby's cousin in Leeds has dug around in her own attic and is now in possession of her own box of family history.

"Her cousin digitized all the family documents and is willing to email me everything to sift through," I tell Celeste.

"That's kind of her."

"It is." I tuck the phone in my bag. I'll respond later.

Our server brings over two glasses and a jug of water, filling them up while we give the menus a quick perusal. The harried man takes our orders, then hurries off.

"So. How's it going at the flat?" Celeste lifts a brow at me. "Lee told me you could cut the tension with a knife."

"If you knew how it was going, then why'd you ask?" I grumble.

"Oh dear. Then it's true? You and Jack are still on the outs?"

"Sort of. We're not avoiding each other anymore. We talk at breakfast, dinner. But it's not the same."

"Look…Abbey," she starts in a voice eerily reminiscent of her twin's, the one Lee uses when I have PMS. "He's not a bad bloke. Jackie, that is."

"I know he's not." My throat squeezes shut.

"Lee said he and Jack chatted over a pint the other day. Jackie told him about his family's financial troubles, how much his mum has struggled—"

"I get it," I interrupt, aggravation prickling at me. "Celeste, I'm not mad he took the money—well, I'm a little mad about it. But what really eats me up inside is the pretending."

"The pretending?"

"He pretended to be my friend." I hate how small my voice sounds. How pathetic. "I thought he was acting protective because he truly cared about me. Especially at the beginning. I thought it was cute the way he didn't want me hooking up with his friend or whatever. I thought it meant he was developing feelings for me."

Her face softens. "Oh, luv. Yes. I can see how that would feel demoralizing."

"Yes. That's the perfect word for it."

"But you're wrong," she finishes, shrugging.

I narrow my eyes at her. "How so?"

"Of course he wasn't pretending. Everybody could see Jack was besotted with you."

My heart trips over itself. "You're only saying that so I forgive him and stop making things awkward in the group."

"If that's what you'd like to believe, all right." She smiles. "But that's rubbish. I never say anything I don't mean."

Fair point. She and Lee are alike in that way.

"All I'm saying is perhaps we ought to allow Jack a wee bit of grace."

I think back on this last month. How painful it's been, running into him upstairs, feeling his elbow bump mine at the breakfast counter. Every time I see him, I'm torn between getting angry all over again or throwing myself at his feet, telling him how much I miss him.

Because I do miss him. Nate too. And each time one of them reaches out to echo that sentiment, it brings a deep ache to my heart.

"On a related note, any word from Nate?" Celeste asks, reading my mind.

"I haven't seen him since he told me he doesn't want a relationship."

And then, because apparently the universe hates me, the bell over the door dings and none other than Yvonne walks into the diner.

Since I'm facing the door, I'm easy to spot. Our gazes meet across the small room, and it's like we both experience a brain stutter between recognition and remembering we hate each other.

"What?" Celeste turns to look. "Oh shit. I didn't even think... I'm sorry, Abbey. I should have picked an establishment not so close to campus."

Yvonne pauses at the door before making her way toward us on a pair of brown leather riding boots. She looks as elegant as always, with her hair perfectly styled. Clad in skinny jeans and a slinky sweater beneath an unbuttoned knee-length peacoat.

"Should I...?" I trail off, biting my lip.

"Hide in the bathroom?" Celeste whispers. "Maybe?"

Too late. In a few strides, Yvonne weaves through tables to stand at ours, her eyes never breaking contact with mine.

"I'm not here to fight," Yvonne prefaces, which does nothing to alleviate the adrenaline already accelerating my heart rate. "I should apologize."

Celeste can only stare at me like she's found herself trapped in the peripheral vision of a wild animal.

"So should I," I tell Yvonne, my anxiety dissolving into regret. "I never intended to hurt you. For whatever it's worth, I didn't ask Nate to break up with you. He and I are not even really seeing each other."

"I know." Her attention flicks to Celeste, and I take it to mean Celeste managed to talk some sense into her friend. "I didn't handle it well, and you were an easy target." Yvonne juts her chin. "Showing up at your flat was petty and stupid, and I'm sorry."

"Thank you."

"I don't expect us to be friends or anything," Yvonne says, shrugging in that cool, indifferent way she has. "Just want you to know there are no hard feelings."

"Water under the bridge," I answer with a nod. "No worries."

Once she's said her piece, Yvonne goes to the counter to order a coffee, leaving the diner less than a minute later. Celeste and I watch her go. I think even if Nate and I had never said two words to each other, Yvonne and I were still never destined to be friends. We simply don't click. But it takes courage to admit when you're wrong and try making amends after such an epic tirade. I give her credit for character.

"I honestly thought she was coming to take a swing at you," Celeste confesses, sounding relieved her prediction didn't come true.

"Trust me, I was ready to throw my drink on her in self-defense."

Luckily, the rest of lunch is uneventful. After Celeste and I part ways, I walk back to campus for my next class. Later, I take the Tube home, eager to get in the shower and wash away the grime of the day.

No sooner do I walk through the door than Jack appears and says, "Abbs. You up for a chat? You and me."

I do a bad job at hiding my wariness, but there's an intensity about him that raises my guard. He's in jeans and one of his surf T-shirts, hair messy as if he's been repeatedly running his fingers through it.

"Oh. Okay," I say.

He nods toward the staircase. "My room?"

"Sure."

As I follow him upstairs, I mentally prepare myself for this conversation, which I assume will involve yet another apology. Then I think about Celeste's advice to give Jack some grace, and I have to acknowledge that the recent awkwardness hasn't been entirely his fault, a fact I bring up once he closes the bedroom door.

"I wanted to apologize," I tell him. "For my part in how tense things have been lately."

He shrugs. "It's not your fault. I was the dickhead."

He sits on his bed and gestures for me to join him. After a beat of hesitation, I sink down beside him, keeping a foot of distance between us. He's still one of the best-looking men I've ever seen outside a movie screen, and my attraction to him refuses to dim no matter how resentful of his actions I may be.

I clasp my hands tight to my lap to curb the temptation to reach for his hand and lace our fingers together.

"I've been thinking," he starts, his voice a bit husky.

"Okay. What about?"

Jack glances over at me. "How do you feel about coming to Sydney with me for spring break?"

48

It comes from so far in left field I don't quite understand what he's asking at first.

"Sydney?" I echo dumbly.

Jack runs a hand through his hair, clearly nervous. "Yeah. I leave Friday at midnight from Gatwick. If you'd like to join me."

I stare at him. "Why would I do that?"

"Ah, right. I haven't asked for forgiveness yet." His face is sheepish. "I fucked up the order."

"What order?"

Resting his palms on his knees, he angles his body so he's facing me. "The order I wanted to say things."

Despite myself, I snort out a laugh.

"Let me start again?" he pleads.

I nod and gesture for him to continue.

"I know I've apologized over and over again, and I reckon you're bloody sick of hearing the words *I'm* and *sorry* exit my mouth. But I need to say them again." Sincerity shines on his face. "I should have told you about your dad's emails. I should have come clean the moment we had breakfast together that first morning or at the very least the moment I realized how much I liked you. I'm never going to stop apologizing, not until you stop hating me for it."

My heart lurches into my throat. "I don't hate you."

"You don't?"

"Of course not. I could never hate you."

A spark of hope lights his eyes. "Does that mean I've a chance at earning your forgiveness?"

He's not a bad bloke.

Of course he wasn't pretending. Everybody could see Jack was besotted with you.

I swallow, hesitating, as Celeste's words poke at the back of my brain.

Rather than address his question, I pose one of my own. "Why do you want me to come to Sydney with you?"

He shifts, his elbow jolting mine. "Ah, well, the family's been asking about you, and I thought maybe you'd like to meet them."

"You talk about me to your family?"

He nods.

"Let me get this straight. You're asking me to go home with you? To meet your mom?"

As in the mom *no other girl* has ever met?

The reminder sends my mind reeling.

"Why?" I push, because he's yet to provide an adequate explanation for this unexpected offer.

The corners of his mouth tip upward. "See, I've been giving it some thought, and I think I figured out my problem."

"Oh?" I smother another laugh. "I'm dying to know."

"It's possible I'm in love with you."

I'm sorry. What?

I blink at him. This must be a hallucination.

"I reckon if I'd managed to tell you that, it could have helped." Jack lets out a harried breath. "Helped to convince you I don't view you as a little kid. Far from it, Abbey. I do view you as a woman. A bloody amazing woman."

I'm still gaping at him, my mind still tripping over the words *I'm in love with you.*

Then I remember something he said to me ages ago.

I'd have to be head over heels for someone to introduce them to Mum.

God, I think he's being sincere right now.

He's got me at a total loss. To say I've been sideswiped by this revelation is an understatement.

"You love me?" I finally utter. "When did all this happen?"

"Guess I figured it out when I looked at my phone and it said you were trapped in Ben Tulley's penthouse."

"That might have been a bit overdramatic of me." In hindsight, I'm sure I overreacted to the situation with Ben. At the time, though, it felt quite urgent.

"I was out the door and halfway down the street before the others even checked their phones," Jack confesses. "I didn't say a word, just ran out of the pub. Practically sprinting down the street until I realized I had no idea where I was going. Took me a minute to notice you hadn't texted only me."

Guilt tugs at me. "Sorry I put you all through that."

"I'm not."

The conviction in his voice rocks me back. There's no doubt in my mind that he'd have ripped the door from its hinges with his bare hands to get to me. That's the kind of guy Jack is. Fiercely loyal.

"I'm happy you asked for help instead of being all stubborn and trying to get out of the situation on your own. I like how honest you are, Abbs. Genuine. I like that you can laugh at yourself." He gives an adorable shrug. "I like everything about you."

"So…Sydney, huh?" Because I'm still stuck on the idea of him taking me home to the family. To his mother. "You said you've never brought a girl home."

"I haven't."

"So if I came home with you…that would make us, what?"

"My girlfriend. If that's not too presumptuous."

My breath hitches. I haven't had much experience with relationships, but I'm pretty sure this isn't how most of them start. It feels like we're doing this all backward. Yet that doesn't mean I don't feel a surge of hopeful excitement at hearing the words. The possibility he's serious about this.

Then again, I've been burned before. Kissed within an inch of my life only to have him take it all back. I didn't realize until this moment what a deep scar that left on me.

"This is a lot to absorb," I say softly.

"I'm sorry. Didn't mean to spring it on you all at once."

I want to say yes. To throw myself at him and let it all be true. But I have to protect myself. And that means a healthy dose of skepticism. Never mind that meeting the fam right off the bat is a major test of what would be a brand-new tenuous relationship.

I reach over and take his hand. He immediately entwines our fingers, and the warmth of his touch sends a shiver through me.

"I…" I squeeze his hand. "I can't go to Sydney with you."

I try to ignore the deep ache in my chest as I watch the disappointment wash over his face.

"Oh. Yeah. I get it. No worries."

God, I hate disappointing him. The hurt evident in his deflated posture tears at me, and almost instantly, I'm recalculating if I've done the right thing.

Averting his eyes, he tries to pull his hand away, but I don't let him.

"I forgive you," I say firmly.

Jack's gaze slowly finds mine. "You do?"

"I do. Me saying no right now doesn't have to do with your deal with my dad. I forgive you for that."

Because no matter how embarrassed I feel every time I think about Jack getting paid to babysit me, I finally understand that proverb about not cutting off your nose to spite your face. I'm only punishing myself by not forgiving Jack. By not wiping the slate clean. We still live together after all. And…well, I care about him.

A lot.

"I'm willing to start fresh. But I'm not sure a weeklong trip where I meet your family is the way to dip our toes back into this."

He nods again. "I understand."

"And just because I'm saying no to Sydney doesn't mean I'm shutting down the other thing. The girlfriend thing."

His lips quirk up. "All right."

"But maybe we can table that discussion until you get back?"

"Of course. It's only a week, right?"

He gets up, tugging me to my feet. My knees feel wobbly as I peer up at his suddenly heavy-lidded eyes. I can tell he wants to kiss me. A part of me is dying for him to.

But this reconciliation is still too fragile. So I head for the door before I succumb to the urge.

I awkwardly reach for the doorknob. "I need to shower."

"If you change your mind about Sydney," Jack says, "you know where to find me Friday night, okay?"

"Okay," I echo.

In the bathroom, I release the breath I'd been holding and study my reflection in the mirror, wondering what the heck just happened.

Has Jack really declared his love for me?

Asked me to come home to meet his mother?

I'm not even close to processing any of it when my phone vibrates in my pocket. I fish it out, startled to find a text from Nate, who I haven't seen or spoken to in weeks.

> Nate: Hey. Can we talk?

When it rains, it pours.

After some hesitation, I text him back.

> Me: What about?

> Nate: I'd rather tell you in person. Any chance you can meet me at the bar later? I'm off at eleven. I know it's late, but I don't want to wait till tomorrow.

Wait for what? Curiosity rears its ugly head inside me. Jack's bombshells and now Nate's cryptic request? There goes any chance of being able to focus on editing my research paper tonight. I'm going to spend the next five hours obsessing over what Nate might have to say to me after weeks of radio silence.

It doesn't escape me that I just told Jack I'd consider the idea of being his girlfriend. And I meant it. But that doesn't mean I don't still have feelings for Nate. Confusing, complicated feelings that I can't even begin to sort out until I've seen him again and heard what he has to say.

> Me: All right. I'll be there at 11.

49

At eleven o'clock sharp, I walk into the bar and find Nate still working behind the long counter. He's in a snug black T-shirt, dark locks of hair falling onto his forehead as he concentrates on mixing a drink. As always, my heart speeds up, because I'm a complete and utter goner when it comes to this man.

At the sight of me, his eyes flicker with pleasure, then regret as he explains that the other bartender was a no-show, which means Nate has to stay for another hour.

"It's all right," I assure him, hopping up on a stool. "We can chat while you work. Pour me something yummy?"

"You got it." He returns a moment later and hands me a glass of wine with a raspberry on top.

"Thanks."

"You look good," he says, mixing drinks as he talks.

I smile wryly. "Is that your way of saying it's been a while and you'd almost forgotten what I looked like?"

Nate just winks and pours a line of shots for another customer.

Watching him work is fascinating. He's not one of those bartenders who flings bottles and shakers around, chatting up the crowd and hamming it up for tips. Or maybe that's not a British thing. Either way, his slightly aloof demeanor attracts a crowd of admirers, women throwing themselves against the bar to get his attention.

Seeing it does strike certain chords inside me. It reminds me why I'd been in knots from the moment I saw him on that stage. How quickly I lost my mind the first time I got on the back of his bike and wrapped my arms around him while we sped through the streets of London.

A curvy woman elbows her way in beside me. She's wearing too much makeup and her boobs are hanging out. She tries her hardest to flirt with him as Nate watches me attempt to not look annoyed, grinning like a cocky bastard.

"Point taken," I tell him once he's served her drink and sent her off.

"Didn't say a word."

Cheeky Nate does terrible things to my body. Accelerates my pulse and sends a tickle between my legs.

"So you called this meeting," I remind him, forcing my head out of the gutter. "What did you want to talk about?"

Nate speaks over his shoulder while ringing up credit cards. "Budapest."

"Like the city?"

"Exactly like the city."

"Not my area of expertise, I'm afraid."

He returns to lean against the bar as I take a sip of my wine.

"This wine is good," I say, running my tongue over my bottom lip to lick off a lingering drop. "Really good."

His gaze heats as it tracks the movement of my tongue. "It's my favorite one we sell. Nobody ever orders it because it's also the cheapest and these assholes think the price tag has anything to do with how it tastes."

"So Budapest," I repeat. "Any particular reason?"

Nate tips his head in that sexy way he does. "Want to go?"

I blink. "Tonight?"

"I mean, if you're game, I was thinking next week. That's your break from school, yeah?"

Holy déjà vu.

If I was the suspicious type, I'd think these guys planned this. Conspiring to test my affections.

"You just came up with this?" I search his face for more clarity.

He shrugs. "I thought if we made it a week in Budapest or wherever without killing each other, then maybe I could convince you to come travel with me this summer."

"You're not serious."

My head starts spinning with images of us backpacking through the streets of Hungary, exploring ancient landmarks and popping into dimly lit cafés. Then later, other dimly lit activities. Just Nate and I, caught up in our own adventure.

"Why not?" He's got mischief in his eyes, which is a dangerous thing with a guy like Nate. There's all sorts of trouble a mind like his can get up to.

"I thought you were a solo traveler," I say, still completely shook by his invitation.

"Maybe you changed my mind."

"I'd love to know how I did that."

"Ignoring me for five weeks was part of it," he admits before having to step away for a moment to pour some drinks and ring up orders. Then he's back, watching me with that deep, intense gaze.

"So this is a ploy to get me back. Is that it?"

"I missed you," Nate says under those dark lashes. "Which made me realize how much more I'd miss you if I was on the road for three months without you."

I bite my lip against the blush rising to my cheeks. Damn him, but he's good at this.

"And maybe I realized that feeling I'd been avoiding wasn't going away."

My breath gets stuck in my lungs. "What feeling is that?"

"That I'm in love with you."

God. You have *got* to be kidding me.

Is he actually saying this? Mere hours after Jack declared the same?

Nate meets my startled gaze, taking my hand to rub his thumb over the inside of my wrist. "And if you'll say yes, I want this adventure with you. We can make some memories together. Maybe a little trouble along the way. Whatever we want."

I suddenly grasp the gravity of his offer. What it means to him to make plans. To allow someone else into his sphere and share this dream with me. It's the only thing I've asked of him, and he's handing it to me on a platter.

But the timing is...terrible.

I'm as tempted to say yes and chase the road with him as I was to say yes to Jack and fly off to Sydney.

And the fact that the choice isn't clear in my mind in this instant means I can't honestly say what my heart wants.

"Baby?" he says huskily. "What do you think?"

I think that if he calls me *baby* again, I'm liable to melt in a puddle on this beer-stained floor.

Instead, I swallow hard and say, "If I say no to Budapest, is summer off the table?"

He smiles wryly. "I take that to mean you're saying no to Budapest?"

"I think so." I nod regretfully. "Yeah, I'm saying no. Not because I don't want to go. I desperately want to go. But...it's too short notice. And you've thrown me for a loop here. I need more than a couple days to articulate the jumbled mess of thoughts that are fogging up my brain."

He nods back. "It was worth a try. And to answer your question, summer is still very much on the table. You know...before I met you, my only goal was to save as much money as I could and see the world. Collect experiences. Never wanted to be tied down or corralled while I did that. And now..."

I can scarcely breathe. "And now what?"

"Now I'm recognizing the value of having someone along for the ride. Someone you're passionate about. I meant what I said, Abbey. I've fallen for you. I've fallen bloody hard."

A smile tugs on my lips.

"With that said…I'll still see you when I get back, right?" He reaches for my hand again, rubbing his thumb across my wrist. It's a gesture I've come to understand as his way of saying *I'd be trying to take your pants off right now if we weren't in public.*

"Definitely."

He flashes that cheeky smile. "And in case you change your mind, I don't leave until early Saturday morning. Flight's at four a.m. Find me at the airport if you reconsider."

———————

After leaving Nate's bar, I find myself on a bus bench and entirely disoriented. For a moment, I'm not even sure where I am. I just started down the sidewalk and kept going for several blocks until I looked up and didn't recognize my surroundings. According to my phone map, I'm farther east than I've ever ventured through the city on foot.

Out of breath and a bit overwhelmed, I slouch and stare at the traffic until the noise and car exhaust quiet my frantic thoughts.

I've spent months in limbo, suspended between disparate paths. Struggling with a decision that feels like not just a choice between two guys but two vastly different interpretations of myself. Now, the status quo is collapsing beneath my feet, and if I don't grab for one of their ropes, I'm committing to finding out what's at the bottom on my own. Which I guess is a choice in itself. Maybe even the one that risks the fewest hearts.

I need a sounding board. Grabbing my phone from my purse, I send an SOS to Eliza.

Me: I'm back in the love triangle. Help.

Her response is instantaneous. It's early evening in Nashville, and I imagine she's just returned to her dorm after dinner at the meal hall on campus.

> Eliza: Were you ever out of it?

> Me: Yes. I told both of them to fuck off. But now they both want me as their girlfriend.

> Me: Is this how the Kardashians feel?

> Eliza: Wait, you forgave Hot Jack? And Drifter Nate wants to settle down? Is this an alternate dimension?

> Me: Right??

> Me: So what do I do?

> Eliza: Pick one.

> Me: Gee. Wow. That is some transcendent advice. Thank you.

A moment later, she calls me. I pick up instantly, groaning in lieu of hello.

"Okay, catch me up," Eliza orders. "How did all these new developments come to pass?"

"Well, I just saw Nate at his bar, and he invited me to Budapest for spring break."

"Wow."

"After he told me he's in love with me."

"Double wow."

"Yeah."

"And you said Hot Jack's also back in the picture? Please don't tell me he got down on one knee."

"No, but basically. He asked me to come to Sydney to meet the family and be his girlfriend."

"The nerve."

"Right?"

Eliza's amused chuckle tickles my ear. "Okay, so what are you going to do?"

"Well, I turned down both trip offers but not the rest of it."

"Meaning?"

"Meaning I forgave Jack and told him I'd consider making things official between us. And I told Nate I'd consider going away for the entire summer with him."

"Aren't you ambitious." She laughs again before her tone becomes serious. "What choice are you leaning toward?"

"If I had the answer to that, I wouldn't be sitting on a bench at midnight bothering your ass."

"Good point. Then we make a list. Pros and cons."

"Doesn't that seem a little…dispassionate?"

"Because you've done so well without my help?" Eliza snickers when I don't answer. "Thought so. Never question my methods."

So we do it her way. I arrange for an Uber and then, while I wait for it, Eliza and I make a list. Matching Jack's steadiness against Nate's spontaneity.

Jack's cocky laughter versus Nate's rare cheekiness.

That mellow, silly, comfortable way I feel with Jack compared to the excitement and passion Nate sparks in me.

And once again, it comes back to who I envision myself to be when I'm with them.

But who am I, damn it? What do I most connect with? The

allure of the free spirit I can be, trotting the globe and living life to its fullest? Or a simpler, laughter-filled, everyday existence appreciating the little pleasures?

Both have their appeal.

Ultimately, what this exercise tells me is that I still don't know myself at all.

Three days later, my anxiety has peaked, and I'm no closer to figuring out what I want. I know my dad is convinced you can't love two people at once, but the longer I obsess over Jack and Nate, the more I doubt Dad's conviction.

I think he's wrong.

I think I'm in love with them both.

I keep waiting for my heart to put me out of my misery. Give me an answer. A sign. But I'm as torn today as I've ever been, and I have no clue what to do about it.

So I've fallen back on old habits of avoidance. Sequestering myself in the library under the pretense of homework and research. Hiding from the conflicting emotions I'm unable to understand or to process.

But these past few days, a creeping feeling has crawled its way into my brain and burrowed deep. The awful, unsettling nausea of wondering if I've made a terrible mistake by not choosing to go to Budapest with Nate.

Or Sydney with Jack.

I should've just agreed to go.

To Budapest.

Or Sydney.

I release a silent scream as I trudge down the sidewalk toward the Talbot Library. I'm liable to drive myself mad at this point. Whatever. Fine. I didn't say yes to either trip. That might be the least of my concerns right now.

Because they'll both be back in a week wanting an answer to the question that matters: Do I love them too? And if so, which one?

As I'm approaching my usual table, Mr. Baxley spots me and marches over with unusual haste.

"You're late, Ms. Bly," he reprimands me, adjusting his glasses on the bridge of his nose.

I eye him in amusement. "Am I? I didn't realize we'd made an appointment."

"You didn't receive my message?"

Brow furrowed, I pull my phone from my bag. "I didn't see any message. Maybe you sent it when I had no service on the Tube—"

"Forget that," he says, dismissively waving at my phone. "I have news."

"You do?"

"Indeed."

"Okay... What is it?"

Mr. Baxley bestows me with the rarest of gifts.

A smile.

"I do believe I've learned the fate of your Josephine."

50

Mr. Baxley puts a *PLEASE CALL AGAIN* sign up on his desk and escorts me into the special archives section. Excitement gathers inside me as we walk past familiar doorways and delve deep into the bowels of the library toward areas students aren't otherwise allowed. By the time we reach our destination, I'm nearly jumping out of my skin. The anticipation is too much.

We enter a locked room under harsh white lighting where equipment covers lab tables.

"What is all this?" I ask, a bit awed as I examine our surroundings.

"Document authentication, restoration, and preservation."

I resist the urge to let out an excited squeal. I doubt Mr. Baxley would appreciate losing the use of his eardrums.

"Over here," he says, and my gaze follows his gesturing hand.

On a table, inside a clear plastic bag, is a leather-bound book. It's warped and tattered and looks like it was flushed down a toilet a hundred years ago.

"A friend of mine recently had access to a collection of artifacts from the *Victoria* that have never been on public display before. This journal was among them."

I turn toward him, my jaw gaping wide. "This was on the *Victoria*?"

"Recovered from the wreck." He bats my hand away when I

reach for the precious book. "I can't let you handle it. However, she did agree to provide me with photos of its entries. These were among them. I suggest you read the top entry first."

"Am I allowed to include these in my paper?"

"Indeed. These copies are for you."

Mr. Baxley hands me a stack of printed papers featuring close-up photographs of the yellowed journal pages.

"There's almost no water damage," I say, marveling at the legibility of the handwriting.

"The journal was kept in a safe. It remained remarkably watertight for years on the ocean floor. They suspect the seal had only recently begun to fail when it was recovered. Just a small amount water had been inside, according to the report at the time. Much of the damage is the result of depressurization when the safe was brought up and opened."

My heart is pounding as I lower my gaze to the page Mr. Baxley indicated.

The journal entry is short. Written by a noblewoman on her way to America aboard the *Victoria*, it describes an evening on the ship at the captain's table. With a rather dry wit, she provides observations about members of her dinner party.

A banker distracted by the wife of the British general who had excused himself from dinner due to a bout of seasickness.

The stage actor she suspected was spending his last precious pennies to travel first class to America in hopes of reviving his fading career.

A railroad magnate who wouldn't stop talking the captain's ear off about steel and Irish labor.

None of it seems to be of much relevance until she mentions bumping into a young man on the main deck after dinner. A young man who happened to be the middle son of her good friend, Duchess Tulley.

A young man called William Tulley.

Who was joined by his lovely young bride, Josephine.

They had just eloped and were setting off to America to begin a new life together.

I look at up at Mr. Baxley's expectant smile.

"Eureka," he says.

I rock backward, utterly winded by the discovery. I feel like someone swung a sledgehammer at my chest. Along with the elation of discovering who Josephine chose, I feel a sudden pang of loss. Heartbreak. Josephine followed William and his wanderlust across the ocean only to perish beneath the icy black waves. Their love was a tragedy, and they'd been driven to their deaths by class and circumstance. Rivalry and expectation. Cursed.

But maybe it's also romantic. What little time they had together, they seized it, undeterred by the unknown. She and William left the safety of his wealth and everything she'd ever known for whatever trials lay west. They fled as a married couple, eager to meet the challenges of postwar America together, with their love and fortitude to guide them.

Yes, their young lives were cut short, but they left this earth together, and maybe that's enough. It's certainly more than a lot of people get.

And much more than many of us will ever attempt.

Mr. Baxley leads me out the door, back through the archives toward the main room.

"Is it the answer you hoped for?"

It's the first thing he's said since I finished reading the journal entry, as if he knew I needed time to absorb it all.

I inhale a slow, pensive breath. "Do you think she ever regretted her decision?"

He questions me over the rim of his glasses.

"When the water was pouring in over the side and filling the hallways. Do you think she wished she'd never heard the name Tulley?"

"I'd like to believe"—Mr. Baxley takes off his glasses and pulls a small handkerchief from his breast pocket to wipe them—"in our final moments, we think of the people we love and what we leave behind. That it's far too late for regrets."

"Thank you, Mr. Baxley," I tell this odd, serious, perceptive man who has become a friend. "For all your help."

"My pleasure. I presume you have what you need?"

"I think so. Now I just need to write it all down."

Which is the first thing I do when I get home an hour later. I'm still riding a high from the discovery, so pumped full of adrenaline that I race upstairs, grab my laptop, and start writing. My paper will finally have the resolution it so desperately needs. The closure *I* need.

I update the last section, sourcing the journal entries from the *Victoria*, my thoughts flying out faster than my fingers can accommodate. I type like a madwoman, revealing Josephine and William Tulley's ill-fated journey, the tragic ending to their love story.

After I hit Save, I stretch out my fingers and crack my knuckles, damn pleased with myself. I'm done.

No.

Fuck. Maybe I'm not done, I amend, suddenly remembering the emails I received earlier in the week from the shipping company and Ruby Farnham. I totally forgot to go over them.

Damn it.

"Lee," I call out toward the hall. I can hear him puttering around in his bedroom.

"Yes, my love?"

"Can I send something to your printer? It's…ah, looks to be about eighty pages. Is that okay? I'll buy you a new box of paper tomorrow."

"No problem. I'll turn it on for you."

Thirty minutes later, I return to my room with a crisp stack of printouts courtesy of Lee's color laser printer. The paper is still warm to the touch as I flop back on my bed, flipping through pages.

I start with the documents courtesy of Steve from Global Cruise Initiatives, which seem boring at first, until something catches my eye and wrinkles my forehead.

It's a minor detail. Or maybe a coincidence. I'm not entirely sure yet, so I shift my focus to the family papers provided by Ruby's cousin Catherine.

I go through them one painstaking page at a time until it becomes glaringly evident I'm not dealing with a coincidence here.

Gripping the last page, fingers trembling with excitement, I stare at the unmistakable truth. Right there on the page.

"Oh my God," I breathe.

51

I MANAGE TO GET AHOLD OF HER EARLY FRIDAY MORNING, BUT SHE says she can't meet me until later that evening. She invites me to her flat in West Kensington, a gorgeous, airy apartment in a pretty, posh building with a doorman. She'll be moving soon, Sophie admits, as she ushers me into what she calls the receiving room. It looks exactly like a living room, but who am I to judge?

"So," Sophie says pleasantly, setting a delicate ceramic cup in front of me. Steam rises and warms my hands as I reach for it. "What brings you here tonight, Abbey? You sounded quite agitated when you rang."

"I know. I'm sorry. I hope I didn't worry you." I wrap my fingers around the coffee cup. "It wasn't agitation so much as nerves and excitement."

"I see. Now I'm well intrigued." She picks up her teacup and takes a small sip, smiling over the rim. "Please, enlighten me."

"I have some updates about the Tulleys."

Instantly, her face darkens. "Bloody menaces, that lot."

I falter. "Oh dear. Did something else happen with Ben?"

I knew she was quitting, but I haven't seen her since the morning she showed up on my doorstep in a panic. Guilt tugs at me for not touching base until now.

"Benjamin refuses to honor the terms of my contract, which

state he's obligated to pay for my father's housing for six months following termination. He's maintaining the clause only applies if I'm laid off as opposed to resigning. And the language is just vague enough that both of us could be correct."

"Fuck. Does that mean you're getting lawyers involved?"

She shakes her head. "It'll cost more to retain a lawyer than to simply pay for it myself. I have some savings. We'll make do. But enough about me. You said you have an update about the Tulleys, and I completely derailed you. This is concerning your research project, I presume?"

"Yes." I set my messenger bag on the glass coffee table, then realize I should have asked first. "Is this okay?"

She waves a hand. "Yes, of course."

I unzip the bag and pull out the file folder containing all the documents I compiled last night.

"All right, this will sound very convoluted at times, so try to follow along as best you can, okay? I promise it's all heading somewhere."

I can barely contain myself. I'm exhilarated. Practically vibrating. Jack and Nate are right—to me, history is akin to sex. That is very sad but very true.

"So. You already know the beginning of this story. Josephine was a maid for the duchess and, at some point after starting to work at the estate, fell in love with both Robert and William Tulley. The eldest son and the middle one. Josephine knew she had a decision to make, and it was eating her up inside, as evidenced by her letters to her mother."

I set down the photocopies from Ruby Farnham's attic trove, laying them out in front of her.

"And do we finally know who she chose?" Sophie looks utterly transfixed.

"We do." I slide the latest journal entry, courtesy of Mr. Baxley, across the table. "It was William."

She gasps. "Then…that means…" Some of the luster leaves her

expression, replaced by the pall of sorrow. "She died with him on the ship. They both drowned."

"Yes."

Sophie leans forward. There's a brief silence while she reads the entry, her elegant features creased with sadness.

"Those poor souls." She raises her gaze to mine. "That's it then? You've solved the mystery."

A smile lifts the corners of my mouth. "Not quite. There's still the matter of Robert."

"I believe Benjamin mentioned a private investigator tracked Robert Tulley to Ireland. Is that not correct?"

"It's correct." I pull out another sheet from my folder and lay it down. "That's the PI's report. But we're going to take a little detour before we get to Robert." I grin at her. "Remember, I said this might get confusing."

She reaches for her tea again, watching me curiously as she takes a sip.

"I got these records from the shipping line that owned the *Victoria*. It's the insurance payouts to the survivors. About eight hundred people survived, while seven hundred perished. Their payouts varied. First class passengers received much more—"

"Wankers," Sophie grumbles.

"Right? But the lower classes were well compensated, or at least they would've felt that way judging by these sums. It was enough for a lot of these folks to transform their entire lives. Build a new life in America. Anyway, we're getting into the weeds. I pored over the list of survivors, and one name jumped out at me. It made no sense at first. I assumed it was a coincidence."

"What was the name?"

I hand her the paper. "I highlighted it in yellow."

"E. Farnham," she reads out loud, then lifts her head. "And that is?"

"Josephine's younger sister. Evelyn."

Eyes widening, Sophie says, "She was on the ship?"

"It appears so."

Sophie skims the list again. "What do the numbers in parentheses mean? For example, here, it says J. and C. Forbes, with the number two in parentheses. M. Gregory, parentheses one. E. Farnham also has a one."

I beam at her. "I had the same exact question. I couldn't figure it out at first, so I went back to the passenger manifest, the list that William—and, by extension, whoever he was traveling with—wasn't on. After a lot of cross-referencing, I discovered that the numbers in brackets refer to children. For example, M. Gregory is actually Marie Gregory, who boarded the ship with her husband and young son. The husband died, but she and her son survived. Forbes is Joseph and Charlotte, and the two corresponds to their two daughters. The kids' names are on the manifest, but for the insurance purposes, they're just numbers."

"So Evelyn Farnham had a child with her?"

"Evelyn Farnham was fourteen years old when the *Victoria* sank. I highly doubt the child was hers."

The teacup rattles the saucer as Sophie sets them down. I can see her growing excitement as understanding dawns.

"Josephine."

"Yup. I suspect she and William were passing the child off as her sister's, at least while on the ship. But once they arrived in America, I bet they planned on raising their son together, with Evelyn as the baby's nurse. That's why she came along."

"Their son?" Sophie raises a brow.

I smile. "We'll get there soon."

"But how did Josephine have a baby without the duke or duchess knowing about it? Especially the duchess. Josephine was her maid. She wouldn't have been able to hide a pregnancy." Sophie pauses. "Well, no, perhaps I'm wrong. She certainly could have hidden the fact that she was pregnant. But not the birth."

"I believe she hid the pregnancy until the last possible moment. And I think this is why William raced to get them passage on that ship. She likely gave birth in secret, and they packed up in the middle of the night and left with Evelyn and their son."

I reach into my trusty folder for several more sheets of paper.

"Now this is where it gets wild," I tell the rapt Sophie. "I got these family documents from Ruby Farnham's cousin. They only raised more questions, as usual, so I stayed up all night yesterday hunting down the information I was missing. This is what I found. Ready?"

"I don't believe I've ever been more ready in my life. This is extraordinary."

"Just you wait."

Grinning, I pull out my carefully constructed family tree. Not the one for the Tulleys, which I agonized over for months. But a new one I created last night.

"This is the Farnham family tree." I don't hand it over yet, reading from it instead. "Josephine had two siblings, Matthew and Evelyn. Ruby is a descendent of Matthew's—he's her grandfather. Ruby's cousin Catherine Kerr, however, is a descendent of Evelyn's."

"Brilliant. So then we know what happened to Evelyn after she survived the *Victoria* disaster! She returned to Britain?"

I rest the family tree on my knee while I scavenge for a few more papers, which I lay down one by one.

"This is the amount Evelyn received from the Northern Star Line. This is the receipt for the passage she booked two weeks later, a one-way crossing back to England. Which, by the way, is fucking ballsy of this girl. Imagine almost drowning at sea and then turning around and boarding another ship? Hard-core."

Sophie laughs. "Indeed it is."

I slap down another paper. "This is a page from the diary of Josephine and Evelyn's mother. It was in the original paperwork Ruby gave me but didn't jump out at me because I was more focused on Josephine than her little sister. But see here? Mrs. Farnham laments how Evelyn has chosen not to return to the employ of the Tulleys, nor is she choosing to remain in England. In fact, Evelyn doesn't even visit her mother upon her return to England. She gets on another boat—this one headed for Ireland."

"To Robert?" Sophie breathes.

"Yes. And no. This part tripped me up for a while before I figured it out. In Catherine Kerr's paperwork, I found a birth certificate for who I believe is Josephine and William's son. The date of birth listed lines up with when William booked their last-minute passage on the *Victoria*. The child's name is Alexander, and his parents are listed as Evelyn and Henry."

A groove appears in her forehead. "And we believe Henry is Robert?"

"Judging by this"—I hand her a copy of a small family portrait Catherine Kerr found in her attic—"I'd say so."

The portrait shows a young woman, eerily similar in appearance to Josephine, and a man in his midtwenties, eerily similar to the paintings I've seen of Robert Tulley.

"I think he was living in Ireland under an assumed name when Evelyn tracked him down. I wonder if she already knew how to find him," I muse. "He may have told Josephine where he was going after she rejected him and chose his brother. Anyway, and this is all supposition at this point, but I think Evelyn showed up on Robert's doorstep with his brother's infant son. She couldn't risk taking the baby home to her own family, because she knew her mother would take the child right to the Tulleys. And she also knew the Tulleys would never love or care for William's bastard son with the maid."

"You believe Robert, now called Henry, took her in."

"Not only that, but he married her." I lay down another page. "This is a wedding announcement in a small local newspaper of a small Irish village, heralding the union of Evelyn Farnham and Henry Brown."

Sophie's entire body tenses.

It takes a moment for what I'd said to register. When it does, she stares at me in confusion mingled with disbelief.

"Did you say Henry Brown?"

The enormous smile I've been fighting this entire time breaks free. "That is precisely what I said."

She shakes her head. Stunned. "But…how…? I don't understand."

"Robert Tulley changed his name to Henry Brown after Josephine broke his heart. Also, he was being pressured to marry a royal princess and wanted none of it. I suspect he had every intention of living the rest of his life alone until Evelyn came to him for help. They proceeded to raise William and Josephine's son as their own and ended up having four other children. One of those kids was Amanda Brown, and she's Catherine Kerr's mother. But the first-born son, William's son…that son, Alexander Brown, was—"

"My grandfather," Sophie finishes, her breath catching.

"Your grandfather," I confirm. "Who had one son of his own—your dad. Is it safe to say your father is Irish?"

"He is. Yes. He came to London in his late teens."

Once again, I beam at my brilliant sleuthing. It's cocky, yes. But after an entire night spent researching this stuff, I'm allowed to gloat a little.

"Grandpa Alex was William Tulley's son?" She's shaking her head repeatedly, visibly floored.

"I believe so. You told me your grandfather is the one who got your dad the job with Andrew Tulley?"

She still appears astounded by everything I told her. "He did, yes. When Dad left Ireland, he worried he wouldn't find work, but Grandad assured him he had connections."

"Robert had connections," I correct. "He kept his distance from the Tulleys after he moved away, but clearly he hadn't cut ties altogether. After all, he did speak to Lawrence Tulley's investigator. It's not a stretch to believe he may have maintained some contact with his brother Lawrence over the years and therefore not a stretch that the Browns and Tulleys remained somewhat connected."

"This…is a lot to process."

"God, I bet. I'm sorry to drop all this on you without warning. I couldn't even believe it when I pieced it all together."

"Perhaps you're wrong." She voices it as a question.

"A DNA test will easily answer that," I point out with a shrug.

"If it's true…"

I grin broadly. "If it's true, that means your father is the true heir to the Tulley land and titles. But at the very least, this information could serve as excellent leverage should you choose to use it against the Tulleys. Because if you are who I think you are, you're entitled to something. Your father"—I soften my voice—"is entitled to something."

Tears glisten in her eyes. "Jesus, Abbey."

"My advice? Get that DNA testing done. But unless all this"—I wave a hand over the sea of documents lining her table—"is merely one whopping coincidence after another, then I'm confident in everything I hypothesized."

"If this is all true, then I owe you a debt I'll never be able to repay."

I brush that off. "Oh, hush. There's no debt. This was fun."

It's her turn to grin. "Fun," she echoes.

"You have no idea how much." I start to gather up the papers, tucking them back in the folder. "I'll leave these here with you. They're copies. And you know what? There is one way you can repay me. Call me the moment you find out whether I'm right or not."

"Absolutely," she promises.

A few minutes later, I'm stepping out into the cool night air, absently arranging for an Uber to take me back to Notting Hill. A whirlwind of information and chaotic thoughts clutters my mind. And along with the mental overload comes a sense of satisfaction so deep and pure it triggers a rush of tears.

I solved the mystery. Months of turning over stones, digging in every nook and cranny, driving all over the country, setting up camp in the library. It's all culminated in this moment.

I've never been prouder of myself.

But perhaps the most satisfying part is I truly believe everybody got some version of their happily ever after in this story. Josephine may not have chosen Robert, but he got his happy ending, or some semblance of it. He got a family. A wife who I hope cared about him, although based on the Farnham correspondence, Evelyn did seem sweet and kind. I hope she was kind to him.

And Josephine got William. Because as she'd told Robert in her note, her destiny lay with William. *Where he goes, my heart will always follow.* Most importantly, their son, the product of their love, survived the tragedy. So in a sense, the two of them lived on.

I stand at the curb waiting for my ride, my mind drifting to what Mr. Baxley said in the library yesterday. Our conversation stays with me on the drive home. During my shower before bed. When I slide beneath the covers. It buzzes in my brain for hours, until it's all I'm thinking about, those last minutes between Josephine and William on the sinking ship.

Our final moments, our regrets. I imagine what my thoughts would be if they were the last I'd ever have. What I'd want to leave behind. Whose hand I'd want reaching out for mine.

Then I exhale. And I know what I need to do.

But first, I have to pack.

52

It's quite late when the black cab pulls up to the airport terminal drop-off. I've nearly drawn blood from the imprints of my nails in my palms during the ride here. The moment the car comes to a stop, I jump out with my suitcase and dart through the automatic sliding glass doors.

Before I left the house, I texted to say I had something important to tell him.

He agreed to wait for me.

Now, every minute that's passed feels like an infinite opportunity for him to change his mind.

Overhead signs point the way toward the security checkpoint as I jog the waxed concourse, navigating an obstacle course of small children and stalled tourists. Black-suited businessmen and women swinging oversize purses. I'm surprised by the number of energetic travelers I encounter at this hour.

A voice in my head taunts my every hurried step. What if he doesn't want me to come with him anymore? What if he decided I wasn't worth the effort? Concluded that he can do way better than some nerdy American with a smart mouth?

But I tamp that shit down. I remind myself that if it's real, it doesn't matter how we got here. Only that we did.

As I approach security, I scan the crowd for his face. With every second that ticks by, the claw of fear and anxiety tightens its grip around my throat.

Until I spot him by the planter.

Jack's eyes lock with mine, and a guarded smile spreads across his lips.

As I approach, he takes note of the rolling suitcase in my hand.

"Off somewhere?" he asks lightly.

With a trembling hand, I pull the paper with my printed boarding pass out of my back pocket.

"It's a nonrefundable ticket," I tell him.

His crystal-blue eyes twinkle. "That's a major commitment."

I manage a tiny hopeful half smile. "If the invitation stands, I'd like to come to Sydney with you and meet your mom."

"What changed your mind?" He pauses, a groove appearing in his forehead. He's clearly reluctant to go on, but finally he asks, "And what about Nate?"

"I know it took a lot longer than was probably fair, but I figured out what I want. I had all these confusing feelings between the two of you, but my dad was right. We can't be in love with two people at once." I exhale in a fast rush. "And I'm in love with you."

"Is that right?" Jack says, biting back a proud grin.

"I think I was fascinated by the idea of being with Nate," I admit.

I swallow, trying to find the right words, even though I'd practiced so much of this in the cab ride over. But it's hard to explain what I feel for Nate. Wild physical attraction aside, I was fascinated by him. Or rather by the idea of who I could be with him. But it was a costume, a part to play in a parody of my life, painting myself into scenes I didn't belong in. It was no more real than living vicariously through my dad's long-past exploits.

"Abbs?" Jack prompts when I'm quiet for too long.

I shift my feet, fidget with my boarding pass, because it's awkward discussing this with him. But I've always expected honesty from Jack, and I owe him the same.

"Being my dad's daughter, I thought I was missing out on something all those years he kept me sheltered. But I've realized I'm not that girl."

Saying it out loud is more cathartic than I expected. But it's the truth. I'm not that girl. Speeding through the streets on the back of a motorcycle to parts unknown is fun and all, but I like my research and catching a rugby game on a Saturday afternoon. Being tucked away in a library late at night and grabbing a drink at the neighborhood pub. I like sitting at home reading on a rainy day. Watching movies on the couch. Dinner with friends. Simple things. Enjoying the company, not the chaos.

"My biggest fear when I moved here was that I wouldn't fit in. Wouldn't find a home. But I have. You make it home." Emotion clogs my throat. "You screwed up, definitely. But I know it didn't come from a bad place. I know who you are. And when I'm with you, I know who *I* am. I like who I am. I know I'm still young and have a lot more to learn, but I want to learn and grow and do all that stuff with *you*. I love you, Jack. I know it took me a while, but if you're still up for it, you're the one I—"

He doesn't let me finish.

Before I can blink, Jack lifts me off my feet. Strong arms holding me tight, he kisses me deeply, with the same urgency and relief coursing inside me. I wrap my legs around his waist, entirely unbothered by the hundreds of spectators.

I'm wholly at peace with my decision. Absolutely confident that for the first time in months, I know where my heart is leading me.

I pull back to peer into his gorgeous eyes. "According to one of her letters, Josephine's mom always told her that the heart never leads us astray. I think she was right."

He ponders that, then flashes that cocky Aussie grin that never fails to make me melt. "I mean, it makes heaps more sense than the heart being a bloody windmill."

That cracks both of us up. Our hungry kisses become

intermingled with bursts of laughter, which is our relationship in a nutshell, I suppose. But I love it. I love *him*.

I tear my mouth away again. "I'm sorry I took so long."

"I would have waited," Jack whispers against my lips. "As long as it took. You were always worth it."

APRIL

EPILOGUE

OUR TIME IN SYDNEY ENDED TOO QUICKLY. I MEAN, I COULD definitely have done without the enormous bugs that look like they crawled out of some radiation experiment gone horribly wrong, but overall, the city was beautiful, and Jack's family was wonderful. I had a very long flight to fret about what would happen if Jack's mom hated me, but from the moment we walked in the door, Traci Campbell was warm and welcoming.

The only snag—once I confessed to being Gunner Bly's daughter, the conversation took an awkward turn. Traci sent Oliver up to the attic for the box of vintage memorabilia from every single Australian concert or appearance my dad ever did. Turns out Jack's mom was a superfan back in the day. Obsessed, actually. Charlie made a crack about their mom getting a shot at Gunner, and they proceeded to spend the week teasing us that Jack and I were going to end up stepsiblings if we let her near him.

Needless to say, Charlie isn't my favorite brother.

It's good to be back in London, though. For starters, it was nearly impossible to get a second alone while we were staying in a house with Jack's mom, younger sister, and two of his three brothers. We found out real quick that the walls in the house were too thin to enjoy our new official status as a couple.

Now that we're home, we can't keep our hands off each other, much to Lee's dismay.

Lee wasn't quiet about his objections when we called a house meeting to lay it out for them. The words *or else* were thrown out quite a bit during his tirade. But we've assured him that this isn't a fling counting down to a fiery expiration date. With everything we've been through already, I'd say we've both had ample time to figure out what we want. This is it.

Which means I'm now giving serious thought as to how I might permanently transfer to Pembridge to finish my degree. With summer fast approaching, I'm not ready to be an ocean away from Jack. I might need to call Dr. Wu for his advice on how to break the news to my poor dad. But hey, at the very least, that confrontation can't possibly be as difficult as the one I had with Nate the other day.

He and I met up not long after I got back from Sydney. Swapped stories of our trips, talked about his plans for traveling this summer. He said he misses me. I think maybe he was testing the waters to make sure I'm not having second thoughts. I assured him I'm exactly where I'm supposed to be and content with my decision. In the end, I think he'll be happier on his travels going it solo. Nate's a free spirit. He can't be bound. I have a feeling that eventually we would have held each other back from our true paths.

Saying goodbye was hard, though. And literally a day later, there was another goodbye in store for me. After yet another house meeting, we agreed it was time to part ways with the tiny terror monster that prowls our house, his feline lordship Hugh. A week as the cat's sole caretakers almost broke Lee and Jamie. Leading the charge, Jamie whined that he wants his sex life back and he's tired of explaining all the scratches on his body to his bedmates.

Lee, in a rare moment of maturity, announced he was going to be honest with Lord Eric and confess that he does not—and never has or will—raise show cats.

So we took a vote and unanimously agreed to give Hugh to Mr. Baxley. I swear the stuffy, reserved man I've grown to adore almost shed a tear when he saw the murderous feline's furry scowl. Something tells me there aren't two more perfectly suited companions.

Almost as satisfying as Mr. Baxley's new family member is the news I received from Sophie Brown at the beginning of April. My sleuthing proved fruitful: Sophie and her father are indeed blood-related to the Tulleys. The shocking part of it is Andrew Tulley, the duke himself, was overjoyed to learn his old friend Daniel Brown was actually a long-lost cousin. The duke assured Sophie that her dad, his cousin, would be taken care of for the rest of his life, no questions asked.

The cynical part of me thinks he extended the offer in order to stop Sophie and Daniel from going after his land and titles, but Sophie doesn't want any of that nonsense anyway. All she ever cared about was ensuring her father was happy, healthy, and well looked after.

When I take stock of this last year, it still feels improbable that I arrived to where I am now. That a guy I was never supposed to meet would become such a vital part of my experience and the person I'm beginning to understand myself to be. Those are the happy accidents, I suppose. The twists of fate that conspire to trouble us, break us, and then fortify us. Make us stronger at the seams.

For so long, I thought what I wanted were stories of adventure and exploration, but what I needed was to find myself in the quiet moments. To find contentment in myself when I'm alone with my thoughts and there's nowhere else to hide.

It was the only way I could truly understand my heart and bring myself around to where I was always meant to be.

ABOUT THE AUTHOR

A *New York Times*, *USA Today*, and *Wall Street Journal* bestselling author, Elle Kennedy grew up in the suburbs of Toronto, Ontario, and holds a BA in English from York University. From an early age, she knew she wanted to be a writer and actively began pursuing that dream when she was a teenager.

Elle currently writes for various publishers. She is the author of more than fifty titles of contemporary romance and romantic suspense novels, including the global sensation Off-Campus series.

Website: ellekennedy.com
Facebook: ElleKennedyAuthor
Instagram: @ElleKennedy33
TikTok: @ElleKennedyAuthor